Praise 1

MW01142168

"A story of two women who live centuries apart but share a journey towards resilience. The depictions of Ruby and Rubina, as women travelling arduous paths to understand their needs and aspirations, are as painful as they are accurate. The character of Ruby Malkhana beautifully portrays the tragic experiences of women of colour in Canada, people who are invisible and othered in their own homes and communities. Taslim Burkowicz's novel encourages us to consider our own journey, the paths that lead us away from ourselves, and the paradigms that explain our choices."

— Kimia Eslah, author of *Sister Seen, Sister Heard*

"In Taslim Burkowicz's enchanting novel *Ruby Red Skies*, two distant places and moments in time—a wildfire-ravaged, contemporary British Columbia and the courtly interiors of seventeenth century Mughal India—are artfully juxtaposed, making for a highly inventive and readable tale driven by questions of paternity, mothering, marriage, race and the quest for self-affirmation. Burkowicz skillfully embroiders each context through the memorable characters of Ruby, a South Asian-Canadian housewife facing a loveless interracial marriage, and Rubina, a dancing girl determined not to fall prey to a concubine's fate, each of whom reminds us, at every turn of their intersecting stories, that the here and now is often powerfully reimagined by the histories we carry within us. A deftly crafted novel that expands the historical echoes and cultural geographies of Canadian literature."

— Dr. Mariam Pirbhai, author of *Isolated Incident*

RUBY

RED

SKIES

RUBY
RED
SKIES

a novel

TASLIM BURKOWICZ

Roseway Publishing
an imprint of Fernwood Publishing
Halifax & Winnipeg

Development editing: Fazeela Jiwa
Copyediting: Amber Riaz
Text design: Jessica Herdman
Cover design: Tania Craan

Printed and bound in Canada

Published by Roseway Publishing
an imprint of Fernwood Publishing
2970 Oxford Street, Halifax, Nova Scotia, B3L 2W4
and 748 Broadway Avenue, Winnipeg, Manitoba, R3G 0X3
www.fernwoodpublishing.ca/roseway

Fernwood Publishing Company Limited gratefully acknowledges the financial support of the Government of Canada through the Canada Book Fund, the Canada Council for the Arts, the Province of Nova Scotia, the Province of Manitoba and Arts Nova Scotia for our publishing program.

Library and Archives Canada Cataloguing in Publication
Title: Ruby red skies: a novel / by Taslim Burkowicz.
Names: Burkowicz, Taslim, 1978- author.
Identifiers: Canadiana (print) 20220262217 | Canadiana (ebook) 20220262225 |
ISBN 9781773635606
(softcover) | ISBN 9781773635804 (EPUB)
Classification: LCC PS8603.U73776 R83 2022 | DDC C813/.6—dc23

For my three sons,
Anjay, Alek, and Augustyn Burkowicz,
without whom I would not have written a large portion of this
book in the driver's seat of a car between drop-offs and pick-ups.
I also would not have had to break up fights between edits,
offer an array of car foods, and hear about their day.
And I wouldn't change this for anything. xxx

When, far down some glade,
Of the great world's burning,
One soft flame upturning
Seems, to his discerning,
Crocus in the shade.

— Ebenezer Jones, from the poem
"When the World Is Burning"

Mughal Family Tree

Babur (1483–1530) m. Maham Begum
(b. unknown–1534)

|

Humayun (1508–1556) m. Hamida Banu Begum (1527–1604)

|

Akbar the Great (1542–1605) m. Mariam-uz-Zamani
(1542–1623; aunt of Maharaja Man Singh of Amber Court)

|

Jahangir (1569–1627) m. Jagat Gosain (1573–1619) m. — Nur
Jahan (Mehrunissa; 1577–1645;
aunt of Mumtaz Mahal)

|

Shah Jahan (Khurram; 1592–1666) m. Mumtaz Mahal (Arjumand
Banu; 1593–1631)

|

Aurangzeb (1618–1707; he and his brother Dara Shikoh were kept
as hostages by Nur Jahan and Jahangir until Shah Jahan took the
court.)

Notes on the Mughal Family Tree

For simplicity, this tree only mentions the ruling kings and their wives (other wives and siblings are not listed).

Maharaja Man Singh of Amber Court (1550–1614) m. Bibi Mubarak (1564–1638). He ruled Amber Court, and while he had a good relationship with King Akbar the Great, he had a fraught one with his son, King Jahangir.

Jahangir's brother Daniyal (1572–1605) was Akbar the Great's favourite son, and the royal chef in this novel was named after him.

Persian was the official language of the Mughal Empire; however, Hindustani (a precursor to Urdu, which did not exist yet) was widely spoken. Hindustani and Urdu were influenced by Persian, Dakhni, Turkish, Arabic, Sanskrit, and others.

Though it went through many name changes, the place in this novel referred to as al-Qandahār (which was formally referred to as such in the second half of the nineth century) is what we know to be modern-day Kandahar.

Ruby's Plan for Driving from Vancouver to William's Lake

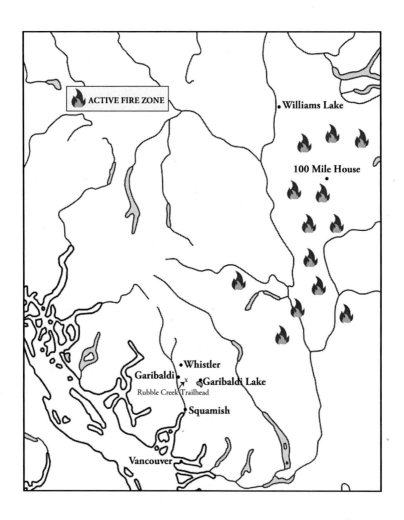

Chapter 1

2017

Trevor sighed heavily. Low and grey as it was, Ruby felt like the sky was closing in on them. Tree shadows decorated the back window of the car in moving patterns of vintage lace.

The rain had just started to fall, syncopating with the rhythm of the classical music emanating from the speakers. The drops splattering against the windshield added a dulled drum beat.

"It's getting late, all right," he said. It was a fact. The drive had run its course.

Ruby glanced over at her husband. He had one hand on the wheel, the other clasped a cup which he periodically tipped to his lips. They had started taking these long drives when Leah was a baby to put her to sleep. Back then, when they were alone in the car, Ruby hadn't felt like they were just teens who had had a shotgun wedding, forced to live in Trevor's mother's rec room. She continuously chased after that feeling these days. Even though they lived in a house of their own now. Even though Leah was already nineteen.

"But," he offered, "happy anniversary, and all. *Cin cin.*"

Cin cin, salud, cheers, and all that jazz. Trevor's toast at their wedding. Ruby turned to look out at the scattered rain. It seemed like only yesterday Ruby was choosing her wedding gown with her mother-in-law. Eleanora liked the buttercream colour. Ruby, the white. In the end, Ruby went with Eleanora's choice. Ruby was a chesty bride and had already begun to show just a few months into pregnancy. The champagne colour Eleanora had chosen washed out her skin tone, and the piece itself — bought to hide all of Ruby's bumps — made her look as if she was encased in a frilly, lacy potato sack.

If Ruby wanted to be more in charge, maybe her father should have been around to offer to pay for the wedding, or perhaps she should have waited until she was the right age to marry another South Asian, not a white person. People were supposed to marry people who matched them; hadn't Ruby ever played Pick Up Pairs? It went without saying that she shouldn't have gotten pregnant in grade 12. These unspoken thoughts had bounced around that cheap bridal salon Eleanora had driven Ruby to while all the other girls Ruby's age were scrambling about, trying on last-minute grad dresses. Eleanora, terrified that Ruby would ask to include an Indian custom in the wedding, had suggested her future daughter-in-law try on some of the ridiculously ornate jewellery pieces on display, advertised as being "made in Morocco."

"Just the perfect cultural touch from your side," Eleanora had exclaimed. Ruby had asked for satin gloves instead.

Ruby had not been planning on having pakoras or saris or even Bollywood music at the event. Ruby's own mother, lips drawn in a permanent straight line after her daughter's pregnancy revelation, had no interest in inviting a single person, Indian or otherwise, to the celebration. Trevor favoured gangster rap at the time, but Ruby's interests in the nineties was confined strictly to what her mother called "white people music," and picking out the playlist (Radiohead, Soundgarden, Counting Crows) had been her favourite part of the wedding. A rushed, embarrassing event filled with teenagers getting drunk in the bathroom, Ruby's wedding had concluded with Coolio's "Gangsta's Paradise" playing on repeat. Now that she thought about it, her playlist had been largely ignored on her wedding day.

Ruby giggled in the car — eliciting an enquiring look from Trevor — as she remembered the extravagant top hat Trevor had worn that night. Hadn't he talked in slang those days — an urban drawl that had clashed with his skinny, white frame? She thought of the modest rose bouquet she had tossed into the crowd. Most girls, having just celebrated graduation, had jumped away from the bouquet like it was an incoming firecracker. Her best friend Belle had rescued it off the floor and held it up like the Olympic torch to Ruby as if to say: *Look, this isn't mortifying at all — see?*

"Hey Trevor," Ruby said suddenly, "do you remember my bridal bouquet?"

"Not specifically."

"Well, Belle scooped it up. Isn't it funny that she never married?"

He turned to her with a cocked brow. "Back then, Rubes, our friends were busy being teenagers. Don't tell me you believe that bullshit about whoever catches it first, marries next."

"Yeah," she said, not bothering to explain that Belle had snatched it off the floor and never caught it. "But we aren't teens anymore," she mumbled. "Belle's almost forty ..."

"She just turned thirty-eight. What's your point?"

"Nothing."

She turned away from Trevor to gaze out the car window. The sky was blotted out by spongey grey clouds. The stormy skies reminded her of the fantastic scenes in the bedtime stories her mother once told Ruby. Her mother had spent a lot of time describing details to her — the million shades of sky, or the way people in medieval India dressed. It had been years since Ruby had thought of those tales — slices of India's past studded in the *sultanat's* rubies and topped with roses from the harem's garden. Out of nowhere, today of all days, snippets of the stories were coming back to her. The stories, invented to distract Ruby from the dysfunction of family life, stopped when Ruby disappointed her mother just as much as her father had.

There hadn't been much happiness in her childhood days, Ruby reflected now, watching water pool into the dips in the concrete, what with Ruby's father having left her mother for a white woman named Julia. The stories that Ruby's mother told had quickly filled the space where her father's box of premium brand cigarettes had once sat right next to his fake Coca Cola, both of which had been purchased at a fraction of their regular cost from a vendor across the Vancouver border, somewhere in Bellingham. There were no trips to Bellingham after Julia, but her father had sent Ruby CDs in the mail every year for her birthday, up until the very year she moved to Trevor's rec room. Ruby had put them in a shoebox she labelled Julia's Choice. While Ruby preferred alternative rock bands, Julia sent her CDs of frazzled white female vocalists who were finding a space for themselves in the world. The Virginia Woolfs of the nineties as Ruby liked to think of them. Sarah McLachlan. Tori Amos. Björk.

The car suddenly jerked, bringing her jolting back to the present.

"Fuck!" Trevor had dribbled coffee on his beige pants, sprinkling them with milky brown drops.

Ruby, thinking of Julia's burgundy and plum lipstick, didn't attempt to dab the spots clean, nor assure her husband she'd take care of them later. "Are you okay?" she said absentmindedly.

"Ruby, it's getting dark." Trevor wove a sigh through his words.

"Hmm," she replied. Indeed, the sky was changing colour. Her mind drifted to the descriptions her mother had given of the skies of medieval Agra. Rubina was the starlet of those stories Ruby was told after her father packed his bags and left to live with Julia. Her mother had claimed lineage to the dancing legend, one who had captured the hearts of the members of the royal court in early seventeenth century India.

Looking up now at the pregnant clouds, Ruby embraced her resurfacing memories of Rubina, recollecting the strong rainfall in the last story her mother told. There had been a battle. Rubina and

4

Empress Nur Jahan had been fleeing on an elephant. Nur Jahan had held a baby while riding it and had shot weapons at men. Wasn't there some great love of Rubina's there too? Some man who tried to save Rubina when she fell into the fast-flowing river? And Rubina had to fight to save herself? How had Rubina become so close to the empress? Rubina had always been presented as brave and fearless in her mother's stories, and Ruby, tucked into her soft bed, had felt quite the opposite. Her mother's voice, warm and buttery, had transported her to past days where majestic elephants battled one another in sport. Words had whizzed out of her mother like the arrows raining down on the enemy below, and Ruby had been able to see the past as clearly as she saw her own life.

Ruby sat up straighter in the passenger seat. She could suddenly, with absolute clarity, remember details about the building of the crimson Agra Fort, of how the castle's red sandstone and white marble walls were precisely carved by skilled masons, but constructed offsite to avoid disrupting royalty's lives. About how the city of Agra had formed a perfect square, protected on all four sides by high banks erected to ward off raids.

"Are you even listening to me, Ruby?"

Where were all these memories coming from, so tactile she could taste fire-roasted nuts on her tongue and feel the dusty plains between her toes? While Ruby couldn't explain her sudden interest in Rubina this evening, she had to admit it was a welcome distraction from the monotonous routine that had, over time, consumed Ruby's life: laundry, dishes, sweeping, mopping, obligatory acknowledgement of her spouse, repeat. No matter how she tried to kid herself, romance between her and Trevor was nearly dead.

"Rubes?"

How intriguing to imagine an era where cities changed rulers over and over again as Mughal conquerors and sultans swept through! Where the royals that went to battle had plain-clothed servants ride behind them to show off their majesty's jewels — heavy gold pieces covering them from head to toe. One sultan invading Agra and levelling the land, destroying the Hindu temples and sculpted gods. Another building ornate mosques and tombs with overlooked treasures left behind by those fleeing the new invaders. A new leader, once again destroying monuments to rebuild yet more in their place. Some of these structures had stood the test of time though Ruby had never visited them: Akbar's Mausoleum, the Agra Fort, the Taj Mahal. How unsettling it must have been to live through a time of such fragility!

She turned up the heat in her excitement and watched as Trevor, annoyed, turned it back down. The driver decided the car temperature, an Andrews family rule. Ruby's reign was restricted to the laundry room. When they got home, she still had to throw clothes in the dryer, she thought flatly, taking a sip of her coffee. After that, while the heavy rains of Vancouver fell, Ruby would have the company of cable television, thick blankets, and pearly milked Earl Grey tea. No crazy adventure here. Her mortgage was paid monthly by her husband of twenty years, garbage brought out properly to the curb by him on the right day. In a dispassionate life, she had the passion of stability. Stability and Ruby were having a hot love affair.

"Jesus. You're lost in your own world again, Ruby. It's like driving with a goddamn zombie."

"Pardon? Ah, yes, I'm not sure that it is my world, per se," she said chuckling, wondering whether to bring up her mother's stories. She had mentioned them in passing but never gone into details with Trevor. "But I suppose I'm lost somewhere."

"Such a fucking daydreamer. Unicorns and rainbows taking up your thoughts, Rubes?"

She winced at the open mockery. "It's hard to put into words, but I guess I'm thinking of the rains. They're reminding me of medieval India. And I'm thinking of what a crazy time all of it was in contrast with how predictable my life is. *Our life*," she corrected quickly. "I'm wondering if predictability is such a bad thing."

"Yes, I see the connection."

Ruby ignored the thick sarcasm. Trevor had always told her she wasn't particularly sharp at catching it, but when she did, it made her flinch as did the scent of cheap cologne. Ruby looked out the windshield, each swipe of the wipers clearing away the old view and replacing it with a sparkly new one.

Trevor snapped his fingers in front of her face with his right hand to make his point, left hand still on the wheel. "What I've been asking is, are you okay with ending our anniversary date early? I'm running low on gas."

Thunder echoed in the distance. Ruby looked out the window, watching the summer rain hammer the pavement. "Sure, we can go home," she said, trying to keep the hurt out of her voice. Trevor logged his hours with her like he was punching in at work.

After a while, she said, "Do you like your anniversary present?"

"Yes," he answered, tapping the breast pocket on his trim blazer.

"It's kind of cheesy to get you an engraved pen ..."

"No, I like it; no one will steal a pen that says *Happy 20th, Sugar Bear*."

"You hate it."

"Oh, for fuck's sake, Ruby, how much reassurance do you need?"

Dollar store chocolates sat on her lap. She was supposed to have gotten china for this milestone, but who had the patience for finnicky dishware? She shrugged to herself, opened her gift box, and popped a sugary chocolate seashell in her mouth. It didn't dissolve easily, so she began to bite at it.

"Is this piece by Handel?" she asked, mouth full, pointing to the stereo. As usual, it was up to Ruby to change the mood. In all honesty, if she had control of the stereo, she would have put on Nina Simone's "My Baby Just Cares for Me." She loved the lyrics, the catchy piano riffs, the perfect pauses.

"It's Ravel's 'Bolero,'" he answered, bored. His lip was upturned, his face showing the strain of annoyance.

She shrugged. She probably got the century wrong. The music layered itself in flutes and violins. Or maybe it was trumpets and trombones. Ruby had no idea. The piece made her feel anxious, like she was climbing a tall mountain on the way to fighting a battle, but she wanted to contribute something positive to the conversation. "Well, it's interesting all the same."

Trevor tapped his finger on the wheel, veins of irritation in his forehead now visible. "But it's not all the bloody same, Rubes, is it? That's the point. Ravel is impressionism, Handel is baroque. Two totally different styles and time periods."

"Which came first?"

"Pardon?"

"I mean which period came first?"

"Oh. Well, obviously baroque came before impressionism." A sharp turn.

"OK," said Ruby measuredly, "so Ravel could have been inspired by Handel and thus sound like him."

"What?"

"I said, Ravel might have been influenced by baroque ... couldn't that be possible? The type of music is called impressionism, after all."

"I don't think you even know what impressionism means."

Ruby sucked air in, watching her belly contract inward under the lap belt, skinny if only for one second. Trevor talked about classical music as if he was the only one allowed to discover a new interest; as if he was the only one ever to drink sour white wine and eat under-salted nuts in a symphony lobby; as if Ruby's best moments had passed in high school, and so now she should accept herself as the woman who dressed in mom jeans and loose blouses to hide the pregnancy weight she had held on to. It was as though she was literally carrying around her past with her, unable to transform into a new person like Trevor had.

If Ruby could have chosen to be anyone she wanted, she would have picked a Paris lounge singer in the 1920s. She'd be a charm of a woman who would be able to do many variations of the Charleston, drink champagne on Tuesdays, and wear faux fur coats for no reason at all. She liked having something to love that was all her own. After a while, she had stopped feeling the need to tell Trevor she liked things other than reality shows and romance novels. She stretched her arms out in the car now, imagining wearing gossamer gloves so fine her skin would show through.

"Isn't it funny how thunder sounds just like a standing ovation? It's like we are at our own private concert." She dug her tongue into the groove of her back teeth, dislodging the cheap chocolate. Ruby imagined this to be an intelligent observation; Trevor usually went for this kind of cheap poetic metaphor when someone else made the comment.

"Ruby, if you please don't mind, I quite enjoy this part in the piece. You're welcome to retreat to your dreamland. As romantic as the rain may sound to you, the lightning is probably starting up wildfires in BC forests. Besides, classical music demands silence to be best appreciated."

A minute passed between them.

And then Ruby could not resist pitching in, "But that makes no sense. Wouldn't the rain put out the fire?"

Trevor looked at her.

"What?" she said, inspecting her teeth for chocolate using her cell phone.

Trevor shook his head. "I just can't understand if you're pretending to be dumb because you think it makes you look cute, or if you really don't understand how weather works. If you assessed the weather with a more careful eye, you would see that this is merely a quick flash rain. In the mountains, where the clouds are closer to the earth, there won't be enough moisture to put out any fires. Think of the forest bed as a blanket of dry matches just itching for a spark to light it."

Ruby bit her lip. "I thought people started fires."

"People cause climate change. The storm is a result of that, as are the dry conditions. You'll hear people argue that forest fires have natural cycles and burning clears out decaying matter and prevents larger catastrophes. I guess humans are the idiots for changing from wandering peoples to the type of species that build large resorts or hometowns on forest beds and then cry later about everything burning down. But the sheer number of fires happening now are a direct result of climate change. However, I'm sure lots of assholes will light bonfires and fireworks in the forest anyway and add to the problem."

"Yes, that makes sense ..." she said falteringly.

"Interesting how the one thing humans have that differentiates us from other animals is our ability to make fire, and yet we have used that very gift to burn the whole world down. It's going to be a hot, dry, long summer, mark my words. Don't be fooled by this short piss of rain. 2017 isn't going to be any different from the last few summers."

"Well, I hope this summer we stay fire-free. It's still only the beginning of July."

Trevor made a strange noise through his nose — his reply to anything stupid Ruby said whenever he lost his desire to school her.

Five minutes later they were in their driveway. Trevor was already slamming his car door shut and running inside, tenting a newspaper over his head as protection against the elements. He left the main door open, the mouth of darkness gaping at her.

Chapter 2

2017

Inside, the house was pitch black. The storm had knocked out the electricity. Trevor searched through a drawer and lit a few candles. His face glowed and, for a second, Ruby remembered him the way he was at eighteen — his face marked with acne, his unsure gaze. But when she looked again his skin was smooth, his suit jacket crisp, save for a couple of raindrops on the shoulders. Straight sandy hair complemented his tall, lean physique. *Time is a funny thing*, she thought. If she chiselled away at him with a trowel like an archaeologist, would she find that sweet boy from high school hiding underneath?

"Darn," Ruby said, placing her empty coffee cup and chocolate box on the counter. As she did, her arm brushed against her own waist. No doubt Trevor would regret the chocolates he had gifted her. But chocolates were meant to be enjoyed, not saved, and besides, she never understood what men saw in skinny, hangry, self-obsessed wives. A whole life filled with salads and calorie counting was depressing. "I hope Leah is okay."

"She isn't a kid anymore, Rubes. I'm sure she can handle a small power outage."

"Hi guys," Leah navigated toward them casting a cone of light.

"Leah," Ruby hugged her close. "You're okay, right?"

Leah pulled away. "'Course I am."

"In a way this is perfect. We can play board games tonight over wine. Leah, you're old enough to have a glass."

Leah shrugged, glancing at Trevor. "Not much to do, now that you can't watch *The Bachelor*, huh, Mom?"

Trevor's laughter pierced the air. "C'mon, Leah, don't make fun. You and your mom used to love playing Scrabble together at night."

"I outgrew three letter words."

"Leah," scolded Trevor. But his eyes shone with mischief in the candlelight; intelligence was something that only Leah and he shared, with Ruby just looking in.

"It wasn't always this way," Ruby spoke her thoughts aloud. She was thinking that when she first met Trevor, she had been the smart one; the one who knew all about bands, the one who had impressed Curtis Simmons, her first boyfriend in high school. Curtis had been in a band that landed opening acts in garage rock shows. Trevor had been just a pimply white kid who thought he was Black, working as a stock boy at the local Green Savers store, listening to Dr. Dre on his Walkman.

"God, Mom, people grow up," sputtered Leah, as if she had read Ruby's thoughts. Trevor massaged Leah's shoulders gently. "I'm going to Rick's to work on a paper."

"Is that such a good idea? Don't you have a crush on him? It might not send the best message, studying together after dark."

Leah's pale face coloured pink. She played with a stray blue-black hair that had escaped from her ponytail. "A crush? Don't study after dark with a boy? What are you, a 1950s housewife? Where's your crinoline dress?"

Ruby gazed down at her pilled pullover. She wanted to say she preferred vintage looks, not vintage values, but it wouldn't make sense given her current choice of clothing. "I'm only looking out for you. Is that such a crime?"

"Mom, back off. Leah's old enough to make her own choices," said Trevor.

Mom. Trevor had actually called her mom.

Ruby's back stiffened.

"I'm going to drive down to the office to catch up on some last-minute work. I'll give you some gas money, Leah."

"Dad, that's okay. I'm teaching soccer camp again this summer. I have money."

"Just wait by your car. You're my little girl. I got you. I'll be right out." Trevor rushed over the words, as if by speaking quickly he could erase the reality that he was walking out on his anniversary date.

Ruby knew a blackout did not mean courtly behaviour on Trevor's part. Once again, she reminded herself that Trevor paid bills and put out the trash, including the organics.

"Thanks, Dad," Leah was saying. "I think I need an oil change, too."

"Well, I'll check it for you," he said, rifling through his wallet to find money for Leah.

"What do you think I should do about the dinner party tomorrow?" Ruby cut in. "I was going to prep dessert tonight."

Trevor stared at Ruby by candlelight as Leah walked out. "It's your idea to host these mundane events where no one discusses anything deeper than the fucking weather."

"The dinner party will be fun ..."

"Making balloon animals is also fun. Doesn't mean it's my cup of tea."

"What am I supposed to tell Belle and John?"

Trevor looked rattled for a second. Belle's newest boyfriend challenged Trevor on every point, be it details of fine liquor or historical facts.

"We can order in. Eat by candlelight." Trevor had veered off script.

"Okay, good idea," Ruby said, relieved to have a backup plan if the electricity didn't come on. "Maybe Chinese or Thai, not pizza."

"Belle hates pizza."

She looked at him, puzzled.

"On account of her throwing up in the high school cafeteria. She swore she'd never eat it again. Who could forget that? What did you guys drink the night before? Gin, was it? Poor girl still can't look at the stuff." He jingled his keys, signalling that he was ready to go out again.

"She's *my* best friend. Of course, I remember that."

"You guys were so dumb, drinking in high school. Thank goodness Leah is nothing like you. She hasn't even got your colouring." He smiled, attempting to soften the blow.

"Back then my *colouring* used to be the thing you liked best about me. Made you feel pretty damn special dating a girl who was *exotic*." She surprised herself. "Although in those days you used to confuse Black and Brown as being the same thing. Remember how you used to say that Lenny Kravitz song 'Black Girl' reminded you of me? You *loved* that song. It was the only non-rap song you tolerated."

He flushed, the tinge visible even in the dim lighting. "What does that have to do with anything? I was just a kid; my tastes weren't developed yet. You're the one who hasn't changed much, Rubes. In those days you used to follow Belle around like a puppy dog, and you still do."

"That simply isn't true. Belle used to admire my intellect ..."

"God. Do you guys, like, always have to argue?" Leah had returned. "Come on, Dad."

"Coming, Leah. Anyway, you're going to be okay on your own in the dark, right Rubes? The gas barbecue is on the patio if you get hungry."

This was such a stupid comment that she couldn't answer. Her diet didn't differ much from a ten-year-old girl's: Skittles, gummy bears, and ice cream — none of which needed to be cooked outside. Chewing the inside of her cheek, she tried to think of what kind of food would comfort her most right now.

"Bye then," he said, kissing her on the cheek. His lips felt like paper brushing against her skin.

"No time like an anniversary date to catch up on work," she snapped. Sarcasm. She could use that just as well.

He didn't respond.

Ruby scanned the countertop for her phone. *Do you have a power outage too? If not, maybe I could come over and watch* The Bachelor, she texted Belle. Once this season of the show ended, another chapter of her life would also be over. Another day of Trevor telling her she was getting fatter gone by; another day of pretending Trevor still loved her; another day where she was no longer young Ruby Malkhana, whom Trevor had looked at wide-eyed with fascination. Where had that wild, free Ruby gone? And why had everyone forgotten she had been something interesting once upon a time?

Trevor has a deadline and our anniversary plans ended early, her thumb rapidly selected the letters on her phone, feeling the need to explain. *But it was still romantic.* She set the phone down. Over the years, Ruby had learned to omit her marital arguments, inflate her happiness.

Her phone buzzed with Belle's reply. *I still have power. Romantic in a physical way?*

She ran a finger over her lips. She could imagine Belle's exact expression as she teased her. Belle loved to discuss sex and her candidness sometimes took Ruby by surprise. *Did a thin-lipped cheek kiss count?* Ruby wondered. *Superhot kissing!* She typed in, before she could regret it, and hoped that Belle would at least laugh at this. *Martinis and* The Bachelor: *yes or no??*

Her phone remained silent for two minutes. When it buzzed on the counter in the dark, she jumped.

Grrrrl, you know I don't watch that trite bullshit. But I could use the martinis...

Trite? Since when? Ruby fingers danced over the letters. *You watched the whole freaking last season with me.*

I'm trying to refine myself.

Yoga pants 24/7, you're so refined, Ruby wrote, a small smile tugging at her lips.

Rubes, take note: a nice ass is timeless. Audrey Hepburn's cigarette pants were glorified leggings. You had me at the martinis, though. Especially if you brought something top shelf. That's refined, right? Too bad I already have plans. With John. My boyfriend-of-the-week! ☺

Ruby placed the phone face down on the counter.

Alone.

Again.

Chapter 3

2017

"This is delicious," said Belle, forking a mouthful of Ruby's dinner party lasagna into her mouth.

The power had come back that afternoon. The oven clock had beeped; the alarm clock had flashed midnight. Odd lights that Ruby had forgotten she had turned on showed themselves, reminding her that her existence was real. She had made a difference in her immediate environment, even if it was minute.

Ruby had lost her excuse to not make food. She had thought she enjoyed cooking until she realized how relieved she had been at the idea of just ordering in. While she was hurriedly making the meal, she had shattered an olive oil bottle that took ages to clean up. When she rinsed the dustpan with hot water, little shards of glass fell into Trevor's precious European bathtub, and she worried about the damage she had caused. Trevor was always reminding her where things were from, how much they had cost. But now, after a few glasses of wine, the worry had melted away. She imagined a piece of glass piercing him and found herself accidentally smiling as she passed around more salad.

Belle's long legs were in John's lap. All Ruby had been told about John was that he worked with kids with autism. The first time she met John, the four of them had drinks at a downtown bar. John and Trevor sat next to one another, arguing ferociously the whole night and Belle barely had a chance to bid Ruby goodbye. Tonight, Belle was wearing a periwinkle dress — or maybe it was cornflower blue. Ruby had no idea. What she did know was that the dress perfectly matched Belle's bluish violet eyes, which she always said were her trademark feature. What the fuck was Ruby's trademark feature? Frumpy and Brown, she felt like the one who didn't belong in this group of friends: the fruit in a group of animals or perhaps, the circle in a bag of cubes. She assessed her dinner guests. Blonde and thin, Belle looked like she was of the same genetic makeup as Trevor. John didn't comment on the food; he wasn't much of a presence. Truthfully, he was like every other "John" Ruby had met: average-looking with brown hair. He was more dressed up than Trevor was, for what that was worth. When John took off his suit jacket, he revealed black suspenders over a crisp white shirt, and she could tell this immediately annoyed Trevor.

She shrugged at Belle's compliments. Her guests would have been really impressed had she made an Indian feast, as was expected of her — some sort of spinach curry with fried cheese, fragrant cumin rice, and hand-rolled breads. But this was only lasagna, a lazy cook's cheat to a dinner party. She had had no energy left to make lasagna dough after the olive oil bottle broke. While non-cooks were amazed by the layers of spinach and ricotta, real home cooks knew how easy it was to stack a casserole dish with oven ready pasta. Ruby had tossed together a green salad and a bocconcini salad in minutes. Belle was only impressed because she was a non-cook, not counting the four-week course she took on French cooking only because it had been rumoured the instructor was hot. Ruby absentmindedly dipped her fork into the balsamic vinegar left on her plate while offering her friend the last piece of garlic bread.

"Ah, Ruby," said Belle, tearing off a small piece, "what am I going to do without your cooking?"

"What do you mean, 'do without'?"

"I mean," she looked at John quickly before she rushed on, "John proposed."

Trevor and Ruby stared at her.

"He did what now?" Ruby said.

"Proposed — that we go to Italy!" Belle burst into laughter. "I said 'yes' naturally. I really had you guys! Rubes, listen though, did you really make this bread yourself?"

"I have a bread machine; it's not that hard to make, really. Soon you are going to get more authentic pasta than this thrown-together dinner." She stood up to top everyone's glasses with merlot. "It looks like Trevor's more shocked than me. Here's to hoping spending all your money on renos was worth it. Or are you dying of jealousy, sugar bear?"

"Yep, I've always wanted to go to Italy. After all, my mother is Italian. You really had us." Trevor cracked a kink in his neck.

"Wait, did I say Italy?" Belle shook her head at herself. She pulled her hair up off her neck and let the champagne curls fall again. "I meant India. Is that what's meant by a Freudian slip? Is it because Ruby made Italian that I said Italy? Or does Italy just sound a little better?"

"It'll be great fun, Belle. Nothing to be afraid of once you've had your boosters. Have you been, Ruby?" John asked, turning to face her. "There's this amazing place in Goa called Seva Ashram. It's a magical place; you'd love it."

"I would?" Ruby asked, a little taken back John had addressed her. "Um." After waving the bread one last time at Trevor, who fervently shook his head as if Ruby was offering up a syringe of heroin, Ruby finally put the bread on her own plate, examining the place where Belle had ripped off a small piece. "No, I've always wanted to, though," Ruby finally said, knowing that Indians were all expected to have some story of their homeland. "When my mom passed, I found a box of photos from when she was there, of the Agra Fort and the tombs. I was born here," she said for John's sake, "but I grew up on these vivid stories my mom used to tell about a dancer in India." She wanted to say more but could feel Trevor tense up when she mentioned the dancer. "But gee, how lucky that you and Belle get to go."

"John is a hippie at heart. Don't let his snazzy outfit throw you off; he always has his nose in a meditation book or is reading up on Indian history, like the 1600s or something, right John? He's fascinated by how the Indian royals lived and how they were, in his words, more advanced than the Europeans back then."

"The Mughal Empire, yes," said Ruby, smiling. John hadn't struck her as a granola type, but there it was — to go to India as a white person you had to be searching for spirituality. She squinted at John, imagining him with a ginger-tinged beard and woven sandals. "It's actually a time that quite fascinates me as well."

"Honestly, I don't know that much," said John, looking a bit put on the spot.

"The royals were quite something back then ..." Ruby said.

"Are you disagreeing that we can be both alive and dead at the same time?" Trevor said to John, going back to their previous conversation and effectively cutting Ruby off.

Trevor pushed his plate to the side, and Ruby made a mental note that she should clean up in a few minutes. As usual, her husband had taken to aggressive bantering with Belle's date.

"I never said that," John said. He took his time sipping the red wine everyone had drunk far too much of, especially Ruby. Everything had become rather fuzzy and blurred to her, like a scribbled drawing version of real life. "I just view time as a forward moving continuum rather than as overlapping."

"Time overlaps, of course it does. It's not one minute the priest is marrying us and next we're married; it's a blend of time."

John scowled. He was clearly tired of discussing Schrödinger's cat. He didn't look like he gave two fucks if, for one moment in time, the cat was both alive and dead. When Ruby saw he was as annoyed as she was with Trevor, he suddenly became better looking to her. He had warm brown eyes that reminded her of chocolate or a good cup of coffee. And not Dollar Store chocolate, either — the gourmet kind that a chocolatier whirled around in a pot with vanilla essence, crushed tangerine, and roasted almond splinters. She wanted to shout at him to heed Belle, that she would chew him up and spit him out as she did every man, but then men liked to be used in that certain way, didn't they? The French chef sure had.

"Each second is a death of the one before it," Ruby found herself saying, pulling back her tousled long waves so that she appeared tidy. "Every time I finish a book it's a mini death, something sadder to me than the passing of my birthday. I can't go back and flip the page the other way. Because I know the ending, and once I put down the book, I can't change the fact that I have read the book. I can't undo it. That is why it is nearly impossible for me to reread books or look at old photos. At the same time, I do think moments are a chain link of things; they connect. When Leah was born, I truly saw that there is a moment someone is a part of you and a moment they aren't. Every second of time during which she was being expelled from my body, I felt her leaving me. Seconds intersect the ones before them; they aren't separate events. Just because each second dies as the next is born, it doesn't mean it wasn't connected to the one that's happening now. You know what I mean?"

"What I'm saying," Trevor plunged ahead while Ruby felt her stomach sink from being ignored, "is that when you go to the paint store and look at shades from black to white, they're placed on a sliding spectrum. It's not like, well, here's the black, and then here's the white. There are shades in between."

"What about a bomb?" said Belle, tapping her pinky nail against her eye tooth. "It just goes off. One minute there's no bomb, and then another minute there is."

"If you slow it all down and watch it happening in slow motion you'll see in the microseconds where the bomb blends into time. Like a water balloon popping. If you film it and freeze the frame, you can see that moment where the rubber splits, that nanosecond where the water is in the air and hasn't even dripped yet ..."

"So fucking what? That doesn't prove time overlaps. It just proves you can slow down events to see how they connect, Trevor. If it overlapped then there would be a million versions of our own bodies, just bumping into one another slowing down the system. Time's always going forward." John's face was animated.

Ruby's stomach felt worse. She stood up. Her hand clutched the edge of her red cardigan, which after glass two; she had thought made her look sexy. Ruby was her name, after all, and her cheeks were ever so flushed. Maybe they were her *trademark feature*, but now, after more wine, she felt just chunky and Indian, clownish and balloonish. Okay, balloonish was not really a word, but that is what Ruby figured she looked like — a big, fat, red balloon ready to pop. She was supposed to clear the table, *be the perfect hostess*, but everything was spinning. John turned to her with concern on his face, a frown spreading his lips into what would be a smile if it weren't for the furrowed eyebrows. She could make out two dimples piercing his cheeks. How could she have missed that? Not that he would ever give her a second look if hot blondes were his thing (and whose thing weren't they?) but right now, at this moment in time, minutes overlapping, colliding or not, he was looking at just Ruby.

"I'm agreeing with both of you. And neither of you hear what I'm saying," she said, gripping the table hard.

"Are you okay?" John said. And time stopped. It really did. He saw her.

"I'm not feeling ..." She paused to enjoy freezing time again, her finger pressed on the seconds just enough to keep them from going forward. For once, everyone was waiting for her to speak. What if she just started stripping off her clothes and doing jumping jacks naked? What if she started to sing some Beyoncé song? That one about putting a ring on it, and performed that dance that went along with the song? Or what if in the next moment she forgot who she was entirely? She used to have that fear when she was taking care of Leah alone when she was a baby. It surfaced usually when she was driving to the grocery store alone, and she would be deathly afraid that she would forget how to get home and who she was, completely. Ruby would be paralyzed with fear, and yet she would keep going — driving on until she reached her destination. She never forgot who she was, but would she ever know if she had?

Belle and Trevor had exchanged a look with one another. Ruby was being annoying again.

"I'm not feeling that great," Ruby said, realizing her stint was up. "I am retiring for the evening." *Retiring for the evening? Who was she? Scarlet O'Hara in* Gone with the Wind? "I do declare, I feel ill," she couldn't stop herself from saying the words. She put her hand over her lips just as a hiccup surfaced.

"Let me help you get to your room," said John.

They were all in the dining room, located on a floor elevated by just a few steps from the living room, which was in the centre of the house. John led her to the left, toward the kitchen, accessible directly from the dining room through a set of French doors. He selected a door and turned the knob, shutting it quickly behind the pair, and suddenly they were in their own world. Trevor had discussed sliding French doors versus traditional ones for six weeks before committing to the latter, which, as far as Ruby could tell, only made her feel more like a servant, as she was the one forced to continuously open and shut them to bring dishes in or out. Next to the kitchen was a solarium. Walking toward it, John helped her sit directly on the bare floor. There they sat side by side, facing a glass wall exposing the patio, a glass domed ceiling above them.

"This should help you feel better. Gosh, it feels like we are practically outside. I need a stick to roast marshmallows," he joked. "If you have some, I could get a fire going."

Feeling a little woozy, instead of responding, she fell directly on him.

Chapter 4

2017

Once upon a time, inspired by the TV show *Love it or List it*, Trevor had added an extension from the kitchen. To make his dream solarium a reality, he knocked out the pantry wall and put in a glass pane that rounded out from the ceiling and glided all the way down to the floor. When all the lights were switched off, you could see the entire galaxy spread out. As gorgeous as the house was it was just as pretentious. Grand double staircases climbed up gracefully from the foyer to meet at the upper floor, accented in black wrought-iron railings. In the solarium, Trevor displayed an antique telescope, which he never used for anything except to tell stories about. The house was all Calacatta marble this, and stained glass windows that, stolen from cathedrals and a whole bunch of other places that sounded freaking amazing but meant nothing to Ruby — not really. But the view was nice. Even Trevor couldn't fuck up the natural beauty of Vancouver's mountains with his bullshit stories. If it weren't nighttime right now, she would be privy to a view of them in their icy blue glory, jagged purple boulders lining the sky. She felt like a teenager suddenly and wished she had long skinny menthol cigarettes to smoke with John. They could lie back and look at the sky and blow smoke up and not care about what happened next.

She collected herself and sat upright. "I'm okay." She hiccupped again, feeling John's concern. At the same time, John whispered,

"You're not okay."

"Look," Ruby laughed. "We just made time overlap!"

He laughed. "So, we did."

"You should be with Belle right now."

"It's okay, she's with Trevor and I'm with you right now."

"I guess we are dividing our time," she offered.

"If time can be divided. Maybe we are multiplying it?"

"Maybe. I think time works differently for all species," Ruby said. "Like hummingbirds. You know how they manage to fly above a car, and you are so sure you are going to hit them, but you don't? They probably experience the world at a completely unique speed. I bet mosquitoes live ten years in a day. Really. How would we know?"

She tugged at her red sweater so he wouldn't see evidence of her tummy rolls. But he was looking at her face.

She went on. "Don't you think it's so weird how people can travel at fast speeds in cars or airplanes, but inside those spaces, time moves at the same pace as it does for people who are stationary?" The wine, Ruby figured, was making her thoughts come out smooth, unwrinkled. "One hour of talking is still one hour of talking, here or inside of a jet. But when you look outside, you see blurs of cars and planes just soaring by, obviously because those people are clearly moving at a rapider pace ... yet how can they maintain the same speed of conversation in their air bubbles?"

"You make really cool points."

"I do?"

"Very much so." His eyes were shining. "The things you said at the table, I could see where you were coming from."

"I didn't think anyone was paying attention. I belong on a different planet."

"You know what we need right now, Ruby?" He glanced up at the ceiling of stars. "That Frank Sinatra song. To take us away from boring Earth where people have very ordinary ideas. 'Fly me to the moon,'" he sang out, his voice clear. It was then that Ruby realized John was as drunk, if not drunker, than she was. "Let me play among the stars."

"Let me see what spring is like, on Jupiter and Mars," she continued, her voice coated in wine.

"In other words ..." He stood up, grabbed her hand, helped her stand, and smoothly twirled her around the solarium. "Hold my hand!"

"Look, I'm really not much of a dancer," she said apologetically, falling into him. The walls were glowing purple. Ruby usually lined the edges of the solarium floor in coloured Christmas lights during winter, but there was nothing in this summer's night that could account for the hypnotic glow of the room. Even in the winter, Trevor found the lights too whimsical for his liking, so she'd never brought up the idea of white summer lights. "Honestly though, I have always wanted to dance, especially when I listen to this kind of music."

"I was surprised you knew the words. Here I thought I was the only nerd who listened to old-timey music. What do most people our age listen to?"

"I don't know, but Belle listens to Drake and Lil Pump."

"Little who?"

"Wait, there are others." She put a finger to her lips. "There's Smokepurpp and Fetty Wap. She calls it trap music. Says it makes her feel young. Me ... only big band music."

"Ruby, the suburban rebel."

She laughed as he spun her again. "I know, I'm so bad-ass, secretly listening to Louis Armstrong and Billie Holiday. And when I want to get super wild, I put on electro swing."

"I'm a Cab Calloway, Chet Baker, Sammy Davis Jr. guy myself."

"Ah, 'That Old Black Magic' takes me right back."

"Exactly. You know, I'd take Betty Roché scatting in 'Take the

"A" Train' any day over jabbering along with silly lyrics that have no
relevance to my life. Or going to see a bunch of bands I once saw as a
teenager; how do people do that?"

"They like the nostalgia?" she offered. "It's like time travel but
travelling to the past one has already lived through."

"The older I get, the more I gravitate toward blues and jazz. The
clothes, the style of dress — they hit a note with me."

"I agree," she said, thinking his suspenders made a little more sense
now. She caught the whiff of something like mangoes on him, but
maybe it was the fruity wine they'd had earlier. "Would you believe
I bought a flapper dress and I have nowhere to wear it? I should've
just worn it to see the symphony. Trevor used to take me all the time,
you know ..." She was babbling but she couldn't stop.

"With a cigarette holder to go with it. To smoke at intermission."

"Yeah," she said wistfully, "but who the hell smokes anymore?"

They were still dancing to the imaginary song they'd stitched
around themselves. "Why don't you just wear it?" John said a little
too loudly, the wine enlivening him. "Seriously, so many venues play
swing nowadays. What's stopping you?"

"Trevor," she said simply.

"We should go. To a ball where everyone dresses in vintage attire,
like its 1927. Or 1936. Or 1948 if that is the era that tickles your
feathers best. Where people dance Shag, Lindy, Charleston ..."

"Do you mean tickles your fancy? Do places like that actually
exist?" He tipped her back and the wine went right to her head again,
making things swim. "We'd go?"

He roared with laughter, "I mean, we could all go. Belle, Trevor,
you, me, if we sneak it in before India ..."

"Oh. Well, Trevor. He'd never go for it."

He moved her around the room. "I'll talk to him."

"I don't think he cares much for you." Her hand went to her
mouth. How had she said this aloud? Her mind continued to spiral,

unfiltered. *Why are you taking Belle to India? Her favourite yoga instructor was trained in fucking Brooklyn. She can't survive without kale smoothies. She'd be more impressed with tickets to see Jay-Z than a goddamn flight to India.* These sentences, thankfully, did not escape her lips. It felt like a spell had been cast on the solarium — the wine, the stars, the mood, the dancing — she might say whatever popped into her head if she took her hand away from her own mouth. She couldn't trust herself.

"You think your husband and I will always be at each other's throats?" he leaned in grinning conspiratorially, "You and I get on quite naturally don't you think?" The stars above her were spinning out of control. A natural connection with John had been even less predictable to her than Belle being proposed to. She felt the lasagna coming up in her throat.

"John," she broke free. "I'm going to go now." Pulling away from him, she rushed around the bend toward one of the grand staircases that led to the bedrooms.

"Are you okay?" he called out after her. "Hey, I think Belle is staying behind to look after you."

"I keep saying I'm okay. I don't need anyone to look after me," she called down when she reached the top floor. *Two staircases, what could be more pretentious*, she thought, contempt for Trevor's architectural style surfacing again. "I'm fine on my own, you know," she added, leaning over the banister, once again feeling like Scarlet O'Hara. "Go on back to Belle." Saying this had made her remember Rhett Butler's Belle in *Gone with the Wind*. Being transported to the past wasn't as idyllic as John and she had made it out to be, she thought, remembering the slave trade and its depiction in the film, but it was too late to bring this up to John now. She felt like a conversation thread had been started and never finished. She imagined he was already in the dining room with the others, Belle curling her body once more toward him like a cat.

Turning the corner, she ducked into her bathroom. Immediately, she threw up in the toilet. After she was sure nothing was left, she managed to brush her teeth, shed her red cardigan and pants, put on pyjamas, and slip into her bed. With the lights switched off, the world as she knew it evaporated.

Chapter 5

2017

Ruby woke up with a massive headache and cotton mouth. She reached for her phone and looked at the screen. 2:45 a.m. it said, plain and simple in white writing. It was a nice way to tell time, unlike the red blinking lights of the obtrusive alarm clocks she grew up on. She found her way into her slippers and robe and selected the staircase closest to her room to descend. Her dreams, infused with wine, had sketched herself atop an Indian elephant, clutching John. He had a brassy, thick beard, and a confident look upon his face. She smiled, then frowned. Her head was throbbing. Stupidly, she stored the Advil in the kitchen with the vitamins. It was not in Ruby's usual routine to drink so much; she hadn't planned out clever ways to kill hangover headaches before they hatched.

The moon was the only light that filled the solarium next to the kitchen. She could hear the appliances humming, like the Persian grandfathers who played cards in the Tim Horton's down the street. Trevor had tucked in a study at the very end of the solarium. It shared the same glass rooftop that led down from the ceiling and curved straight to the floor, and it gave him great light to do his writing. He was an accountant by trade, but he spent evenings working on a novel about a man on the brink of an existential crisis. When she opened the cupboard door to get out the pills, she heard giggling coming from behind the study door. Her back straightened and she rubbed her eyes. It figured that Leah would have late night conversations with her father and leave Ruby out. She dashed past the glass sliding door leading toward the backyard — where she had been with John earlier — and rushed toward the study door, ready to catch them playing Scrabble.

The study was an ostentatious room, just like the rest of the house. Hunter-green velvet wallpaper, a wooden moose head, an antique brass globe, and a case of Cuban cigars usually featured on the large mahogany desk all sounded very elegant, but Trevor had tucked an old pull-out couch in the corner and put up a flat screen on the back wall to which he had hooked up a new PS4 console and a retro NES system. The addition had taken the room from academic classy to man den in five seconds flat. He argued that the glass wall facing the stars was why he chose to sleep on the couch every night. His claim that art was being created in the room was essentially just "man play-ing *Legend of Zelda* and *Super Mario Kart* all night long." But Ruby had never pointed this out, not even when he mocked the lavender, lime, and lemon chiffon book covers of the novels she was reading, with their big bubbly titles and embossed doodles of stiletto heels and shopping bags. There was no use in pointing out to him that she read other types of books, too.

Ruby saw what looked like a miniature lake glimmering before the closed study door, purplish-blue, mesmerizing. Still just a wee bit drunk, she slid her slippers along the wooden floor like an ice skater toward the mysterious pool of water. It turned out to be a dress, splayed in a pond-like shape of plum and cobalt blue in the night. She dipped her big toe in it. And then, before she could think twice, she flung open the door.

A naked Belle was straddling Trevor on the old pull-out couch. Ruby's first thought was about how stunning Belle was, with her arched back and sandy blonde hair curling all around her shoulders. Pink dime-sized nipples on creamy skin — so unlike Ruby, whose everything was painted different strokes of brown. Belle looked like a divine mermaid sculpture — a goddamn goddess — the moonlight rippling over her body, unmarred by childbirth, in small silvery waves.

It was only after that initial reaction that Ruby realized she should have a proper reaction, one of disgust, shock, anger. But no feeling came immediately, so she tried to pick one out like a particular coffee mug from a shelf. They saw Ruby right away. They didn't even try and cover up. Ruby tried to think back to the last time Trevor and she had had sex. She came up with nothing. She was supposed to flee now, cry, escape to her room, but she couldn't take her eyes off the scene. She was the intruder, coming across two people who had won the genetic lottery, two people who should have starred in *Gattaca*, where everyone — except the geneticist — was perfect, beautiful, white. She was the odd woman out: a human cotton ball but Brown, wrapped in her fuzzy robe. She opened her mouth, but no sound came out.

"I guess it's time you know about us, Ruby," said Belle, sighing as if she was tired of pretending Santa Claus was real for a preteen. She had turned to face Ruby, perfect breasts shining like luminescent shells in the moonlight. She had an inconvenienced look on her face, the same look she'd had in grade 8 when Ruby walked in on her making out with Roger Lopez in the closet during Belle's birthday party.

"Yeah, I suppose we can't go on hiding and sneaking around forever," Trevor added.

"Rubes," Belle sang out, "why'd you lie about you and Trevor being intimate on your anniversary?" Belle was reaching for a shirt to cover up with. It was Trevor's. She rolled up the cuffs and suddenly she looked all Julia Roberts-like, straight out of some bloody romantic comedy. "Such an odd thing to fib about."

She hadn't meant to be dishonest when she had said superhot

kissing. Ruby had been embellishing, joking, maybe even being sarcastic. Her mind was stuck like a car in a ditch and it desperately wanted to back up and just get out. Go anywhere but stay here in the present where she was frantically trying to process and un-process information simultaneously. Oddly, the Sinatra song John had sung was still in her head, replaying the same line "on Jupiter and Mars ... on Jupiter and Mars," like a broken record. If that part of her night had felt like a dream, what was this?

Ruby started twitching. She felt her face flush with shame. It was as if Belle and Trevor were chanting "Liar, liar, pants on fire." It was Ruby who was caught, and she felt like her whole body was burning — flames flickering on her cheeks and heat travelling right down to the tips of her toes.

Chapter 6

1610

Cooking fires were burning, black smoke travelling up along the bank carrying smells of singed flatbread and spiced lentil stews. It was a long walk back from the Yamuna River, and Rubina's hands were tired from carrying her wet clothes in her clay bucket. Agra, the city that had housed Rubina for all her fifteen years, was spilling over with people. She passed by rows of homes made of clay and mud. The floors, patted down with cow dung and the roofs, thatched of straw, made the huts vulnerable to fire. Some of Rubina's neighbours would have chosen to burn to death in their dwellings if a fire broke out rather than risk unveiling to save themselves.

Rubina looked over at the Agra Fort as she walked by; dusk was dressing the brilliant red castle in sashes of sheer pink and purple light. The surrounding grounds were covered in an array of almond, peach, and pear trees. Flowering vines and panels of flowers were selectively planted to match the colours of a peacock — turquoise, purple, gold. The Mughal king, Jahangir, would make an appearance on the balcony of the Agra Fort at dawn tomorrow. If a villager wanted to see the king before the dawn appearance, he could simply shake the golden justice bells attached to the stone pillars next to the riverbank. King Jahangir would be whisked out of the comforts of his palace to listen to his complaint, and the villager risked an impulsive ruling.

From the east side of the river the church bells would be ringing out. But from where she was standing, Rubina heard the Arabic call to evening prayers instead, harmonizing alongside the sounds of working animals — cows and elephants — and her own dance instructor's vocal beats. She heard his warm-up before she even unlatched the gate.

Behind her, white oxen carried patrons to the Agra Fort, with nobles sprawled out in their palanquins, the satin beds carried by slave boys up and down the dusty road. *How would it feel to lay out on a bed of the softest fabrics?* Though Rubina often thought of life in the Agra Fort, she was grateful for the sanctity of the brothel and dancing house she lived in. Khushi owned this dwelling that housed foster girls. Rubina called Khushi "mother," as did all the orphaned slave girls living there, but Rubina was the only one that Khushi had developed any emotional attachment to. Rubina knew this was purely a result of Khushi's narcissism; Rubina, being a skilled dancer much like Khushi herself, was able to execute the technically complex moves with quickness and grace. The older Rubina became the more she looked like her mentor, and this year she had begun rubbing kohl around her eyes when she danced, just as Khushi did, thick and cat-like.

The dance master nodded at Rubina in the entrance hall. It was no secret he appreciated Rubina's ability to anticipate the next sound that would come from his mouth even before he made it: *tha thicka THA THA tha, thik thikka, THA.* Rubina was able to shift poses quickly, executing Bharatanatyam moves seamlessly through the various sequences. She was a natural at the expressive, dramatic movements. Rubina had thus been moved to dance in Khushi's troupe very quickly — by age thirteen she was a fulltime member, saved the fate of dancing on the streets on a Sunday afternoon to fetch a price for her virginity. Instead, she and the group performed at religious festivals and at weddings of the nobles. Prostitution, however, was Khushi's more profitable business, one she made excellent commissions from.

Though Khushi never made Rubina feel indebted to her for escaping the trade of selling her body, watching the hall turn into a makeshift brothel at night always sobered Rubina. Rather than earning fame as being only a whorehouse, the dance hall was also better known as one of Agra's best places to gather at night, called a *nashaghar*. Men, drinking wine and smoking opium, would watch the dancers perform in the main hall, as they spread out on the floor on Persian rugs, cushioning themselves with pigeon-feather-stuffed pillows. Whilst being entertained, they would discuss who the king was to see in court the next day and who had gotten a share of more land or holdings. The dancers at Khushi's house, trained at the highest skill levels, were often invited to perform at the king's court. To date, Khushi had refused invitations, and — perhaps more surprisingly — the king had never punished her for her refusals. Khushi had two armed men working on the premises to remove patrons if they got rowdy; it was rumoured they were Jahangir's own Rajput soldiers, but Rubina could not work out how Khushi could possibly have managed support from the king to run this type of establishment.

Rubina walked by the storage hall to go outside and dry her clothes on the line. Her nose was met with the sharp sweet scent of ripe berries being pummelled; in the backyard, Khushi kept fruit wines hidden in large oil barrels, along with many more that sat on the dance hall verandah. Though it was well known that King Jahangir drank wine, he had prohibited his subjects to consume it. Khushi thus sold the product illegally. The liquor was so sugary and tasty that, occasionally, Rubina had seen even women come disguised as men to join the festivities at Khushi's brothel just for a taste of her wine.

Swinging back her long dancing plaits, finely braided and slick with coconut and lavender oils, Rubina pinned her washed *lehenga* to the drying cord. Peeking through the layers of pink and yellow sheer fabric, which blew in the soft breeze and superimposed a temporary sunset, Rubina had a full view of the Yamuna. Once again, she was mesmerized by the Mughal castle. Her eyes lingered on the gardens and fountains that hinted at the likely proximity of the Agra Fort's harem. From her viewpoint, although she was very far away, she could still see over the tall fences where guards were posted and make out the fields of mutlicoloured roses, bred solely for the harem's pleasure. She often wondered how sweet the lives of the harem children must be, to grow up amongst flower beds as deep as water pools.

Rubina had no memories of her own childhood — Khushi had never told her how she had arrived at the dancing hall, or who her parents were, leading Rubina to guess she had been sold or abandoned at the gates as a toddler. Her earliest memories were of being handfed variations of simple dhal and rice or coarse flatbread with salted vegetable stew, the daily meal at the hall, by the older girls. She had never owned a toy and she could not remember a day without chores. Khushi ran a tight system whereby the mature girls, whom everyone called "*baajiyaan*," cared and prepared meals for the young, regardless of their fate — which was either to become a dancer or a prostitute, or in many cases, both. Rivalry and intolerance of others was not permitted in the hall, and the slightest act of malintent would mean being cast out onto the streets. In this way, Khushi made it so the bullies were either turned away or reconditioned.

Sometimes Rubina wondered about the girls Khushi had washed her hands of. It was rumoured that one of Khushi's foster girls had made it to the Agra Fort to work as a slave girl. Rubina wondered what her life was like. Even now, she could just see herself dipping her toes in the distantly visible cooling pools if she squinted hard enough. She stood on her tippy toes, straining to catch a better glimpse. Stepping backward, her bare feet hit cool clay. This was the packed terracotta floor where the orphaned girls had taken their meal earlier. Poised just so, Rubina felt she could almost smell the fragrance of ambergris perfume that the concubines were known to rub over their bodies. The scent, she imagined, was foreign and mystical. The women who lived in the imperial harems were known to be Persian, Turkish, and Rajput. It was said they all dressed in gauze-thin, embroidered gowns and had milky white skin and hair as black as the cast iron pots used for cooking food above open fires. Though no one had seen them in person, of course. The harem was a wondrous place that many of the girls at the dance hall dreamt of whilst they slept on the floor worrying about who might purchase them the following day. As Rubina spun around, dancing amongst the many translucent *dupattay* hanging from the clothesline, she imagined herself to be a person worthy of the king's approval, performing in court, wearing gowns designed solely for her.

The sun was getting lower. She headed towards her personal room. Rubina's space was a walled off compartment separated from the younger girls, who slept huddled in the main hall. The side halls were quiet. The foster girls, the youngest of whom would usually jump on Rubina by now and beg for sweets, were nowhere to be seen.

"Mother?" she called out. "*Koi haye ghaar pe?*"

She blinked. Something urged her to turn around. In the space where she had been hanging clothes only seconds ago, a man was now visible, sitting atop a grand beast. With a scarf wrapped around his head and mouth, he jumped down from the great height of the elephant, unassisted. His robust elephant had chalky makeup that decorated her eyes in two lilac tear drops, with flower markings on her trunk made with saffron water.

The bandit darted past her towards the dance master seated in the main hall. Still humming, the dance master was warming up on his tabla for rehearsal. Rubina tried not to scream, afraid she would call attention to herself. The dance hall was about to be looted!

39

Khushi must have locked the foster girls away in the secret crawl space below the kitchen to keep them from being stolen. Given her relatively older age of fifteen years, Rubina could claim to be a senior prostitute, as Khushi had trained her to say should a raid happen, in the hopes she would be considered a worthless steal. Virgins, everyone well knew, fetched the best price.

Rubina rushed into the dance hall following the bandit. Knowing the back exit was blocked by the bandit's men, she hoped she could escape out the front. Much to her surprise, Khushi was standing in open view. Her face sharpened with anger when she spotted Rubina. Khushi was dressed in her finest silk emerald gown, decorated with a thousand tiny pearls. Her hair had been freshly painted with crimson henna, and she smelled of rose oil.

This was no surprise attack, but a planned rendezvous.

Clearly, Khushi had received a message from this masked visitor via a runner, for she had had time for the dance master to prepare her a perfumed bath and massage. When Rubina reached home just a short while ago, Khushi had been dressing in her chambers. The bandit was an expected guest. Rubina saw the evidence of the preparations through the open door leading into Khushi's private corridor. Residue the colour of peacocks floated atop the water sitting in the cauldron, indicating the bath had just been used. Khushi's eyes were heavily made up with kohl, reserved for special occasions. Rubina saw that the black had bled into the fine lines surrounding her eyes. And yet, Khushi was still a breathtaking beauty. Rubina faltered. She had interrupted this meeting but she had nowhere to hide. Khushi was not pleased. Even the foster girls had been smart enough to take to roaming the city to give Khushi privacy, and Rubina, who did what she wanted without reporting to anyone, had failed to notice anything amiss. The dance master was always too immersed in his music once he started playing to pay the natural world he belonged to any attention. He simply went to another dimension, where only his music and the moves of the dancers would reach him.

"Ah," said the stranger, unravelling the ribbons of cloth that had been covering his mouth, the ends tucked into his turban. He was a young man, only a few years older than Rubina. He had a fine face, sharp eyes, and a trim black beard. He looked like royalty. But Rubina's insides cringed — the man looked at her the same way as did the old men who came for the youngest virgins.

He sank to his haunches, a typical peasant's pose. Had it not been for his shoulders, which he held upright to the sky, it might have been a believable act. "This precious jewel," he pointed at Rubina, speaking in a strange, high-pitched tone, "belongs in my court. Why have you kept her from me, Khushi?" he whined. "My men, who are waiting for me outside, can escort her immediately to the castle."

"My dearest *jaan*," Khushi said in refined Hindustani. Peering at her own reflection using the largest mirror in the dance hall, she carefully placed a fine-toothed gold comb in her hair. It sank down immediately in her locks from sheer weight. Rubina noted the hair piece was new, encrusted with rubies, diamonds, sapphires, and emeralds. Khushi's polished voice echoed in the dance hall as she addressed the man: "Do wait for my reply to this, my sweet love, whilst I fix my hair for my prince."

Rubina wondered again where Khushi had received her fine education and training. Khushi had taught Rubina to make a man wait whilst she beautified herself for him to see her true worth. Had it not been for Khushi's sandy skin, Rubina would have thought her foster mother to be of noble descent.

Khushi removed the golden comb and put it in her hair so it would hold more firmly, placing it closer to her temple. Her spirals shone red because of the oil burning in the glass lanterns. She took a moment to stare down at Rubina before she turned to address the prince, who was clearly entranced with Khushi's abundant tresses. "Your father, the king, wanted me in the royal court years ago, and do you know what I told him then about caging his most prized bird?"

The prince dismissed her with a wave of his palm. "I need a full-time dancer in the court. The girls in the harem are the most terrible performers. Perhaps this gem can teach them a thing or too."

"You have not even seen her dance, *jaan*. She has much left still to learn ..."

"Dance!" he pounded his fist on the earth floor, making Rubina jump.

Rubina was not dressed to dance. She was wearing a faded yellow blouse and *ghaghara*, and it being washing day, her only set of daily overlay cloths were hanging out on the lines.

"*Beti*," said Khushi in a harsh tone. "Why did you wait so late in the day to do the wash? Do you expect the moon to dry your clothes?"

"I had to wait for space to clear by the river, *Amma*," Rubina whispered.

"Speak up when you address me! How do you expect to dance for the prince dressed in your undergarments? When he sees you dance for the first time you must be wearing your fineries; the grandiose silk slips and the gold anklets that the maharaja himself has gifted me over the years. So heavy will they be, you will struggle to move under the weight and your leg muscles will have to work twice as hard to hold poses."

"Yes, Mother."

"Prince Khurram, we will arrange a different time. The eve of the full moon next month, during the Moon Festival, my house's most precious diamond will dance in your court. However, I am setting the condition that she must arrive a fortnight in advance to prepare." Khushi twirled a crimson strand around her finger, and the prince followed it like a kitten eyeing yarn. "*Filhaal*, I must teach her how to dance for aristocrats, in both manner and dress, *nah*?"

The prince took in her words and gave Khushi a brief nod of consent. Rubina's stomach flipped as she realized they were in the presence of the king's favourite son.

"*Beti?*" Khushi returned her gaze to Rubina. Rubina saw now what she perceived initially as rage was far worse. It was terror. "Please leave us now. *Jaldee se jaaow.*" The dance master struck his meaty palm upon the drum and Rubina caught Khushi's flame-red curls fly back as she arched her back seductively.

Chapter 7

1610

The camel that Rubina sat upon scuffled its hooves. She was in full *niqab* atop the animal. A beautifully dressed guide with pom poms hanging from his turban pulled the camel with a rope. She dug her fingers into the camel's fur, matted from where the carpet saddle that she sat on slid against him, the hairs of the beast dyed cayenne from the morning sun. It was cool yet, and Rubina was grateful for the cloak that Khushi had placed on her before they set off on their journey towards the Agra Fort.

Rubina had only been able to see a small portion of the Agra Fort from the backyard of the dance hall. Surprisingly, in person the golden tiling and turquoise fountains were exactly as she had pictured. Each mosaic square was hand painted, so exquisite they could be sold individually as art pieces. She had the odd sensation of having been on the premises before. The prince had honoured the deal Khushi had struck, and both women were fetched to be ridden to the castle two weeks before the eve of the feast. Khushi had, in detail, outlined the conditions needed to prepare Rubina personally at the Agra Fort: she wanted an empty outdoor hall, and only her dance master could lead the performance. Rubina was touched by how her foster mother was concerned for her welfare.

"We must arrive at the Agra Fort together. Coming early will allow me to build alliances within the harem and secure our safety," Khushi

44

had told Rubina, just before the camels had arrived. "Once your performance is done, we must leave together. Your home is here, with me, not in the harem. Do not be lured by the *shahzada's* promises."

Never had Khushi shown Rubina outright affection. Yet before their trip, she had offered Rubina the first bath and braided fresh flowers into her hair. Rubina could not understand Khushi's spontaneous hugs or tears, and though Rubina remained polite, after years of a mostly formal relationship, her body was rigid after her foster mother's embraces.

But after arriving by camel, both disguised from the prying eyes of the commoners in heavy cloaks, Khushi was whisked away in a separate direction by the Rajput soldiers. Rubina went on her own journey, observing with silent awe that nearly everything in the imperial harem was built of white marble, the long rows of pillars embedded with gems and precious crystals. It being summer, silk drapes hung from the curved windows as did woven grass screens down which the attendants would drip fragranced water to cool the occupants. Khushi had told her that the Mughals preferred dimmed conditions, for in the winter, thick velvet curtains would hang from the archways. Try as much as she could, Rubina had never been able to truly visualize the grandness of the great palace. Yet here she was now, looking at the very water channel that Khushi had described to her countless times, seeing the water running through the castle and passing through the harem — a shallow yet steady moving internal river that connected the entire fortress.

Rubina, brought in first through the main entrance, was led around the large building by the camel, and then made to disembark at the harem entrance. Servants carefully guided her through the heavy wired gates separating the harem from the rest of the castle. Her cloak only exposed her eyes, yet Rubina could hear smatterings of various dialects: Persian, Bhojpuri, Hindustani, and Dakhni, but none of the rough countryside dialects of old village-style

Hindustani that she was used to hearing in Agra. She scanned the area, her kohled eyes shifting from side to side. Older women, whom the king had presumably outgrown, were seated now against the wall staring at her, chattering amongst themselves. The official language of the court was Persian, but many members communicated with each other in a refined Hindustani. This suited Rubina, as Khushi spoke eloquent Hindustani. The women of the harem were content to watch Rubina like one would watch a bird dip into water, amused but not excited, busily stuffing their mouths with green folds of betel leaf filled with scarlet areca nuts.

The small children these old ladies were looking after (special beings, for they had been selectively spared rejection by the king's wives or other more powerful concubines) were being taken to the children's nursery by the maidens. The children, dressed like dolls in their *angarkhay*, miniature versions of the silky long gowns their elders wore, filed forward like wooden puppets from a toy maker's shop. The boys had kohl dancing around their eyes, painted carefully with adult fingers that had dug into tiny compacts, and the girls had oiled ringlets, made with careful caretaker's hands that had twirled over and over them with coconut. Pampered but well educated, one day these children would rise to play powerful roles within the court. It was likely they were going to take care of those who paid good attention to them during their time in the harem. Through the small window afforded by her *niqab*, Rubina could see one toddler sucking on a mango treat and another playing with a ball which was almost certainly made of pure gold.

She was standing alone in the centre of the harem.

Despite observing her with open, chewing mouths, not one elder had acknowledged Rubina's presence in the concubine quarters. Perhaps they were waiting to see what position she would hold in the kingdom before they devoted time to engaging with her. Without Khushi to guide her, Rubina wasn't sure how to proceed.

She was certain her foster mother would send word soon, but until then, should she unveil herself and approach a matronly concubine for instruction?

"*Adaab,* young mistress." An apple-shaped woman, dressed in a heavy, multicoloured gown, rose slowly. Rubina felt she had passed a test by not losing her cool and waiting to be addressed first before she sought to make connections. The older woman bowed to Rubina, raising her cupped hand to her head. Never had Rubina been addressed so formally. The speaker, round-faced with a big bosom, appeared to command great respect, for the other concubines were now copying her, also raising their cupped hands to Rubina in silent greeting.

"I am Moti Ma. I am, informally, head mistress of all the concubines, and if you want to know how I earned that title, feel free to ask any other ladies in the harem." The woman smiled, showing Rubina ruby-capped teeth, tainted from betel juice. "You must be Rubina. Khushi *jaan* herself asked me to show you your quarters." Moti Ma led Rubina down the maze of halls. "Here they are. Though barely furnished, at least they are private."

"Do you live here also?"

"Here?" Moti Ma laughed, her hand going to her large chest. "Goodness, no. I have my own apartments. I come down to the main harem quarters, the *zenana,* only to socialize."

"Thank you for accompanying me. What are my instructions?"

"Instructions?" Moti Ma laughed again like Rubina had just performed a magic trick. "My dear, you really are serious? Well, if you want instructions, I suggest they be to bide your time. Until you see what life the harem has selected for you, stay out of sight. I bid you farewell."

Moti Ma left behind a perfumed aroma. Rubina inhaled sharply, taking stock of her surroundings. She had a room that just fit a charpoy, which was pressed up against the red sandstone walls. Elegant turquoise and green pillows decorated with peacocks and a thin sheet dressed this woven cot.

Almost instantly she missed her old dance hall, with its cracked mud walls and cranky dance master who had just started to show signs of grudging respect to Rubina, saving her Khushi's bath water or offering her Khushi's leftover henna in pots should Rubina want to condition her hair. At the dance hall, she had been the top girl, but here she was the lowest in the hierarchy. She sat on her bed and, finally alone, uncloaked herself. Then, searching out the bath house she freshened up quickly, grabbing dates and sweet breads to eat alone in her space to avoid questions about why she was in the ladies' quarters. She had a strong feeling the women would find a new dancing girl a threat, and besides, she was not even sure that she had that title to begin with.

Moti Ma did not attempt to reengage with her, but she nodded mildly when she saw Rubina pass in the halls. When days went by without any word, Rubina began to worry. How was she to perform for a kingly audience without knowing what to? During the hours when the harem ladies were listening to poetry recitals or gathered in the garden, she took the opportunity to explore the chambers, and orient herself to her surroundings.

In the early evening, when it was just beginning to cool, the ladies often gathered in the shaded *zenana* garden to seek amusement. Presently they were occupied by a juggler and magician that the king had commissioned. This marked the start of the festivities, for today was both the moonlight party and the eve that Rubina was supposed to debut her dance. As such, she was not tempted by the fluttery laughter or gasps that came from the entertained ladies, soft and tinkering, made to please the king. She peaked out into the garden and saw a lady wearing a delightful moustache. This trained woman, dressed like a foreigner in odd-fitting *churidar* pyjamas, was pulling coloured silk scarves out endlessly from the sari waist of a particularly large concubine. The king himself, though she could not make him out directly, was stretched out on a day bed, nestled by an array of concubines, each attending to his needs.

Rubina realized anxiously that she had to find Khushi before it was too late. She turned and ran barefoot against the fragrant Persian rugs infused with sandalwood and rose water, searching the building. Darting quickly past the Mughal art, embellished floral carvings with Arabic engravings, her foot nearly tripped on an unravelling silver rug cord. Looking outside the octangular cut-out window, Rubina could see the champa, cashew, fig, palm, and mango trees, leaves outlined in the pink sherbet sun. Earlier in the day, the honey scent of the many flowered trees and bushes attracted the sweet songs of red and blue birds who skipped on the shaded divans and many terraces, but now the courtyard was empty. The setting sun's amber reflection trembled upon one of the harem's numerous outdoor pools, where the ladies were safe to remove their veils and dip their feet in during the day.

She took a turn down one of the corridors. These secret halls, she had overheard, were to be used only by the king to access his favourite women separately, through a complex system of winding underground tunnels and channels. There were no eunuchs guarding the pathways lit with ornate candelabras now, the king having enlisted them to assist with ceremonial duties pertaining to the eve's upcoming festivities.

Rubina's face was flushed, her clothes damp under her armpits. She knew that on the outside entrance of the harem stood two armed female guards, one a Turk, the other an Uzbek. Both were built like men, thick limbed like the elephants that were to compete against one another in the contest at first dawn, when the grounds were still clouded in morning mist, in the arena built not far from the castle. Both female guards were trained to kill. Despite this danger of being caught, Rubina continued her search, losing count of the turns she took, exhausting almost every area of the harem, but she saw no clue to where Khushi could be.

Rubina rounded the tight corners trying to navigate the corridors. There was but one room left. The physician had a place in the harem where he tended to issues faced by the harem's occupants, his duties ranging from prescribing opium to assuming the role of a fakir and making predictions about a said concubine's fate in the castle. Rubina hoped that today he would be able to divulge the whereabouts of her foster mother.

Heart in her throat, she found the chipped door and pushed slightly, throwing up a tall shadow of herself on the candlelit wall of the room. The room smelled sickly, of old goats and rotten jasmine flowers.

"*Amma*," gasped Rubina. She had immediately glimpsed Khushi's face, cradled with printed scarves. Her skin looked indigo even in the faded light. "Is it really you?"

The physician stepped out of a dark corner. "I am terribly sorry," he said in halted Hindustani. Rubina gathered he was from overseas judging by his strange hair, the colour of gingerroot, but even from her experience dealing with foreigners at the brothel, she could not gather where this man was from. She had never seen such skin. It was devoid of any colour and had pink veins stitched over the nostrils, forming webs over his cheeks. "She is no longer with us."

"I do not believe you."

He shrugged. "I do not know you well enough to want to lie to you."

"How did mother end up in this bed? She simply cannot be dead! Did she leave behind any message?"

"Khushi left behind nothing but her diseased body."

"Moti Ma says you save lives, not end them." Moti Ma had not said this directly to Rubina, but she had overheard this sentiment when she was rushing from the bath house to her room. Moti Ma had been referring to the prescriptions of opium the physician advised her daughter, Sabina, take, because the girl was weak of mind and low in energy. "That busybody Moti Ma might run the harem, but she is not god. I cannot save what is already departed."

Rubina considered throwing herself on the floor to grieve for her foster mother. But years of bracing herself for raids and attacks on the brothel had sharpened her senses. "I am supposed to have my dance debut in the court tonight," she rambled. "Mother did not have the opportunity to prepare me to dance in front of an aristocratic audience. Nor do I have the proper clothing or jewellery. Have you any idea how hard it was to live amongst the other concubines knowing that tonight I would be presented to dance especially for the prince? The others might have slit my throat from jealousy! How will I return home now? Am I doomed to live in this harem as just another one of the prince's concubines?"

"It's rather difficult to understand your long list of problems that I cannot solve, nor do I desire to. But did I catch in your nearly non-sensical dialogue, 'just another one of the prince's concubines'? You could get whipped for saying such a thing! Boiled alive in a bathing cauldron! Have you no idea what an honour it is to live on these lavish grounds? You have access to the rose gardens, the courtyard, the bathing pools ..."

Rubina fixed her eye on Khushi's face. It looked thoroughly inhuman, as if it had been treated with blue dye, and it had widened unnaturally, with wrinkled lines cutting every which way in a pattern that Rubina had never previously noticed. Had Khushi been older than Rubina realized? Without dancer's face paint, her foster mother's face looked like a dried date. She swallowed, though her mouth was dry. "Has Khushi *jaan* been ... poisoned?"

The physician shrugged. "*Pousta?* Poppy extract? What would a young girl such as yourself know about such matters? More importantly, how did you get past the eunuchs?"

It was Rubina's turn to shrug. She had hoped the physician would act as a type of prophet, and that was why she had sought guidance and help from him. Realizing that the physician was not going to budge, Rubina looked down at her overlay skirt that she wore when dancing — she had not changed since arriving at the harem — and decided to unveil herself to show the physician she was at his mercy. This kind of act always impressed the men at the *nashaghar,* who in their opium-fuelled states, would tip Rubina extra coins should Khushi be short of money to keep her business operating. *Dupatta* lowered, Rubina's wavy hair — unusual for a Rajput — fell to her shoulders. This was perhaps the only tidbit about her ancestry that Khushi had imparted to Rubina: she was Rajput, like Khushi herself. Also like Khushi, Rubina was not ivory skinned like most of the others in the harem; her skin was the colour of tea when you poured in cow's milk.

Rubina spoke once she was certain the physician's eyes were upon her. "I have responsibilities in Agra," she said. "Since *Amma* is no more, I need to train the other dancers and be the head performer. We have a dance hall filled with abandoned young girls, and with Khushi *jaan* gone, who will tend to them? I cannot be stuck here. I have no idea how to perform, and more importantly, *Amma* told me I must return home after I have danced." Trembling, she could not control her racing thoughts. "Was *Amma* poisoned? Truly, I must know. Did she kill herself? What were the circumstances of her death? I plead with you in the name of Akbar the Great, lover of all the world's religions, to please tell me!"

"You have just moved to this harem from the filthy streets, watered by urine and decorated by garbage. Do you not have any fear, running through these halls that only the royal guards and staff are permitted to occupy? Have you no mind at all talking to a royal physician without proper reverence?"

Rubina lowered her eyes as expected and kneeled. She covered her head with her scarf, knowing her loose curls were spilling off to the sides. "I am terribly sorry. I have no one else to whom to turn. *Mu'aaf keedjiyay ...*"

"*Aap ki amma,*" the physician said, thawing, but only slightly, "the famous dancer, took her rightful claim as a concubine and re-entered the court. Here you have no danger of catching the king's eye or that of his promiscuous son. Your mother has told the court you are the king's offspring, a Rajput one at that. The records have been consulted, and it appears that Khushi had a long-standing affair with our great king. It dates back over twenty years, predating the time before he was even crowned. She lived on these grounds for three years and indeed, she was pregnant with you when she left. Or you were a young girl ... this part of the records remains hazy. But what is undeniable is that Khushi is of Rajput noble ancestry. The king granted her permission to live off grounds. They had an arrangement."

Rubina put her hand to her throat. After a moment, she whispered, "You said she left no message."

"Not left. She made sure it was delivered to the right people." The physician smiled, showing rotten teeth. Rubina hated that he was enjoying his power in the kingdom and using it to toy with her. "No one will dare bother you. You need not worry about the prince; he has been notified you are his illegitimate half-sister."

Rubina stared at her feet. How had Khushi fabricated such an elaborate lie? Khushi's daughter? It simply could not be true. Why would Khushi risk her own life with such a fib to keep Rubina safe living amongst the royals? "But what happened to my mother? How can you be sure it is on formal court record that I am of the king's blood?"

"Do not go around boasting of things that might have you killed. It is true that before King Akbar's time, any child of a concubine and royalty might have the chance to have power or take the throne. But nowadays the queens do not allow concubines to hold any sway. Here, in the Agra Fort, you are still nobody. Nonetheless, as I have mentioned, and you should well know, the harem life is far grander than one on the streets as a commoner."

"Did she suffer? Khushi *jaan*?"

He sighed. "She threw up until her insides were on the outside. The dogs on the premises would not eat her vomit."

Rubina backed up, her hand accidentally touching the soft Kashmiri shawl and furs that lined the bedside table. A copper jug sat on top. She suddenly felt an insatiable thirst but could not bring herself to quench it with Khushi's water pot. Her foster mother had saved Rubina by claiming her as her own, and whether this was true or not, all Rubina felt was disgust for her weathered, malformed face.

"*Aur abh*," said the physician, smiling with his decaying teeth, "do you need a checkup whilst you are here, or would you prefer to do it later? All the members of the harem must go through a rigorous inspection."

Rubina did not hear the lechery in his voice, for she had already turned to run.

"*Ruko! Muth jaaow! Muth bhaago!*"

But Rubina was already gone. She had received some answers, but now had more questions than before. Lifting her skirt, she ran back through the maze, for the first time noticing the scent of saffron rice and curried dhal permeating the halls. The thick smell of death lingering in her nostrils was replaced quickly by new scents. Roasted cumin. Fried ginger. Clay-baked naans with caraway seeds, poppy seeds, and nuts. Savoury and strong, they made it so Rubina's very head was filled with the culinary fragrance. She had not realized how hungry she was, but she had a feeling it would be a long while before she would get a chance to eat.

The harem, it appeared, was going to be her new home. And now she had to find out how to make it work. Or find a way to escape, just as the only mother she knew had managed to do.

Chapter 8

2017

When she awoke, Ruby felt she was anywhere but home. Her comforters were alien to her, damp with night sweats. Her lips dry. She licked them and swallowed. The inside of her mouth felt as if it had been stuffed with tissue soaked in old cough syrup. She had fallen asleep in her robe, hot, half-drunk, the sheets tucked around her body like she was a sushi roll.

It was sometime in the mid-morning and the house was empty. Leah was at the community college and Trevor was gone. Evidence of his packing was everywhere; drawers left open; shirts pulled off hangers. Suitcases — unused since their honeymoon to Calgary — had vanished. Only the boxy vintage trunk she'd bought online had been untouched, clearly unattractive to him with its paisley pattern. He had entered the room while Ruby was sleeping. Picking through to find his own things, Trevor had thrown aside Ruby's barely used Indian clothes, leaving them on the floor much the same way he had rejected her. As Ruby swung her legs over the side of the bed, her feet were tickled by the mesh lining of her green *lehenga* and the minuscule, hand-sewn pearls covering it. Ruby's mother had gifted her these items years ago, right after she'd gotten married, even though Ruby didn't have many Indian friends or Indian occasions to go to. She raised her fingers to her temples, feeling light perspiration at her hairline.

"He would've told you sooner," Belle's voice rang in her head, a sour reminder from last night. "But he didn't want to leave this house. My tiny condo just doesn't live up to all *this* fabulousness, apparently."

"We'll have to work out the details of our living arrangement later," Trevor had told them both calmly, as if they were sister wives on a reality show. Ruby had watched him as he warily eyed the stars through the glass ceiling in the solarium. A perfect slice of the universe had been visible from where the three of them were standing. Belle had put her hand on Trevor's shoulder, illustrating the change that had taken place in their relationships with one another. The moonlight had washed lavender streaks over Belle's collarbone. The arrangement of their relationships with one another meant zero to someone looking down at them from outer space, Ruby had thought. Even ten years ago, in the very spot they were standing, there was an older house that had been torn down to build this one. One day there would be something new standing where they were now. And still, no one would give a fuck about the relationship that Belle, Trevor, and Ruby had exchanged, traded, swapped.

"You were my best friend," she had said to Belle somewhat lamely, her words jamming in her throat.

Belle had looked at Trevor. Trevor was still staring out at the stars. She had sighed irritably. "I *was*, Rubes — we had a high school friendship that didn't carry forward quite the way it should have. Do you really feel we have that much in common?"

"Well, we have Trevor in common, so there's that."

"There's that," echoed Belle. It had pained Ruby to see her face. The teeth Belle had straightened in high school with braces and periodically whitened, the eyebrows so fine she had to darken them in with pencil. Ruby knew her expression well, lip turned up like Elvis. It was the same look Belle had when she was so over something: French cooking lessons, trip hop lounges, her brief stint as B-girl in her twenties, and now, Ruby Andrews. Why hadn't she noticed that Trevor had been making the same face at her lately?

Now, in her bedroom, Ruby glanced over at her light pink curtains, the ones that her husband made no secret of hating. Trevor swore their bedroom would be the next thing he would renovate in their house and expressed great delight in the anticipation of tearing down the salmon 1980s drapes she'd selected. They had been the first thing she had bought as a married woman, and she felt so grown-up buying the packaged drapes. They were also the first thing Trevor started mocking when he developed an eye for interior design. "Those ugly things you hung up that look like the mandatory coral couch in a Florida doctor's office," he used to say, or "Cyndi Lauper called. She heard you have her prom dress hanging in the window." But then Trevor had started sleeping downstairs and stopped nagging Ruby about the curtains. The bedroom had become her one, uncontested space within the house. Sure, the kitchen was hers to cook in, but she had not selected any of the fixtures or even the dishware — Ruby couldn't be trusted with such tasks. She ran her hands over the comforters. They were practically the only thing she'd chosen after the curtains; white, fluffy, non-offensive. If Ruby had still slept in the same room with Trevor, he would have eventually installed blackout blinds. She had always thought it funny that he spent so much time convincing her of the merits of the blinds when he himself had relocated to the den, which was essentially nothing but a glass house facing the garden. Ruby had argued strongly that blinds would mess with their natural sleep patterns. Why had she been so adamant about that? Why had they fought about such unimportant matters?

Today she regretted not giving in to the blackout blinds. The room was filled with happy, blissful, passionfruit sunlight. Birds were chirping as if she lived in the middle of a bloody nature sanctuary. A waste truck honked the horn before driving past her driveway.

Had Trevor taken out the garbage before he left? It didn't matter — life was progressing. It stopped for no one, not the death of a relationship, superstar, or prime minister. And who was Ruby, anyway? She wasn't Michael Jackson or Elizabeth Taylor. She wasn't even dead. And, in the aftermath of everything, she was less worried that her husband had just left her for her best friend than she was about people's reaction when they found out. She had — despite every effort made to avoid it — become her own mother.

Ruby pulled her white robe tighter around herself and shuddered. She felt like she had the flu. She pulled her legs back up onto the bed. For the next three hours she sat there, playing out her life with Trevor, trying to remember when things had gone wrong. In the beginning Trevor had liked her curves; he had called her his Baby Mama and his Shorty, but those were the days when he talked like he was from the hood and aspired to live his life out like Eminem. And of course, that was when her shapely areas were confined to her tits and ass. The years had made her body more blobby, less defined. Consequently, the shedding of Trevor's hip-hop skin had him looking at different women with awe; Ruby had seen the way he ogled Kate Moss in lipstick adverts. Even if Ruby lost the pounds that she had gained over the years, she'd never be white or model glamorous. But if Trevor had changed, so had she. Her concert tees had been packed away and eventually donated; her CDs had gotten pushed to the back of the shelf, replaced first by Trevor's accounting books, and later, his classical music CDs. Motherhood had drained her ability to care about bands. Chasing a three-year-old made Nine Inch Nails sound like their lyrics and music were being hacked into strings through a cheese grater, dismembered, deconstructed, and discombobulated. She just couldn't take her old favourites seriously anymore.

In high school she had cared so much about music that she would give a single CD her undivided attention, listening to it from beginning to end, lying on her bed with the jacket cover in her hand. Sometimes she had partaken in this ritual with Curtis Simmons in his car. Memories of her first boyfriend, the one before Trevor, had almost entirely faded away. She knew if she tried to prove they had once been something, she wouldn't find anything — not even a photo of the two tucked in her yearbook. Curtis had been above preservation of such pathetic, nostalgically inducing memorabilia. He had accurately predicted these things would be particularly appealing at the onset of middle age.

At noon, as Ruby continued analyzing her marriage, she realized the change between Trevor and her had not been sudden. Like the example used during last night's debate about whether time had overlapped or was a forward trajectory, the failure of their relationship had been gradual, a continuation of shaded colours on display at the paint store. The Andrews had lived for some time in the grey category, slipping from silver to slate. But now, if their relationship was truly Schrödinger's cat, and if someone bothered to lift the lid to have a look, it would be pronounced officially dead. No doubt about it.

Her stomach rumbled, interjecting. Her mouth tasted like vinegary grapes. Acidic, sharp. She tightened her robe even though no one was home and went to the bathroom to haphazardly run a toothbrush over her teeth. Then she slipped down one of the staircases to heat up a can of vegetable stew she had bought on sale.

Belle didn't care about deals, Ruby thought as she stirred. She bought whatever she wanted, whenever she wanted. Belle indulged as far as her money could take her, never saving for the future — the classic grasshopper in the Aesop fable. But perhaps by investing in her beauty, like some practical witch in a book-turned-movie, Belle had been magically preparing for the security of her own romantic and financial future by poaching an attractive mate. Belle's dinners were almost always some linguine Weight Watcher's bullshit. She went to the gym. She wore all those snazzy outfits the young women wore, looking like some exotic animal on a safari, with her geometric painted tights and matching bra tops. Of course Trevor would be drawn to her: she was everything Ruby wasn't, presented right in front of him almost on the daily. Up until now, Belle had engaged in whimsical romances with French chefs and travelling John types. Ruby had tuned out Belle's recent talk about wanting a man and a house, about wishing she no longer had to work so she could indulge in yoga classes all day long. *If I were you Ruby,* Belle's voice played in Ruby's head, *I would be spending my time getting Botox and perfecting my head stand. I'd sleep in 'til noon, and binge watch Netflix. And I'd buy fucking Citizens of Humanity jeans when I bloody well wanted, not just when Aritzia's having their goddamn year-end clearance sale. I'd be all, peace out, bitches! You don't even know how lucky you are.*

Maybe she hadn't known. Maybe Ruby had wasted her opportunity at being a housewife by focusing on clipping coupons rather than cultivating the perfect body. Even today, the morning following the great betrayal, her body clock had woken her up, telling her the place needed tidying. Ruby took her heated stew to the breakfast bar. It warmed her stomach, providing temporary comfort. She followed it with leftover chocolate cake and room temperature lasagna from the dinner party. Nothing had been refrigerated but she didn't care. What was salmonella compared to a completely failed marriage? Almost immediately, she experienced the feeling of contentment established years ago in her mother's kitchen while eating twenty Oreos frosted over with Twinkie filling.

But not long after binge eating, the usual remorse set in. What had happened that day of the cookie binge, so many years ago? Oh yes, Curtis Simmons, her high school romance, had gone to Portland and never come back. How quickly Trevor had filled the gap. Her eyes roamed to the dinner party dishes stacked in the sink. Belle and Trevor had, in an act of domestic couple role-playing, carried in the dishes through the dining room French doors and into the kitchen. They didn't see the need to wash them. That was Ruby's job. Well, why should Ruby wash them? She thought briefly of John. Did he know anything about Belle and Trevor? Should she seek some type of connection with him on social media and reveal it? Was Ruby still even listed as Belle's friend on Facebook? In a world where your social media activity was as important as your real-life presence, one had to upkeep broken relationships both in person and online.

Ruby put a pause on these questions and decided to have a drink. Trevor had quite a collection, but she proved to be a weakling. She could only drink the Malibu rum and worked herself up to some kind of Russian vodka. She would have gone for the wines (she wondered when Trevor would give in and come home for his vintage collection), but she had no idea how to use the wine opener (another stark reminder of how dependent she was on a man who didn't love her). As she kept drinking, she giggled, remembering John's dimples — how she had been tempted to dip her pinky finger into one at the dinner party.

Chapter 9

2017

"Mom," Leah called out on day four. Or maybe it was day five? Ruby had lost track. Leah walked in through the large entryway to the sunken living room and then back up to the dining room; Ruby was in the family room, a pocket nestled into the right wing of the house. Was family room really a good name for this space with a television and couches? She was a family of one now. Having run out of dishes, Ruby had taken to eating from paper plates with spooky ghosts leftover from Halloween and Baby Elmo from Leah's second birthday.

"What the hell is going on here? For real, Mom."

As it stood, Ruby was watching *Intervention Canada* reruns. It thoroughly went with her mood; here were people who had way more fucked-up lives than she did. Or more daring lives. She was too spoiled by the creature comforts of cable television and central heating to take a hit from a crack pipe. If she could be any animal in the animal kingdom, Ruby would not be a lion or wolf — she would be a calico house cat. The Hallmark movies had been making her weep even more than those about the druggies who kept botching up their last chance. Screw the greeting card movie franchise with their Christian families who all looked like Belle and Trevor. Or all those blended families where every divorce was celebrated with a Christian prayer, a new puppy, and a beautiful single woman who took over the absent — whose absence was never explained — mother's family. And why was some handsome bachelor in a flannel shirt always raising three girls alone in a cabin in the wilderness? It was the kind of remark she would have made to Belle before suggesting Belle try her hand at camping to meet a hot guy.

"I should be asking you, young lady," Ruby forced herself to respond to her daughter. "You've been gone for days without a reply. Don't you think you owe me at least a courtesy call to let me know where you are? Huh? Or should I just assume a young girl is safe just because she thinks she's too old to check in?" It did not escape her that it took sipping vodka and pineapple juice from an old Christmas paper cup for her to find the courage to try out her new mom voice.

Leah looked at her for a long time without speaking. "I told Dad I would be staying at Rick's for a few days. I just came to get the paper I was working on from the computer in Dad's study onto my memory stick." Leah eyed the left wing of the house, as if wishing she could just transport herself to the other side as fast as possible.

"Well, he never relayed the message."

The world came slowly back into focus. She saw the world as Leah did, her semi-drunk, robe-clad mother drinking from a cup on the couch, ignoring the dishes stacked on the table. The television blaring, showing a case study of a twenty-year-old heroin addict injecting dope into herself hiding behind a trash can, only caring about her "right now." Much like Ruby herself. But in the back of her mind, Ruby was worried that she didn't know how to do her own taxes or change her car oil. She wasn't even sure if the organic waste truck came on the same day as the garbage truck. Ruby waited for Leah to console her. She closed her eyes and tears of self-pity rolled from her cheeks and landed in hot drops on her hands.

"You had to have known things were over for a while. Dad has been sleeping in his study for ages," Leah said, her voice harsh, tight.

"But he was playing video games down there late at night and didn't want to wake me up when he got into bed. And I don't know if you know this," she fixed her eyes on her daughter's glossy blue-black hair, "but he left me for Belle."

"Mom," Leah said coldly, "you need to get yourself together. The house looks horrific."

"Leah, did you know about Belle?" In her head she continued, *Belle, the cool one who knows The Weeknd's latest songs and offers to take you to dance classes where people wear stripper heels...*

"Mom, you don't have your own hobbies. You don't have a job, friends — an actual *life* outside of what goes on in this house. And you might lose this place. You can't sit around in a robe and let life pass by you. When is the last time you had a shower? Pull yourself together."

Ruby hugged her arms around each other and pinched the fat under the arms through her robe sleeves. "Do I need to call a lawyer or something?" And then quietly, like a spooked-out child, "Oh why are there so many French doors, glass ceilings, and staircases in this house?"

Leah sighed. She started picking up the empty wrappers. When had she eaten candy bars?

"Sorry, Leah," Ruby said, unsure if she was apologizing for the mess or her existence in general.

Leah sighed again. "It's okay, Mom."

But Ruby knew it wasn't okay. Leah's lip curled in distaste. Everyone who had loved her, or so she thought, looked at her this way.

"I'm going to Rick's."

"He's untrustworthy, you know," Ruby said, suddenly feeling like a roadside fortune teller. "He's going to break your heart."

Leah narrowed her eyes. "Stop meddling in my life. Worry about your own. I know what I'm doing."

The landline rang as Leah walked to the study. Ruby picked up the phone and cradled it between her soft robe and ear.

"Hello," she whispered, verifying she was present. She hadn't even looked at the call display. Did Ruby have the guts to hang up if it wasn't someone she wanted to talk to?

"Rubes, it's me." Trevor. His voice sounded like it already belonged to a different time in her life. "Listen, I didn't want things to go down the way they did. I mean you shouldn't have found out about Belle and me the way you did."

Ruby could hear murmuring in the background. Belle, prodding him, but she couldn't make out her words.

"Uh, I just feel bad for how it happened," he said. Was he talking to Ruby or Belle?

"Why are you calling, Trevor?"

"You don't need the house, Rubes. It's too big for you. I mean, I don't want to involve the law so early on. I could get a smaller place for you. The condo's too small for Belle and me ..."

"Are you imagining that I trade spots with Belle and just move into her place?" Trevor's pause was terrifyingly long. "I wasn't goddamn serious, Trevor. There's Leah, too," Ruby's voice kept shrinking but Trevor apparently could still hear her. "You know ... our daughter."

"Isn't she staying at Randy's?"

"Rick's. And not forever."

"She mentioned she wanted a space with us."

"Oh," she said softly. "Oh."

"I'm sorry, Ruby."

"Don't say you're sorry!" Belle.

"Trevor?" Ruby said, her voice suddenly loud.

"Yes?"

"Leah's not your real daughter."

"Are you fucking kidding me? Really, Rubes? I mean that is a desperate move. Even for you."

"Get a DNA test if you don't believe me." And she hung up. Just like that.

65

Chapter 10

2017

The next afternoon, Ruby fixated on the clock in the kitchen. 2:30 p.m. And now 2:31 p.m. Time kept on slipping, like that bloody Steve Miller Band song. Curtis Simmons and Ruby had listened to that song a lifetime ago, in his car, kissing, each lip lock starting at the exact place another ended. After Steve Miller Band they had listened to old reggae, Ruby recalled, in that secret area you could pull into just past the main area at White Pine Beach, their hair still laced with fine sand. Bet that place wasn't there now ... everything was now regulated and fenced off. There were no wild places left.

What would have happened if she had chosen to go to Portland with Curtis Simmons way back when and taken a risk? What had stopped her then? Her own feelings, quite simply — as wonderful as Curtis made Ruby feel, he made her feel just as uneasy. She was worried if she pursued him to Portland, he would break her heart. It had been much easier to leave their relationship on a wonderful high and escape becoming someone he'd grow tired of — which, to Ruby, was the thing she feared most of all: Curtis Simmons staring at her like she was the most ordinary person in the world. Which also, Ruby realized with dawning clarity, was how a man looked at you even when you produced the most impressive feats of humanity: having a baby and breastfeeding. Instead of being in awe because you performed such magical acts, a man transformed his fantasy vision of a once-coveted hot thing as someone that turned into a boring, maternal, and eventually, uninteresting woman. No one needed a degree to be a stay-at-home-mom, as Trevor had been fond of reminding her; it did not put actual food on the table — it was about as sexy an occupation as perhaps that of a middle-aged stocker at a supermarket. No man found it an awesome adventure to watch their partner's body swell with child, or if they did, they would soon grow disenchanted when they saw the folds of skin a baby hurriedly left behind. Wide terrains of puckered folds and crisscrossed maps of silvery stretch marks; an abandoned human nest that did not always dismantle with time. Perhaps, having an inkling of this at eighteen, Ruby chose Trevor. Trevor, who achieved excellent marks in Accounting 12. Trevor, who even in the height of his obsession with watching *8 Mile* every evening, called home if he was running late. A rock star Trevor Michael Andrews was not. And yet, even predictable, sensible Trevor Andrews had eventually gotten tired of Ruby.

Now Ruby had time, and lots of it, to imagine a parallel life with Curtis. One where the two remained passionate about each other, consumed to the point where time intensified to absolute nullification, where each minute in the day could be spent indulging in the sheer pleasure of touching the other person and losing yourself in how good their skin felt against yours. Remembering Curtis, Ruby now realized, made her feel alive again. Lost in her fantasies for the next few hours, Ruby sat at the kitchen bar and imagined herself as someone who achieved perfection and kept up with it. Her dreamt-up self was someone skinny but nicely toned; someone fuckable and also emotionally available; someone who read the news and had strong views yet was engaging to talk to. Someone who maintained arched eyebrows, hairless legs, and freshly painted nails without chips. A person who didn't surrender to a life of comfortable clothes and no makeup fulltime. But most of all — in this imagined timeline of hers merged with Curtis — she was someone who was eternally lovable. Someone who had value and worth.

She stared at the marble ripples on the bar counter. There was no way to measure, in this dreamt-up universe of hers, whether Curtis would have loved Ruby if they'd stayed together. Love could be measured by the extent of dilated pupils or a rise in chemicals, but no one could truly apprehend how a person really felt it. Time could likewise be measured with clocks or the pathway of the sun, but how could anyone say how each person experienced one minute or ten years? Before the Big Bang, Ruby reminded herself, there was no time, nothing was moving. No humans fucking shit up with their rules and rituals, fences, and signs. No Ruby. No Curtis. No Trevor. Time was supposed to be a measured interaction of the earth's rotation around the sun — a relationship between two moving objects. Was love a measured interaction between two people? It was nice to fantasize imagined projections of a life with Curtis, but she no longer had interactions with him. Not anymore.

If Ruby decided not to be an object anymore and killed herself, she wouldn't feel time. Would anyone in her life even miss her? She got up abruptly and started fiddling with the block of knives near the oven, sweating at the possibilities. Ruby was again experiencing every second of time individually, painfully, horribly.

Ruby suddenly remembered hearing an interview with a released prisoner of war. This woman explained how, without a society around her, she had lost complete sense of who she was. The woman had talked at length about how she had started to forget how to read. The books left behind in her cell no longer made sense to her; words were just nonsensical symbols.

Without being plugged into a social structure that helped her recognize what role she had to play, Ruby realized that not only was she *not* an individual, she wasn't much of anything at all. She had just been the sum of all the parts around her. And now she had no parts around her anymore to move her motorized clock bits. Time had altered for her, expanding and contorting, and her sense of self was being sucked through a blackhole. Who the hell was Ruby supposed to be now? Was she to cling to being Trevor's wife and so continue being Ruby Andrews? Should she go back to being Ruby Malkhana, daughter of Indian immigrants, and reclaim the surname of a father who had left her when she was a young girl? Could she claim to be a mother if her daughter didn't want to be mothered? Was this how her own mother had felt when her father had left the family for Julia? And how exactly had Ruby's mother felt when Ruby had popped Julia's CD by Everything But the Girl in her stereo, the techno beat slithering through the crack of her closed bedroom door? How much worse would it feel to see Leah physically spend time with Belle — Belle, who Ruby once had a genuine relationship with?

Ruby forced herself to leave the kitchen and take a shower. The steamy water washed away who she had been minutes ago, along with her dark thoughts. She slipped on wide pants and a summer sweater and went down to the solarium. There, she slid open the glass door leading to the outdoors. The summer sky was clear. There were no flowers — just a barren rock garden that Trevor thought would be the perfect backdrop for meditation and relaxation. Neither had ever taken yoga, though Ruby could no longer say with certainty that Trevor hadn't gone to a class with Belle. Ruby sat cross-legged on the bare concrete. She opened her palms to the universe. She saw Belle on top of Trevor behind her closed eyes. Fuck. "*Om*," she said out loud instead. Then she shouted, "Zen, Ying-motherfucking-yang, earth mother goddess!"

She opened her eyes. Something was distracting her. It was the glare of her wedding ring. Gold with a small diamond mounted on the band; it was the housewife standard, albeit a bit small. She always doubted that it was real but pointing this out to Trevor at the time would have exposed the fragility of their relationship, taking it to a place neither could come back from. He had been trying then, hadn't he? He had only been a boy when he proposed to her.

She squeezed her eyes, trying to concentrate. Fuck Belle for taking yoga, the one thing Ruby should have known how to do, being Indian and all. She sucked air through her nostrils. Fuck Belle for using white-girl words like "chakra" and "kismet" in her daily language. For wearing goddamn leggings painted with the image of an Indian girl with a *bindi* on her forehead. For acting like she was the most cultured person in the world because she was pro-immigration and generally stood for progressive ideals. Fuck her for being in love with all things multicultural and getting excited about getting free samosas on Vaisakhi and for knowing that authentic chai was way better than chai lattes, because she had an Indian best friend who made tea for her regularly. *We had a high school friendship that didn't carry forward quite the way it should have.*

Fuck fucking Belle!

She pulled at her ring and chucked it far into the square shaped hedges. Then she released air she had stored in her nose, flaring out her nostrils and puffing the air out in one go like the wolf in "The Three Little Pigs." Although, really, when Ruby thought about it, it was Belle and Trevor who were the wolves. Ruby was the pig with the brick house — or, more like the glass house — trying to hang on with all her might.

She shook out her fingers. The weight was gone from her finger. Her mind felt clear. She rolled her neck and massaged the arches of her feet. She was approaching yogic tranquility. Or so it seemed. Whatever it was, she'd take it.

She let her mind go to a place she would have much rather been.

Chapter 11

1610

Moti Ma stood hovering over Rubina's charpoy in the harem. "*Aap kay naachnay kay kapray*," she said in aristocratic Hindustani, words sung out like poetic verse. She held a stack of dance clothes in one hand and tucked her sari back over her ample waist with the other. She stopped talking for a moment to chew the betel leaves in her mouth. "Well, Khushi's dance clothes, but the physician tells me these are yours now?"

Rubina eyed the stack in Moti Ma's arms, and had a sudden recollection of Khushi *jaan's* body in the physician's bed earlier. Drapes of crimson material spilled from the older woman's chest like a bloody waterfall. Rubina could see that the pieces were decorated with rare shells and silver bells from *jhanjar* anklets. On her cot lay an intricately carved mahogany jewellery box. Behind Moti Ma, through the opening of her room, which had no door, Rubina could see some of the older concubines giggling, legs outstretched as they reached for their toes.

"What are they doing?"

"Yogi Bandeer was here. If he was not a million years old and tested to be one who follows *brahmacharya*, the practice of celibacy, the king would never have permitted him to enter the harem." Moti Ma smiled, exposing browning teeth, yellow at the roots. "The Nath Yogi has taught the ladies some moves for health and wealth of the mind. Hurry! It is almost time for your dance performance. I need to lace your *choli*. Your dance master arrived by palanquin just minutes ago. He is in the main hall, and there are several musicians, sitarists and tabla players. Are you quite ready?"

"Quite," Rubina lied, stretching her arms above her head. She undressed, her plain yellow top slipping to the floor, not feeling shy as Moti Ma hurriedly tightened her new *choli* that fit her breasts and shoulders surprisingly well and fastened her *dupatta* to her hair with jewelled pins. She stepped into the new slip and dancing skirt that Moti Ma held open. When Rubina unclasped the tiny ivory hook on the jewellery box, she cried out. "I think there has been a mistake. These anklets look to be made of real diamonds and rubies." She held up two bands five fingers wide, encrusted with walnut-sized jewels. "But they are so large they seem to be *naqli*."

"Nothing in this royal court is fake, except perhaps the people."

"But I move quickly. These could fall off."

"You are in the royal court now, dear. The dance floor is painted with genuine gold and there are jewels implanted in the pillars. The king will obviously send you such rarities to match your dress every performance. He cannot have you wear anything less. The dressmaker has designed this outfit using your mother's measurements."

"My dance teacher's?"

Moti Ma did not meet her eye. "Is it true you are Khushi's exact size?"

Rubina nodded. Years of dancing had made her frame small and her arms and leg muscles strong, like Khushi's. She sat still whilst Moti Ma delicately rubbed kohl under her eyes using her thumb. Moti Ma then flipped open Rubina's palm and made a *tsk* sound.

"No one came to do my henna," Rubina said quickly. "The local henna artist did mother's the night before she performed."

"We have black henna here," said Moti Ma. "From Zinjibār. The Portuguese brought it. I will do it myself for you next time. Today, we will make you gloves." Moti Ma reached down and touched her own scarlet skirt. It was made of thin crepe silk, just like the clothing of all the concubines. She ripped a strip expertly, and wrapped a piece around Rubina's middle finger, proceeding to do a bandaging action until she reached Rubina's elbow.

"Do not squander tonight's performance. Prince Khurram might have asked some time ago for you to perform, but he has already forgotten you as he does many of his other whims. It was I that put in his ear that you were worth watching."

Once Moti Ma was done perfuming Rubina with her own bottled rose scent, made from the foam left on top of boiled rose petal water, Rubina could not understand why so many of the other girls were whispering warnings to each other, telling tales about how the head concubine could not be trusted.

Chapter 12

1610

The pavilions in the main dance hall were meant to kiss the sky. Rubina could not imagine the number of men it would take to stand upon one another's shoulders to reach the white marble inlay of the airy and light domed ceiling. She was ushered in via the side partition, surrounded by a parade of eunuchs, each dressed in a white muslin *kurta*. The shirts were tucked into Hindustani-style pantaloons, each a different colour — pink, green, gold. Looking through the crisscrossed rosewood fencing, Rubina could just make out the setup designed to please the king.

Silver and gold threaded Persian carpets cloaked the walls. On ivory stands stood silver urns and kettles filled with red rose perfume. Girls in sheer leaf-green saris waited near the walls holding gold washing pots should the king and his court choose to freshen up before the performance. The musicians and dance master were already seated on a wool carpet so fine it looked like silk, with a filigree design of gold grapes woven in. In front of them stretched a vast area of marble flooring for Rubina to dance on. Off to the far side of the wall stood a massive throne flanked by smaller thrones, glistening with a master inlay of jewels that Rubina could see even from her distant vantage point. Other members of the nobility, all men, were already seated across from the throne on yet another finely patterned rug. Each noble was outfitted in a decorative dress suit more elaborate than the one worn by the man beside him.

The king and his procession arrived. Rubina saw the court rise and bow, all performing the *taslim* together, as if in prayer. At once she spotted Prince Khurram, recognizing his sharp black beard and straight nose. He walked behind his father, his shoulders high. Once the court was seated again, the eunuchs pushed Rubina out onto the marble floor, her face and head still hooded by the red *odhni* that Moti Ma had arranged on her face. She felt sick with nausea. How could she perform as she had at the dance hall? She had not been prepared as Khushi had promised she would be. Never had she danced with the accompaniment of multiple musicians. She was not just performing for local city folk, potters, and tea makers. These were the noble members of the great empire!

Her old dance master began humming, his mouth an instrument. His voice was comforting, gentle, and firm. He was going slow, purposefully giving her time to recall what they had practised so many times at the dance hall. But he was humming the notes to Khushi's most intricate number, an item she had watched with awe and only learned in segments and parts. Rubina swallowed, missing the first bar. She could not risk hesitating now. Her place in the court was dependent upon tonight's performance.

With a sudden jolt, Rubina remembered the sixty-four principles of specialized dance positions and arrangements of her limbs, torso, and face. She imagined her body as being separated into triangles. The sitar and tabla players joined in, and Rubina bent her knees, spreading her arms outward. She began carefully, tapping only her feet, enticing her audience, until the ripple continued upward through her abdomen. Bringing her hands to her mouth, she moulded them to perform the act of playing keys on a flute, then morphed them into a bird, next a kite, contouring and moving her body across the floor. As the music picked up, so did she, taking care to celebrate each rhythmic move in a pose. Soon she was twirling wildly, and her *chunni* fell from her face.

She had taken over Khushi's piece, putting in her own design and imprint. Balancing carefully with her left leg, she raised her right leg in the air. She held it in her hand, high and straight. Emotion passed through her face rapidly: anger, sadness, happiness. This dance was about two lovers, separated by a battle, but now they were reunited, and Rubina danced as Khushi had taught her — the hours spent daily in the studio coming to her in muscle memory. Move right, then left. Finger poised to her lips. A kiss. Arm extended out to show she wanted to receive love, and her grand finale: dozens of perfectly executed spins, taking care to spot so she would not get dizzy. She paused so suddenly that her skirts were still swishing around her, and her hair, long and curly, was wild about her face. She bent down to touch her forehead to the dance floor in a sign of respect, and brought her hands together in prayer position, her eyes cast down and away from the emperor.

The royal court went wild in its appreciation. Loud, enthusiastically uttered words of praise, and flowers and coins were thrown her way, clear signs of the attendees' approval; the noise, trapped dully by the domed ceiling, echoed back down, thundering around Rubina in a second, more intense, wave. *Va-vah! Kitnee khoob-sooret! Jiyo hazaaron saal! Wo-wow! How Gorgeous! May you live a thousand years!* The finely dressed eunuchs were suddenly back, each with a jewel pinned in the centre of his turban, clean cheeked with sweet, boyish features. One reached out to pull Rubina's *dupatta* back over her face and another sat her on a large, cushioned pillow. Then, in one mighty swoop, they hoisted her up, seated, above their heads. A moving team of humans that now resembled a grand elephant or camel, they headed back behind the crisscross patterned wall.

"Hurry, Raj," one whispered. "They will eat her alive!"

"We are moving as quickly as we can," the one named Raj said. He had an accent Rubina was used to hearing on the streets of Agra. She was comforted by this, and looking downwards, saw his golden slippers sliding across the marble floor.

Once Rubina was safely out of view behind the fencing, they lowered her to the ground. The eunuchs scattered, but Raj remained, pulling at his pale rose gossamer pantaloons.

"Quite a performance! *Buhoth barrhiya*!" he cheered. He spoke with a gulley-accented Hindustani, the preferred but unofficial language of the court, choppy and filled with slang. "Exquisite training! You will be commissioned to dance at every feast. Soon, you will be a star. You will get requested to dance in Amber, in front of one of the Navaratnas, the nine gems of the royal court, no less. Each gem was designated by King Akbar himself to have a special meaning in the kingdom. And one gem in particular — the one I am referring to — is the maharaja of Amber Court, Maharaja Man Singh. You do know that Akbar the Great married Man Singh's aunt, Mariam-uz-Zamani? She is the mother of our present ruler, King Jahangir."

"You are telling me so much so fast. I do not know which maharaja you refer to." Rubina was still trying to catch her breath. She was embarrassed that she had never learned much of the royal order or lineage beyond the name of the old king, Akbar, his son the current king, Jahangir, and Jahangir's favourite son, Prince Khurram. The first time she had seen Prince Khurram had been in Khushi's dance hall two weeks earlier.

Raj handed her a copper cup filled with clear water brought in from the mountain tops. Rubina drank greedily.

"Maharaja Man Singh of Amber! He has conquered many lands on behalf of the Mughal army, crushed many rebellions and destroyed small kings! He was appointed Governor of Bengal, Orissa, and Bihar. In fact, he fought alongside our King Jahangir himself when the king was just a prince." Rubina was still seated. Raj helped her up by her elbow off the large pillow, speaking to her in rapid fire whispers. "Maybe I am confusing you."

"No," said Rubina, grateful for a chance to understand royal politics and get her bearing. "Tell me more."

"It is a good thing you want to learn more, young bird, for knowing such details will help further your position in the kingdom. King Jahangir and Man Singh have a fraught relationship. Man Singh never wanted Jahangir to take the throne. The maharaja said he was a wastrel, a scoundrel who was too much into opium. But Jahangir won the throne! When Akbar, Jahangir's father, was alive, Man Singh had much power. Now, out of spite, Jahangir has stripped many land titles from Man Singh, including taking Bengal from him. Man Singh has invited Jahangir to the Amber Fort to try to reconcile things. Rumour has it that Man Singh has hidden away many of the treasures from his plunders of the Afghan tribes, secreting them in his fort that the Mughal dynasty has never discovered. Imagine if Jahangir takes you along on his expedition!"

"What expedition?"

"The royals are always going on expeditions." Raj flicked his hands rapidly like butterfly wings. "To hunt, to fight war campaigns, to visit Kashmir, to relax. They spent more time on the go than they do here at the palaces. They only really settled down during Akbar's time, for we even speak what is known to foreigners as the 'language of the camp.' Do not look so afraid. They are fashionable and well-seasoned travellers. Just you wait and see."

Rubina's head was spinning from all the information. "Why are you telling me all this?" Suspicion crept into her.

"I do not seek to hide my motives. I want to hitch myself to the most talented dancer in the kingdom."

She felt the first sensations of flattery flushing her cheeks, "But I cannot imagine I will ever be sent to dance in another court."

78

Raj squeezed her arm playfully. "Surprisingly, you have an opportunity to do so awaiting you! As I told you, Maharaja Man Singh is desperate to please his majesty. And his majesty does owe many of the great battles won to the maharaja. Jahangir will not refuse the invitation to the Amber Fort. They must address their issues. Play your cards right and you will not be stuck living in a harem as a hidden virgin your entire *zindagi*. You will see great jewels in the fort if you indeed go away, and you will be invited to dance in the hall for a private audience, in the Sheesh Mahal no less! Did you know, the interior walls are made from coloured glass imported from across the seas? Imagine when the nobles see you dance in that room. All your elegant moves reflected countless times over — you will be a *sitara*! It is said that the candles lit in that hall glow in the mirrors like a thousand stars."

"Really?" Rubina imagined a ceiling reflecting countless flames. How had her virginity been so obvious to Raj? Before she thought to ask him, a small voice in her head told her she was supposed to head back to Khushi's dance hall in Agra. Perhaps she should aim to perform terribly so that the prince would forget her dance talents and she could slip away, no longer needed or wanted by the kingdom.

"But you must not forget me. You must bring me a bauble from the Amber Court, a souvenir, to prove the value of our new union. I take care of you, you take care of me. Imagine my glee if this bauble is from the loot the maharaja is sure to be hiding in his fort! A wild bird like you should not find it hard to bring back your new *dostar* a present, *nah*?"

Rubina lifted her veil and peeked up. Raj boasted shapely eyebrows and a delightful smile; he was wonderfully easy to look at. "Is the harem not a good place to live? My Khushi *jaan* also warned me to not to stay here, but now the prince has taken notice of me. However, the city of Agra is cutthroat and dangerous."

"Dangerous?" Raj asked, toying with the bangles on Rubina's arm.

"*Kaisay khatarnaak hai?*"

"Your accent tells me you grew up in Agra. Do you not remember what it was like?"

"Not really," he sighed. "I was brought here when I was nine years old. My mother saw I looked better in the dresses I stole from my sisters than they did and sold me as a eunuch. It is no shame to be a eunuch in the court; she is very proud of the title I now hold. My mother wishes for me to go to high places in the court. She says that she had a vision that one day I will serve the king and queen directly. A great eunuch can hold much power in this court. When I was young, I did not leave my home to explore the streets as I was content to play with my sisters' fineries instead. My castration, however, was still performed after I entered puberty, just so the kingdom could ensure I was right for the position. I could have told them I was born for the role. Tell me, tiny bird, about Agra. What happens there?"

"Lootings," Rubina said, pulling him closer to the candles nestled in the corner. "Rapes, murders. My mother ran a dance hall. A woman running such an enterprise alone; you must understand the dangers ..."

Raj shrugged. "Yes, but she was protected by the king. Everyone knew Khushi sold virgin girls. The king himself shopped for night companions for his nobles at your hall."

"She was a dance teacher, too," said Rubina, pulling back her glittering arms from Raj.

"Was she not the mother-head of a nighttime brothel house? What were the evening parties like, my *chakli*? You lived in the *nashaghar*. What things you must have seen and heard!"

"Nevertheless," Rubina avoided the question, "the streets of Agra are never safe. They are overrun with disease, beggars, thieves, the likes. My mother warned me against staying here but, I thought, well ... hoped," she said sheepishly, "that the harem was the safest place in the world."

Raj let out an astonished laugh. It rang out in the air: the laugh of a man, not a boy. "The harem? Safe? Well, you might have a fine bed to sleep in at night, but the ladies cannot be trusted, my little bird."

"Rubina."

"Rubina, you are indeed my little *chakli*. A sweet and beautiful baby bird that has fled her old life. I have heard how Khushi protected her favourite dancer. She sheltered you from a hard life, did she not? We all know how pure she kept you! How will you take to living in the confines of this jailed royal harem? These women will hate you for your beauty. Especially once they hear you can use your outstanding talent in dancing to please the court. Each will scheme to strip you of your jewels. They will yearn to be you ... but perhaps you can use this to your advantage. Teach them how to move, keep them wanting more — tell them they can learn dance moves from you to entice the king and to please him sexually."

"I know nothing of that!"

Raj smirked. "You had better learn. I can get you some scripts. With illustrations. Would you like lessons? You know some members of our court have the great honour of recording the couplings between the king and his partners. They watch moving flesh live, right in front of them. Everything is written meticulously in the record. Every position, every ..."

"Where do *you* sleep?"

"With you, in the harem. I am safe. The physician has made me outwardly more like you than you can begin to imagine. I have the strength of a man, the desires of a woman." Raj looked down at his trousers and Rubina's eyes followed his. "I did not mind the procedure. The others, they were not so lucky — the surgery was against their wishes. Dinesh, for instance, thinks more like a man. Beware Dinesh. He will lust after you, but he cannot deliver satisfaction."

A strange gurgling sound interrupted Raj. "What is that horrid sound?" he asked, reaching over to play with the bracelets adorning her wrist.

"My stomach," Rubina admitted. "I have not eaten in hours. I have been demanding answers from the physician regarding Khushi *jaan*." An image of Khushi *jaan's* sapphire-hued poisoned face flashed in her mind. "Not that I received any good answers."

"Well, *aajaayay, jaldi say*. I know a back route to the royal kitchen and we can get there quickly. I think Daniyal *bhayya* will take a liking to you."

"Daniyal?"

"The royal chef!" Raj winked. "You absolutely must win him over. Then we can get our fill of sweet *mithai*. I want the pistachio and mango ones, okay?"

"I would prefer savoury dishes."

"But they are my favourite, and I am your new friend, right, *chakli*?" Raj did not wait for her reply. "Remember to appease Daniyal *bhayya*. Do not fight with him. Agree with everything he says. Or we will not get anything. Do not argue with him. Repeat it."

"Do not argue with the royal chef."

"Good." He took her hand in his, locking his pinky through one of her sparkly bracelets. Before the night was over, he would claim one as his own. They fled down the candlelit labyrinthine corridors towards the seductive scent of spiced curried stews that Rubina remembered from earlier — the smell of fennel, buttery biryani rice, and creamy almond puddings that cut clear through the fragrance that the rose fountains were spewing into the air. A eunuch guarded a door that led to a dimly lit passageway. He nodded at Raj, who knocked a succession of eight taps.

"Are you sure this is safe?" she whispered.

Raj smiled playfully at Rubina. "Nowhere in the harem is safe. Not even your own bed. What you need to ask from now on is,

82

'how can I make this situation safe for me?' Only the ruthless survive the court. Now we are best friends for life, and we must look after each other."

It was a statement, not a question. He turned to rap on the door once more.

Chapter 13

2017

"Open up, Rubes, I know you're in there!" The pounding continued. "Open. Up!"

Ruby tried to remember what day it was. The house was clean. She didn't remember tidying up, but she must have. She rubbed her eyes. She looked in the closet for her trusty robe, surprised she'd fallen asleep naked. When had she last slept naked? She felt so uninhibited with no one around. Wrapping the robe around herself, she stepped down the staircase and looked over at the identical staircase across from her with disdain. It was like looking at a mirror and finding that her reflection had disappeared.

As she reached halfway down, she caught the scent of Indian spices — tikka masala — remembering that yesterday she had reorganized the jars. Wiping them down and rearranging everything last night had made her feel catatonic, at peace. How lovely the items smelled in the glass jars: the fennel seeds, licoricey and sharp; the turmeric, bitter and dizzying. She had kept her mother's incense in the same cabinet; the word her mother had for it came to her now: *agarbatti.* The sticks of camphor mixed with dried chili conjured up the image of an Indian marketplace. Even the next day the scent had managed to linger, filling the corners of the house, in spite of all its wings and French doors. These were parts of herself that had nothing to do with Trevor, no matter how many staircases he built.

The television, she could hear, was blaring in the family room, filtering through because Ruby had chosen not to close the French doors as Trevor had instructed her to do. He asked her to do this for no other reason, she suspected, than that he liked opening them to remind himself he'd had them installed. The television was reporting wildfires spreading through interior British Columbia. Ruby remembered watching yesterday that Kamloops was on fire. People had been evacuated. There was a woman in tears claiming that she had already lost her first house in the fire in Fort McMurray the year earlier. How could her house, newly built, burn down again? The camera had zoomed in on a helicopter dousing a raging orange fire with water. The flames were such a brilliantly appealing vision to her — she was surprised they were so destructive.

The pounding on the door continued. "Ruby!"

Ruby bristled. She looked down at her hands, bare, no ring to nervously toy with. With a jolt, she remembered — she had thrown out her wedding ring. Trevor had left her. Her head spun. Instinctively, she looked up at the ceiling as if someone was watching her from above. She didn't really believe anyone was. It was a socially conditioned move she had picked up from her mother, and it made her feel the same way smoothing down a dress to make the wrinkles go away would.

Ruby, like many other Indian Muslim girls her age, had been sent off to Madrassah — Muslim school — on the weekends and had her head filled with images of burning hells and renegade angels, but instead of being terrified into indoctrination, she had merely grown impatient with the simple plot line of the stories. *Woman tempts man in paradise. Man eats apple. Humanity is punished.* They sounded just as made up as the stories about Rudolph and Santa that the teachers at school were recycling. Symbolic or not, she couldn't subscribe to them. Her mother did not have the time/interest/conviction either to keep the myth of Santa alive or to solidify the terrors of a hell should Ruby not obey religious rules. Rajput Muslims had a history of mixing Hindu traditions with Muslim ones, and this practice had added to her mother's flexibility about beliefs. There had been, however, promises in prayer, something ambiguous her mother muttered into her hands and to the sky periodically, even toward the end of her failing cancer treatments.

But who, Ruby wondered, was she to pray to? The same god that had created a raging hell? The very one that collected prayers from bowing humans, chanting humans, humans who beat themselves in his name? What was this god doing with all these fevered prayers? Was he building himself a castle like a tooth fairy did out of children's milk teeth, or burying himself under them, like a hoarder who collected stacks of newspapers? And how fair would it be that Ruby got what she wanted when thousands of "heathens" died of starvation around the world? Could she accept the help of a god that hierarchically graded subjects on their obedience? And what if she prayed but it all went unanswered because god had a better plan? Then what was the point of any of it? Surely her own mother had prayed to get Julia away from her father, and that had gotten her nowhere. When Ruby asked her mother all these questions about the injustices of patriarchal history, selective prayer answering, and mythological legends that were reminiscent of the tales of the Greek gods, she was given but one answer: it was better to do something than nothing at all.

Instead of praying, Ruby had put a more than weighty pressure on herself over the years to not make any errors and stay in control, and if she fucked up, then for x number of nights she had strong bouts of anxiety and self-blame awaiting her. She envied the people who put their energy into praying — they were allowed the ability even as adults to believe in something as magical as Santa, keep the hope of having things fixed or make sense for them: cancer, divorce, war.

"I know you're home! For godsakes, your car's in the driveway!"

Today, more than ever, Ruby wished she had a god to believe in so she could believe in a better plan. Because right now she felt like she couldn't breathe, goddamn it; it was like that time she had the stomach flu and was so sick she literally wanted to die — she was completely all for medically assisted dying after that illness. This was the same thing, except a sickness of the mind. How first world of a problem was it to have a panic attack, anyway? People in the developing world were concerned about their day-to-day survival; they did not have the luxury of panting dramatically on one of two staircases trying not to pass out from stress.

She. Had. To. Go. On.

The person at the door would not let up.

Ruby briefly wished she had a mother to call now. Not that calling the mother who had not supported Ruby's choice to have a baby in her teens and then marry Trevor was all that appealing. She lifted her head high. This was just a fucking pending divorce. A betrayal. *Just* that. Millions of women endured it every day.

By now she had talked herself to the front door.

"Ruby, we need to talk! Have a heart!"

A heart. Ruby was standing on her tippy toes; the peephole was built with Trevor's height in mind. Belle stood there, caramel blonde hair glowing like a halo around her animated face.

"You never leave the house at this time. Your routine is totally predictable. Just open the door! Look, I didn't want to do this to you. If I hadn't have found out about the baby, I would have broken it off with Trevor. I didn't set out to destroy your life, you know. I tried so many times to break things off with him. But we keep getting drawn to one another … it's like this weird cosmic energy," Belle was saying. "You know, kismet …"

Ruby opened the door a crack. "Did you say baby?"

Chapter 14

2017

"Thank god," Belle said, pushing past Ruby. She had on a short floral dress. Skinny heels, shiny.

Ruby felt exposed. Belle had come in full makeup, dressed to go to her massage therapist job. Eyebrows drawn using brown liner. Pink, glossy lips. Ruby touched her upper lip, feeling fuzz. She reknotted her robe, feeling it mildly funny that this time, she was the one naked under a housecoat and not Belle.

Last month Belle had been a receptionist, and besides, who wore heels to massage people? And didn't you need specific training to massage people? But who was Ruby to comment, being virtually jobless, since, well, forever.

"Look Ruby, there is one of you and soon-to-be four of us, counting Leah. We need a bigger place. You don't need all this space. Why are you being so difficult?"

"What are you saying?"

"Ruby, please don't be thick. It isn't a good look on you," she sidestepped Ruby with this double innuendo. "I'm having Trevor's baby." Her feet tap-tapped all the way to the kitchen.

"How do you know it's not John's?" Ruby said, feeling like a stuffed animal in her robe. She rubbed the velveteen sash between her index finger and thumb.

"Are you fucking kidding me?"

"Oh, how I wish I was."

"John," Belle said, reaching for the kettle, "used condoms."

Ruby recoiled like she had been shown a graphic page in a pornographic manga book; a man making love to a woman who was part octopus, tentacles swallowing him in a passionate embrace. The image of Belle and John sleeping together was more offensive to her than Belle and Trevor. Ruby plucked the kettle back from Belle.

"You're saying you and Trevor didn't."

Belle sighed, hands on hips. "I'm saying I need a cup of green tea; it's a stress reliever for me, and I have a long shift ahead. And, frankly, I don't care if you believe me. Unlike you, I don't *lie* about my sex life. John was meticulous about protection. Ridiculously level-headed, even in the throes of passion. He didn't lose himself in me, like *other guys*, you know?"

"Actually Belle, you did lie about your sex life. You neglected to tell me you were sleeping with my husband."

"Well, you overtold to the point of lying," Belle was rummaging for a cup. "You said you were making out with Trevor on your anniversary."

"I was kind of kidding — never mind. Please leave my house, Belle."

"Kidding?" a snort. "It's not *your* house, Ruby. Trevor pays for everything. Hasn't he taken care of you long enough?"

Ruby bit her lip.

"We need the house, Ruby. Just think about it, and you'll see it's rational. You won't need to clean the house for hours. You can start working and learn how to support yourself, you know? It'll be good for you. You'll see life is more than organizing your linen closet so neatly that it could be featured in a catalogue. Although," she said, poking around again, "it does look rather mesmerizingly shiny in here." She sniffed. "It's smells of curry spice, but cleaner, somehow."

Ruby was relieved Belle hadn't stumbled on her a few days back, in the glory of her binge drinking and paper plate–using days. She brushed her finger along the spotless counter. "Yes, us Curry People can never be too clean given our wild cooking habits."

"Please don't be cheap and make this a race issue. What I meant was, Leah told me when she saw you here last the place was a dump."

Leah. Talking to Belle. About what Ruby thought were private family matters. But those family boundaries were crossed now, intermingled, blurred. Wires fucking intersecting. Ruby felt suddenly dizzy. The world was spinning around her, just like the night she had too much wine. How could that have only been just over a week ago? She held onto the countertop. It was grey and white, swirls mixed together like a galaxy. Trevor had picked them out himself. It had taken him weeks to decide on the mirrored brick-style backsplash. Ruby had called Belle to complain how absorbed Trevor had been, how she was fed up with him using up all the PVR space to tape home improvement shows. *I'm so fucking over Mike Holmes.*

"Are you okay, Ruby?"

She wasn't. If she let go, she would pass out, a naked heap on the floor covered only by a fluffy robe. Belle would see her unshaven legs and unshaven, well, everything else. After the dinner party Ruby had seen firsthand how Belle had maintained her pussy parts. She blushed at this thought, sweat forming on her upper lip.

"I need you to leave." Ruby said through gritted teeth.

"You look like a deranged frothing pit bull," Belle said, hand over her almost indiscernible baby bump. "You're freaking me right out. Relax, I'm leaving. Don't get your panties in a knot."

"For once, it's me that isn't wearing any. Now please, get the fuck out."

"That was a really dumb thing to say about Leah not being Trevor's, you know," Belle said, reaching into the fridge and pulling out the last bottle of the mini smoothies Leah liked. She walked to the door, shoes echoing on the marble tiling. "There's no need to get nasty about all this and lie."

"How do you know it's a lie?"

Belle snorted again. "Please, Ruby. Next you are going to tell me you had Leah with Brad Pitt. Someone real rich and famous, right?"

Ruby's ears burned. "Maybe."

"Sure, Ruby, sure."

The door made a soft click as Belle finally exited. Ruby looked up at the ceiling. She knew it was low of her, but she couldn't help but mutter, "Thank god."

Chapter 15

2017

After Belle left, Ruby forced herself to take a shower and drink tea. Momentarily refreshed, she sauntered into Trevor's study. She switched on the desktop and logged into Facebook. She ground her bottom lip under her teeth. Typed a name into search. *Curtis Simmons.* Too many hits to narrow down, so she scrolled. But then she recognized him, even in the thumbnail. He had the same lopsided smile, hair so black it had shades of blue, like Veronica in the Archie comics. Three mutual friends. Clicking on his profile photo, she caught glimpses of pewter mountains, a line of pine trees, still emerald water. And of course, there was Curtis himself. Head tilted, hands shoved in pockets; in this shot she could make out tattoos on his arms. Ruby gasped, touching her finger to the screen. In red ink, she could make out what looked almost to be the letters of her name. The rest of both of his arms were covered in full blue tattoo sleeves. It was odd seeing him standing there without a guitar in his hand, which is how she pictured him in her mind, crystallized forever as a teen statue with his trusty prop.

Ruby scanned the photo for more information. Curtis had made a comment replying to a friend under the photo. "En route to Williams Lake. Garibaldi Lake is a wicked place, man." Heat rushed up Ruby's neck and face. Curtis still talked as he did in high school. The snapshot had been posted about a week ago — the same time that Ruby had walked in on Belle and Trevor. Ruby closed her eyes. Behind her eyelids she saw a neon grid popping out in the blackness, like she was on a hallucinogen. She hadn't seen that image in years; all she usually saw when she closed her eyes was a vague reddish blackness. But there it was now. The jumping green squares she used to see when she kissed Curtis at the beach. It was the only proof she needed that he had been real after all, given that the rock star Ruby had once dated had faded from her memory faster than a summer tan.

She walked out of the study and passed through into the solarium. Hand pressed against the glass, she paused to look outside. There was a Buddha statue in the rock garden. Ruby hadn't inspected the Buddha carefully before; she never realized that he had moss at his base, or that the stone used to make him was more purple-hued than grey. It was then she realized how little she came outside, even in the summer. The Buddha sat among the pebbles, fat and happy, smiling at Ruby like she was the joke. She stared back. There were rules about taking Buddha statues out of countries, Trevor had confessed to her once, but he justified buying this statue on the grounds that he would meditate out in the garden, bypassing the obvious charge of using a religious cultural icon as yuppie decorating art. Not that Ruby would have accused him out loud. If he had ever bothered to ask her opinion on anything, he would see she didn't put much stock in belief systems of any kind. Ruby had given up telling people her zodiac sign after grade 9 and quite openly declared herself as atheist; in fact, her very musings about the lack of a god had once intrigued Curtis to no end. Trevor, meanwhile, believed in God, read the horoscope, and had insisted on baptizing Leah — using the same argument that Ruby's mother did: it was better to do something than nothing. Now Trevor fancied himself a modern-day man, moving easily from the category of Christian schoolboy to Richard Gere Buddhist, meditation his new salvation.

She touched her ring finger and winced. Throwing her wedding ring away had felt victorious in the moment — she'd felt free, in control. Now guilt enveloped Ruby. It was the same feeling that came after consuming three chocolate iced doughnuts bursting with cream. Unlike eating the doughnuts, she could potentially undo this action — she could put things right. Turning away from the glass, she remembered she still hadn't turned off the television in the family room.

Leaving the television on lately made her feel like someone was home. She walked to the family room and looked up at the screen to see images of flames ravaging pine trees in the central interior of BC. Highways were closed. Helicopter cameras captured the flattened images of scarred homes, some reduced to cigarette ash trenches. Forest fires were growing fast due to hot and dry conditions, devouring the stretches of land separating them, merging into colossal fire balls. Ruby paused to catch a video shot by a couple riding their car through a tunnel of orange flames along Hwy 20, twenty kilometres from Hanceville, narrowly escaping death. She shook her head in disbelief. The fires were out there, swallowing BC in a golden roar, and yet the sky outside her house was blue. Birds chirped. Her mouth went dry when she imagined Curtis amid the wreckage. Where was he when the fires erupted? Williams Lake was close. Trembling, she turned the TV off.

Making her way back to the solarium, she went outside, trudging carefully through the rocks near the manicured hedges sectioning off her yard from her neighbour's, searching for her wedding ring. Her fingers glided over smooth, wet stones. She upturned them, seeing them painted with the cool earth. The ring had symbolized love, even if it was falsified love. Fake or not, she wanted it back. She tried to think back to what Trevor had said when he had first given her the ring, but her mind was buzzing with anxiety.

The ring wasn't anywhere. She couldn't press a button and undo her actions. Unlike Belle taking Trevor, throwing the ring was something she had absolute and direct control over. She could, therefore, dedicate significant time to beating herself up for her actions. Plopping herself next to Buddha and his nest of stones, she rewound time and replayed the moment that she pitched the ring, a piece of her literal past, and then pinched her skin, remembering. This was her game of regret and guilt, and she knew how to play it well. It was all about hating yourself for not being able to change things. A box of doughnuts eaten in under ten minutes. Crop tops thrown away because she felt sure she would never lose enough weight to wear them ever again. The moments where she felt content after she rid herself of belongings or consumed the dessert section of her refrigerator were short-lived, replaced quickly by self-torture. What if her ring was a real diamond? Would Leah want it someday? What if Ruby and Trevor reconciled? What if one day she did lose all the weight she wanted and could wear those crop tops from the nineties and Trevor fell back in love with her and asked to mount her original ring with the mother of all diamonds?

Please, please, please! Where could that fucking ring be? She had worked herself up into such a frenzy she was about to throw up.

She heard the door slam in the foyer.

Chapter 16

2017

"Mom? Mom!"

Ruby bit the skin of her unoccupied ring finger. Then she shouted, "I'm coming!"

Leah wasn't a girl who dressed up. A tall, athletic girl, she had played soccer since she was three. Today she was wearing jogger shorts that showed off the ample muscles of her legs, and her hair — so black it was tinged with sapphire streaks — was pulled into a crisp ponytail. Her back was to Ruby as she scavenged the fridge.

"Everything's expired in here, Mom. The yogourt I like's gone bad. What the heck?"

"No one's been here to eat it." Ruby bit her tongue before she added, *You all fucking left me, remember?* Instead, in a respectful, calm tone, she said, "The eggs are still good, and I have some bread in the freezer. Do you want me to scramble some eggs up for you?"

Leah looked around and wrinkled her nose at Ruby. "Why are you covered in soil? I can't eat all that oil and salt."

Ruby looked down at her blue palazzo pants and dusted them, "Since when?"

"I'm trying to lose a bit of weight."

"Where is there weight to lose? I just don't get it. You're the poster girl for a sports magazine."

"Well, you wouldn't get it, would you? Look, never mind, I just ...

there's this girl. She is always hanging around Rick at college. She is all tiny and petite. Her name is Vanessa. I don't know, I thought I'd start showing everyone that I could wear dresses and stuff too. Not that I see a point showing up all decked out to go to flipping college ... I guess I just came back to raid my closet and see if I had more clothes to wear than just gym gear."

"Are you still staying at Rick's?"

"He has a big house, and his parents and sister are away for the summer," she shrugged. "Yeah, mostly I'm at Rick's."

Mostly. Ruby tried not to think of her daughter staying on Belle's pull-out. She swallowed again, pushing ahead. "You can't change your build, Leah. You're a sports girl. What are you going to do, lose muscle to be like Vanessa? Bet Vanessa would kill for your legs. And she doesn't play soccer like you and Rick. What does she do when you guys go to practice?"

"She shops, texts, repeats. You are right, she is a little twiggy." Leah smiled. "Seriously? Like all my fruit and seed yogourt is expired? Didn't I have a smoothie bottle in here? That's gone too."

Ruby decided not to mention Belle's visit. "I could make you scrambled egg whites."

"Okay," Leah said resignedly and tapped her phone on the bar. "How are you, Mom? You're wearing real clothes and the place is clean."

"Are you saying that because a little birdie came here and reported back, or are these your own observations?"

"Good god, Mom. My own."

Satisfied with this, Ruby turned to crack an egg against the side of a bowl. "You know when I was your age, I was pregnant with you ..." What points could she make about this? That she was once young too? That Leah was more naïve than she was because Ruby had been a teen mother forced into responsibility?

"Yes, I know."

Ruby used the top half of the broken shell to prevent the yolk from slipping through and poured the white into a bowl. She repeated this step three times and tossed the liquid onto the pan. The pan was so hot the liquid immediately turned white. Running her spatula through them, she lifted the pan above the element so as not to overcook the eggs. Then she put them on a plate and added salt and pepper. "Seriously, you don't want even a slice of bread or cheese? The yolks are my favourite part! With the free range eggs that we buy, I bet they're also the healthiest part of the egg. Normally, I like to add fresh basil and cherry tomatoes to my eggs, but you can see I haven't been shopping ..."

"I'm good."

"As it is, there is so much food going bad because I'm the only one in the house. I have good truffle oil ... maybe now with you and Dad gone, I can finally go from being a vegetarian to becoming a vegan," she offered Leah a mild smile.

"Mom, I'm good. No extra oil, remember? You were saying?"

"When I was your age, I really liked alt-rock music. I know — you probably can't imagine that. I was thinner. I had big boobs, not that I don't now, but back then I didn't look like a pillow. I had a defined waist and I used to wear these real cute, tight, black band shirts." Ruby remembered how, after one epic house party, she had tailored all the baggy band shirts bought off Granville Street using her mother's sewing machine. "Oh, forget it! I wanted to interview musicians. Become a writer. Maybe write biographies?" She laughed at herself before Leah could.

"Uh, huh," Leah said, barely chewing before she swallowed. She drained the glass of water Ruby had set next to her.

"Anyway, I knew this guy. He played the guitar and was a singer. He liked me. A lot. He asked me to go to Portland with him."

"Okay."

"Well, he's a rock star now." She paused. "And he's really well known. Famous."

"So, I take it you didn't go? To Portland? On account of you marrying Dad?"

"Yeah, no, I didn't."

"And now you are wondering what if?"

"It's not entirely like that ..."

"You think you and the rock guy could have another go at it? Or maybe Dad will be so jealous he'll leave Belle? Dad and you haven't been a real couple in years, Mom."

"What?" Ruby registered her daughter's appalled face. "No! I know very well what I look like. I know the famous guy would never go for me." She pointed down at her wide pant legs to prove she knew her limitations in both fashion and figure. "Anyway, I don't *like* him. I just wanted, you know, like, closure." She winced at her own accidental imitation of talking like her daughter. Speaking like Leah was no way to gain her daughter's respect. She cleared her throat and tried a firm voice. "There are things he needs to know."

"Right." Leah picked up her dish and put it in the square-shaped sink. She wiped her mouth with a paper towel. "I'm sure he's just dying to meet you. Where is he, anyway? This hot rock god?"

"Williams Lake. At least that's where I'm guessing he is headed."

"Isn't that where the fires are?"

"It appears so," Ruby said.

"God Mom, I thought you were above this. I mean I should have known after finding you coming apart at the seams the other day you were going to pull such a stunt. You really are looking for attention in the wrong spots! Why would you need closure from some guy you dated in high school?" She held up her hand so Ruby could not interrupt. "You know, this is a lot for me too, Dad talking about remarrying, me getting a new brother or sister, but I thought I could deal with it all because I knew you and Dad were all unhappy and stuff. And Belle's been so torn up about you finding out ..."

"How long have you known about all this?"

"But if you can't be happy, you don't want anyone else to be happy either. You'd rather Dad stay with you because you are going to throw yourself into flames if he doesn't? Is that really the woman you want to be, Mom?"

Ruby paled. "Honestly, I was thinking you'd be proud of me, embracing an adventure, dealing with my past ..."

"Mom, it was *high school*. You really think he remembers you?"

"There was this song he wrote, 'Ruby Red Skies.' I heard it on the radio when you were a toddler. It was the first time I heard him sing other than in person. I felt like he wrote it about me. About us. We had this one particularly amazing night out once when we were together. The sky was crimson, everything felt so magical, we had been talking ..."

"Oh, for Christ's sake!" Leah slammed the bar stool against the back wall of the counter.

Ruby drew back. "But that isn't why I'm going. I have important stuff to tell him. Honestly." She reached out, attempting and failing to touch Leah's shoulder.

When they were young, Trevor and Ruby hadn't waited long to have sex. Ruby had already been pregnant with Leah, but she hadn't known it because she took the pregnancy test too soon and her periods had always been irregular. Ruby hadn't even known Leah was Curtis's until she was born earlier than Ruby expected. Leah should have been put in an incubator. But she wasn't; she was a fat, happy full-term baby with blue-black hair. Ruby's guilt was written all over her face when the nurses expressed shock that Leah's lungs were fully developed. But the physician — he knew. He looked at Ruby while everyone else was still marvelling over the fact that Leah was already lifting her neck up on Trevor's chest. The physician locked his eyes with Ruby — she still remembered the colour, grey like sheet metal, with thick, black eyebrows. The physician had shaken his head ever so slightly at Ruby, and Ruby had kept her mouth shut. After all, Ruby's family wasn't even at the hospital. She was a South Asian teen whose father was absent, and whose mother had suddenly become prone to intense migraines that Ruby was made to feel she was responsible for. What the fuck could she have done? Tell Trevor and Eleanora the minute she saw Leah that she'd made a big mistake?

"Whatever," Leah closed her eyes. "I came here to look for dresses in my closet."

"Please, let me help you."

Leah fixed Ruby with a cold stare. "Do you plan to help before or after you pack your fire-retardant suit?"

Ruby waited for tears to spring to her eyes. Instead, a cool sensation washed over her chest and rose to her neck. It gripped her, paralyzing her, so she could only watch in silence as her daughter's face contorted with anger.

"Have a good trip, Mom."

"Wait ..."

The front door slammed shut and Ruby heard Leah peel away in her car.

Chapter 17

1610

The hard sound of cooking cauldrons being thrown down made Rubina jump. The head chef, Daniyal, was not what Rubina had pictured in her mind. He was not old, fat, or bald. He was dressed in a simple raw cotton shirt. It was handmade by a worm gear roller, the front of it styled with genuine gold buttons. He was from al-Qandahār. He boasted black hair, pale skin, and hazel-green eyes that burst like stars with anger. Weaving through the candlelit halls with Raj, Rubina had learned Daniyal was named for the king's brother, who was born before the cook was. Rumoured to be King Akbar's favourite, Prince Daniyal had died five years ago, after consuming strong liquors that were transported into the imperial castle in a rusty keg. He had been a lover of parties and wines, much like many of the members of the royal family, who Rubina was learning would do anything to their siblings to take the throne for themselves. But this Daniyal, the royal chef, only used alcohol for cooking, throwing it into cooking pots of food to release the flavour of fermented grapes.

There was a screen separating the cooks and staff, and Rubina was ushered behind it into the kitchen by Raj. She stared with surprise at the apricots, nuts, dried fruits, dates, pomegranates, and oranges sitting in various jade bowls. Mughal cooking was influenced by an array of cultures and had incorporated Asian root vegetables into curries, roasted kebabs from Persia and al-Qandahār, spinach from Kashmir, and recently, potatoes, which were being brought in by traders from the Americas. The room smelled intoxicating. Scents of tarragon, marjoram, bay leaf, and garlic seeped into Rubina's scarlet gown, perfuming it.

She watched as Daniyal expertly mixed coloured peppers into a mashed gravy curry, adding in sugar and lemon, turning his attention then to the tamarind lentil stews, and checking on the rice, to ensure each grain was buttery and separated, all for the Dastarkhān, the grand Mughal meal spread. She was mesmerized. He moved like she did, a graceful dancer. She watched as he smothered chicken in almond paste, next checking to make sure the charcoal stove was lit. Once he was certain his gold leaf plates were nearby, he reached for his seals and made sure the calligraphists were ready to draw up labels with a list of ingredients so that meals could not be switched for the king. Only then did he give his attention to Raj and Rubina.

"Women," he snapped at Raj, "are not allowed in the kitchen." Daniyal shoved past Raj towards the crew that was gathering the heavy plates into their arms to carry to the main hall. With their fair skin and Islamic caps, these servants were apparently from North India. However, the court did not discriminate between religions, and the concubines themselves practised different religious rituals within the harem; some had prayer mats, others, idols they made offerings to. This evening at midnight, King Jahangir was getting three of his dead brother's sons baptized by Jesuit priests as part of the celebration.

Behind Daniyal stood three handsome men, likely the food tasters, who looked more bored than they did nervous. Rubina thought they should be worried, for even living in the city she had heard stories of attempted poisonings that had occurred since Babur's rule. There were tales circulating of the royal kitchen being intercepted by traitors during each monarch's rule. First, Babur's son Humayun had been targeted, then his son Akbar, and now, there were concerns about the current ruler, Jahangir. Rubina tried not to stare at them, wondering who would volunteer for such a dreary position. Were they prisoners? Hungry city folk? The men surely were not dressed in street urchin clothing; rather, they were adorned in matching gold and burgundy balloon pants, with crisp *kurtas*. All three had shapely moustaches, and Rubina imagined they would look better on horses riding in a battalion than in the kitchen.

"These three are the prince's food tasters," confirmed Raj, seeing Rubina watching the men. "They are the exact build as he is to ensure they will react similarly to the composite of poison, should it exist in the food." To Daniyal he said, "Oh, she is harmless, Daniyal Master. She is soon to be famous, this new dancer. The ravishing Rubina! Do you not wish to meet her? Surely you can make one exception to your 'no women' rule."

"I was talking about you, Raj. No 'ladies-made-of-boys' in here. Out! Now!"

"But she has not eaten for hours," said Raj, making his voice sweet like a child's. "She cannot possibly wait for the concubines to be served after the men at the midnight feast, for she will positively die of hunger. Besides, the ladies will make a great fuss of her. They will starve her whilst they examine her every part."

"The concubines only stare at their own reflections in those tiny, mirrored rings they wear on their thumbs; they care only for their own looks." At this comment Rubina laughed and her veil slipped from her head. Daniyal stared at her. The three food tasters looked up.

"She is really going to be a star, you know," said Raj, pushing Rubina out as he adjusted her *dupatta* back on her head. Quickly, he grabbed walnuts and pears from the heaping bowls, pulling his billowing pants out and folding the treats inside. "You will be sorry for treating her like this!"

Chapter 18

1610

When they were safely in the harem quarters, Raj took one of Rubina's peacock patterned cushions and positioned himself against the charpoy, half-reclining, letting go of the folds of his pants, and fruits and nuts spilled every which way onto the ornate Mughal carpet, fast, like hard rain. The concubines, as Daniyal had suspected, indeed were preoccupied with themselves and had gone to the fragrant iris gardens bordered by jasmine bushes and pagoda trees to enjoy their feast.

Raj put a lamp shaped like a conch shell and made of red pottery between the two and handed her a piece of the bounty, a slivered pear slice embedded with coconut shavings. Rubina lay on the cot with her belly down, her head close to Raj. Rubina's tiny, partitioned red sandstone alcove was now lit warmly by orange light.

"The prince has taken a new wife," Raj said in a hushed tone. "She is a Persian princess. But everyone says he is obsessed with the idea of marrying the beautiful Arjumand Banu, daughter of a Persian adviser. The two are said to have met in early youth. Now the prince swears that no matter how many wives he is forced to take, he is eternally betrothed to Arjumand."

"Arjumand," Rubina whispered, trying out the name on her tongue. It tasted like sweetened almond paste on her tongue. It even sounded to her like the word for almond in Hindustani, *badam.*

"But how would the prince have met her?"

"At the Royal Meena Bazaar during the celebration of Nauroz, the New Year's festival. The prince's grandfather introduced the event to celebrate the entering of Aries. Prince Khurram met Arjumand when he was but fifteen. But perhaps Arjumand snuck in another visit to remind the prince of her beauty and charms, who can say?"

Rubina had heard of the eighteen-day festival marking luxury and opulence. Khushi had, Rubina remembered, loved to share tales of the harem. She had heard that the concubines and wives and noble women would all sell treasures to male aristocrats under maroon velvet tents during the event. Underneath coloured lanterns and beautifully shaped candles, the women would enact the goings on of a true bazaar, haggling with the emperors and would-be suitors. It would be one of the only times the women would be allowed to uncloak their hijabs and parade their decorated faces to the men.

"Are they truly engaged?" she asked.

"The king himself put the ring on Arjumand's finger on behalf of the prince."

"What are they waiting for then?"

Raj smiled, the light playing on his face. "An auspicious time. But the prince is truly lovesick."

She could smell the ghee fuel burning from the light source. How lovely to believe in such a powerful love — but there was something amiss with the news. "The prince came to see my mother, Khushi *jaan,* before I came here," Rubina whispered, though no one else was in the quarters. "I feel he is lecherous, a woman chaser."

"Yes, yes," said Raj, dismissing Rubina. "The prince has his lusts. And Khushi is, sorry Khushi was, the queen of delivering these heavenly pleasures. That does not mean the prince cannot love the captivating Arjumand. She is a perfect image of paradisal angel, a beauty schooled in Persian poetry and literature. You know how the Mughals feel about the language they rule the court with. You see, the prince is full of pain *precisely* because he cannot have his true princess. He needs distraction."

"Love does not work like that," snapped Rubina, remembering the prince's perfectly trimmed beard and black, shining eyes. She could not dismiss the prince's spoiled behaviour, and frankly, Raj's infatuation with Arjumand was becoming tiresome. "But it seems no one here has love for anyone, or respect for any life form. Look what happened to my Khushi *jaan*."

"You have such a naïve view of love," he sighed. "Tell me, *chakli*, who could have had a vendetta against Khushi to have her poisoned? Has anyone in the harem spoken?" Raj leaned his head back and popped a seasoned nut in his mouth.

Rubina stared down at her bangled arms. "No one speaks of Khushi *jaan* at all. It is like she never existed. The women in the harem refuse to acknowledge her."

"Khushi's ghost will find her way into the harem and soon you will find your answer, *chakli*. Trust me. Let me distract you with other news. The king himself has become entranced with Arjumand's aunt, Mehrunissa. She is another educated, captivating woman. Some people say they have not met," Raj's beautiful eyebrows wiggled up and down with wicked mischief, "but I am sure the king had her husband, Sher Afghan, murdered in Bengal."

"This seems like gossip, Raj."

"Do you not want to understand the workings of this empire? There is a history here. Rumours often lead to legends, which I am helping you learn. And you should learn the cunning ways of Arjumand and Mehrunissa, how they enrapture men and will likely use this to rise to the top of the Mughal dynasty. For if Arjumand has her eye on Prince Khurram with the hopes he will be the next king, Mehrunissa has her eye on the very king himself!"

"Look, Raj, I only want for Khushi's ghost to find me and tell me the truth! What is the point of learning about royal politics when a bigger danger might still be lurking here? I need to know who poisoned her!"

"It was me."

Daniyal stood in the entryway to Rubina's hovel, a madly stoic expression on his face. He was holding an offering: a gold leaf platter heaped with a mix of curried vegetables, *jeera chawal*, smoke charred meats, and tandoori roti. "The king wanted her gone. It was a death far better than being walled-in, believe me. Here, eat some food. I took pity on you. Beware of telling stories, Raj. You know better. As for Khushi, I am afraid she had to be taken care of."

"Taken care of!" Rubina leapt off the bed just as Daniyal pulled the plate away so she would not tip it.

"I could not travel down another road," he said, illustrating his point with the Hindustani expression. Hindustani was influenced with a mix of many other languages — Arabic, Dakhni, Turkish, Sanskrit, and Persian — and members of the royal court, no matter where they hailed from, used it to bridge the gaps in communication. "She was carrying on with the young prince without discretion. Khushi was the king's property. That was their agreement. The king will absolutely not tolerate the prince playing with one of his concubines."

"Property!"

"Just as you are now property," said Daniyal, shifting away before Rubina could accost him.

"But mother had no choice! The prince gave her no option."

"Just as I had no alternative with the poison. Now, pull yourself together," he said, the chamber flame glinting in his brown-green eyes. He set the large dish down on a white calico mat covering the blooms of wisteria flowers racing along the Mughal carpet, allowing the scent of sandalwood powder and parsley to travel up Rubina's nose. Despite herself, she shrank down next to the plate and with shaking hands reached down to eat with Raj, hoping Daniyal did not take this as a sign she had forgiven his treachery.

"He is a disgusting murderer," she said to Raj, watching as Daniyal left the room, his shoulders held stiff. She took food to her lips. Her mouth betrayed her anger with singing flavours of ginger and tamarind that popped on her tongue. She mixed rice into the yogourt and cucumber before bringing it to her mouth to cool it down.

"You must understand, *chakli*, this monarch is ruthless about betrayals of any kind. Daniyal *bhayya* is right. Khushi was playing with fire by dillydallying with the prince. Khushi died a good death. Kings have been known to suffocate their own nobility in the bodies of other animals, skin people alive, or even quarter humans by use of four camels. What have you heard of the Mughal dynasty?"

"That the king is a discoverer. He digs up roots of the banyan tree to see where they lead to; he designs fine monuments and superior artifacts; he studies elephant's birthing periods ..."

"Sure," Raj scoffed, "when he is not fighting them against one another in sport and scarring them in jest." Raj took a bite, licking the fingers of his right hand. "He has had lions hunted and cut open, their innards studied to see where their courage comes from. He has cut his own child with a knife to see if he would not scream out — who is telling you such great things about King Jahangir?"

"I have overheard Moti Ma talk about his greatness."

Raj dropped thinly sliced lemons and vinegar doused onions into his mouth and smiled jeeringly at her. "The concubines adore the king. His majesty spends a great deal of time here, showering the women with his fine jewels. He has bags filled with them to spare, after all. Some of the king's concubines remember the day when the king was a child, and the small children that loll about sucking on sweets all day are truly the prince's brothers. Why, the prince's very nursing maids live here. The women of this harem worship the king and prince like gods! You cannot trust these ladies — they have never left the perimeters of the harem as you and I have, *chakli*. We know another world. Or Khushi would not have warned you of the harem. Daniyal *bhayya* was helpless."

"Daniyal has crazy eyes, and he cares only for himself and his cooking. He is not to be trusted." Her mouth suddenly stung with spices as if Daniyal had lashed at her tongue for speaking such words aloud. Desperately, she reached for a copper jug filled with special water, taken from the mouth of the Yamuna River, where it was cleanest. "I have no one to guide me here, Raj," she said, pouring liquid and drinking from a brass cup, "I do not know what path is safest." She had not meant to show weakness, but there was chili caught in her throat and her eyes had begun to water. "I cannot even talk to my dance master with privacy. What will become of me? Everything I hear contradicts what I know."

"You have me," said Raj, pulling a sparkly bracelet from her wrist and squeezing it onto his hand.

"I have you," Rubina repeated, to give the words weight.

"And if you want to survive in this palace you will have to listen to my stories. They are not merely gossip, for in my own way, I am guiding you."

"Okay," she agreed.

"And to this end, you will have to marry Daniyal *bhayya*."

"What?!" she nearly dropped the food clenched between her right fingers.

"That 'murderer' is your ticket to freedom," proceeded Raj calmly. "He is yet unmarried, and you will be granted freedom to leave the harem. And I saw the way he looked at you. It is a rare thing, that look a man gives a woman. He brought you food which he never does, not personally, not for anyone. You must use his desire for you to your advantage. You do not plan to be a dancing girl forever, now do you?" Raj said.

"What of our friendship? Do you not want me to stay on with you in the harem? I thought you wanted us to rise to the top ranks here."

Her mind was spinning.

"The royal chef is a high-ranking official, *chakli*. Daniyal *bhayya* serves the king's tastes directly. If you move away from the harem, perhaps I can be summoned as your personal assistant. You will live luxuriously off the citizen's taxes and be outfitted in the best jewels. As will I. As your friend, of course. This is one way to rise to the top."

"Not as high as I would be if I stayed in the harem. Here, more people will recognize me as a dancer, and I can gain more favour. Perhaps even from the monarchs themselves."

"True, but my plan is a safer route. Heed Khushi's warnings."

"But the harem seems a better place for me. I cannot trust such a treacherous soul as the royal chef."

"The royal chef can never refuse orders that come directly from the king," Raj placated. "Look not at what the royal chef did but rather how life went awry for your beloved Khushi *jaan*. And," he said, putting his hand over Rubina's mouth to keep her from interrupting, "if this fails, I will rethink another plan for us."

"Are you quite sure?" she said when his palm had stopped pressing her lips. "What of me going back to the brothel?"

"How do you plan to run the brothel without the king's protection?"

"I do not know."

"Besides, Daniyal *bhayya* was positively entranced."

Before Rubina could use more profanities to describe Daniyal, Raj quickly covered a cinnamon stick with rice and offered to feed her a mouthful. She obliged, opening her lips. He smiled as she bit uninhibitedly. Quite suddenly, she was shocked by a spicy, sharp taste. A second wave of heat washed over her, and the cinnamon took away her ability to argue any further with Raj. Full of laughter, he enveloped her as she tried to recover.

Chapter 19

2017

After Leah left, Ruby blinked once more at the computer screen in Trevor's den. The air still smelled of the cinnamon musk cologne Trevor favoured. When had he started to wear fragrances that gave off the scent of sickeningly sweet money? When had she stopped smelling his neck? Had she ever? Could smelling a man's neck be a way to discern supposed compatibility? For though she could not remember Trevor's scent before the cologne, now that she had remembered Curtis, she could not forget how his dizzying scent of saltwater ocean had made her knees go weak. The pillows in her own room had long since lost Trevor's scent and she was surprised there was still a place in the house where his presence lingered so strongly.

Next to his computer were a couple of books to inspire Trevor to write his novel: Hemingway's *The Garden of Eden* and Miller's *Tropic of Cancer*. She picked up the latter, skimming through. There was a lot of mention of cocks, cunts, and pubic hairs. Did Trevor think his life was as exciting as these men's, travelling around writing about their womanizing ways? Perhaps by sleeping with Belle, Trevor was trying to make his writing better. Ruby winced, remembering Belle's naked body shining silver and midnight blue as she sat atop Ruby's husband. In this very room. She shook her shoulders and arms out. Put the books back next to the mouse. Switched on the computer.

Her fingers pressed the sequence of keys that matched their wedding anniversary. Trevor's password for twenty years. Curtis's Facebook profile picture, she saw, was still the same. She exhaled, in part relieved that the digital Curtis was exactly where she had left him. Her eye roamed over the message icon, but Ruby dismissed the thought; no one messaged to say: *I have a nineteen-year-old daughter and you're the father.* Did someone as famous as Curtis even check his own messages? Ruby cocked her head imitating Curtis's pose and stared at the photo, as if it could tell her more. In BC, fires had spread to other regions and more communities had been evacuated; currently, nearly 200 fires were actively burning. Was Curtis safe? Had he reached his final destination, or was he still at Garibaldi Lake?

She opened Google Maps. There were a few routes to get to Williams Lake. The one that was the shortest and most scenic was likely the route Curtis had taken, particularly because it passed by Garibaldi Lake. It was a six-hour drive straight to Williams Lake. She drew points on the pad from Vancouver to Williams Lake, with Vancouver at the bottom, Williams Lake at the top, dotting all the main stops along the way: Squamish, Garibaldi, Garibaldi Lake, Whistler, 100 Mile House, Williams Lake. She wrote *active fire zone* under and above 100 Mile House and Williams Lake, which were the furthest northern points.

She wondered if it was possible to make it to the active fire zones. But for now, Curtis was in Garibaldi Lake. *Curtis stopped at Garibaldi Lake,* she scrawled in cursive on Trevor's notepad. It looked like you could only access the lake via a hiking trail. Searching the Internet, she spotted Rubble Creek parking lot as a potential place to begin the hike. She circled Rubble Creek twice on the pad. Not that she figured she'd be going on any hikes. She had never been outdoorsy. But maybe she was. How could she know without exploring wilderness? Whenever Trevor had suggested they go camping, Ruby had always found excuses. He had labelled her a house mouse who didn't like to go out, and she'd accepted that. It was much easier to accept that than ponder why she had been reluctant to be alone with him under an endless black sky. Silence made or destroyed couples and perhaps she had subconsciously heeded the keen sense that the two of them could not outrun the noise of the quiet.

She traced her finger across the pad. This route did not account for road closures or detours due to the active fires. Opening one of Trevor's drawers, she looked for another sheet of scrap paper to write down exact directions. A Cuban cigar case. She opened the box and put a cigar between her lips. Chomped down. Hoisting her legs up on the desk, she rolled up her white yoga pants, and leaned back in Trevor's leather chair. *Sexy*, she thought, searching for a lighter. Fuck Belle and Trevor — she could be wild in this room, too.

A dark figure covered the glass window and peered into the den. She shrieked and almost dropped the cigar. A black outline tapped on the glass. She rushed to open the study door and ran into the solarium, attempting to flee the intruder. It followed her across the glass like her shadow, past the den, pressed up against the solarium, leading right up to its sliding door.

She screamed.

Chapter 20

2017

"Oh, for godsakes, Rubes, open the door. It's me!"

"Trevor?"

"Who else? A fucking stalker?"

She slid open the sliding door, her heart in her throat. "Why the hell didn't you use your key, Trevor?"

"I didn't want to sneak up on you."

"Oh, good plan. I can see you really thought that through."

"I haven't thought much of anything through." Trevor peeled off his camel trench coat and followed her to the kitchen. He sank onto one of the breakfast stools at the centre island. He had a five o'clock shadow and his hair, nearly the same colour as his jacket, was mussed. "What the heck were you doing with my cigars?"

She flushed. One of her pant legs slipped down. "Why were you wearing a jacket in summer?" she deflected. "I was living life."

"Your new motto?"

"Something like that." She set the cigar down on the counter.

"They have the A/C on full crank in the office and the A/C in my car is strong. Well," he said, eyeing the cigar, "you can have them. Belle doesn't want anything of that nature around her belly. But make sure you cut the cigar before smoking it — hey," he interrupted himself, suddenly noticing her, "you look different."

Ruby turned her back and looked down. Today she was wearing

clothes again, real ones; white yoga pants that one could wear in public and an off-the-shoulder white sweater that Trevor had always liked on her. An almost 1950s look if you ignored the pants were Lululemon. They fit better since she hadn't had to cook for a family. She exhaled, surprised she could "look different" on a sour key and alcohol diet alone. She unrolled her other pant leg down to make both the same and shook her head at him. "Aren't you supposed to be at work? What do you want, Trevor?"

"A decent meal?" he cracked a smile. It quickly disappeared when Ruby didn't return it. "I took the day off for another one of Belle's obstetrician appointments. I was supposed to drive back to work and the house is on the way."

The house, she thought.

"Aw, come on, Rubes. I am starved. Don't you have any of that soup you make during the week? The bean one?"

"Afraid not. Cooking for one excludes using the slow cooker."

"Any leftovers at all?"

"No," she squeezed her eyes shut, trying to stop herself from finding a solution to Trevor's problem. But she spoke anyway. "I do have some wraps I froze ages ago for Leah's lunches. But she hasn't ..."

"Been around?"

"She's been around," she said, immediately recovering. "I meant to say she hasn't been eating carbs. I just saw her."

"Oh. Are the wraps the ones you make with the samosa filling? I'd love one."

"Yes. I'll heat one up." As she moved to the fridge, Ruby realized her instincts to take care of Trevor had overtaken her desire to completely shun him. But it satisfied her immensely that he missed her food. So, she added, "But don't get used to this." She reached into the bottom section of her refrigerator. "I thought you hated my Indian cooking. It's all I really had left of my Indianness but even that you hated."

Trevor blinked at her. "I just have a sensitive stomach is all; no one is trying to rough ride over your identity. It wasn't like you were hiding behind a hee-jab when we first talked. You were wasted drunk and wearing black eyeliner, for godsakes."

"Well," said Ruby, clutching the frozen wrap to her chest. "Then this is far too spicy for you — you may get indigestion."

"I can handle it. Look, Belle doesn't even know I'm here. I'm not supposed to eat your food. Can you maybe not mention it? Oh, and could I get a coffee, too?"

"Don't push it."

"Okay," he threw up his hands. "Look, for what it's worth, I'm sorry. I can't believe it all came down to this. I owe you a huge apology. Things got out of control, you know?"

Hands shaking, she turned to the microwave and put his wrap on a plate, undoing the wax paper. "No, I don't know, Trevor. An affair? A baby?! She was my best friend."

Trevor winced. "I never pictured myself a cheater, Rubes. You and I just didn't connect anymore, and Belle was just ready to listen to me. She was always around, dressed up, ready to do fun things. She made me feel young again and I've known her for years ..."

"Trevor, please. I don't need to live out the romantical progression of your relationship." Was romantical even a real word? Never mind. If Trevor decided to correct her right now, she was going to throw the spicy samosa wrap right onto his stupid beige pants. Ruby pressed her fingers into her head, waiting for the ding of the microwave, thinking vaguely of her mother's trauma-induced migraines. When the ding sounded, she turned around and slammed the plate in front of Trevor. "What the hell do you want? You didn't come here just to give me an apology. That much I know." Her eyes rested on a spot on his pants.

"The coffee stain never fully came out."

"What?"

"My pants. The night of our, erm, anniversary. I spilled coffee on them. And I guess the stain set in."

"Do you really think I notice every little detail about you?"

He grabbed the wrap with both hands without waiting for it to cool, ignoring this. "I honestly came here for your food," he smiled sheepishly. "I sleep on a junky bed in a 600 square foot condo. Belle's a certified hoarder, I swear. I have no room for my things. My back hurts. I have no place to shave because she has seventy-five bottles of nail polish crammed on the bathroom counter. She doesn't cook."

"Seriously?" Ruby's face went hot.

But he kept going. "She wants to do all these tests. For the baby. In one of the tests, this needle goes into the belly, and it tells you if the kid has Down syndrome. She's killing me with paranoia. Bloody weighs everything she eats and is on a thousand vitamins. She has the Canada Food Chart pinned to the fridge and has exactly the right servings of fruits, veggies, and grains a day. Did we do all that with Leah?"

"Are you actually coming at me like I'm your friend? I'm your goddamn estranged wife!"

"Did we do the tests, Rubes?"

"No!" said Ruby, putting her hands back on her temples. "I mean, I was just a kid. I think those tests are for when you are a mature mother. Probably I was too young to be scared of all the million things that could go wrong with a fetus. I was more worried about my mom disowning me. But, look, I am NOT your therapist. You can't come here and do this shit with me!"

"No, I know," he put down the wrap. Wiped the corner of his mouth with his thumb. "I'm sorry, okay? For all of it. I know you don't even have your mom to talk to about all this stuff."

"Yeah, well, if me getting pregnant as a teen didn't kill her, my marriage ending surely would have. A baby," she added, shaking her head.

Trevor raised his brow. "She died of cancer, Ruby. Not because you were a teen mom."

Ruby's eyes hardened. "She died because she gave up. It was the perfect exit."

"You don't really believe that she wished cancer upon herself and died as some revenge ploy against you, do you?"

"When I told my mother that I was pregnant and that I was marrying you and moving into your mom's rec room, she told me that she held herself together when my dad left only because of me. Then she said: 'I don't have to hold myself together anymore.' Pretty sure she checked out of life at that moment. My mom maintained a strained relationship with my dad after he left us solely on the hope the community would match me up with an Indian lawyer or banker. Not a doctor ... she had already given up hope I'd ever marry that high."

"Sorry I was such a disappointment for your grand plans."

"They weren't my grand plans. Anyway," she said, annoyed she had said this much, "I'm not buying that you came here for my food alone. And surely you didn't come back here for the pen I got you for our anniversary."

"Pen?"

"Ugh. Never mind."

"We need the house, Rubes." He took the wrap back to his mouth and broke into it. Steamed spilled out. "It's got to happen. And we probably ought to discuss the whole 'Leah isn't your kid' thing."

Ruby blew air upward and pulled away the long waves that had fallen on her forehead. She folded her body over the countertop. "I can't get into this right now."

"That's okay. I know this is a lot for you take in." He smiled generously, as if she was a Girl Guide that he was buying cookies from and had to take time to find the right change. "Grief makes people say stupid things. But don't bring the kid into this, you know? Leah's the best thing that came out of us. Please don't fuck with me about her not being mine again, okay? Just think about it. The house part, I mean."

"The house being too big for me?"

"Yes." He had the decency to look away when he spoke. Ruby had to give him credit for that.

"I'll see you, okay?" he leaned in, either to kiss her cheek, or maybe to squeeze her shoulder. Ruby would never know, because she pulled away.

Chapter 21

2017

When Trevor left her with his dirty plate, worry crept up on her. How long was Ruby going to stay afloat? She rushed into the study. Signing on once again to the desktop and logging into their personal banking account, she confirmed that Trevor must have spent the last few months funnelling their savings into a secret account. Their joint account still had a sizable chunk left — she counted rapidly in her head — at least enough to cover the mortgage and her car insurance and the utilities for two months. If Trevor wasn't so predictable with his password, she would not have been able to access the information. Looking after the bills was not her part of the traditional division of roles ascribed in their marriage.

Ruby felt a sense of relief in knowing he wasn't exactly like her father. Trevor was better. Ruby wouldn't have to work at Subway like her mother, or apply for income assistance, or sell her car. Not yet, anyway. But, for how long would he continue to pay? Was there a grace period when you had to take care of both your wife and your mistress, and when did it expire? If she gave up the house, would Trevor buy her a condo? Would she own it fair and square? Would they get lawyers and do things through a court system, or would handling things amicably mean more money would be left over? Perhaps, she sighed inwardly, she should just throw up her hands and accept the terms and fill her life with new things, like a cat or knitting lessons. And start to look for a job, though she wasn't sure what she could do given her qualifications: *I make good food my husband misses only after leaving me. I can expertly organize spice cabinets and break into bank accounts. I have a knack for spying on my high school exes. Well, ex. I only have one. I love the jazz era and reading loads of books but no one I know wants to talk to me about it. Everyone in my life has pegged me for a reality-show-watching housewife. Which, let's face it, I am, so can I just do whatever this job I am applying for requires from the comfort of my own sofa?*

She walked back to the kitchen. Odd to think that Trevor had sat on the bar stool a short while ago, speaking to her, not running away like he had always been. His fingers — she hated that today they had seemed so attractive clenched around her wrap, so manly, strong. Was that because she no longer had claim to them anymore? There he had been. Only two hours earlier. His body. Right there. She switched on the spotlights in the kitchen and watched them shine down on the island, making little stars glitter on the slab. Brushing her hand over it, she absentmindedly checked for crumbs.

She made a choice: it was time to find Curtis Simmons. She was temporarily done with this house, all its nonfunctional doors and plural staircases. Or maybe permanently. That remained to be seen. Her hand wavered over the light switch habitually before she realized she wasn't going to flick it off. Better for robbers to think someone was home.

Ruby rushed up one set of staircases and pulled out her retro trunk with the flowered panel before she could rethink her decision. Looking up one of her favourite songs on her phone, "Why Don't You Do Right," sung by Peggy Lee, with Benny Goodman and His Orchestra, started to play. She spun on the hardwood floor and shimmied. Inspired by the 1942 song, she sorted through the impractical vintage clothing she had bought over the years. Into her trunk went a vibrant lime 1940s dress, capped sleeves with tiny buttons running down the front and a thin vinyl matching belt. A black halter dress with a tulle underlay that had little cherries and a gingham belt. She hesitated before throwing in a slip of a creamy beige vintage flapper dress with exquisite champagne fringe and gem work done on it, which once, in another lifetime, she had planned to wear to the symphony. She remembered how when Trevor had first seen it, he had asked her why she'd ordered a Halloween costume in April. She had been too embarrassed to admit she'd wanted to wear it on their date.

Not giving herself the chance to change her mind, Ruby changed into a butter yellow, sleeveless 1950s tea party dress that had a fabulous spinning skirt and adorable collar. All these clothes she'd had just hiding in the house, never worn. After applying basic makeup, she put on the red lipstick with a blue undertone she had bought and only worn when no one was home. Ruby Jewel, it was called, like her name. She hunted for the white satin clutch with a rhinestone handle she'd bid for on eBay, remembering how she hadn't shown it to a single person when it had arrived. She slipped her feet into a red pair of three buckled 1940s shoes ordered from New York in the hopes that she would one day go swing dancing in them. They had sat in a shoe box for nearly five years, absurdly the exact colour of the lipstick she was now wearing.

Ruby glided down the staircase she usually avoided, her hand caressing the wrought-iron railing. Hurriedly, she locked the door even though she wasn't late for anything or expected to arrive anywhere. She put the trunk packed with her clothes, makeup, and toiletries into the back of her blue Nissan and threw her purse with her passport and wallet onto the passenger seat of the car. The car, a gift from Trevor when he had made partner at the accounting firm, was just his old vehicle with replaced tires and new seat covers. While most wives would have been annoyed at the hand-me-down nature of the gesture, Ruby was relieved he hadn't bought her a new car. New things made her nervous.

She put on white cat-eye sunglasses and, pulling a red scarf from her purse, tied it around her neck. Carefully, she looked down at the directions on how to get to the Sea-to-Sky Highway she had written on the back of an old cable bill — her car had no GPS. She started the ignition and backed out of the driveway and onto the road. Her house, white and large, was now a small square image in the corner of her rearview mirror. Green moss covered the brown roof, which Trevor had claimed gave the house an "English manor" feel. She had no temptation to turn around and look back.

Twenty years ago, when she left her mother's house for Trevor's, she had looked back one last time, freezing the image of her bedroom in her mind, noting the frilly pink curtains her mother had never let Ruby replace, claiming it would be a waste of money to change a perfectly good thing. Ruby had hated those curtains so much and yet sheer pink curtains were the first thing Ruby bought to replace the navy-blue blinds in Eleanora's dingy rec room window. The pink curtains would follow Ruby and Trevor first to the places they rented, and then to the house he would eventually purchase for the two of them. Back at her mother's place, Ruby had left behind all the CDs she didn't listen to but wasn't sure she was finished with, a stereo that crackled when you turned the volume too high, and boots that, while wearable, had worn down at the heels from the way that Ruby dragged her feet when she walked. Ruby's mother hadn't complained about her leaving behind junk, and she never told her daughter goodbye. As if not uttering the words made it not real. Almost exactly one year later, Ruby had learned what it was like to come back to a house with no one living there anymore.

Trevor's mom had offered to help pack the house after Ruby's mother died, but Ruby had adamantly refused, asking her to watch baby Leah instead. Ruby wasn't interested in Eleanora's words of consolation — which hadn't been fair, what with Eleanora having already battled breast cancer and all, and thus knowing the pains of battling cancer better than anyone. But Eleanora had survived, and Ruby's mom hadn't, which to Ruby meant that Eleanora had wanted to live and her own mother hadn't. White people weren't martyrs like Indians were; Eleanora was very practical about her life. Back when Eleanora had thought she might not live, she'd asked for a Celebration of Life funeral. Something classy and falsely upbeat, with a picture slideshow of Eleanora's momentous life occasions, followed by mildly funny speeches and bittersweet invitations to make donations to a cancer foundation in Eleanora's name. People would eat sandwiches made with Swiss cheese, honey mustard, and peppery arugula on French bread and drink sauvignon blanc. They would say quaint things, like white roses would always remind them of Eleanora. Ruby liked that Eleanora was logical about the cycle of life; she was not melodramatic, clinging to it like fangs sinking into meat, unable to let go. Ruby knew her mother pictured days of wailing and mourning to take place after her own death. Ruby was expected to beat her chest and collapse. Ruby's mother wanted a shrine of flowers commemorating her death, not some anonymous donation to a charity where there was no knowing who gave what in her name. Ruby was left with more than a funeral that she dreaded participating in — she was burdened with the feeling that she and Leah weren't worth fighting cancer for. That Ruby's father was nothing more than a worthless cheater who had abandoned his family. That Ruby had also participated in the act of deserting her mother. Ruby's mother managed to be the eternal victim even in death.

Ruby remembered systematically packing her mother's clothes in a box, not wanting to cry, because when she was finally alone, she cherished not being expected to perform the ritual of sadness for an audience. Ruby knew she'd never wear oversized Indian pantsuits, not even as maternity wear if she ever got pregnant again, so she packed them away on autopilot, one set after another, pistachio green, creamy almond, cotton candy pink. There were photo albums of relatives whose names Ruby had never learned, places in India she'd never go. These, she put in a box marked "later." That box now sat on the top shelf of her bedroom closet. None of this had made her cry. It had been a dented can of cream of broccoli soup that did her in, the only Canadian food her mother subscribed to. How was Ruby supposed to eat seventeen cans of it? What had her mother been planning for — a natural disaster? Ruby hated the idea of eating the soup, knowing the stringy fibrous threads of broccoli would not break down no matter how much she chewed on them. And standing in the kitchen, realizing that her mother had been alone night after night heating up the soup in a small saucepan, had finally made Ruby break down in genuine tears.

A lifetime later, driving on a highway in the right lane because she wasn't brave enough to fly by with the cars in the left, Ruby realized her mother had died long before the cancer got to her. With her whole family gone, Ruby's mother had given up on making dinners. Ruby knew this because she was doing the same thing now with a bag of sour keys, fending off hunger pangs as best she could, alternating between licking the keys until they were gelatin sticks and crunching on them until the gummy substance moulded onto her back teeth. Leaving sticky sugar dust on the wheel of Trevor's old car, going ten kilometres under the speed limit on the Sea-to-Sky Highway. Feeling a loneliness that she had felt acutely for years but that she had a name for only today — abandonment.

It was twilight now and the sky was the blue of a Cadbury mini egg, the setting sun lighting mountain tips yellow. Everything was sublimely clear now, as if Ruby had on focused lenses, just for those few minutes before blackness would descend. Ruby turned on her headlights. It was better to do the drive at night; now she wouldn't have to see people in their cars and speculate about their amazing lives, the trips they were going on as a family, their sweet kids plastering handprints on the windows. Now that the road would soon be swathed in a black blanket, she could concentrate on just the section lit by her headlights, one segment at a time.

In her mind's eye, Ruby pictured her own house standing in dark shadows. In the rear of the house, she imagined the golden light from the kitchen spilling out of the solarium window and onto the backyard. The windows were uncovered so anyone could look inside from the outside.

A perfectly lit glass house. Someone's forever home. It was never hers to begin with.

Chapter 22

1610

"All of these can be yours. These are created by the most famous jewellery designers in the world," Moti Ma said, showing Rubina an assortment of fine jewels: a gold necklace strung in pearls, heavy diamond and emerald bangles, loose topaz jewels, a ruby headdress. "Just become the king's favourite entertainer. Outdo the acrobats, the mimes, the singer, and the poetess, and the Koh-e-Nur will be yours."

"Isn't the Koh-e-Nur, or as Khushi *jaan* called it, the 'Mountain of Light,' missing?" Rubina asked. Khushi had told her the 793-karat diamond had been lost and found numerous times during the Mughal Empire's rule. The last place it had been seen was in the flowered purse of King Humayun, the grandfather of the current king, before it had disappeared to some corner of Persia.

"It is just a figure of speech. Great Akbar, nothing gets by you! Never mind, we have found you a place to practise your dance, to train night and day. Your dance master has agreed to live close to the fortress in the quarters near the river. You can have use of the cooling room by the big fountains; it has marble flooring. It is outdoors but covered. Only the songbirds will disturb you there; they tend to fly in and get stuck in the rafters under the domed ceiling."

Rubina ran her finger along the jewels laid out on Moti Ma's double charpoy, their edges sharp and cool. "What is the point of owning all these jewels if I shall never leave? Then they are not mine to begin with."

Moti Ma chucked her under her chin. "Why would you want to leave? You think you will have a better life anywhere else, *haan*? Stupid *lurki* thinks living on the streets with dogs is better than a *mahal*."

Rubina thought of asking Moti Ma about the royal chef, Daniyal — he was such an enigma — but she decided now was not the time to broach the subject. Moti Ma led Rubina out of her beautifully designed apartments, passing by several Portuguese vases. Moti Ma's status as a senior concubine had granted her one of the larger dwellings within the fortress, which, Rubina noted, still had an entryway for the king to access her through secret corridors. Moti Ma followed Rubina's eyes to the door and under her gaze, Rubina blushed.

"You know, there are more useful ways to service the king than erotic intimacies. Your majesty seeks advice from me. I update him on the goings on here in the harem. I tell him which concubines are acting rude or insolent and which are carrying out illicit activities. Shanti was carrying on with Dinesh, the eunuch. It was I who told him. Can you imagine? He is not even a full man, what pleasure could she derive from him?"

"Where are they now?"

Moti Ma shrugged, lifting the *pulloo* of her sari to wipe paan juice from her mouth. "They are awaiting trial. Each will be permitted a chance to explain themselves to the royal court."

Together, they went to Moti Ma's private garden entrance to walk under the many canopies of cloth, interwoven between the almond trees, next to the bluebells. The sun shone through the thin, red material, as it was meant to lend the harem a warm atmosphere, and Rubina and Moti Ma's arms and faces glowed an orange shade as they passed through.

"She was your birth mother." The sun hit Moti Ma's face with white light before they passed under another row of trees cloaked with green sashes. "You do know that, right? Khushi was your real, true mother."

"Of course," Rubina said quickly, looking at the tented outdoor bath houses. Large kettles of hot water, tended to by diligent servants, was a tradition that dated back to Timur's time. Before Humayun ruled, there was Babur, who was related to Genghis Khan. Babur's great-great-great grandfather, Timur, who reigned over the Barlas Turk tribe, had cemented an empire across the region almost all the way to a place referred to as the Ming Dynasty, which Rubina had heard was unconquerable. Apparently, Timur had started military conquests to capture this impenetrable dynasty but had died on the way. Whilst the concubines did not know many of the details of Timur's conquests, they all knew he had introduced bath houses.

"When she lived here Khushi looked exactly like you, same slim waist and same skin tone, not fair like us with our Persian ancestry. Did you know she was your birth mother? Or did you think she had adopted you?"

"I always knew," Rubina muttered, and perhaps she had always known. After all, Rubina had Khushi's mannerisms and dance style, and Khushi had clearly favoured her. But Khushi had never directly claimed to be Rubina's biological mother, and for this Rubina was suddenly hit with a deeper sense of grief.

"It is a relief to me to know she had your best interest in mind. When you first arrived here, there was gossip amongst us that you were to be sold at the bazaar to the highest bidder for your virginity. It was said that one of the nobles was going to purchase you as a present for a landowner in another region."

"No," said Rubina, suddenly embarrassed by Khushi's other business ventures. "If that were true, she would have sold me a long time ago."

"But you must know Khushi rented out her own body."

"But *you* must know she had no other choice. She would never force me to do such a thing." There was a terrifying silence, filled by birds squawking overhead, wafting over from the tended farm area where the king grew jackfruit, pineapples, pomegranates, and oranges. Rubina saw Moti Ma clench her jaw, and she worried Moti Ma would cast her out for her disrespectful tone.

Yet Moti Ma smiled at Rubina, chewing her fragrant betel leaves mixed with Indian spices. "Yes, *beti*, no choice. She was already a concubine. But she begged the king to let her raise you away from harem property. And now, you find yourself back here. Do you think this worked out for you for the better? You do not know how to conduct yourself here. You do not have proper education or the ability to read prose in Persian. You are a street girl."

"I am a trained dancer."

"Why bring you back if she wanted to be free?"

"The king respected her wishes. It was the prince who went back for Khushi *jaan*," Rubina reasoned. "She was in no position to refuse his advances. Once the prince spotted me, he wanted me here."

"And once the prince has touched the king's spoils, those spoils are rotten. The king will destroy those spoils."

"Yes," said Rubina, remembering her mother's wide, wrinkled face at death.

"It appears the bird is once more caged," said Moti Ma, looping her arm through Rubina's.

"It appears she is," said Rubina, pushing a smile through her lips, wondering if she would ever be free to walk by the Yamuna River alone again.

Chapter 23

1610

Having been raised a street girl, Rubina did not have a fear of travelling the underground channels in the Agra Fort built for the king, which the eunuchs guarded with their lives. She was used to being in Agra, winding through the paths where street merchants sold their wares on wagons, past the camels with backs loaded with fruits, up and along the riverbank to do her washing. Khushi had not prescribed curfew rules on Rubina, only that she be home in time for her dance training sessions. Rubina had the free will to come and go as she pleased, especially loving the time before Hindu festivals when vendors sold painted clay masks of the heroes and villains in the Ramayana story, and when the city folk themselves would act out the great stories of Lord Rama and Princess Sita. As a young girl, she would marvel at the faces of commoners, coloured with turmeric to look like monkeys, the tails pinned on their behinds, mimicking these wild animals that fought to save their lord during battles. Plenty of good times were had during such festivities; milky sweets were handed out in and around the many shrines and temples. Just like his father Akbar before him, King Jahangir did not bother the Hindu priests, who were able to rebuild from the rubble the Muslim ruler Razia Sultana and her armies had left behind when they looted centuries back. Sultana's people had pillaged many grand pieces from which to build their own mosques.

Sultana herself was the first female to head a sultanate. Khushi had told many stories of this great figure who wore men's clothing and made coins with her face upon them.

But peace was never guaranteed. Local robbers and travelling thieves still took to the streets, and the city folk were always wary of invading armies. Riding on great horses, they might even find their way over the fortress walls meant to safeguard the city. Despite these dangers, Khushi did not prevent Rubina from mingling with those on the streets. Rubina was so well taken care of at the dance hall, there was never any worry that she would not return, and Khushi had taught Rubina how to navigate the streets well, prizing this skill as highly as she did dance training. For this, Rubina was now grateful. She was different from the concubines who had spent their lives in purdah, hidden in noble howdahs before they came to the Agra Fort. These women, even the young ones, had no in-born curiosity or inner fire that would make them want to peek through the tunnels and find adventure through the halls. These girls only wanted fine oil rubbed in their hair and skin by the servants, satisfied with the pleasures offered within the confines of the harem. As a result, they all had white skin unmarred by the sun, and ample curves from rich sweets fried in ghee and dipped in honey. At the bathhouse Rubina saw even the young ones had white rolls on their waists from never doing much physical work besides taking walks through the rose garden.

Rubina, darkened by her outdoor excursions, sinewy and untamed, ran through the chambers now, looking for any sign of Raj. The other eunuchs, alerted to the fact that Rubina and Raj were fast friends, did not arrest Rubina. Some looked the other way, others offered her a greeting, and the oldest eunuch, whom everyone called Sardar, gave Rubina a small orange whenever he saw her.

Raj was standing in front of the physician's hovel. By now Rubina knew the way to the physician's doorway easily, and she could likely navigate her way through the maze using just her hands to pat down the cool walls should the halls ever be unlit. But they never were. A small ledge was built at the top of each staggered wall to hold a candlestick, and even now, the light favourably highlighted Raj's high cheekbones and painted, thin brows. His eyes shone when he saw his good friend.

"You have seen Sardar *ji*."

"Yes," said Rubina, opening her palm to reveal the orange globe, so sweet even the skin could be consumed.

"Well, what are you waiting for?"

Rubina put her thumb into the skin and peeled it away, placing a slice that glistened with sugar water into Raj's mouth. "And?" she said, barely allowing him a chance for the juices to dissolve on his tongue.

"*Mmm, kitnee meethee hai.* Sardar *ji* always finds the best oranges. Which tree do you think he picks from?"

"He will not reveal his secret. He says the grove of trees from which he picks them have their soil sprinkled with 24 karat gold by the king's gardeners; that is why the oranges are so marvellous. Who, pray tell, is in the physician's hovel?"

"I will not reveal *my* secret."

"Raj!"

"*Theek hai, theek hai,* please do not pinch my arm. I work hard to keep my skin smooth. I scrub crushed date shells all over my body, followed by the dates themselves to achieve this texture ..."

"Raj!"

"Okay, okay! It is Daniyal *bhayya*."

"Daniyal, the royal chef?"

"Who else? You look frightened, not elated. Should you not be thrilled Khushi's murderer is in poor health?"

"He is in poor health?"

"So, you do care?"

"Well, of course I care. I care to know!"

"It is love sickness. A heavy bout of it, apparently. He has told that European doctor he needs to be permitted to work in another area of the great palace. The royal kitchen is too close to the harem. And he has developed an infatuation with one of the concubines. He is confessing before anything unholy occurs."

"Raj!"

"What, do you not believe me? Or are you more afraid this concubine is not you?"

"I am not a concubine."

"You have better moves than a concubine. What is that thing you do with your leg?" he extended his foot, surprisingly graceful, she thought, for someone born a boy.

"Just tell me the truth!"

"Fine, fine. He cut himself. A gash on his finger. It is not serious, but he needs medical attention."

"Oh."

"Were you quite worried?"

"Of course not. I was hopeful the murderer got a taste of his own poison," she forced out, dismissing the memory of Daniyal's brown-green eyes and the explosion of fire that shone through them.

"Well, that is a good thing, I suppose. I just found out Daniyal Master is betrothed to another. Seems we need to revise our plan, *chakli.*"

"To another woman?"

"I was not altogether lying earlier when I said Master had a case of the flutters. I sincerely thought he would be your meal ticket out of here. In more ways than one — have you had his *haleem* before? His bronze coloured mash made of mixed lentils, barley, and shredded soft meats cooked for hours in two dozen spices are a taste of *jannat.*" Raj sighed with delight.

"Is your day spent thinking of food?"

"Yes," Raj admitted, looking defeated by his own desire. "But I spend a great deal of time thinking about clothes and jewels, too." He fingered the gossamer gown Rubina was wearing, the colour of lemon sherbet. Now that she was a member of the harem, she was required to wear clothes made by the royal tailor master. Each outfit was graceful, made to accentuate her dancer's physique.

"Did you hear about Dinesh?" Raj continued.

"Yes, I heard."

"*Tsk.* It is one thing to dream about possessing fineries but acting on the impulse?" Raj shook his head. "Carrying on with a concubine? Concubines are the ultimate prize, the jewels of the castle itself. The royals would chop off his man parts for his indiscretion if he had any to begin with." He grinned, his expression looking sinister in the soft candlelight.

"Who is this woman that Daniyal is entranced with? Surely, she is not a concubine? Must we really revise our plans?"

"Well, you seem suddenly more interested. It will cost you. I love this overlay vest on top of your gown. Let me have it. And since when were you a fan of the plan to marry Daniyal Master to begin with?"

"Raj!" Rubina exclaimed, but she dutifully peeled off the sheer vest, as thin and clear as a slice of lemon.

"It is Moti Ma's daughter," he said, shrugging it on. He twirled in the narrow hall, imitating one of Rubina's dance moves, hopping and moving his arms from side to side. "Sabina. She does not possess your lovely curls, of course," he pulled one out from under Rubina's *dupatta.* "But she is as fair as Kashmiri snow. She has never left the harem. She has lived in purdah her whole life. She does not have your wild sense of spirit and wonder. She is educated in Delhi Sultanate history and knows Persian poetry. Daniyal may have a chance to marry her, for she is the king's illegitimate daughter."

"Marry her?" Rubina tried to make her voice come out as even as unrippled water.

"After all," Raj plunged ahead, "Sabina cannot very well have relations with Prince Khurram, him being her half-brother. And having such a beauty around will tempt that lusty fellow! Have you seen her generous bosom and hips?" Raj sighed, cupping his hands over his chest. "But, in any case, imagine how a girl like this will live away from the harem? She will have to live with Daniyal Master in one of the quarters by the Yamuna River. Sabina, swamped with jewels and feasts — how do you think she could survive such a life?"

"Where do they meet?"

"Under the banyan trees, at midnight. Sometimes, at first light."

"He loves her?"

"Terribly so," Raj pulled at Rubina's headpiece, a shimmering jewel that was clipped into her parted hairline. She had become so used to the fine pieces left for her to wear that she barely noticed Raj's hands in her hair. It was strange that just a few short weeks ago she did her own washing by the river, clothed in only her yellow undergarments; her *choli* and skirt.

"You love him, little bird."

"I do not!"

"Yes, you do, my *chakli*. I saw it from the moment you two first met."

"You are mistaken."

"Perhaps you will have a chance yet to win him over. I wholly welcomed an opportunity to live in the royal apartments with you, should you have married Daniyal Master. Maybe you could have started a small dance hall; Daniyal Master would surely have never let you perform here or for others. But I suppose you would be happy never dancing again if you had your Daniyal Master," Raj made a kissy face.

"Stop with the fantasies, Raj."

"Do you really fancy him?"

"You said yourself he is spoken for."

"Listen to me very carefully, then," said Raj, dropping his teasing tone immediately. "If you want to make Daniyal Master yours, and I have no doubt that you have the power to do such a thing, you have another opportunity. The royals are packing a caravan. In a few days they will depart in a large group. The king travels with his favourite concubines, wives, servants, and chef. Camels, horses, and elephants will be packed for the trip to reach Amber Court. Along the way, you will have to camp in tents. But do not worry; the lifestyle is just as luxurious as the one you are living now."

"What does all this have to do with me?" she said.

"You, *chakli,* are performing for the Maharaja of Amber, Man Singh. Sardar *ji* himself revealed that the king has put you on the list of performers. Do you remember I told you about our King Jahangir being angry and taking away the maharaja of Amber's titles? Man Singh has lost Bengal and is desperate to get his lands back. Jahangir is still angry at Man Singh for not backing him for the throne. This meeting is vital for the future of the Mughal kingdom. Man Singh will undoubtedly go to great lengths to win our great king's heart. And I have another good tidbit of news for you." He paused to put his mouth to her ear. "There will be no Sabina on your trip. You have a chance to change Daniyal Master's mind."

"And what of Sabina?"

"Moti Ma's daughter," Raj pushed Rubina gently, "is a lover of opium. She will not stray far from her first love."

"Oh," said Rubina.

"Now go from here before Daniyal Master comes out of the physician's room! Pay heed to what I have said. Remember, he will be alone in the camp. And hungry for the touch of a woman. Use this to your advantage."

Rubina looked at Raj, wearing her see-through yellow vest, petting it like it was one of the sweet kittens brought into the harem for the concubines to fawn over. She turned to run back through the castle corridors. She imagined Daniyal's lovely, angry eyes, fixated on the dishes he was preparing, and she remembered how he had looked at her with annoyance. How did he look at Sabina? Did his eyes soften? Rubina imagined he touched Sabina with the care he used when preparing royal feasts. Feeling a strange sensation in her heart, she pictured Daniyal enjoying Sabina's voluptuous hips, of him taking in the sound of her voice reciting Persian prose over and over to him until she simply could not stand to picture Daniyal engrossed in Sabina any longer.

Tonight, she would ask the others about Persian poetry.

Chapter 24

2017

A haunting sound, filled with sad notes made by the kamancheh filled the car — the ancient sounds of Persian folk music had taken over the radio, created by someone the announcer called Tasnif Hanuz Hosein Nourshargh. There was a history in the music — rich, deep, mysterious, painful. Lost in it, Ruby forced herself to pay attention to the exit signs. She had driven for about an hour and wanted to stretch her legs, maybe eat something besides gummies.

She felt strangely beautiful in her yellow 50s dress, ruby red lipstick, matching scarlet shoes. But she wasn't delusional; she didn't expect Curtis to see her and fall in love. For now, she just wanted to surprise Belle and Trevor. *See,* she imagined herself saying, *you don't know me at all. This handsome rocker is the father of my daughter.* Maybe she'd say *fucking handsome.* No one was used to Ruby talking the way she really did in her mind. Maybe she'd say nothing at all and let Curtis do the talking, his arm casually slung over her shoulder as he spoke. She edited her daydream, adding intimate touches exchanged by her and Curtis, as she drove by grassy meadows with mountains sketched in the periphery. They reminded her of the Heidi stories she'd read as a child, of Swiss mountains and villages tucked into valleys and slopes. She breathed through her mouth, one hand covering her nose, as the smell of blueberries, manure, and petroleum fumes seeped into the car.

Ruby took the exit for Squamish. Sliding her car around the snug bend, she saw the usual fare of small-town restaurants: a chain breakfast joint, a McDonald's, a mom-and-pop diner. She spotted a small pub she imagined aged cover bands and local people were attracted to. A place where Curtis would place his full-sleeved tattooed arms on the bar and order a sleeve of beer. She parked and stepped out of the car. The night air hit her afresh. Through the propped open pub doors, she could see old hardwood floors stained with spilled whisky and marked with crushed cigarette butts from back in the day when people were still allowed to smoke indoors. Bills were tacked to the front of the doors listing the upcoming performances: open mic rap, spoken word, and an indie rock show. Ruby squinted as she walked in, wondering if Curtis fit any part of the puzzle.

"Drink?" A young girl with old eyes approached Ruby. She said the word like a dare, and Ruby shrank back, reminded instantly of her daughter.

"I'm here to, um, look for someone."

"Sure thing," the girl said. A natural redhead, the server's hair glowed like a glass of brandy with sun shining through it. "Just give me a shout when they show up."

"No, I'm not waiting for anyone. I'm trying to find someone."

"Underage kids show up past midnight with their fake IDs." She gave Ruby a wry smile. Her small nose stud softened her lightly freckled face — the opposite impression she had probably intended. She was Leah's age, surely, but she talked like a waitress in her fifties or from the fifties — Ruby wasn't sure which.

"It's an adult I'm trying to locate," she said, hating that she had been instantly branded a mom. "His name is Curtis Simmons."

"You know Curtis?"

"Used to know him pretty well, actually." Ruby winced once she heard how braggy this sounded aloud.

"Then you'd know he went to check on his family in Williams Lake."

"I gathered as much from social media." Did young people use words like social media? Ruby wasn't sure, but she forged on. "I figured he drove through here on the way." She ran her thumb over the smooth wooden seat of one of the bar stools. "This place is just his style." Worrying she sounded like a stalker, she added, "We were friends in high school."

"You do know about the fires that spread across the region, right? Roads are blocked. Lines are down. But Curtis thinks rules don't apply to him. I told him he should just sit pretty. You can try messaging him on Facebook, but he isn't replying to anyone."

"You saw him recently?" Ruby said, registering the girl didn't see her as any kind of threat. Probably rock star groupies didn't come in wearing old-lady dresses. She wondered if she should revamp her wardrobe with distressed skinny jeans like Belle had, all slashed lines showing thigh skin. Belle, she thought, would look credible enough to be Curtis's lover. She frowned at this. Back in high school, Curtis hadn't even looked at Belle.

"Curtis is always here. Never forgets his roots. He played a lot of gigs here first when he wasn't as famous. Now he always stops in on his way up to Williams Lake. Old habit I guess." The girl rubbed her neck, showing a splatter of freckles that spread down to her collarbone. Ruby realized she was beautiful in the way Leah was, the understated way, where you didn't need makeup or fancy clothes.

"As soon as I saw this place, I knew he was connected to it somehow," Ruby said almost to herself.

"So," the girl pushed in the stool that Ruby had touched. "You knew him in high school?"

"We were good friends. And then he got a gig in Portland and took off."

"What was he like back then?"

"Always one step ahead. If everyone was into grunge, he had moved onto industrial."

The girl nodded, wiping down a table. "And you're following him into the fire zone because…?"

Ruby faltered, feeling her act falling away. "I want to catch up with him. It's been twenty years and like I said, we were once close."

"If you say so. Are you staying to eat?"

Ruby had wanted to make it to Garibaldi tonight. She wanted to check out the town and get her bearings before she figured out how to get to the lake, but she was tired of eating candy. "Do you have a veggie burger?"

"Surprisingly, yes. Sweet potato or home cut fries?"

"Home."

The girl nodded. "We have some beers on tap …"

"I hate beer." Ruby pulled herself up onto the stool, trying to act as if she came to pubs every day. She smoothed down her dress. "I'm a wine person, you see."

The server shrugged. "We have two kinds. House red and house white."

"White." Ruby hadn't been planning on drinking at all, and now, in some odd pursuit of proving she was interesting, she had accidentally ordered a glass. *I'm a wine person, you see.* She grimaced. What did that even mean? She was nothing of the sort; it was Trevor who was the wine person. Why had she extended this to herself? They were no longer a pair.

She started to feel a bit silly in her old-fashioned dress, like she'd come off the set of a period piece sitcom, but an obscure bar in Squamish where people wore plaid shirts and beards was as good as any for its debut. The girl went behind the bar and Ruby stared as she poured a generous cup.

"No one orders wine here," she said, half smiling, when Ruby struggled to bring the glass closer to her without tipping fluid.

"Thanks," Ruby mumbled as the server bent over to scoop ice into glasses. And then, touched by the generosity of the wine given to her, before she could stop herself, she called out, "You know, you remind me of my daughter. You're an old soul like her." She didn't add that like Leah, the girl tried to hide this fact about herself, putting on a tough girl act that Ruby could see right through.

The girl straightened her posture and looked fixedly at Ruby. She folded a piece of flaming orange hair that had come loose from her bun, behind her ear. "Look," she sighed, "you seem like a nice lady. Curtis isn't who he used to be in high school." She ran a finger over the arch of her brow. "The thing is, he is kind of an asshole now?" she said, using a questioning inflection to try and soften her words. Or maybe she wanted Ruby to argue with her.

Ruby didn't know how to argue or agree with this. "An asshole?" she said, feeling like repeating the words was the only thing she could do.

"But me, I don't fall in love easy like the other tarts in Squamish. Everyone else falls for his charades so easily ... not Brandi Lavigne."

"I have family stuff to share with him," Ruby admitted, taking Brandi for a jaded woman scorned by someone famous. "I don't need him to be a reformed saint. Who he is now is his business."

Brandi made a "whatever" gesture with her hands and Ruby felt as if she was wearing the scent of naïvety. "He stops at Garibaldi Lake every time he goes up to Williams Lake. He thinks that nature nurtures his creativity?" Brandi said, adding another questioning inflection. "But he might already be at Williams Lake by now. You know, given the urgency of the fires and all, he probably wants to get to his parents right away. But then again Curtis doesn't think the rules of natural disasters apply to him. He probably went back to fuck every groupie in Garibaldi first." She looked to see how this news affected Ruby, who was trying to keep her face impassable. "He's basically the most narcissistic man I have ever met."

"I was going to check there first, just in case."

"I hope he gives you a chance to talk, hun. He is a moody guy. The only reason I get along with him is I've never had any kind of relationship with him. Once he has slept with you, he's done with you. And if he doesn't want anything from you sexually, he isn't interested in conversating. That's his style."

Ruby tried to calculate where she might fall on the Curtis spectrum.

"Wine, eh?" A heavyset man with a long beard pulled up next to Ruby. Ruby wanted to ask Brandi more, but she had walked away.

"Pardon?"

"Real fancy. Nowadays they put them berries and stuff in beers. I used to make fun of it all but then I had a raspberry-flavoured beer at my niece's and guess what?" His voice was low and gravely, like it had been processed in a mixer with small rocks. "I actually liked it."

"I'm happy for you."

"You don't really care none. But it's nice of you to pretend all the same. The waitress don't even bother," he tugged at his black and grey beard.

"No, she sure doesn't," Ruby agreed with a faint smile.

"So, where ya from?"

"Just Vancouver."

"There's a few people in Squamish with your skin colour. They look like you ... Poonjabs. Work out here on some farms."

"Punjabi," she corrected. It was funny to her that people saw her as being Indian when all the problems she seemed to be currently experiencing would be classified as white people problems featuring actual white people. Even her own daughter presented as more white than Brown.

"Actually, we don't have as many farms as people think we do. Common misconception. All the people coming up to the farmer's market are from Pemberton or out of town. Only a few homesteaders we got here."

"I'm Rajput Muslim, not Punjabi."

145

He shrugged as noncommittally as Brandi had and Ruby wondered if dismissive shoulder shrugs were a characteristic of Squamish people, much the same way Vancouverites overreacted to snowfalls or ignored each other even when their shoulders touched under a crowded bus shelter. She wanted to explain her complex relationship with religion, for while it defined her cultural upbringing, it did not define her current belief system. Sometimes, people would ask her why Rajputs were Muslims and not Hindus, and she would patiently explain that in medieval India, tribes were attacked by foreign invaders and many Hindus converted to Islam but kept some of their sacred traditions alive. Conversions were motivated by political and economic gains; some were forced and others elective. While Ruby admired Rajput Muslims for picking religious rituals to practise as if they were selecting foods from a Hindu-Muslim buffet, she knew this made people suspicious of Rajput Muslims.

But once the man had pointed out her skin colour, he was finished with the topic of ethnicities and had moved on. "We used to get tourists in the summer. But the fires. They don't get out this far, at least not yet. We're on wildfire watch. The farther up ya go, the more dangers. Tourism gets hit hard. I mean as do our lungs and the greenery and our ability to just go out, but never mind, I'm rambling. Where ya headed?"

"Williams Lake."

"It's a death wish driving up there this time of year."

Brandi set down Ruby's burger. The bun appeared to be sweating, like the wine. Ruby fumbled with the basket. She wanted to ask Brandi more, but she felt Brandi's views were too biased to be trusted. "I don't know what the hell I'm doing."

"Does anyone? Eventually the sun'll explode, and everything'll be gone. We are at the halfway point."

"Halfway point?"

"Of the sun's life. It's been burning fer like five billion years. We have about six left."

Ruby looked up at her existential motorcycle dude. "Yeah, I have gone over the 'we all die in the end' anyway point of view in my mind a few times, but it doesn't help my situation."

"Maybe you oughta accept your situation."

Ruby thought of the baby in Belle's belly. Of telling Curtis the truth about Leah. Of being ejected from her family home while her daughter, husband, and best friend continued to live there. She wrapped a napkin around her burger to catch the drips and brought it to her lips. "Believe me, I'm trying."

"Do you know who Shevek is?"

Ruby picked out a sliver of pickle and looked at him thoughtfully. "I'm trying to figure out why that sounds familiar." Was he a character on Star Trek? A Ferengi maybe?

"He's a character in an Ursula Le Guin book."

"Ah," Ruby said. "I knew he sounded familiar. I don't go out much, but I read a lot. You read science fiction?"

"You think I just read *Zen and the Art of Motorcycle Maintenance*? Look, focus on how Shevek in *The Dispossessed* looked at the planet that he went to that was supposed to be a critique of our Earth when he visited. Have you read that book?"

She had. All the time she wished someone would talk to her about books and now she couldn't think. Ruby tried to sort through all the dystopian fiction she had read. *1984*, *Brave New World*, *The Dispossessed*, and *The Handmaid's Tale* all bled together into one novel.

"Let me remind you. Shevek thought everything about people was so wasteful, plastic items wrapped in plastic; the custom of giving people gifts they don't need wrapped in more plastic; the waste of water like it was an infinite resource. What I'm saying is, we waste so much time worrying about the wrong things when we can fix the right ones, like Earth."

"But we need human relationships."

"We are consumed by our own problems while the world burns down. Look at the wildfires happening! And you're ignoring them, looking for some, as I overheard, movie star?"

"Rock star." Ruby was too tired to feel annoyed at being spied on. Suddenly she realized who Shevek had reminded her of — Trevor. Trevor's entitlement, taking Belle. "Shevek," she said pointedly, "was a flawed character. No saint like you're making him out to be. I didn't like the way Shevek felt about that one woman on the earthly planet. She was so adorned and beautified, he simply could not resist forcing himself upon her. Like it was her fault for being so available — he felt entitled to have her. I don't remember much about the book, but I sure remember that." Ruby wiped mayo from the corner of her lips and took another bite. It was the best veggie burger she'd ever had, and she'd never have it again. That's how it was with amazing burgers.

The man nodded. "And do you think that focusing on the movie star will help?"

"You're saying I shouldn't waste my time fixing my personal relationships because the world is on fire and that is way more of an issue." As she said this, Ruby pictured masses of conjoined water bottles skimming across the surface of the ocean; dolphins with bellies filled with garbage; turtles with shells cinched by soda pop holders. "That rock star happens to be the ... never mind. Forget him." She tipped her wine glass back to her mouth, swallowing it like juice. Her head tingled. The last time she had a proper glass of wine was at her dinner party, and she could have never predicted her life turning out this way back then. "The short end of it is my best friend is having an affair with my husband and they are having a baby."

"The long end of it is my wife and six-year-old son got killed by a drunk driver," and then he raised his hand before she could respond. "Books don't disappoint you like people do. I have a whole library.

Imma a fucking book hoarder. It's not very environmentalist of me. So, I don't actually abide by the advice I dole out. I don't even share my books."

"Ever?" asked Ruby, seeing that he was silently begging her not to dwell on his loss.

"I have paid the price too many times." He held out his fingers. "Let's see, I lost a Ken Follett, a Murakami, a Vonnegut, and a Márquez, indefinitely. I remember the authors but not the crummy people I sent them off with. How sad is that? But," he said, "I suppose books are communal, like umbrellas. You can't develop a forever relationship with them because someone might need them more than you do at the time. Yet I'm still an individualist when it comes to my books. I've learned my lesson about sharing. I refused the last person who asked me if they could borrow something."

She set down her burger in its woven basket. "I'm sorry about your wife and son."

"People have a way of disappointing you even if they die."

Ruby thought of losing her mother and nodded.

"I'd do it all again, though," he said gruffly.

"The thing is I'm not sure I would ..." Ruby trailed off.

Brandi walked behind the bar and topped up her wine glass. "Don't talk to Harvey about books. He told me I reminded him of a character in *The Sun Also Rises* and then refused to lend it to me."

Ruby was about to make a comment to Brandi, but just as she opened her mouth, the server had swivelled and was headed back into the kitchen. Ruby looked at Harvey.

"If I got a do-over, maybe I'd go back in time and choose the rock star."

149

Chapter 25

1997

"Angie Rodrigues?"

"Here."

"Dave Travers?"

"Yo!"

"Curry Masala?"

"It's Ruby Malkhana," Ruby said. The class tittered.

The homeroom teacher flushed even redder than Ruby. She had rookie written all over her — newly pressed white shirt, short pixie hair that tried to show she was in with the current look but which only resulted in giving her Elven features. She cleared her throat. "It appears someone pencilled the original name out."

Dave's nickname for Ruby irked her not because he had named her after an Indian dish — which could be seen as both a racist jest and misguided flirtation — but because truthfully, she never got curry for lunch. She got strawberry jam and butter spread on white bread. And a fruit that she couldn't consume, like a hard orange you needed a knife to get into, or a banana that was so brown it looked almost like Ruby. She envied the Asian kids who brought their native food to school. Like her, they also sat in the hallway to eat lunch, but in groups of ten and more. She stared at their decorated bento boxes with pickled daikon and sushi rolls and chopsticks rolled in neatly printed napkins and tossed her lunch into the waste basket next to them.

Ruby could not outright fault her mother's bad lunches. Parveen Malkhana's passion for cooking had died when Ruby's father left them. Ruby saw a picture of Julia once — she had wine-coloured lipstick and a haircut like Rachel on *Friends*. Her dad had once commented that Julia liked the same music as Ruby. "Julia likes The Cranberries," he had said, "like you." Ruby hated the band, but she hated it even more that her poor mother thought The Cranberries was a fruit picking festival. Ruby didn't talk to her mother about her dad leaving; one didn't talk about their feelings in the Malkhana household. Instead, she wondered why her mother cared enough to try to protect him. The guy was an asshole. Yet Ruby's mother went through all sorts of efforts to ensure that the community thought she was still with her husband: calling him to make sure he attended wedding functions, having him meet her at their place for appearances' sake, just for her parents. In the end, it turned out it was all to protect Ruby: to make sure that Ruby had a chance at marrying a respectable Indian boy.

Ruby didn't want to marry an Indian boy. If she could marry anyone, it would be Curtis Simmons. He wore plaid lumber jackets, and he would never be caught dead watching *Friends*. He saw Green Day at a rundown bingo hall on Granville Street before they were famous, and he played in a garage band. He was the type of guy constantly saving money for amps and noise proof insulation. Ruby wished Curtis noticed her — naked, preferably. Then he would see she was one of those few people who looked better without clothes than with them. While many women used clothes to narrow their waists or perk up their breasts, Ruby always thought that disrobed she looked like a woman in a Renaissance painting: soft and curvy, stomach and legs free from binding clothing and lusciously inviting.

Then again, Curtis didn't acknowledge her best friend, Belle, either, who was anatomically perfect but chose entirely the wrong clothes. Belle dressed like a trippy hippie; striped flare sleeved shirts paired with floral pants were her specialty. Belle had beautiful purple-blue eyes, the colour of wisteria flowers, but the more she wanted people to notice her beauty, the more they were turned off by her. She hugged everyone she knew hello, flirted with the teachers, and was on every team the school had to offer. But Curtis's glazed eyes passed over everyone except the five people he regularly exchanged some form of greeting with. Hesitantly, Ruby had accepted Belle's friendship because the more Belle sang and shouted and skipped, the more Ruby could blend into the walls sitting next to Cecilia Wong and Vivian Nguyen every lunch hour, wishing she could trade one of her jam sandwiches for a fucking bowl of noodles or pho or whatever it was they were eating.

The bell rang, and Ruby saw Belle turn the corner. Ruby's first thought was that Belle had forgotten her pants at home. Her dress was lilac and skimpy, and it stopped exactly one inch after her bum ended.

"What *are* you wearing?" Belle laughed as she pointed at Ruby's oversized Alice in Chains concert tee. "It's like a garbage bag with fancy turquoise designs." Belle was grinning so wide, the elastics at the back of her braces showed. "There's a party tonight, you know. I wore this dress so people will take note of me and remember me later in the evening. I'm going to wear a super short black dress tonight."

"Party?" Ruby slammed her locker shut, trying to sort out all the info Belle had thrown her way. "What party?"

"Heffner's parents are out of town."

"Who's that?"

"I don't know. That super tall kid who doesn't say much and listens to rap with his lame friends — you know, those white kids who think they are Black. People will be dropping acid. You *have* to wear something better than that."

"Yeah, I don't really want to go," Ruby said. "I have a curfew and all that ..."

"Curtis Simmons will be there."

"I see."

"*I see*? I imagine he'll be wasted. It'll be way easier to talk to him. I know you guys like the same bands and stuff. No other girl in grade 12 studies bands the way you do."

"Curry Masala!" a group of short eighth grader boys shouted, waving at Ruby. Dave snickered behind them.

"Shut up, will you!" Belle glared at them. They were staring at Belle's legs and couldn't speak. "You can't just eat lunch at your locker by the FOBs, Rubes."

"I like it here ..."

"Just think about it, okay?"

Chapter 26

1997

The party was indeed at Dan Heffner's house, behind the football field of the high school, where all the middle-class white kids lived. They had problems too, but they didn't hide dads that walked out on their families like the Malkhanas did; they happily labelled their families with the appropriate afflictions: Single Mom Household or Blended Family. It was all very regular around these parts. The moms here proudly loaded up their squad in the car for hockey practice on their own, and the ones who had remarried seemed spiffier, somehow. Shinier. These jolly, pastel-lipsticked and teased-hair women were a far cry from Ruby's own mother, who wore Indian sleeper sets to go out shopping after Ruby's father left. If Ruby complained about her mother's dishevelled appearance, Parveen Malkhana would declare white people did not know her Indian pyjamas were night clothes.

In Dan's case, it was his mother who had left his father, but only Ruby seemed to make note of this detail. Dan Heffner wasn't a conversationalist, but word had spread that his dad had gone out of town for a conference, and it felt like the entire high school had flooded his house. Kids were oozing out of closet space, drinking tequila out of Solo cups, smoking cigarettes in Dan's bedroom without even bothering to lean out the window.

Belle had cut five slits into Ruby's Alice in Chains shirt. She had knotted the front of the shirt to give it more shape and cut holes in Ruby's jeans at the knees. She had made Ruby wear blackish red lipstick and black eyeliner. Ruby felt like a complete and utter imposter. Like it was Halloween.

"My mom's going to expect me home at ten," Ruby warned, as Belle reached into her backpack for a bottle of gin she had stolen from her father.

"Ruby," she said. "You're the smartest person I know, and I admire you, I really do; it takes guts not to want to belong."

"If I'm not home by curfew, she's going to worry. You don't know Indian moms."

"My point is just try taking a swig. Forget about being the perfect daughter for once. Walk around. Meet people."

The prime space of the living room couch had been taken up by all of Curtis Simmons's friends. Curtis, however, was still nowhere in sight. Nirvana cranked up full blast, the kids were thrashing to the music in flannel shirts and dirty pants. The words of the song all jumbled in her head like bingo balls in a machine, out of order, out of synch, nonsensical. *El albino, half of stupid, entertainer, a mosquito.* Besides Belle, Ruby didn't talk to anyone else. No one had yet called her Curry Masala, so obviously Dave had not come. Feeling her belly press up against her jean's button, she sucked in her stomach. She tried the gin and her mouth stung. For a second, she felt invincible, a character from *The Outsiders.* Or maybe that was just the gin burning a hole in her stomach.

Belle pulled at her tiny black dress. A lampshade on her head and she would have been the lamp from *A Christmas Story.* It was far too adult for this party. Then, Curtis walked through the kitchen. He stopped and leaned his head back against the wall where Belle and Ruby were standing. He banged his head lightly against the wall a couple times, testing for something. Firmness?

"Hey!" Belle said cheerily, turning to him. "Do you want some gin?"

Ruby started perspiring. She put her hand on Belle's arm, but Belle pulled it away.

"Gin ain't my thing." He looked away from Belle.

"You play the drums, right?" Belle pushed on.

He didn't correct her to say it was the guitar. Ruby wasn't going to wait for Belle to humiliate her. She slid away from the two and decided to leave the party.

"Hey, nice shirt," he called after her. "You mutilated it pretty good, but still."

Ruby turned back slowly to face a very drunk Curtis Simmons smiling at her.

"Oh yeah?"

"I'm so over 'Teen Spirit.'" He pointed at the stereo. "I mean, why can't the 'burbs move on? Let the guy rest in peace? Our high school's so behind the times."

"I'm more of a Hole girl, but, you know, maybe kids find Cobain relatable ..." Ruby sputtered, running out of words. She took the gin from Belle and swallowed, allowing the fire to spread into her gut.

He sighed, leaning his body toward her. "Fame's the death of good bands. What's your favourite non-famous band?"

"Pavement." It was an easy answer for her.

"'Crooked Rain, Crooked Rain,'" he whistled through his teeth. "No one here knows Pavement. Play them fucking crap bands like Live. Or Garbage."

"You're not 'Only happy when it rains'?" She swigged again and handed the gin back to Belle, like they were sailors used to sharing bottles of hard alcohol. She wiped her eye, surprised to see black eyeliner on the heel of her palm, and then looked up at him. "Hate and anger would be more believable if the singer didn't look like an adorable handmade doll."

He laughed. "Isn't that what you are going after with your look?"

"My look?"

He had black hair, so dark it looked blue. Longish, it brushed up against the collar of his plaid shirt. Curtis was holding a beer bottle by the neck, casually, like he lived in Dan's house. He did that in biology too, slouching in the chair as if it was his own personal sofa. "Who are you, anyway?"

"Ruby Malkhana," she said, her name coming out foreign on her own tongue. She could sense Belle wanted in on the introduction too, but Ruby swallowed the urge to include her.

"Do you want to talk more upstairs?" His eyes looked frosted over.

"Sure."

Wordlessly, they wove their way between people, Curtis guiding her back toward Dan's staircase. As they climbed, Ruby took great pains not to acknowledge Belle still standing by the wall, mouthing *oh my god!* The two came upon a bathroom at the landing. It was clean and new, but it lacked a female presence; there were no perfume bottles or pink towels. Curtis, unsteady, leaned on Ruby and asked her to close the door behind her.

Rumours flooded their high school the next day. Ruby and Curtis had sex in the shower. Dan Heffner slept with not one, but two girls in this father's bed. Mickey Wu had done so much acid he tried to fly out the top floor window. But the truth of it was, as soon the door shut behind them, Curtis, relieved he no longer had to keep himself together for the sake of others, hung his neck and stopped talking. After throwing up multiple times in the toilet while Ruby ran the shower to hide the sound of retching, Curtis had fallen asleep on her lap like a soft black cat. She didn't dare move for fear of waking him. Shortly after this, the cops were called because a boy, likely Mickey Wu, was dangling from the window. In the chaos of the sirens and shouting kids, Ruby opened the bathroom door and Curtis fell onto the carpet like spilled Jenga blocks. Immediately, he was scooped up by a group of guys and carried away. Ruby bolted as fast as she could into the night, hoping she wouldn't get arrested, cursing Belle the entire way. She had never been able to bear the dramatic tears her mother dissolved into if she was even a little late; the thought of what she might do if Ruby was hauled to a police station was unbearable. She could just hear all the things her mother was sure to tell her that clearly made her "just like her father."

But when she looked down at her watch, struggling to catch her breath, she saw it was only nine-thirty.

Chapter 27

1997

Curtis showed up at Ruby's locker on Monday. The hallway smelled, as it always did, of seaweed, ramen, and kimchi.

"Ruby Malkhana, is that your lunch? It's abysmal."

"Fucking abysmal," she responded, surprised he had remembered her name. Hadn't he been wasted out of his mind?

And then, as if answering what she was thinking, he said, "I couldn't forget our conversation about bands. It's why I came today." In his outstretched palm was a nicely packaged container holding perfect hand-rolled sushi. "Wanna share my lunch? My stepmom's Japanese," he explained when he saw Ruby's shock.

Ruby imagined him living on the same street as Dan Heffner with all the other divorced families. And then, Curtis looked embarrassed and added, "Thanks for helping me throw up."

"You mean hide the fact you can't hold your liquor at all."

"Yeah, that too."

"That isn't going to bode well for you being in a band and all."

"I'm working on it."

"I apparently lost my virginity to you," Ruby confessed, still surprised Curtis was holding out a lunch she had dreamt of for months. She examined the black sesame seeds dusting the roll she now had in her hand like they were black diamonds. It should have been mortifying for her to blurt something like this out, but the air between her and Curtis felt intimate, like they had known each other for years, "and consequently, my reputation."

"You lost your reputation to me?"

She smirked. "Technically no one knew me before Dan's party. Maybe I gained a reputation."

"Gosh, I'm sorry. High school can be brutal." He slid down next to her. "I hope I was at least good enough to lose it to." He winked. "I guess I owe you lunches. Two weeks' worth?"

"Try two months," she said, reaching for another avocado roll.

That was how Ruby was introduced to Nature's Valley peanut butter granola bars, fruit salads, Snapple tea, sandwiches made using bakery soft buns and farmer's cheese, and best of all, Japanese food.

Chapter 28

1997

Two months later, Ruby was seated on the hood of Curtis's car.

"What you want," Curtis paused to blow smoke into the air, "is to replicate the past but add something new to the music. You just have to know what that new thing is. Catch on to the sound before people know they are looking to hear it. But you have to be quick. Music changes fast." He passed Ruby the joint.

She sucked in, feeling warmth spread across her chest. It made sense to call marijuana weed. She imagined she was breathing in the meadow, and she felt the grass coat her chest with honey. She cleared her throat, enjoying the sensation. "History repeats, sounds come back," she said. "Why not look in the past and try to bring back an old sound?"

"The Dirty Cavemen are revolutionary. We aren't just going to pull up sitars used in the seventies or throw in some synthesizers from the eighties and call it a day."

"Ah, yes, the age-old quest to be unique. The name is so masculine. Are you guys going to rip into chicken drumsticks on stage or something?"

"It's ironic. Philip is gonna wear a skirt on stage. They wanted me to do something too, but I don't know what." He pulled at his ragged black hair and sighed. He didn't even dye it that deep colour or add the indigo strands. Curtis's mother was Iranian. He didn't talk about her much, but from what Ruby could make out, she had moved back to Iran after divorcing his father. "Like, what the fuck am I supposed to do? Wear a goddamn dress? Put on face makeup and make like I'm Kiss? The whole point is to do something new."

"Hmm," Ruby put her hands behind her head and leaned back on the car. The sky was crimson, like it was on fire. Pink clouds smeared the horizon as an orange disk slipped through. It was quite possibly the most magnificent sunset she had ever seen. "People underestimate the talent it takes to replicate the past." She stuck her finger in the air, wishing she could taste a piece of the sky. She was certain the red sky would taste like blood. Metallic, sharp.

"Rad. Sunsets happen every night so maybe you have a point. Something the very same occurring at the end of every day, and people still manage to be amazed."

"Yes, but it isn't the same sunset every night. Imagine how hard it would be to produce the same kind of circumstances." She turned to him. "You know I heard on the radio that this guy got busted for making the past so believable that he tricked people into believing his version really existed?" She took a deep breath and tried to sort out her thoughts through the hazy corridors of her mind. "Let me explain. I don't know what artist it was, but he painted perfect knockoffs of original paintings and then sold them for millions. Like, he copied brush strokes, got the exact paint shades correct, even managed to age the canvas. People bought the work thinking it to be authentic. I think someone spilled something on one of the works, literally years later, and a sample was taken. That's the only way anyone uncovered the work was not original, by accident. The law is now in hot pursuit of the guy! Can you imagine going to jail for something like that? I mean, I think he is a genius!"

"A genius of imitation! There is nothing endearing about a cover band, Ruby."

"If you genuinely fool art curators then you are the real deal."

Curtis bent over to trace her lower lip with his finger. "I love The Cure but trust me I don't want to be them. But I could inject pieces of what I like of them into my music. I mean, in music we are always building upon what has been done before. I'm so over grunge, and I don't care if everyone in our dumb high school is feeling it right now. *Vitalogy* was a nice fucking save for Pearl Jam, with that gimmicky CD book. It's been years since anything good has come out. Let's face it, grunge has overstayed its welcome."

"I love that book." Ruby thought of the hours she spent in her room listening to Pearl Jam, flipping through the pictures of anatomy and bones, of Indian chiefs and archaic medical advice.

"I have gotta be on the next new thing." Curtis squeezed the roach between his fingers. Ruby tried to concentrate on his voice; there were crows squawking in the distance, frantically trying to find home before the sun went down, and she could only isolate one sound at a time. "And that," he said, "is techno. Obviously it's a repetitive dance beat, but Philip and I are overlaying punk and vocals. Like industrial rock and shit. Still want to keep it hardcore, but people can move to it, like The Crystal Method. We're playing at a rave in Portland."

"A rave." Her words hung in the air, dry, disconnecting from her mouth.

"I mean, yeah, it might be weird for us to have a band where there are normally only DJs, but we gotta take the gig. If we catch on, we'll be huge! There are so many raves in Squamish that we could play after that. The West Coast would be ours."

"Ours," she said, finding a single word from everything he had said.

"I need you to come."

"Oh, I can't leave my mom behind."

"You're the only person I can talk to like this." He leaned on her. "Feels like the world is on fire, Ruby," he said, sinking back to look at the sky. "I picture such big things happening for the both of us. No one else I know gets music like you do, you know?"

When Ruby closed her eyes that night, she saw diagrams of brains and charts of bones. She saw green grids, too, stacks of them, lining up. She heard her mother letting herself in past midnight and pictured her peeling off her brown pantyhose like they were potato skins and leaving a new bus pass for Ruby by the kitchen phone. Always with a new laminated card for her to place it in, even though she still had the one from last month. She remembered how earlier that night the crows had flown above her, blue-black clusters across an orange doughy sky. Like balls of Curtis's hair. If the world was indeed on fire, she didn't feel like big things were happening for her and Curtis.

Curtis was the only person she had ever truly connected with. And she was certain he was going to leave her behind.

Chapter 29

1997

Trevor Andrews had been stocking shelves at Green Savers when he had his first conversation, if you could call it that, with Ruby. No one had said anything to him about not wearing headphones while he worked, so he listened to Snoop Dogg and N.W.A. with his banged-up Walkman tucked into his apron. After work, he planned to use his spending money to buy a $10 bag of weed and smoke it on the grassy hill between his old second and third grade elementary school classrooms. Heck, he might as well invite Dan Heffner and Jamie Kronsky to come smoke with him. Dan had hit a bit of stardom after his epic party, but his fame had dwindled out, and he had time for Jamie and Trevor again. It was Friday night and Heffner might have some of his dad's beer to drink. It was triple x something or another, totally gross, but if they drank enough, Heffner and Kronsky would start rapping along with Trevor. The boys were not rolling down any street smoking endo and sipping on gin and juice, like all the guys on tracks they listened to were, but in a couple of hours it would sure feel like they were.

Trevor imagined the boys who were truly living the street life would trade anything to sleep in Dan's big-ass house and have access to beer and video games galore. Instead, Dan moped around like being unsupervised was such a bad thing. Maybe it was the ghetto condition that made it so you could create good art. Trevor wished, not for the first time, that he had been born someone else in some other place, like Oakland or Compton. For the time being, it felt fly for Trevor to imagine sitting back on the grass in a couple of hours, watching how Vancouver's grey clouds had become blotted out by the inky black sky — but he would be imagining a Californian sky with palm trees crisscrossing overhead instead. When they got high, Dan and Jamie would turn into real homeboys, letting more slang come out unrestricted, tongues thick with ghetto phrases that had found a place in their lives. Maybe when the three were older they could move to LA, get jobs as grip boys or something.

He sure hadn't expected that Indian girl to come in, five minutes to closing, mascara running down her cheeks. Ruby Masala. Or maybe it was Malkhana? Dave had a nickname for her, but he couldn't remember it. She was a nice-looking girl, light brown skin and round face, cute enough body. Thick and juicy popped into his mind. Chipped black paint on her nails. Not Goth, but something close. He had always wanted to date a Black girl, and it occurred to him Ruby was as close as he could get at his mostly white high school. She'd been a bit of a nobody, but the last couple months she'd been seen chatting here and there with Curtis Simmons at school. Trevor waved at her before he had a chance to feel self-conscious about his lanky height or the terrain of angry purple-red acne marking both sides of his cheeks.

She ignored him. He felt like a clown, but at closer look he saw she was visibly distressed.

"Everything ok?" he asked, pulling off his headphones.

"I'm fine."

"Are you drunk or something?"

"Something. Yeah."

She had taken to wearing heavy eyeliner to school and it was smeared across her cheeks like football paint. She was wobbling dangerously.

"Do you have to pee or something?"

"Something. Yeah," she said again.

"Look, I'll just take you to the backroom; I'm off in a couple minutes anyway. Okay?"

She burst into a fresh bout of tears. She was really very adorable in her ripped denim jacket and choker, and instinctively he put his arm around her.

"I came here to make a purchase," she whispered into his shoulder.

"What were you gonna buy?"

"A pregnancy test."

"It's the next aisle over," he said, as if she was a customer and her asking was the most regular thing ever. He led her down past the condoms, adult diapers, and tampons. The cycle of life confined to half an aisle of the store. He coughed, "You pick one, we'll take it with us."

"I can't." Her eyes filled. "I'm too wasted to read anything."

He scanned the products. "Well, let's go with the most expensive pee stick they have." He shoved it between his apron and shirt and pushed her past ice creams and frozen pizza, which the other stock boys called "the munchie aisle," and down toward the backroom.

They were now by the storage lockers, and a couple of men were loading things off the trucks for the graveyard-shift stock boys who would be coming in soon. The sound of boxes hitting the floor made a dull, heavy sound. The cashiers, the gossips of the employees, were thankfully still ringing in last-minute customers up front.

"Let's go, okay?" he said quickly.

"The bathroom?" she croaked.

"It's too risky, we just gotta go." He changed into his sweatshirt, dropped the pregnancy test into his backpack, clocked out, and suddenly they had gone out past the loading dock. The air was crisp and cold. She shivered.

"I really need to pee."

"Seeing as I stole something and ducked out early, I can't hang out at the crime scene. Just across the street there's my old elementary school." He jutted his chin toward the destination. "There's lotsa bushes; no one'll see you."

They went through a hole in the wire fence leading to the underground play area and ended up on the hill where Heffner and Kronsky would have camped out tonight if Trevor had scored and if he had called them. If. Now Ruby Masala/Malkhana was pulling a pregnancy test from his bag.

"Will you help me?"

"Of course." He pulled open the box and ripped the package with his teeth and handed her the stick.

"Am I just supposed to pee on it?"

"Probably." He turned around and could hear her pee hit the rocks.

"Ok." She handed him the stick. She looked better. Not so green. She even smiled. "Thanks. I can't believe I am asking you to help me with this. You won't tell anyone, right?"

"Nah," he said.

"Because I just finished living down a rumour, and it sucked. Trevor Andrews, right? You're in my biology class."

"Yeah. Let me see the stick." He matched it to the box feeling real adult-like. "If it shows two lines crossing, you are pregnant. One line is a negative."

She looked green again. "What does it say?"

"It's too soon to tell. Whose is it? If it's a plus, I mean."

She wouldn't answer. He figured he knew. Probably Curtis Simmons. He'd heard the rumour that the two of them had done it in the shower at Dan's house. Not that it would have done him any good saying so. They stood there, waiting. There was the buzz of the light in the lamp post above them. A gutter pipe gurgling water that reminded Trevor of the sound his water bong made when he took a hit.

"Anything yet?"

"It's a negative," he declared.

"What?!" she pulled the stick from him and stared at it. The fuck? But it was.

"You must be relieved."

"Yeah," she sank down on the grass. "I thought I missed my period. I really thought ... wow. Like wow."

"Well, now you have your life in front of you again." He crouched next to her.

"Uh huh." She sank into his chest with a thud. Her teeth were chattering. He pulled her to him and held her tight. "I hate that asshole," she whispered. "It was my choice not to go to Portland...but still, he didn't seem upset when he left. He hasn't even written me."

"What a fucker."

"I never want to talk to him again." She had no way of knowing then that she might not. That the rave in Portland had the potential to turn into more raves, which could turn into an opening act at festivals, and possibly, a full-fledged tour.

This time Trevor didn't ask her who she meant. He just kept hugging Ruby, letting her cry. It had been so easy, her settling onto his chest like she was always meant to fit into him. He knew his sweatshirt smelled like an unwashed pillow and hoped Ruby would instead pick up the scent of brewed coffee from the supermarket backroom that his mother always claimed seeped into his clothes.

What he didn't expect was that she'd say yes to his invitation to play pool with Heffner and Kronsky that night in his basement rec room. When she looked up at him and nodded, he saw that the mascara which had bled under her eyes had now caked, making her look like a panda anime character. On the way to his house, Ruby talked about going to a concert where Blind Melon's lead singer had pissed on the crowd in Vancouver and got arrested. Now, she informed him, he was dead of a drug overdose. All she did was talk about bands that Trevor had never listened to. She seemed to know so many details that even though Trevor found most of the music cringeworthy, he couldn't help but be impressed.

Years later, when they would reminisce about the night, Ruby would joke that she was the one that helped Heffner and Kronsky realize they were white again. "It took a Brown girl to get Trevor's friends to put down Eazy-E and Dre," she was fond of joking. "Trevor and I kind of knew each other at school but we really fell for each other at closing time. It was like that song was written about us, a few years after we met, you know, by Semisonic?"

Neither would mention the first pregnancy test in their memory of the night, not even to one another, hating to recall that Curtis was responsible for their connection.

"Like I was saying, we met at closing time. At the supermarket," Ruby would go on. "I really had to pee, right Trevor? And you helped me find a bathroom?"

Trevor, squeezing her hand, would always back up the omissions.

Chapter 30

2017

"Are you really wishing that if you had a do-over, you'd be pregnant with the movie star's kid?" Harvey stroked his beard and Ruby saw the world as it was currently served to her: an old bar in Squamish playing an outdated Deee-Lite song.

"Who is to say I wasn't?" Ruby frowned. "I took the test wrong. I took it too early." She rubbed the bottom of her new glass of wine into the ring of water it had formed on the table. "I'm trying to set things right again, find Curtis Simmons. When I knew the baby was his, I should have gone looking for him, you know? Can you imagine how different my life would have been?"

"It's an answer you'll never have."

"For a while in the beginning, I guess things were good between me and Trevor. But eventually, Trevor got bored with me. I have given it a lot of thought and people who get bored of their partners just get bored with themselves and they find new people as a means of distraction. The real problem, if you ask me, is with him. Not me," she said pointedly, shifting her thighs. "Not fucking me. I'm loyal. Stupidly loyal. I would have been happy to try to invigorate our relationship with passion. But he checked out. Trevor ignored my needs for so long that I became a piece of bleached wood lying on a beach. I don't know ..." her words meandered, and she wiggled on the bar stool. "Maybe there was nothing he could do to bring us back. After all, water won't do anything to a piece of dead fucking wood. In the end, maybe it was karma." She made a face realizing this was more in line with Belle's type of thinking than her own. "I lied to him first."

"I don't believe in karma much," said Harvey. Ruby was sure he was thinking of the accident that had killed his family. "Have you figured out what will happen after your big reveal to Trevor?"

"I already told Trevor, but he doesn't believe me."

"Oh. Wow, well that must be a hell of a doozy for Trevor, finding out some deadbeat celebrity is his daughter's father. What'll happen next?"

Ruby hadn't figured out much past proving to Trevor she wasn't lying. She couldn't help but see Curtis as her new friend did, an immature fame seeker cloaked in the smell of skunky weed, caring only about his right now — as the asshole Brandi kept declaring he was.

She thought of Trevor's caring blue eyes shining through his teenaged, acne-scarred face. Ruby remembered that the night she told him she was pregnant he had claimed it was his fault. Admitting he had no prior experience with condoms, he said he failed to put it on right when they had sex in his rec room. All of it had happened so fast. Ruby had consoled Trevor. After all, she was the tough one back then. She was the girl who played better pool than Dan and Jamie. The girl who had schooled them on rock music and convinced the two of them to switch within weeks. When Trevor had proposed marriage to her in the rec room, sun sneaking through between the dark blue blinds — minutes after she confessed that she was really pregnant this time — it was Blind Melon that was playing on the stereo behind her: "All I can do, is drink some tea for two, and speak my point of view … "

But what difference did it make that Trevor might measure up to be the better man compared to Curtis if, in the end, Trevor had not loved Ruby the way she had deserved to be loved? Curtis hadn't known she was pregnant when he went to Portland; he couldn't fail a test he never took, could he? Her mind churned this over as she sat next to Harvey, and the wine wasn't helping make things clearer.

"Top up?" Brandi asked her from behind the bar. Ruby looked at a couple dancing on the floor, a sloppy bump and grind that looked awkward yet oddly natural. "Groove is in the heart," the words spread lazy sex vibes onto the dance floor.

"I think I'll try the raspberry beer," said Ruby, eyeing Harvey's pinkish amber glass. "It's about enjoying the small things, right?"

"The temporary's all we have. The Earth has six million years left and we have maybe fifty and that's how I think of my priorities. But because the temporary is all we have we obsess about it."

Brandi set an amber-pink drink in front of her.

"We're mortals who can't accept our insignificance, so we create celebrities to worship and allow them to act out of bounds. Allowing us, in some way to believe that this Earth can host immortals. We've been doing it since the Greeks," Harvey said.

"You think I'm chasing the myth of a god, don't you?"

He didn't answer. Was she chasing a fiction? For the first time since she had come up with the idea, she wondered if sharing her most treasured person on planet Earth with Curtis Simmons was such a good idea.

Chapter 31

1610

The sun was about to rise. At the base of the horizon, the sun tinged the sky with the colour of *rasbhari* — cape gooseberries, deep golden and pink. Khushi was the one who had taught Rubina the art of recognizing each step that the sun took when it climbed the sky and to mimic the sun's journey in dance. Rubina would watch in awe from the balcony as the sky transformed from inky blue to violet, from blood-red to scarred pink. Morning light would fall upon the city of Agra, shining through the layer of fog yet covering the densely packed red mud huts. Cows would twitch their ears as sun beams warmed their skin, preparing themselves for the noises of daily activity that would shortly begin. Women lifting buckets to fill at the river. The rush of workers tap-tapping their bare feet against the dusty roads. Oxen, not yet swarmed by flies, pulling carts of grain, causing the wheels to scream shrilly in the still chilly air. Wet with dew, the ground that met the air would give off an earthy smell. Remembering this now, she thought she would never again see something that would awaken people as would the firstborn minutes of an Agra sunrise. On the dawn on her first Mughal expedition, Rubina was lost in thoughts of her home city.

Rubina was not sure what to expect from her upcoming trip, but she had seen moving camps before — nomads crossed Agra on their trips when she lived at the dance hall: people walking in a simple line of camels or horses; some leading the beasts by rope in a caravan, lighting campfires along the route, sharing heated pistachio milk from pots as payment to anyone willing to let them stay on their land. At night, the nomads might light a bonfire by the river and invite the locals to dance with them, accepting coinage for the strange wine drinks they offered. The nomads were always interested in the Mughal coins, on which was inscribed: *Allah-o-Akbar,* which could be interpreted either as God is Great or Great is King Akbar. Even though Akbar's son Jahangir was now in power, the old coins remained in circulation. Many townspeople were afraid to mingle with the tribespeople, who could speak broken Hindustani but were likely travellers from the steppes. Yet Khushi had always taken her best dance girls down, trading handmade dance anklets for the nomad's necklaces made from seashells, or better yet, a lesson in their odd, hooting, jump dances.

Rubina had shared with Raj all these delightful stories about the city of Agra, and in turn, Raj had told Rubina about Sabina; where her room lay within the harem and the best times to spy on her. Rubina had not summoned the courage to do so yet. However, now that Rubina was certain that Sabina, the lover of royal chef Daniyal, was not part of this royal expedition, Rubina was suddenly curious about what the girl was like. Just minutes before her departure from the Agra Fort, she snuck into the chambers to catch a glimpse of Moti Ma's daughter. She had expected the young Persian to be asleep, it being almost dawn. But Sabina's silky white feet were soaking in honey and lotus flower water, and she had a dazed expression on her face — perhaps she was dreaming of Daniyal's upcoming marriage proposal.

"Do you have a message for me?" she had asked Rubina vaguely, barely glancing up. She spoke in a voice dripping with opium. Heavy. Sugar-coated.

The lavish diamond-white gown that emphasized the contrast between Rubina's waist and hips was in vain, for Sabina had taken Rubina for an errand girl. In any case, Sabina's own misty blue gown was far heavier; it looked made up of nine layers, with the top one an overlay covered with genuine sapphires. Rubina wondered if Sabina had been up all night making love to Daniyal by the banyan trees, because everyone knew it was an unusual sight to see Sabina up before midday.

"Um," Rubina said. What had she hoped for by coming to Sabina's chambers? That the girl would look upon Rubina and see her as a beauty to be reckoned with? No, Rubina had just wanted to inspect the girl that Daniyal was infatuated with. To see if the girl would infect her with a fit of jealousy. Instead, Rubina's breath grew stifled, and she immediately covered her mouth with her hand. The air smelled of lavender and intimacy, though it was nearly impossible Daniyal could have ever entered these corridors. The scent of sex was overwhelming.

"Are you here to massage my feet?"

"I am here to bid farewell," she recovered. "Perhaps you do not recognize me? I am the dancer for the royal court. I am Rubina, daughter of Khushi *jaan*."

"Safe journeys then," Sabina said, cupping her right hand to her forehead as a sign of goodbye. "But if you have the time, I would love to ask you for a present from the Amber Court."

"But of course. What does your lady's heart desire? A bauble? A jewel?"

Sabina smiled, a long lazy grin that made Rubina feel uncomfortable. "Silken undergarments. Can that be arranged?"

"Silken undergarments?"

"Do I embarrass you? You did come from living in a brothel, did you not? I ask you because you are an expert in such matters."

"I am hardly an expert. I lived as a dancer in a dance hall."

"Are you telling me you are a virgin?"

"I am not sure what weight my status as a virgin would hold in this conversation."

Sabina pulled her heavy black hair forward, fiddling with the violet blossoms tangled within it. "It holds weight because if you were a skilled harlot, you would have secrets to teach me. You have the possibility of being an ally to me. Are you a skilled whore or are you not?"

"I ..."

"You are not. You are obviously an inexperienced little virgin who has come here to find out how these fresh flowers from the meadow have come to be laced in my hair." She pulled lavender from her strands to show Rubina before snapping the bright purple swig of flowers shut in her palm. "Curiosity has urged you to find out about me. Perhaps you want information about my lover. Something intrigues you so, and you have not the experience to hide it. I see it in your eyes. What thing are you seeking to take as yours? My experiences? My man?"

"You have mistaken my intention!"

"You want to learn my lovemaking specialties, so you can use them to seduce someone. Who?! Daniyal? Another man? You keep shaking your head? Then why do you become shy when I ask you for fine quality undergarments? Why did your face look so upset when I asked for them? Why do you appear out of nowhere to wish me farewell, huh? Speak now, or I shall strike you!"

"You completely misunderstand me," Rubina cried out, wondering how everything was quickly slipping from her control. She backed up towards the entryway. "You are right, the place I used to live in, indeed it was a house where virgins were sold to pleasure seekers. My mother ran the hall. My real mother. I am not driven by the desires you have imposed upon me ..."

"For what purpose did you come into my quarters unannounced? Do not waste my time in making me guess. I do not intend on being a piece for your game of chess! Do I look like I would stand in the garden courtyard and act as the king's live, moving chess piece? Well, do I? Do I look like the type of person that the king would dress in fancy clothes and have stand in the hot sun whilst he moved me around like a mere plaything? Calling out moves and having me move to square patches in the grass? No! Then, it is obvious I am not stupid and there is something you want so badly you cannot resist coming in here unannounced. I would have believed you better had you massaged my feet as the slave girl I mistook you for. But my, my, you were eager to show me your position in the kingdom." She removed her feet from the small basin, resting them on the edge with a slam. "And you are ruining my relaxed opium state by making me find out why it is that you are here!"

Rubina began twisting her *dupatta*. Was her interest in Daniyal so obvious? Before she could figure out how to retract, Sabina continued with a sigh. "I have let down my guard and told you I am on an opium high. I do not have opium here. Is that what you seek? Go search elsewhere, you inexperienced little wretch."

"You have me mistaken." Rubina was brought to tears. "Look, I came because I am well acquainted with Moti Ma, and she, being your mother, speaks highly of you. I promised her that I would check one last time to make sure you did not want to join us ..." Rubina came towards Sabina, near her white shoulder, exposed because her sleeve had slipped to one side. "I beg your forgiveness for startling you. I should have told you from the start, but you looked so peaceful. I did not want you to feel as though your mother had sent a spy to watch over you." She fell to her knees and carefully lifted Sabina's ivory feet and submerged them once more in the warm water.

"Oh ..." Sabina said, her voice wavering. She treated Rubina to a long, languid smile. "Mother knows very well that I will not be able to obtain opium if I went on the camp. I much prefer to relax here. The doctor, he never forgets to bring me my dose." She spread her arms over large cushions, embossed in golden monarch butterflies. "I do apologize for my hot temper. It is not easy for me to see my love go on the camp without me."

"I will see what I can do about your silken undergarments. *Adaab*," Rubina said quickly, mirroring Sabina's earlier action and bowing slightly. She watched Sabina sink more comfortably into the divan, a lusty expression settling once more upon her face, her heavy white bosom barely contained in her blue robe dress.

"Oh, Rubina?"

"Yes?"

"I do hope we can become friends. My mother is very careful with who she brings into her circle. If she accepts you, I accept you. Please keep an eye on my beloved. I assume you know to whom I am referring?"

"But of course."

"I worry Daniyal *jaanu* works too hard. He must be in control of each dish. Not too long ago he cut himself in his obsession with perfection. Do see that the other workers do their share."

"I will put in a good word with the kitchen staff."

"Good that we understand each other. He will soon be my husband and then I will not have to live in the harem any longer. I will have freedom. Have you really no experience with silken undergarments? Never mind. When you return, I shall teach you all about them. Bibi Mubarak in the Amber Court has them sent to her from overseas. Have you heard of the Hispanic Monarchy? How about the Kingdom of England? The physician is from one of those lands over the seas and he told me that all the queens there are known to dress in silken drawers! Just try and see if you can snatch me a pair."

"Yes, I will try," Rubina said, the words feeling thick on her tongue, as she imagined Daniyal seeing the European style *kanchuka* on Sabina. Instead of objecting, what she said was very different. "Actually, I do know about silken undergarments. My mother

Khushi *jaan* was buried in a pair handmade for her with love from Prince Khurram. They were sewn with 24 karat gold threads. Not even a queen is buried with such lavishness. Never underestimate the status women who run brothels can rise to. Or," she tossed over her shoulder as she turned to leave, "where a woman raised by her can end up." She walked away allowing this tidbit of information to sink into Sabina's opium-swollen brain.

Still, despite seeing the extent of Sabina's obsession with Daniyal, Rubina felt she had time to win his affections. Raj had told Rubina earlier, in the privacy of her alcove, that Sabina's marriage had not been confirmed yet, seeing as Daniyal had to pass through the proper channels and get the right approvals. First, he had to receive permission from the maharaja. Because Sabina was his illegitimate daughter, King Jahangir had no use for her as a concubine but might want her to remain as a member of his harem yet. Then Daniyal had to seek Moti Ma's approval. Rubina was not sure what grandiose plans Moti Ma had set in motion for her only daughter. Whether they included Sabina leaving the harem and living in the apartments on the riverbank with the royal chef remained to be seen.

Chapter 32

1610

Rubina found her place outside with the rest of the harem. The smell of lavender from Sabina's chambers had sunk into her clothes. She thought of Sabina's half-closed lids, her sultry expression. Soon, she was distracted by the sights unfolding before her. Raj, by *not* sharing every elaborate detail of the Mughal camp in action with his good friend, had managed to shock Rubina senseless, for she now understood that he never could have done the grand procession any justice with words alone.

The camp had prepared to depart at dawn, right after the *adhaan*, the call for Muslim prayers was made. The sun, slow to rise, cast a rainbow of different colours upon the traveller's backs — blue, purple, pink, orange, and yellow. Clothed in her travelling scarves, the first thing Rubina noticed was rows of heads lining up in what looked to be a battalion formation, the men wearing smart shoulder and breast plates. Cannons pulled by wooden carriages went by her, followed by a group of velvet-garbed elephants carrying bundled bags. Then the camels, mules, oxen with carts, each stamped with the tiger emblem, followed — every last one burdened with a share of camp goods, tandoor ovens, fine dishware, foods, and loads of jewels and gifts. Finally, the slave men that belonged to the camp trailed past, already making a show using small weapons to chip away at rocks and minor obstructions. The concubines would find their place in this great line.

"I wonder where all these poor men have come from. Why are they in the back? Do they not need to be in the front of the path to clear the way? They are pecking away at shrubbery pointlessly," Rubina whispered to the girl standing beside her. Though the camp had just begun its march, Rubina's jewel studded overdress was already covered in yellow dust, as was the girl's next to her. The line had stopped and soon the concubines would be ushered into the appropriate palanquins wedged within the procession.

The girl, Rubina now saw, was a concubine not more than eleven years old. Rubina had previously taken notice of the young one at the bathhouse, watching as she shrank back to avoid the others, hiding in her room to eat date cakes alone as Rubina had done when she first arrived at the Agra Fort.

Tiny with a child's voice that matched her straight and narrow looks, the young girl clipped back an answer to Rubina. "The roads here are well maintained, but the king wants to leave with style and show off his helpers. Later, when we start winding around the wild, untravelled areas, the workers will go to the front and make way!"

"They look like mere paupers."

"Yes, they do ... you are correct! Some of these labourers were stolen from villages during other expeditions when they were just children. Others come from sandy mountainous regions. When the Mughal camp passed through, these men joined to avoid a desolate life of hunger where they suffered under the rule of terrible lords. Seeing the Mughal Empire traverse the road is quite a sight, do you not think? Those who do not leave their villages; they will forever remember the vision!"

"But how do you know this?"

The girl stared at her with large eyes that did not quite fit the frame of her small face. "Because that is how I came to the harem! It was announced that a camp was passing through our remote village. There were mountains on all sides of my hometown. There had been famines before, in my grandfather's time, but we were mostly getting by. We had never seen strangers before. Instead of staying in our hut like my mother told me to, I snuck out to see the spectacle, to see the nobles themselves on horseback and hear the trumpets! *Hai bhagwan!*" She clutched her hand to her chest. Rubina strained to follow the girl's excited style of speech. "Prince Khurram spotted me, and he had his guards pluck me out of the crowd. I never even had a chance to say farewell to my parents!"

Rubina remembered the prince's lewd expression when he first laid eyes upon her at the dance hall. "I thought all the concubines are noble-bred? Or, at the least, should they not be cultured in some form?"

The girl was not offended by Rubina's remark. "The prince thinks I can learn the concubine ways quickly, given my youth. He believes treasures can be found even amidst the roughest terrain. He took away my village name and renamed me Heera — diamond."

"Heera," Rubina repeated, testing the girl's name on the wind.

The dark, shirtless labourers passed on, and Rubina and Heera were still standing by the other chosen concubines and entertainers in a huddle near the Agra Fort palm trees. Heera had not initially seemed poorly raised to her. As Prince Khurram could identify her unusual large eyes as being beautiful, so could Rubina. But now she could hear that the way Heera spoke Hindustani was disjointed and rushed, as if by speaking fast and with exclamation she would cover her mistakes. Heera's "s" was pronounced "sh" and her "sh" like "s." No wonder Rubina could barely keep up with her.

"Do the others know you come from a dirt-poor village?"

"I hide myself as best I can!" Heera's large eyes were shiny. If she was going to cry dramatically like a child, Rubina would not be able to bear it. The dance hall girls were like this when they first arrived at Khushi's, wetting their bed at night, crying for the mothers they had, crying for mothers they never had. Rubina had never been able to stand it. She had not mourned dramatically over the loss of her own Khushi. One had to move on. Ironically, this was a lesson Khushi herself had imparted to her.

The eunuchs were guarding the ladies even though they were yet at the entrance post of the great palace, making a big show of fanning the most important concubines with large peacock fans, including Moti Ma.

"You are different like me, I can tell," said Heera.

"Yes, I am a dancer. My name is Rubina. I recently joined the harem."

"I do not mean that. Your mannerisms are different."

"I grew up in a dance hall." Rubina, insulted to be considered a commoner like Heera, found herself adding, "But my mother was one of King Jahangir's favourite concubines. Khushi *jaan* was the only concubine allowed to leave the castle, and she fought fiercely to raise me away from the harem."

Heera stared at her with unconcealed awe. "Are you really of king's blood?"

Rubina guarded her expression. Although this was quite possible, Rubina had not spent much time thinking of King Jahangir as a man who had fathered her. Like all the girls at the dance hall, she had never imagined herself as having a father.

Suddenly, the royalty and nobles and royal chef staff came up past them, carrying the voices of the girls away in the breeze. The aristocrats were surrounded by uniformed guards. Most of these important men were mounted on horses, upon saddles that boasted decorated parasols. A shiver passed over Rubina's skin. A kettle drummer rose to go in front of the emperor, who was safely stowed away in a plush throne on wheels, pulled by an elephant. Following the king came ten horsemen, four displaying royal matchlock muskets, which they then enclosed in gold cloth bags. The other horsemen followed suit, in turn showing off other weapons — bows, swords, daggers, all of which were enclosed in the similar gold bags. Following this was the captain of the guard with his troops. The prince's palanquin would be placed here, and twenty-four horsemen would follow. Musicians traipsed behind the royal crew, eight with pipes, eight with trumpets, and eight with kettle drums. Their tinkling notes cut through the air. Mustard-coloured dust rose like smoke from the marching camp, though the sun had just freshly risen. Rubina, versed in the ability to do simple math sums by Khushi, could not help but count and make records of all the details around her.

Adjusting her eyes to the first light, Rubina could see that the members of the royal family themselves were carried in mini palaces with lavish chairs built inside, resembling portable thrones, by an army of men. They marched ahead of the concubines to fall into line. She was in awe, imagining herself riding beside the queen — but such a thing would be unheard of for a court dancing girl. The royals' travelling camp huts were luxuriously outfitted, in banners of satin, silk, gold, even jewels. Eunuchs were nearby holding sticks to swat away spectators (already gathering in large masses) from gaining glimpses of the beauties hidden away in the canopied howdahs. Rubina did not see Raj amongst the eunuchs. She knew that as exciting as the royal camp was, Raj would do anything to avoid making his way through the dust clouds; he preferred the comforts of the castle in all its splendour. Rubina did, however, see Sardar wetting the chalky plains from time to time so that the royal women would not suffer from having to inhale the poor quality air as the camp forged ahead.

The concubines and wives were the next members of the Mughal Empire to march. If Heera wanted to ask Rubina more questions, she had lost her chance. Drenched in the gold of the morning light, a eunuch hoisted Rubina into a sealed hut palanquin sitting firmly atop an elephant. Rocking back and forth gently, she was able to push aside the satin curtains and stare out of an eye slit cut into the ivory decorated hut which served as a secret viewing panel. She was relieved to know her hut was not situated on a camel, like those of the many other less important members of the harem. Moti Ma was well placed enough in the kingdom to travel in a large hut attached between two poles, carried by two docile elephants, one in the front and one in the back, swaying gently like a rocking cradle. It was annoying to think that if Sabina had come, she would have sat in the same special house as Moti Ma.

Most of Rubina's day was spent jostled atop the elephant, with the sun creating decorative shadows on the floor of her hut, a type of moving art made possible because of the template used to create her *howdah*. Squinting through the divider, she saw that the king's procession only stopped when the royalty expressed an interest in visiting a temple or a mosque. Rubina was tempted at these times to seek out young Heera, but the concubines and performers were not allowed a chance to enter the monuments. She could, however, see that the priests and mullahs were beyond themselves with happiness over the royal visits. Whenever they stopped, King Jahangir threw down coins with his name and lineage inscribed upon them. Raj had told Rubina privately that the maharaja had aspirations to create a portrait of himself drinking a goblet of wine etched upon a gold coin, but Rubina could not imagine the Mughals veering so far from their traditional style of minting monies. She watched as the travelling villagers alternated between throwing themselves at the emperor's feet and fighting one another for the silver tokens.

Just as she began to feel hunger, food arrived for her. Meals were brought by servants for the members of the harem who observed strict purdah. Rubina knew Daniyal's cooking from the first bite: sweet and spicy mixed together, for the royal chef loved the contrast. Rich coconut and lime porridge topped with unripe green mangoes for breakfast. For lunch, a dish so aromatic King Jahangir had called it *lazeezan*: a mung lentil and rice dish sprinkled with pistachios and raisins known as *khichdi*. And then dinner, the grandest feast of all, which was yet to come. Clearly, Daniyal had full access to a portable kitchen and staff as his food tasted even better in the fresh air, cooked over open flames. Eating Daniyal's food made Rubina feel closer to him, and she was eager for another chance to see him once the camp settled.

At last, the sun began to descend, and Rubina was stunned at the royal camp's speed and efficiency in setting up for the night. Within moments, an entire city was erected, emulating the grounds of the Agra Fort, the footmen working quickly in the fading amber light. Secure on all four sides with a full cavalry and tall walls made up of wooden boards and silken cloth, the city was impenetrable, access controlled. A front entranceway was the only route in or out of the camp, and it was clearly marked with flagpoles and guards. A stage was set up within the mini city for evening performances, which Rubina knew she would be a part of. A series of tents fashioned out of poles and cloth were assembled, with the nobles laying first claim to these makeshift houses dressed in gossamer curtains and grand furniture. The king and royalty themselves were to stay in a howdah that was quickly constructed by slave men, comprised of multiple levels and a balcony that the king could appear on — a mini palace. There was also a bazaar set up on the grounds, and a bathhouse where Rubina could see men already beginning to heat water in large cauldrons to fill chai cup–shaped tubs. The labourers, who had not eaten all day and would not partake in the feast that was coming, were starting to cook their plain meals of coarsely ground rolled grain over the open cow- and camel-dung fires. Smoke rose in plumes, the fires scattered through the camp. Rubina was struck by the thought that Heera would have been a common villager, sister to these mountain peasants crouched over their fires, had Prince Khurram not taken possession of her.

The most important landmark in the camp, Rubina noticed immediately, was the Akash Diya or "Light of the Sky." She exhaled. A massive bowl sparkling with magnificent flames, it was lit by cottonseed oil and towered 120 feet, grounded with sixteen ropes. This fire ball served as a symbol for people miles away that the Mughal Empire was the world's greatest. Indeed, as the camps had been set up with precision since Timur's time and the setup had been perfected to an art form, no one could dare contest this fact.

Now, camels were being dispatched to the next checkpoint to start to set up camp for the following night, but for the people who remained on the grounds, the festivities of the night were just beginning. There was talk of staying at the camp for two nights because the king had heard there were tigers to hunt in the mountain region. The king had his own pet with him to stalk deer, a leopard with softly brushed hair and adorned in a heavily jewelled collar, who hunted alongside nobility like a trained dog.

In the bathhouse, Rubina sought out Heera. An idea had begun to implant itself in her mind about how she could seek out Daniyal. She felt a bit like Raj, conspiring to make her plan a reality.

Chapter 33

1610

The girl, so thin she had not yet developed breasts or hips, was braiding her hair near the cauldrons. Heera was dressed in a gown that was too matronly for her frame, a musky scented indigo curtain dress made up of three layers. "The baths are reserved for the main concubines and wives," she said, barring Rubina from entering. She used a matter-of-fact voice that Rubina took an immediate dislike to.

"I am tonight's star performer. I have been permitted to bathe."

"I thought the rhinos and lions appearing on stage were the star performers," Heera said. She had not meant it as a joke, and Rubina could see how naïve Heera was. This reminded her once more of the girls in the dance hall who still liked stories about fairies and animals.

"Well, the star performers are the ones that take rose baths. Can you imagine bathing a rhino?" she said teasingly. "Clearly I am the night's star."

Heera broke into a small smile, hiding her mouth quickly before Rubina could see the rot of teeth at the back from the months her family had gone without enough nutrients. She rose to help Rubina disrobe. "The nobles, they quite like the way you move. What a talent you possess. Do you have a lover, Rubina *baaji*?"

Rubina felt her cheeks warm. Heera would not understand, yet, Rubina's curious feelings for Daniyal. She did not know if Heera could be trusted either, so she said nothing of him. What would there have been to tell, anyhow? Daniyal was not her lover; he was Sabina's. The small interest he had shown Rubina could not have been mistaken for more than a general kindness.

Rubina instead wiggled her hips suggestively. "The Mughal nobles enjoy seeing a woman who understands how to move, Heera. Have you never seen a true dance number?"

"I have not. Are you to perform in front of the Rajput Raja of Amber, Man Singh?"

"Why of course. This is the reason the good king has brought me." Rubina slipped into the warmed bath easily, while Heera fell into the role of a slave girl and took to delicately washing and tending to Rubina's hair. Heera was full of gossip and news just like a loyal house maiden.

"The maharaja has constructed gorgeous temples, such as the one at Vrindavan. He has decorated the court of Amber in majestic fashion. I am eager to see the Amber Fort! Have you heard that the maharaja once stood up to Akbar the Great? Maharaja Man Singh of Amber is one that never takes to accepting direct orders! The time we are living in is so interesting, am I not right, *baaji*?"

Rubina closed her eyes as she imagined Sabina would do. She sighed with bliss. Heera was delicately massaging her temples. "I do not know much of politics, though my dear friend Raj has told me a great deal."

"The eunuch?!"

"Yes."

"You are so beautiful. Of course Raj would prefer your company! He only trails the most gorgeous girls in the harem. He has never even greeted me."

"But the prince noticed you."

Heera stopped playing with Rubina's hair. "It is a curse to be noticed by the prince."

"Who else have you seen Raj talk to?" Rubina felt a spark of jealousy beginning. "Sabina?"

"No, never Sabina. Sabina is lost in her own world."

"How do you mean?"

"Do you not know? Sabina is sometimes not well. Her mind," Heera twirled her finger by her head. "*Vo paagal hai.*"

"Crazy?" Rubina slipped out of the rose-scented water, allowing Heera to cover her in a drying cloth. A eunuch brought Rubina a satin robe, and unashamed, Rubina allowed Heera to dry her hair and body in his stead.

"Would you like me to apply this?" Heera was holding a golden pot filled with something that smelled like Daniyal's rose *faluda*.

"What is it?"

"Sugar scrub. All the best ladies in the harem use it; I know because I have been a spectator in the bath houses for a long time." She lowered Rubina's face down to her lap and began scrubbing her face with the potion in small circular motions. Gently, she washed the scrub away with warm water. She led Rubina to a stool made from animal skin and braided her hair loosely so Rubina's waves would set more softly. "Sabina hears voices. Ghosts, that sort of thing. Remember Dinesh, the eunuch with a man's desire?"

"Yes, I think so."

Heera pulled off Rubina's robe and began cinching Rubina's *choli* using golden ribbons. "He was Shanti's lover, *nah*? Well, as you must have heard by now, Dinesh and Shanti's trial ended, and both were killed by the order of the king. Sabina swears she hears Shanti's voice at night. *Santi ki bhoothni uske shaat baath karthi hai,*" she said, mixing up her "sh" and "s" sounds. In her delight she was unable to hide the true uneducated mountain villager she was. "Ghosts haunt Sabina's mind. They infect her brain. Sometimes she is okay; other times, she is a big mess and does not bathe. You have not seen her in her moods — Moti Ma worries about how to care for her

191

only daughter. Have you really not heard? This is the reason she is allowed to smoke so much opium. It makes her easier to handle. The fire-haired physician himself prescribes it."

Rubina had only known parts of what Heera revealed. Heera was proving herself to be more valuable by the minute. "Tell me more. Do you know anything of Sabina and her lover? Have you seen them ... together? In each other's physical embrace?"

"No, I have not." Heera wrinkled her nose, which made her look very cute. "I know more of the stories of our kings. Do you know much of this Maharaja of the Amber Court?" She began to tighten the waist of Rubina's icy-silver silken *lehenga* using leather strips. The skirt was covered with hand-sewn gold coins and pearls. Rubina took a deep breath as Heera pulled. "The maharaja once saved King Akbar's life you know, by preventing Akbar from stabbing his own chest. Akbar was trying to prove his own bravery during a drinking party by harming himself. Akbar, angry the maharaja was interfering, wrestled the maharaja down, and an elder aristocrat, in turn, saved the maharaja! Are you also the main act to perform in this maharaja's Amber Fort, Rubina *baaji*?" she sped on. "You will see the Sheesh Mahal! I have heard much of the Sheesh Mahal. One hears so much gossip just sitting off to the side at the baths in the harem."

"Sheesh Mahal?"

"Oh yes, the mirrored palace. It is made up entirely of mirrors and coloured glass and one lit candle reflects a thousand stars! The queen cannot sleep in the open night air, so the maharaja has brought the stars inside for her!"

"Ah yes, I think Raj told me about it."

"Surely then Raj told you about the palace's magnificent carvings and art, and of the courtyards, for there is one on every level. We will stay in the *zenana* with the other women. And perhaps we will see the idol of Shila Devi carved from a single slab of black stone. Maharaja

Man Singh won a battle against the Raja of Jessor in Bengal, and as a prize for his victory, the goddess Kali appeared to Man Singh in a dream and asked him to retrieve her image from the bottom of the ocean! Maharaja went searching for the goddess, and deep in the sea he found a large block of black stone from which he made Shila Devi."

Rubina brushed her fingers down the bodice of her garment, put her hands on her hips, and bent her knee back to stretch and practise a few dance steps. When she turned, she saw Heera was staring at Rubina with an incredulous expression.

"It sounds marvellous," Rubina replied. She started doing her hand exercise where she loosened the joints by having each finger meet a point on her thumb. "This is what I have been commissioned on this trip to do, find the marvellous. I am to seek out a bauble for dear Raj in the Fort. Perhaps you can help me, precious Heera? He wants me to bring him back a trinket." She purposefully left out Sabina's absurd request.

"Yes, *baaji*! What an adventure ..."

"And," she put in quickly, hoping she had conversed enough to put her plan into motion, "Will you be a dear and deliver a message to the royal kitchen for me?"

"I regret it is dangerous for me to go, for everything will be monitored closely."

"What about during the performances? Surely the concubines will be permitted to watch the acts. You can sneak away then."

"I would be too afraid to go, *baaji*."

"What of that girl that broke away from her hut to watch the Mughal Empire parade through her village, *haan*? What of the girl whom the prince scooped up from her ordinary, miserable life, fighting for scraps to eat? Is she not a lovely maiden in his great harem now?"

"Truth be told, I wish every day I had not disobeyed my mother, Rubina *baaji*. We were not a prosperous people and we had bad years. But we were surviving."

"Life cannot be squandered in regret, Heera. You must make the most of your life in the harem. It is an honour to be a part of the king's harem." She winced inwardly for sounding like the physician when he had first spoken to her about the loss of Khushi. She bit her lip before she went on to list the harem's exceptional qualities, as he once had.

"Yes, Rubina *jaan*."

"Would you really rather spend your life living in a hut between two mountains never seeing the world?"

"No, Rubina *jaan*. It is with the grace of the gods that I have been blessed to see the world."

The eunuch had left Rubina a sherbet to drink in a goblet on a tray. It was made of the pineapples carried into the camp in animal hide bags by the camels. Rubina thrust the drink into Heera's small hands. "Try this, my young companion. Let the sweetness sink into your tongue. Is it not exquisite? Surely your village had no pineapples."

Heera did. She drank what was supposed to be the dancer's rejuvenation sherbet in three gulps. The Mughals were great believers in concoctions for health and restoration. Rubina did not doubt her decision — she did not need an elixir to dance. At Khushi's dance hall, only after her performance was she offered water. Khushi had kept the purified liquid aside to cool in camel leather drinking pouches for her best dancers. It had tasted sweeter to her than the juices of the Mughal Empire; thus Rubina made it her custom have a drink of water following her performances.

"So fresh," Heera said. "I went my whole life without seeing pineapples."

"We must look out for one another here, Heera. Two girls not raised behind the harem walls. Two girls not raised in the noble world, not raised in purdah. It is important we stick together, *hai nah*? Or we will be ripped apart by the concubines like the hunted meat a tiger has caught." Rubina pulled her fists from one another repeatedly, causing her bangles to jangle. The sound was like heavy rain. Rubina could not remember when she had last seen water hit the earth. The plains were hot and dry though it was monsoon season. Everything was so parched, even in the tent house things were slowly being covered in silky clay-coloured particles.

"I will go now to do your errand," Heera spoke quietly. "It is almost dark. Soon people will have their eyes on the show. The eunuchs do not watch me as closely as they do Moti Ma's tribe. Some think I am their maid."

"Good girl." She brushed stray hairs from Heera's face. She was not yet refined, but one day, under the right guidance, she might become a lady. At the far end of the tent, by the pole, a eunuch was busily setting up an *aa'ina* — a gilded mirror and a small tin of kohl for Rubina to beautify herself with.

Rubina spoke deliberately, "You must find your way to the kitchens. Locate the royal chef and tell him to meet me at the main stage after my dance number. His name is Daniyal Master. And I shall teach you the dance of the snakes later in the evening ... and the tale that goes with it."

"Will you really teach me to dance, Rubina *baaji*? I am a fast learner. Prince Khurram is right about my trainability."

"But of course he is." She squeezed the girl's slender shoulders. "He has a sharp eye for discovering the most talented girls. Heera, I confess the harem is not somewhere I plan to be forever. Just like my mother, Khushi *jaan*, I will also leave. And it would not be bad to leave you behind with a skill you can use."

If the girl was confused about why Rubina wanted to leave the harem after praising it so much, she did not say anything. Heera only stared at Rubina. A eunuch arrived and pushed Heera aside so that he could arrange the layers of lace trimming the lining of Rubina's coin covered skirt. Heera was so focused on watching Rubina, she did not register the eunuch's rude shove.

Rubina almost felt bad for putting the girl's life at risk to make her a messenger. Heera was naïve, as many girls in the dance hall had been, but her loyalty and desire to please others made her stand out. Her eyes had the same hunger as Rubina's: to reach somewhere further than the commoners. Perhaps Rubina would mentor the girl. Take her under her wing as Khushi had once done for her.

Just as Rubina wondered if sending the girl on the mission was a good idea, the girl lifted her arm as she had seen Rubina do. Twirling her wrist seductively, her arm painted the colour of silver coins by the moon, she disappeared into the hubbub of the night crowd.

Chapter 34

2017

Ruby saw it outlined by the moon, like a painting lit by gallery lights. The best place to stay in all of Squamish, as promised by her motorcycle companion. Feathering yellow paint. Bottom half a grocery mart. Top, a dwelling that boasted a large window with heavy lace curtains. There was a wooden hand-carved sign on the window ledge that read: Barbara's Bed & Breakfast. Minutes after registering, she was sitting on the edge of a frilly bed, looking out through the antique cream curtains she had seen from the street. Her eyes focused on the keyholes made from embroidered thread. This was the first time she had checked into a room alone. She had been more independent when she was her daughter's age than she was now.

Leah, as far as Ruby knew, was back in Vancouver, sleeping in Rick's sister's room.

Rick made Leah kale smoothies. He called them Green Dream Soccer Machines, claiming they improved kicking abilities, and Leah, who had initially mocked him mercilessly, was now a self-admitted addict. They drank them before going for the hill runs that were meant to strengthen their quads and calves. Leah talked a lot of Rick, not *to* Ruby directly, rather *at* Ruby; a sort of uninhibited running dialogue that daughters did with mothers when they mistakenly thought they were only being half-listened to.

Leah thought of Rick's place as home. Ruby knew she put her car keys onto one of the hooks designed to hold hers especially, above the laptop nook in the kitchen. Rick's house, older than theirs, was designed in a homely fashion wholly with the intention of being used. The kitchen was painted a pale margarine shade. Rooster wallpaper bordered the ceiling, above the worn wooden cabinets. In the foyer, there was one simple set of stairs that led to the bedrooms. The hardwood floors had dips and scratches, shaped by movement, and never redone to hide this. Every room, Ruby had been told, was painted a different colour. Rick's room a cadet blue, the living room a grey colour that reminded Leah of the Vancouver sky on a rainy day. It wasn't necessarily a sophisticated home, and Trevor would turn his nose up at the outdated hospital green bathroom tiling, but Leah loved every inch of it.

Leah relished telling Ruby how everything about the Dyson's household was welcoming: the couches softer because they were used for family movie nights; the upstairs carpeting more comforting than the full hardwood flooring Trevor had insisted on. Though Leah didn't outright say that the Dyson's were better people, she might as well have. Ruby didn't feel as much jealous as she was curious about the other household; she lingered on the details the way she did over the gourmet granola bars Curtis Simmons used to bring to school to share with her. Her own mother only bought discounted dipped bars on sale, shoved with kiddish ingredients like marshmallow and coloured chocolate chips, and she had marvelled at the idea of parents caring about nutrition over savings. She remembered how she used to touch the wrapper to try to catch a glimpse of his family, whom she'd never meet, huddled together eating the traditional Japanese dishes Curtis's stepmom made.

Leah, Ruby imagined, would complain immediately to Rick about her mother going into some fire to search for her ex-lover. And not metaphorically, she'd emphasize. Leah would not express regret over getting upset at her mother and slamming the door on her. Ruby imagined that, instead, she would despair over not dressing up before coming to Rick's, of leaving what little makeup she owned at her house.

Ruby stared out at the dark Squamish sky wondering if it was possible to convince Leah that although the two had grown apart, Ruby still knew exactly what her daughter was thinking. Had Parveen Malkhana known when it came to Ruby? There was a time when Rubina's stories kept Ruby up through the night reeling with excitement and yet, she had left her mother alone in the apartment where her husband had already deserted her. *I named you Ruby, after the brave Rubina.* How special Ruby had felt when she heard that. She didn't believe in the traditional definition of karma, but hadn't Ruby treated Parveen Malkhana the same way Leah was treating her now?

Chapter 35

2017

"It's literal," Leah said, brushing her hand on the wooden countertop inscribed with knife carvings. Rick's family used their countertops to cut cheese and bread, making it so the very blocks of wood in the house had multiple uses, giving a whole new meaning to the words "lived in." Leah shook her head, continuing, "As in, she is *literally* going into the fire to find this washed-up geezer rock star who was apparently in love with her."

"Rod Stewart old or Axl Rose old?"

"It was the nineties. Remember, my mom is only thirty-eight. So, neither. I guess more like Justin Timberlake old."

"That isn't that old."

Leah ignored this. She took a sip of the smoothie Rick had made, a sliver of raspberry catching between her teeth. "I feel like I'm mourning something, but mourning should be saved for when you lose something, you know? Like a dead mother. Mine's here, but she lives on a cloud. Hearing her talk, I feel like I'm the mom and she's the kid. She's delusional. I feel bad for even saying this, but I understand why my dad would leave her. She spends her Monday nights watching lame reality shows. She doesn't have a life. Of course she'd obsess over some guy she knew for a minute in high school."

"Don't you think you are being a little hard on her, Andrews?"

"Hard? She's going on some attention-seeking trip to have us all worry she's going to throw herself into flames."

"She'll never get through. Just today I heard they sent 300 extra RCMP officers to guard the evacuated zones. Pretty sure most of the roads where the forest fires are burning are blocked off. Where's she hoping to find this guy? Amid the brush fires?"

"See, you get how crazy she is being! I just don't get it. She was getting all nostalgic, talking about how she was so passionate about music when she was my age. That she should have done something with her knowledge, like, I don't know, write biographies." Leah twirled a piece of her hair in her fingers, inspecting the tinges of what looked like blue under the light. "She wanted closure or to tell him something. I don't even know what ..."

"Hey," Rick said. His voice went soft. His hair was the same colour as his skin, bronze. As if one crayon shade had been used to make him from head to toe. It made him appear as though he had a tan all year, but Leah had found out ages ago that he was half-Indian, just like Leah. They belonged to the same tribe — halflings Leah had dubbed them. And while they were different looking, there was still something similar about them — when they were out together, people assumed they were both Hispanic or Persian. He grabbed her ponytail and pulled it. "Remember when we first met, and you said you never met anyone like me?"

"Not because you are the coolest person on Earth," Leah joked. "It's because both our moms are Indian, and our dads are white. Except your mom's a fancy dentist who wears Louboutin to work. And we both play soccer. It's quite the coincidence."

"Well, Andrews, despite your lowly view of me, you are absolutely the coolest person I know. Okay, so you sat in front of me in that first-year psych class for what, two weeks before we talked? Do you know how you got my attention?"

She shook her head.

"You were the only girl I'd ever seen carry a huge sports duffel bag with cleats poking out to every class. The teacher was talking about attraction theories, and how we pick our partners on basic commonalities like finances, proximity, and values. You put your hand up to say the topic should be the 'fiction of love.' You said we all have these lists made up and that we mentally check things off before we 'permit' ourselves to engage with the other person. You said no matter how open each person thinks they are being, there is no way they open themselves up to every person on Earth for love, that the phrase 'I'm open to love' is utter bullshit, you are only open to people that fit your precise boxes. There are social boundaries no one crosses."

Leah blinked hard. She barely remembered this. "Oh yeah? I said that?"

"And when that uber Christian chick started arguing with you, you said: 'like you would talk to a guy with prison teardrops tattooed on his face!' When you said all that, I was blown away by your logic. It's like you took Santa Claus away from me. True love is a concept we've been sold since ..."

"The beginning of diamond engagement ring advertising campaigns?" she filled in, liking that Rick thought of her in such an admiring way.

"Sure." Rick moved away from her to wrap the cord around the blender and tuck it back onto the shelf. "What I'm saying is you are so perceptive, Andrews. Can't you see all your mom wants to go on is a quest for this magical thing called love? The 'fiction of love,' as you'd call it. She wants to experience it because she probably never did with your dad. And if she can't get that, then she is in it for the adventure. She deserves that after everything she's been through with your dad."

"Well, regardless, she's out of touch with reality, and while this rock star might be washed up, I'm guessing he still has his share of lame groupies. She's going to be humiliated all over again when he rejects her. Couldn't she just fucking take up parasailing or windsurfing? Maybe trade in her car for a stupid convertible? Or get a job instead of depending on my dad so much? Deal with her midlife crisis in a more traditional way?"

Rick touched her shoulder and leaned in so close to her ear she felt his breath warming it. "No real adventure in that, is there?"

"No." Leah felt a tingle spread over her body. She couldn't help wondering if Rick might have kissed her had she worn lip gloss. Her mother was going into a goddamn fiery pit of hell to prove she was fearless. And Leah could not get up the courage to wear false eyelashes.

"Why you all dazed and glassy-eyed, Andrews? You gonna be able to keep up with me on this trail run or what? Or has worrying about all this stuff made you go soft? Not worth tripping over, son."

"You better bring your A-game on this run, homie." She shot fake bullets in the air, playing along with the hip-hop lingo they used with one another. "I ain't got time for the stupid shin splints thing you pull mile five."

Chapter 36

2017

After their run, Leah put shampoo in her hair, rinsing out sweat in the Dyson's upstairs shower. Leah lathered in conditioner and closed her eyes, letting water run down her face in streams. She inhaled deeply. All the products in the Dyson's house were infused with jasmine, like they were hotel moguls. Turning off the tap, Leah examined the last of her fresh clothes hanging on the towel rack: cotton underwear, a sports bra, athletic shorts, and a tank. Her uniform. Because of her mother, she had become thoroughly derailed from her plan in bringing over something more attractive. Annoyed, she grabbed them and balled them into her overnight bag.

Rick always put her up in his sister's room. Olivia was in Maui with their parents. Rick was taking a summer course at the community college to transfer to the University of British Columbia on time, in the fall. Leah wasn't entirely sure if Olivia knew that she was sleeping in her bed; most of the time Leah felt like a substitute sister taking up space in the Dyson household, like a perpetual Goldilocks sleeping in a borrowed bed. She found herself switching fantasies between wishing she had been brought up in the Dyson family to hoping they would welcome her as Rick's love interest.

Priyanka Dyson didn't put up with shit like Ruby Andrews; she ran things. She had a calendar on the fridge with appointment times and weekly meal plans. She went to spin class in the mornings. All her own mother did for a hobby was read books. Once Leah caught Ruby listening to a Tool song, "The Pot," and she'd looked at Leah, her eyes misted over with nostalgia, and said, "This sounds like something I would have liked in high school." And Leah had said, "God, Mom, this song is like ten years old." Ruby, in her dated fleece top shrugged. Mrs. Dyson was current, she liked Rihanna, she shopped at Victoria's Secret. Leah had seen her there one time and she was forced to awkwardly wave hello. It was no secret why Mr. Dyson was still captivated by his wife, what with her taste in hot pink lace underwear. Her own mother wore cotton granny underwear with waistbands as thick as tensor bandages.

Leah didn't want to be like her mother. Her hair, still wet, dripped down and left the shape of a continental mass on the back of her borrowed towel. She went to Olivia's closet and pulled the knob on the folding door. Beads of perspiration popped up where the shower water still glistened on her forehead. Dresses hung haphazardly from white hangers. She poked the hangers like a stick at a campfire. A black dress slipped. *Whoops.* It was thin, made of some type of spandex material with skinny straps and had a sort of built-in bra in the front. It could look casual. It could look like Leah owned it. Kind of. She slipped it on. It was tight. Her small breasts popped up. Her muscular legs looked feminine, sculpted. She didn't want to wear her cotton underwear under a dress like this. Maybe no underwear was better than stealing Olivia's.

She sauntered back into the bathroom. First, she simply took out some of Olivia's creams, laying them out on the counter like she was a toddler arranging shapes from biggest to smallest. There was something for the face, so light and fluffy it smelled like cake batter. There were separate lotions for the eyes and lips, too, but she didn't have the patience to segregate her face into sections and instead chose something that read "facial evener" and hoped that was a wise decision. The next cream was for the body; it gave off the scent of lemon meringue pie, and she rubbed it on until her body shone.

She inspected Olivia's makeup kit. Looking like a drug smuggler's silver suitcase, it was filled with dozens of eye shadows and lipsticks, reminding Leah of a Crayola box she particularly loved in the fourth grade, with sixty-four colours and a built-in sharpener on the side. Leah peeked in. She wasn't big on makeup; she usually just stuck with mascara and gloss. Ruby had loved her daughter's natural beauty, but Leah referred to herself as plain. "I am as simple as my name," she was fond of saying, which had started off as cute and ended up feeling like a life sentence. Pulling out a few different lipsticks, Leah inspected the uncapped tubes of waxy colours: bright pink, deep red, and peachy nude, with names like Paris Vacation and F Me Now. Olivia's skin was a copper colour like Rick's, so the foundation probably wouldn't match. She undid some eyeliner, smudged black shadow on her eye lids, coated mascara on her lashes, and settled on a light pink lip colour called Down Under.

Sighing, she wondered if being so clueless about feminine things meant she was exactly her mother's daughter.

Chapter 37

2017

Leah felt the scratches in the wood under her foot. She paused, rubbing her arch against a step. Music was coming from the television downstairs. Earlier Rick had suggested a movie. She had a paper to write, but that could wait.

"Well, that isn't right, Rick!" a shrilly voice.

"Vanessa?" The name got stuck in Leah's throat.

"Wow, like you are really dolled up! You going out or something?" Vanessa was holding a flute of something that bubbled. "Are those even your clothes?"

For the first time, the usually dressed-up Vanessa was dressed down in exercise tights with mesh running down the sides. And a cropped sweatshirt. Her face looked au naturel — she was wearing honey nude lipstick and had on what looked like a touch of mascara, but Leah knew that in reality, false eyelashes were applied meticulously close to her lash line, helping Vanessa's blue eyes pop out. Vanessa had a talent with makeup brushes. She knew how to paint contour lines under her foundation so that her cheekbones appeared high, and her nose skinny and narrow. Most days she looked like a cross between a snow owl and Persian leopard.

"What do you mean?" Leah said, touching her own done-up face. Suddenly she felt like an amateur burlesque dancer.

"I've never seen you in a dress." Vanessa squinted. "Is it borrowed?

And you're wearing black eyeshadow. How gothic."

"Andrews," Rick pivoted, pointing at his glass of peach liquid, "V brought Prosecco."

"What are we celebrating?"

"Today," Vanessa said, as if ambiguous statements added intellect to her mundane commentary.

"Seriously, are you going somewhere, Andrews? You are really suited up," Rick cocked an eyebrow.

"Yeah," as Leah spoke, the lie felt real. "I'm meeting Belle and my dad for dinner. Sorry for springing this on you. They wanted to talk about things with me. Living accommodations in September. The new baby and how I feel about it. And let's face it, eventually your parents are going to come back from Maui." She forced a dry laugh.

"You know you are welcome to stay here as long as you want. Liv is going back to UBC in the fall. And I don't want to live on campus; it's too far for me to get to soccer practice. Her room will be empty and my parents like having you ..."

"That's so weird how you just accept Belle," Vanessa interjected. "Like if it were my dad having an affair, I'd just flip." Leah had never talked to Vanessa about her private life. Vanessa continued, enjoying seeing Leah lose her footing. "A stranger just moving in ... to your life. And everyone just going with it."

"It's rather complicated," Leah said. Vanessa's double-edged dig designed to make Leah feel like an imposer on Rick's family was not lost on her.

She watched as Vanessa went over and sat with her body pressed into the arm of the couch and patted the seat beside her, waving Rick over. Leah felt hungry after the run, and Vanessa was thereby more annoying than usual. Rick was a good cook. He had a knack for throwing things together without measuring or poring over recipe books, much like her own mother. Leah could smell his garlicky pasta sauce simmering. Rick eyed the space Vanessa was caressing with her hand. His hair was still wet from his shower, but golden pieces were drying fast amid the damp ones. Even from where she was standing, Leah could smell him, all laundry-ish and jasmine soap.

"But you are right, Vanessa," Leah said, her voice catching.

"I am?"

"Yeah. I mean I shouldn't just *accept* Belle. I need to think about my relationship with Belle before I decide on what I'm doing for September." Leah pulled her phone from her handbag on the counter and sent herself a fake text.

"What does that mean?" Vanessa tilted her head, the light shining down the middle of her nose.

"It means I'm lying low tonight, homies! Got another glass of bubbly?"

Rick dropped seamlessly into their gangster parody. "V brought two bottles, yo! I'd be happy to get you a glass, son."

"On point," Leah said, doing exaggerated gang signs at Rick. She took Vanessa's offered spot on the couch. Leah's breasts, albeit small, looked like they were going to pop right out of the dress. She was about to get up and change but she caught Vanessa stare at them. She sat up straighter and ran a finger along the built-in underwires in the dress.

Rick passed her a fresh glass and the fizz rose, stinging Leah's nostrils. As soon as he went to stir the sauce, Vanessa turned to her. "He called you 'son' Leah," she said, her voice dropping to a whisper. "You know you're friend-zoned, right? I wouldn't want you to get crushed. You're sleeping in his sister's room, for godsakes. You guys are, like, the same background and stuff. You look like brother and sister."

"I don't know what the fuck you're talking about. We don't have the same genetic makeup, Vanessa. Do you think all half-Indian people are related?

"You're not listening to me. I have a single friend; he'd be so into you. He likes athletic girls with muscular builds. You look like a drag queen in all that stuff. It isn't you. I'm trying to help you."

"You really need to start by teaching me how you apply that war paint on your face you call makeup." Leah hoped Vanessa couldn't tell she was shaken. "Do you look legit tribal when you are applying it? All white and brown lines on your cheeks and nose and forehead before you apply the five layers of foundation?" She had raised her voice so that Rick could hear her from the kitchen. "I saw a YouTube tutorial on it once. It's like an art form, putting on all that makeup. The before and after are like night and day. Have you seen the tutorials on the Internet, Rick? I'll show you, during our soccer shake time, okay?"

"Green Dream Soccer Machine shake time," Rick corrected Leah, sinking in next to her.

When his leg brushed up against hers, she didn't move. "V, are you turning on Netflix or what?"

Chapter 38

2017

After Vanessa left and many glasses of Prosecco drunk, Leah was not able to say who kissed who first. It was as if Rick was kissing not her, but over her, his mouth covering hers so sloppily they were always off-sync. Teeth against teeth. Tongue sliding over her upper lip. Gums colliding. Her skirt hitched up easily, and with her wearing no underwear, everything ended as fast as it started.

When the morning light shone through the living room blinds, it covered Rick's sleeping face in rectangular slits that made him appear like he was wearing a mask. Leah lifted her face from his t-shirt, which Rick had never bothered to remove. She stared at him until he woke up, taking care to remember the small details of him: his laundry scent, his copper hair. She thought he'd be embarrassed to face her, that the change in their relationship would either make him warmer or colder toward her, but Leah had never factored in that he'd have no reaction at all.

"Hey there," he said, a morning grin spreading over his face.

"Hey," she smiled, taking the brunt of the awkwardness for the both of them.

He rose to go to the kitchen, stretching his arms. "Sleeping on the couch killed me. Shake?"

"No thanks." She followed him and rested a hand on the counter. "I'm going to head home."

"Okay."

She shifted uncomfortably in the dress. "We should talk about last night, don't you think?"

"Do you need to?"

"I mean, don't you?" she said, trying to sound unrattled.

"I know how you feel about the 'fiction of love.' Makes things like what happened after too many drinks easy to handle. Don't worry, Andrews, I'm not going to hold you to anything."

"Hold me to anything?"

"I know you find the idea of love to be bogus, and that you think all that Valentine's Day bullshit is propaganda invented by our current capitalist system ... you said so yourself."

"I did?" Her voice was squeaky.

"In psych class. When you got my attention."

"Oh."

How much had she talked in that class? So much that her past-self went and betrayed her future-self. And now, even if she couldn't remember making all those declarations, it was too late to go back on them. Rick's admiration for her, after all, was built on the fact she had no expectations. She was stuck. She couldn't be held to anything even if she wanted to. There was a slight difference in Rick's body language now that she looked closer. Rick adjusted his crotch. He'd never been so intimate in her presence, and yet, there was not an ounce of romance in his behaviour.

"Look, I get you." Rick, apparently, was still talking. "I always liked our connection. You're like a guy but you don't look like one."

She tried to focus. She cut in before he could say more things that she could no longer unhear, "Is this going to happen again?"

He shrugged. "It could. But it doesn't change things? Right, Andrews?"

Right. She hadn't said it aloud. "Right."

"Do you want things to change between us?" His eyes widened.

"No." She reached forward and squeezed his shoulders. Watched him relax. "I'll see you soon, okay?"

After she walked away, all the power she had been holding on to drained from her shoulders. She grabbed her handbag from the laptop nook where her keys hung, all but racing up the stairs to grab her duffel bag. She left her shorts and tank in the laundry hamper, still damp with runner's sweat, which later, Priyanka Dyson would think were Olivia's. After Maui, the set would be washed, folded, and put in Olivia's drawer. Olivia would never notice the addition of athletic apparel, even wearing it to the gym. But Olivia would spend hours looking for her favourite black dress. She would finally rush down the worn hardwood steps, charged and angry, blaming her mother for donating it. A couple of days later, unable to solve the mystery, Priyanka Dyson would hand over a hundred-dollar bill and an apology to her daughter.

But Leah would never know this. The morning after she slept with someone she thought was her best friend, Leah drove in circles for a long time, her throat burning because tears wouldn't come. She felt annoyed with herself because she wasn't technically allowed to miss Rick romantically when he was never hers to begin with. Because she'd traded in a fake friendship for an even faker romance. Because it seemed like Rick would rather disappear to a foreign country and change his identity than to ever discuss his feelings with her again. Somewhere in the back of her mind she knew her mother would say that no real friend would behave like this. She drove home wearing Olivia's dress but her own running shoes on her feet, because she hadn't factored in footwear when she had hatched her make-over plan.

If she had bothered to do so, Leah would have seen right away that a size 6 heel would never have fit her size 8 foot.

Chapter 39

1997

"You did this to me? After Papa left us both?" Parveen Malkhana said in her sing-song Indian accent.

Parveen's feet were tired from pulling a double shift at Subway. Ruby's father was already living with Julia and Ruby would never be disloyal to her mother and stay with them. Not that Ruby was welcome. Though sometimes Ruby felt her mother wished she would go. Her husband no longer sent money; Ruby was a teenager, and he didn't feel they needed it. Parveen wanted her husband to see the challenges involved in raising a teen. Ruby was insolent. Ruby still thought she could control her life and did not yet know that her life would grow to control her. Ruby was fickle; she asked for avocados and ate them every day for two weeks and then didn't touch them and let the new ones go brown and deep purple, like a new bruise on flesh. Parveen Malkhana had zero interest in avocados, which had grown wild and were universally regarded as an inedible part of the tree where she came from. This is how young people were, in Parveen's opinion, disconnected from the reality of how hard it was to live on minimum wage, asking Parveen to waste an hour of her earnings on something expensive that you mashed on toast. The youth were only focused on achieving rich people's posh standards in food and fashion without wondering how it was one would come to pay for these things.

"Did what to you, exactly? Can't you see this is done to *me*, not you? I'm the one who's pregnant, not you!"

"Through your own selfish actions. How will we show our face in the community?"

"Well, you've been showing it since Papa left, and people have been pretending to you that they don't know he left us so far. I'm sure they will probably keep doing the same thing."

Parveen looked like she had been slapped. Slowly, she peeled her knee-high stockings one by one off her feet, like the transparent brown layer covering an onion, tossing them to the floor as if they were kitchen waste. "I know they know. I am not stupid. People have sympathy for a wandering husband. But they don't cut a pregnant teenage girl any slack. The husband is responsible for his actions. You are responsible for yours."

"Yeah, well, they think you didn't keep him here, so that's on you."

"What do you mean, 'that's on you'? I don't understand this saying."

"Of course, you don't," muttered Ruby. "It means, Ma, that you didn't do enough to keep him here."

"But I tried," Parveen met Ruby's eyes with her own. "It wasn't enough."

Ruby took in her mother's saggy breasts and wide hips. "Okay," she managed to say, thinking of Julia, her rhinestone chokers and the lingerie tops she wore like real shirts.

"You think I didn't do enough? I cooked fresh food for him every day. When we came to Canada, we put his education first. We never even bought a house! We've lived here for years in an apartment, and did I complain? Now your Papa has bought a townhouse. He has money and I have nothing. But he knows I won't get a lawyer and let the community know he has left me. I'm stuck, Ruby."

Ruby watched as her mother sobbed, head in her hands. It all seemed put on to Ruby, the muffled wailing, the shoulder shaking.

Not greatly moved by the dramatic act, Ruby forced herself to pat her mother's shoulder.

"Sorry, Ma. I'm here with you, aren't I?"

"No," said her mother in an even tone, lifting her head up, the tears immediately stopping. "You're not. You're pregnant and about to marry some white boy and live in his mother's basement. After I worked so hard to feed and clothe you."

"Well, you should be relieved, then. I'm not your problem, anymore, right? No more double shifts for you."

"That isn't what I meant. But you got what you wanted. Freedom from me. I hope forcing yourself into someone else's family will save you." Parveen pulled hard at her hair, inflicting self-pain.

"Trust me, Ma, this isn't what I wanted. I wish you would not fall apart like this."

"Falling apart is a luxury. I didn't have that option when Papa left. I had to take care of you. Now, I don't have to hold myself together anymore. You get your jailbreak; I get to fall apart in peace."

Chapter 40

2017

Ruby ran her hands over the braille pattern of the lace bedsheet, thinking of her mother hunched over. How different that memory felt looking back now. Back then she had only seen her own point of view. But now, twenty years later, she saw her mother's. Removing her bright red forties shoes, she reached for the beige rotary phone, surprised at its antiquity.

The phone rang twice before Trevor picked up his cell. "Hello?"

"Is she okay?"

"Ruby, what number are you calling me from?"

"My cell's dead. I'm calling from Squamish. Is Leah alright?"

"Why wouldn't she be?" Trevor was defensive.

"Well, when did you see her last?"

Trevor sighed. Heavy, hard. "She's been staying at that friend's house. Ryan. Err, Rick. If you're so worried about her, why'd you leave? Are you having one of those psychic premonitions?" His voice was coated with sarcasm.

"Last time I had a feeling like this, she broke her arm on the trampoline at a birthday party."

"That was just a coincidence. She was eight. Accidents happen. What about all the times you had panic attacks and she was just fine?"

"I'm telling you, mothers know." She heard him huff and then wondered if he was sleeping next to Belle. "Did I disturb you in your

217

lover's den?" she said, borrowing a dash of his sarcasm.

"I was sleeping. Actually, in our own den slash study."

"You're at the house?!"

"Look, I came here to talk to you, but you weren't here, so I grabbed the bills next to the computer. I just lay down for a sec and fell asleep. Why the fuck were all the lights lit up like this place is a bloody showroom? You might as well have hung a sign on the door to invite the burglars in. Or left them a money jar on the table."

"I thought lights on meant people were home."

"Not when you have no curtains or blinds in an open glass solarium."

"Well, whose great idea was that? Or did you expect that I'd always be home like a goddamn family dog watching the property while you had an affair?"

"Look, Ruby, we have to both be adults about this whole thing. Take it easy."

Ruby swallowed. Her mouth tasted like raspberry beer. "I don't know why I have to be a fucking adult about anything. Who decided that? You?" Trevor made a sound and she cut him off and dropped the hostility from her voice. "Look, this isn't about me right now. Just listen to me. Go upstairs and knock on Leah's door."

Trevor harrumphed but she could hear him jaunt up the black railed staircase. She assumed it was the staircase on the right side, closest to the den. It was the one Trevor preferred even though he had insisted on getting two identical staircases. His cell phone was rubbing against something, and the sound was grating on Ruby's ear. A few raps on the door and she heard Leah's muffled "what?"

"What the fuck?" Trevor said, panting into the phone. "How'd you know she'd be home?"

"Did she sound okay?"

"I dunno. How the hell am I to know? I'll take care of her, don't worry."

"You have another family to take care of. How are you going to take care of her?"

"I can be a father to more than one person, you know. She's nineteen, Rubes. Relax."

Relax. Don't overreact. Calm down. Ruby clenched a lacey pillow, burying her face in it. Everything in the room was covered in some form of doily — the cupboards, the windows, the bed. She was told her whole life that Indian people had a distinct smell of spices and curry, and even now, sniffing deeply, she agreed that she couldn't nail an exact white people smell. Maybe, making a snap judgment based on the room she was in now, it was white cheddar macaroni and cheese. Aged, dusty lace curtains. A pilgrim smell of oak furniture and maple syrup, sausages, and baked rolls that said you had a place of belonging in this country, that you could colonize a space and make it yours.

Ruby didn't belong anywhere now. What smell did her house used to have, the one with Trevor, her being technically Brown and him, white? When they used to stay at Harrison Hot Springs when Leah was little, Ruby used to look forward to returning home, hunting for those few seconds when they would open the door, and she would catch a scent of who they were as a family. She found out it was an aroma of blown out birthday candles and something vaguely coconutty. She inhaled sharply now, remembering how she had fondly thought of it as the Andrews' signature perfume, of how she had felt satisfied that she had smelled the house as a stranger would and had been relieved that the scent was welcoming and non-offensive. Not alien, but still a little exotic, which she took the credit for. It was their home. Now Trevor was creating a new smell in a new home with Belle, who would eventually bring her smell into the Andrews' house. It would be that of a yuppie white woman. Body Shop bath products. Lush coffee grounds face masks. The stupid garlic powder in a shaker that Belle sprinkled on food because raw garlic was too offensive. Perhaps, though, thought Ruby, Ruby would leave behind a curry spice smell in the house that Belle and Trevor would only notice if they returned home from a vacation. The ghost of Ruby, haunting the two with her Indian vibes. *Weird, does it smell like someone cooked Rajasthani dhal in here? Can you detect the scent of cardamom rice pudding? No, never mind, it's gone.*

"Ruby, hello? Are you still there? If you aren't going to tell me what the fuck it is that you are doing in Squamish, can you at least tell me when you'll be home?"

"How can I answer that when I don't even know where my home is anymore?" she snapped. She wrapped her finger around the tan phone cord. When was the last time she had coiled a plastic wire around her hands? Nobody had this type of phone anymore. "But tell Leah I'll be there for her. Soon enough. Tell her I love her. And that she doesn't have to worry about me falling apart because it's not a luxury that appeals to me. I'll be there for her always, even when she doesn't want me to be. I'll be there until the end. Will you do at least that for me?"

"Jesus Christ," said Trevor. "You expect me to remember all that? Just come back already."

Chapter 41

1610

Khushi's brothel and dance hall was the only home Rubina knew, but it was a place she had left behind both physically and mentally. At present, everywhere her eye could see was consumed by luxuries: gold coins in carts guarded by henchmen; copper pots filled with rich milk desserts; pots of rose-scented perfumes brewing to wash clothes in. Rubina had only performed for the royal males before. Even at the dance hall the clientele had been, for the most part, male. But today, she was in an open-air camp with a lively bazaar; animals were living amidst the people; camel-dung fires were blazing, and kebabs being roasted and shared. For now, the Mughals were living like true desert nomads, which they had once been for long enough to know how to carry it off, and as such, rules were loosened. The concubines were brought temporarily out of purdah and placed in a tented arena, ever protected by the eunuchs. On this night, Rubina would dance for everyone: the local land-ruling lords whom the king was testing to see if they were following empire rules, the royal staff (hopefully including Daniyal, who would leave his kitchen to the workers) and even the commoners, who would stand on rocks in hopes of catching a peek of the show beyond the fencing.

Feast food was coming in turns. *Pilau* arrived now, fragrant rice cooked with cardamom and cloves, topped with shredded meats and accompanied by potatoes from the Americas. The Mughals were able to feed their empire decadent meals, clothe members in fine materials, and house them in a secure environment precisely because the lords of these conquered lands were taxing and starving poor peasants to death. Along the way, Rubina had seen farmers who had lost their harvest due to the missed rains, each bone in their bodies traceable through their skin. Some of these men gathered the strength to chase the trails of dung left behind by the oxen and camels, fighting one another for the seeds and grain found in the animal waste. Others were so desolate she was not sure if they were corpses, for they did not react when the king rained coins upon them. Although she had naturally seen beggars in Agra, it had been nothing like seeing hundreds of hollow-eyed, knob-kneed skeleton people, most too weak to make their way down from the rocky incline leading from their barren village to properly see the Mughal camp pass by.

"Mind your step at the back entrance here. *Ta da ta da ta da.* There we go. *La la la la la la.*"

She wasn't sure which of the two short, lean eunuchs who were leading her towards the stage had spoken. Each with a tall peacock feather tucked into his turban was virtually indistinguishable from the other. Involved in a comedy act of their own, they swayed a little as they helped her onto the large platform. Giggling wildly at their own jokes, they left her at stage centre. Rubina could not help but miss Raj, who would have left her with sweet parting words. The lords, she could see, were already drinking with the nobles and royalty — a sweet wine made from pomegranates and rice. From the stage, she could also catch a glimpse of the wives and concubines under their own canopied tent, and she saw they too were partaking in cheerful drinking.

When the dance master sang out his first note, Rubina turned her back to the audience. She would dance a third of the song with her back to the crowd to tease and entice them into wanting to see more of her. Like a deer being stalked by a god in a Hindu story, Rubina

222

darted across the stage, her shadow, cast by the large fire ball that was burning in the centre of the camp, creating a spectacular tale of its own. Her curves were further amplified in her shadow twin, a sight that was sure to arouse the lords and nobles. She turned forward holding her sheer *dupatta* between two of her fingers, her neck and hips playfully bobbing, and then she let go of the *dupatta*, at the same time unclipping her hair, causing waves of hair to tumble down her chest.

People gasped in awe. The lords, already drunk, fell into one another's arms. Unused to the fine manners of the kingdom, they hollered and whistled like drunks in a street festival. "*Hai ram!*" shouted the Hindu lords, "Save our dear souls!"

No one reprimanded them. The crowd, ever excitable, became rowdier. Rubina spun out to the front of the stage, tilting her arms at an angle as a submission to the heavens, and then she spun in a pattern that, if one looked from the sky, was of a rose in bloom, and then a butterfly. Gracefully, she ended the dance with her hands in prayer pose, bowing her head. Humbly, she kneeled and touched her forehead to the ground, demonstrating that the stage was a sacred place of worship. She then scooped her hand up to her forehead and whispered "*Adaab,*" in a gesture of goodbye. In the Mughal Empire, goodbyes were just as important as greetings, and as such they were performed with much enthusiasm. To reflect this, Daniyal had timed the end of his fantastic feast to her dance, and she could see mango *kheer* being handed out in goblets to the lords at the front. Sloppily, they were slurping the dessert and tossing the fine brass dishes into the sand, and Rubina imagined the royal chef wincing to know his grand finale was being devoured with such ill manners.

The lords and nobles were still erupting in cheer. "*Adaab!*" they gestured back to her, "*Adaab Mohtarma! Alvidaa!*"

The peacock feathered eunuchs were once more by her side. Her ears were filled with the sound of loud speech in many dialects. A brass horn blared, and somewhere to her left, wild bull-frogs whose home had been suddenly occupied by the travellers croaked their complaints.

The two eunuchs trailed behind her. She now saw that the eunuch's trousers were designed in an additional compliment to the splendid peacock, as they were dyed in multicolours of dark green, gold, indigo, and purple. Prince Khurram, King Jahangir's son, was clearly captivated by peacocks, for the bird was known to have once guarded the gates of the Islamic paradise. Prince Khurram was rumoured to want to snatch the title of the king over his brothers, and there was talk of him scheming to build an ultimate peacock throne, one based on King Solomon's. Encrusted with a multitude of precious gems and weighing twenty-five hundred pounds in gold, his vision was projected to take years to complete. Rubina wished again for Raj to be by her side so she could tell him about these comical eunuchs that were walking announcements of Prince Khurram's love for peacocks. Remembering her dear friend, she pictured him back in Agra, sighing with joy talking about the treasury of jewels that he kept saying Man Singh had hidden from the king, and how Raj's one wish was to ogle each gem separately, uninterrupted. Her jolly Raj had claimed there were nearly three hundred pounds of emeralds alone, stowed away in the Amber palace vault. Rubina turned to examine the eunuchs so that she could describe them in detail to Raj once the two were nestled back on her charpoy in the harem, ever ready to share palace gossips. She raised her eyebrows when she saw the peacocked eunuchs were indeed indistinguishable from the other. Each was a mirror image of the other. Twins!

"We have a message for you!" The one on the right said.

"A good message!" the other chirped.

"*Chup!* What is the point of saying that? I already said we have a message!" the first said shrilly.

"But a message can be bad or good, *nah* Rubina *jaan*?"

Rubina was tickled by the duo. "What are your sweet names?"

"Sukh," said the one on the right.

"Dukh," the other one announced.

"Are you sincerely telling me your names are contentment and unhappiness?" she scolded playfully, hands on her hips. "Contentment, I can understand, but who names their child unhappiness?"

"I am named for pain and longing," said Dukh, sighing heavily and tapping his heart with his left hand. "Also, my mother died right after she birthed me. She named Sukh first as he is the oldest. Dukh is what my father said when I was born, and so the name stuck."

"That is sad," said Rubina, examining the short pair. Golden skinned with eyes framed in kohl, they grinned at her.

"We are not sad, never, not at all," Dukh said.

"Sometimes we are," Sukh said. "When the wine runs out, we feel sad."

"This is true," Dukh confirmed, stumbling a little. "But the *sharaab* never runs out." He held up one finger. "Not for us!"

"What is my message?" Rubina said, worried now she was losing the two in their own mischief.

"Daniyal Master is waiting for you as you asked. He received your message via your slave girl."

"Pray tell, where?"

"Left of the Akash Diya there is an empty tent. Where the goods are stored. We told him to go there as it is safer than meeting at the main stage."

Already she had lost track of which twin was which, as they were swaying and dancing with one another, sloppily imitating some of her classic dance moves. "How can I get there?"

"Why, we will take you, of course."

"But how? Everyone will see me!"

"Yes, this is not a problem for us. We will pretend to be return-ing you to your tent by hiding you in the grand palanquin. We can take you because there are big barrels of more wine in the tent. More spirits! Let us bring the palanquin, Dukh."

From the back of the stage, the twins lifted a spectacular hut fashioned from what looked to be white marble but was light to the touch. It had one pole in the front which one twin would carry on his shoulder, and another in the back for the other. In the middle sat a gorgeous miniature house, fully carved in poetic Arabic scriptures, inside of which Rubina would sit.

"You are quite sure about this plan?"

Sukh and Dukh looked at one another with the same lopsided smile. "Not really, but have you any other choice?"

Rubina sat inside and looked out of the grill. It was very similar to the one within the harem walls where the concubines could peek out if the king was giving a ruling. Rubina wished she had looked out the day Shanti and Dinesh were given their ruling. Had they really been in love with one another? How could the king have been so ruthless to sentence them to death? How had Dinesh made love to Shanti if he was a eunuch as everyone indeed said he was? Once her mind started racing, it wouldn't stop worrying about other things. Could their deaths mean that Raj and Khushi had been right and living within the confines of the harem was more dangerous than living in Khushi's dance hall in Agra city? If so, how in the world could she convince Daniyal to make her his wife? If he didn't, could she and Raj find an alternate way to rise and be protected within the kingdom? Sukh and Dukh, unaware of the thoughts racing through Rubina's head, had lifted the palanquin. Her breath caught in her throat. She was given full view of the hazy camp as they departed through the back entrance of the stage and to the front. All the ques-tions in her mind vanished when she saw what was outstretched in front of her.

Chapter 42

1610

A sea of people. Smoke rising from the fires. The Akash Diya, shining as bright as a second moon, casting a bizarre orange light on faces. Sardar, patting the sleeping camels gently.

Rubina scanned the crowd to see if she recognized anyone else. The royals were hard to miss. There was the prince, dancing and cheering on the lords. He had on a strikingly fine turban, pale blue and gold to match his *jama* coat. Fitted at the chest and flared from the waist down, a jewelled sword hung from the *patka* belt. Multiple strings of pearls hung from his neck.

"I will have my Arjumand!" he was shouting. "She will be mine!"

"Is she not already yours, your majesty? Are you not betrothed?"

"Yes. However, I am growing weary of my father's procrastination in setting a date for the *nikkah*!"

"He shall set it, dear son," an elderly noble cloaked in a pink and purple *angarkha* spoke. "He is looking for the most auspicious time. Be patient."

"But on this night who will be yours, your majesty? Do you not have a whole selection of women to choose from?"

"Indeed!" Through the grate Rubina saw the prince unsheathe his sword and thrust it high in the air. "I have a young, soft fruit. A virgin child. I have named her Heera."

Rubina shivered. Her fingers pulled back from the grill.

The elder laughed. "The oldest fruits are the most ripe, dear sir. Take mango, for instance. It is the sweetest when it is no longer green. But not too old or it will be spoiled. Do you want to waste this fine eve on a girl who knows not how to please a man?"

Prince Khurram considered this. "I have been saving Heera." That childish voice Rubina remembered from the night she had first encountered the prince cut sharply through the earthy mist. "I simply must have her. Who refuses me my diamond?"

The jovial atmosphere had changed. The men began to move away from the prince. A eunuch came to offer more sweet spirits.

"What of the dancer?" another lord said.

"She is not for the taking," the prince said firmly. "She is one of my father's illegitimate daughters."

"Shame."

"Indeed," said the voice of a young, arrogantly dressed noble. "But does such a thing matter, dear prince? Would your grandmother, Mariam-uz-Zamani, care? Or your mother, Jagat Gosain? She is not her daughter."

Try as she might, Rubina could not hear the prince's reply for the palanquin was no longer near the main stage near the intoxicated nobles. Her palanquin bearers, the twins, for all their tipsiness, had moved smoothly, cutting a crisp pathway through the thick crowd. They reached the Akash Diya without incident. The tent the twins spoke of turned out to be unguarded. The watchman, with an empty canteen of what looked like liquor sitting next to him, had dozed off against his camel.

The supply tent was hitched up using twelve-foot posts, and the twins were able to navigate the palanquin into the tent swiftly. Setting it down, Sukh and Dukh bent in to offer Rubina their hands. She exited like a queen, her dancing jewellery tinkling in the musty air. She could get used to such treatment. Bags of supplies were packed on top of one another forming a maze of private corridors.

There was only one kerosene lamp lit, hitched smartly from a rope near the top of the tent and it shone an eerily red light upon the small group.

"What now?" Rubina asked of her adventurers.

"We want our wine. Dukh, go!" Sukh removed a strapped purse from his shoulder. Rubina saw it was a drinking pouch made of animal skin.

"But why must I always be the one to look for the *sharaab*?"

"Because you can locate it faster than I."

"This is true."

"You are indeed smarter," Sukh confirmed. "But I am more beautiful. Is this not correct, Rubina *jaan*?"

"It is I who has the shapely eyes!" Dukh shouted.

"But have you seen my rose red lips? Have you seen the way they kiss the pouch that carries the liquor?" Sukh was speaking poetically, as if he was reciting Hindustani lyrical prose. "My lips kiss alcohol like it is one of the prince's harlots."

"They are wine-stained is all. They are nothing special. You tell us Rubina *jaan*. Which of us is the fairest?"

"Rubina?" The three turned to see where the voice, magnetic and masculine, was coming from.

"Daniyal!" Rubina ran to the middle of the tent, navigating between piles of bagged grains, leaving the twins to fight amongst themselves. Her anklet bells rang out again in the tent, but the hum of the camp crowd was so loud she did not fear anyone would catch them meeting unchaperoned in the tent.

He did not look happy when she embraced him. She but only touched his thick neck briefly before he disengaged.

"Why have you called for me here? Sending such a small girl to come for me." He was rubbing the area where her fingers had been as if to wipe the very memory of her away. "It seems you know of no dangers. I have heard of you running through the king's secret halls without any fear for authority. Clearly you have no respect for your own life, dancing girl, but what of others? I had a younger sister who perished of an illness. My father neglected her and if he had paid attention to my mother's concerns, she might have lived to see adulthood. One should value life."

"Are you concerned for me?"

"I am appalled by you. Once a street girl, always a street girl."

Rubina was thrown off course. She tried again. "Did you have a chance to see my dance? We have this in common, Daniyal. Your love for cooking; your technique, the passion you bring forth in the kitchen," she paused to look him in the eye. "It is the very same I use in my movements."

"I only saw a section of your performance."

"Which part?"

"The very beginning."

"Well, let me show you the rest," Rubina turned and assumed position, her back to Daniyal.

She felt a sharp pain on her upper arm. "I do not have time for this *naatak*," he said. "Save your play-acting for your little friends, the eunuchs."

He was already at the entrance of the tent, leaving with his back to her.

"Wait!" she shouted. "Wait!" She was pulling at his back, clawing at him. Emotion was rising to her throat, choking her up.

"I cannot understand what you want from me."

"I will explain," she said. Sensing the smallest opening, she pulled him near the flour sacks on the floor.

"Go on. Speak then," he said.

She sighed with relief at his compliance. Except now that she saw her charms no longer seemed to affect him, she wondered what she could say.

Chapter 43

2017

Back on the road, Ruby pondered what she would say to Curtis Simmons first. Would she come straight out and tell him he was Leah's father? Or would she talk about her own life first? How would Curtis receive her — with cool enthusiasm or warm trepidation? Ruby did the math and quickly decided the latter was better.

Soon, her thoughts shifted from Curtis to the landscape she was currently navigating. Her motorcycle buddy, Harvey, had been right about Ruby's insanity in heading toward the BC fires. Post-apocalyptic mushroom clouds hovered above Ruby's car, billowing up like beige parachutes. Over the last half hour, the clouds had slowly transformed to jellyfish shapes soaring through the air: orangey-pink and translucent, and strangely captivating. The world was on fire, and at its dying moment, it was most beautiful. The clouds reminded Ruby of the things she had read about when Hiroshima was bombed: how at first sight the nuclear explosion was nothing short of breathtakingly gorgeous. She saw minuscule pieces of ash floating in the air past her dashboard. The daylight sky was filled with a thousand stars; five-hundred-year forests inhaled in one campfire breath, stinging her throat and catching in her chest. Strangely, the more unstable her surrounding environment became, the more Ruby felt in control of her life.

On the main highway there had been no closures leading into the fires, not yet, but Ruby saw silver ash lining the outer edges of the road, places this fire, or an older one, had kissed. In the interior, when she was brave enough to take her eyes off the road and peer into the trees, there were bald patches within the forest where the fires had flattened areas. Trevor was right, BC wildfires were a regular thing in summers now, a trend that was surprising at first and then just stayed on like a permanent houseguest so you couldn't remember life without them, like regular Twitter feed updates or photos of people's meals on Instagram.

Ruby turned on the radio. The news was reporting that the air quality index in the city of Vancouver, the city Ruby was currently driving away from, had plummeted. Young children, the elderly, and those with illnesses were told to stay indoors, shut their windows, and crank their air conditioners if they had them. To survive the environment, people were ruining it further. The hotter the outside air, the cooler indoor malls and public places became, as people used more energy to regulate temperatures so they could remember what shivering felt like. Ruby always wondered how desert places like Dubai managed to sustain large indoor water parks and ski resorts — she would have asked Trevor to explain this mystery to her if he wasn't perpetually annoyed with the stupidity of her questions.

People calling into the radio station said it looked as if someone had wrapped a green piece of cellophane over the sun in Vancouver. When Ruby left Vancouver the day before, it had been an ordinary summer. The Vancouver sky now, people said, was lime and yellow, like a child's popsicle treat. Others said the air reminded them of roasted nuts. Like Africa, one caller declared earnestly, it smelled like Kampala. The radio broadcaster claimed that parks were mostly empty, except for children and parents who hailed from places accustomed to more polluted skies: Beijing, Mumbai, Shangai. Ruby thought of domed parks on the top floors of Chinese towers, built to protect children from pollutants in Beijing, where children could play safely under the sun, guarded from debris — an image akin to something out of a sci-fi novel. Getting closer to the epicentre of the fires, it was difficult not to think about how little she knew when she'd talked to Trevor about wildfires on their anniversary, and she was embarrassed by her former naïve nonchalance.

She took the exit marking the turnoff for the Garibaldi Townsite. Brandi and Facebook had both confirmed this was where Curtis likely was. She hugged the car around the bend of the road leading off the highway. Rolling down to the first intersection, she spotted a gas station. It looked like it doubled as a 1950s diner. Ruby could make out the restaurant's mint walls, a black and white checkered floor, an old juke box. She needed to eat. She parked her car in the lot and rifled through her white vintage purse. Her hand brushed over the smooth navy-blue Canadian passport before she checked for her wallet and phone. She had packed very light, but if she wanted, she could get on a plane to anywhere and never come back. Paris. London. New York. Tokyo. Anywhere listed on one of those fashion t-shirts that people like Belle wore with yoga pants to do errands.

Biting her lip, she thought of the possibilities. Ruby had suddenly gained Belle's freedom. It was like one of those kids movies with twin sisters who had been separated at birth, then went on to switch spots: one went to secretly live with the rich parents, the other, the working-class parents. Ruby wondered how Belle was coping with the duties of playing house and having a middle-aged man and teenage daughter to tend to. Neither was an easy person to take care of.

She opened the door to the diner, sounding off chimes. Inside were vinyl booths and a wraparound bar with chrome stools. It was the type of place where cops would meet on a TV murder mystery, ordering milkshakes and cherry pies. It was almost a shame smoking wasn't allowed indoors anymore, or that poodle skirts were no longer in fashion. She could almost see hazy cigarette smoke and hear skirts swooshing. She picked the last booth to slide into, her back against the wall. Beatles artifacts lined the shelves.

"What can I get for you?" A skinny Indian boy in an old Pink Floyd shirt came toward her. His disengaged modern disposition startled Ruby, who had already imagined a blonde waitress with red lipstick who would say, "Hi honey, d'ya wanna hear our specials?"

She scanned the plastic placemat menu in front of her. "I'll, uh, I'll have the all-day breakfast, with orange juice."

"'Kay."

"Are you from this area?"

The boy narrowed his eyes as all Indian people did when they were asked where they "really" came from. "I was born here."

"I meant, well, I'm of Indian origin. I thought you were, too. Not even sure why I said that. A bit idiotic of me to think people like us can't work at a place like this."

He softened. "My parents are from Agra. They actually own this place."

"Agra! I've always wanted to go there, see the Agra Fort. The Taj Mahal. Maybe go to Jaipur and see the Amber Fort." *God, Mom, you're rambling on and on*, she heard Leah say in her head. She pushed Leah's voice aside. "I know a lot of stories from the time the Mughal Empire ruled. Been thinking of them lately."

"Cool."

"Have you ever been?"

"To India? Nope, I haven't." He looked like he might say more, but instead he just shrugged. "How do you want your eggs?"

She was impressed at her boldness. Already she had managed to snag some sort of dialogue out of a few people since she had left home. She smiled at this. "Over easy?"

"Hash browns or toast?"

She wanted both but was afraid to look greedy; the curse of being what was considered a bigger woman. "Toast. Sourdough. Is the orange juice freshly squeezed?"

"It's from a bottle. My parents buy Tropicana juice in bulk. Maybe in India people make orange juice freshly squeezed."

"You think?"

"I imagine."

"Hey, I know you're a young, really cool guy. And I should know, my daughter's around your age," Ruby realized the more she spoke the more the boy was looking at her like she had horns on her head. She shrugged to herself, deciding to keep going. "I was wondering if you maybe heard of this person I'm looking for?"

"Really cool guy?"

"Well, you're wearing the same Pink Floyd shirt I used to have, so I think I am complimenting my own taste rather than yours. I'm trying to find Curtis Simmons."

The boy tapped his pen on his short order notebook. "Course I know him. I play the drums and have followed him for years. Local star and a controversial guy."

"What do you mean?"

"Well, he pushes some buttons, singing about police brutality and all that ..." the boy trailed off.

"Oh, yes, I guess you have to be a certain kind of person to enjoy him."

"Remember when he was in that band The Dirty Cavemen? They were industrial punk back then. I like him more as a solo artist now. His stuff still hits the same points, but he's mellowed out a bit."

Ruby remembered Curtis on the hood of his car describing how he and his bandmates were going to wear skirts on stage with spiky dog collars. "Yeah, I know, his old stuff sounded a bit like a confused Trent Reznor. But they struck a chord with the young kids back then."

"Now he reminds me of a male Karen O from the Yeah Yeah Yeahs. I still like his music, but he probably shouldn't have started sleeping with local girls."

"Oh," said Ruby, feeling jarred. "So, you meant a little more than musically controversial."

"Apparently one of the girls in town had his baby but he denies it's his and wants nothing to do with it. Said the girl is just after him for his money. The girl got some DNA test and is in the middle of suing for child support. It's quite a fiasco. Simmons's lawyers have managed to keep it out of the media so far. I don't know how though, since the whole town knows about it, but things are about to explode."

Ruby hadn't pictured Curtis would turn out this way. Would he deny Leah was his after what this server had told her? Would he think she was chasing him for money? Would he make it so Leah, Trevor, and she were dragged through emotional turmoil? "Is Curtis out here a lot?"

"Yep."

Ruby felt self-conscious. When she had woken up in the Squamish B&B, she had pulled out her 1950s black halter dress covered with cherries, with a tulle underlay and a gingham belt that pulled in her waist. She'd applied her vintage makeup — cherry red lipstick and pencilled-in dark eyebrows — arranging her hair in a retro style by pinning the sides of her curls away from her face with diamante clips. Now she felt self-conscious and gimmicky. She was sure she didn't look like any of Curtis's jilted ex-lovers, in their skinny jeans and crop tops. The last time she had almost worn this dress was five years ago, and Trevor had stared at her calves so hard she worried she had cankles, and she changed into pants. But still, when she imagined what she wanted Curtis to see her in, it was this tailored dress, the kind that she believed suited her curves.

The boy standing in front of her was tapping his foot now. He had black hair that stood up and waved over in a manner only achieved by time, persistence, and the high heat setting on a blow dryer. He was looking at her like Leah usually did: *silly, stupid Mom, hurry up and say what you have to say.* The way he was spinning his pencil around like a baton, Ruby understood he truly was a drummer. She swallowed. "I knew him once, you know."

"I was surprised you knew his music so well. Yo, my mom thinks listening to U2 makes her cool. I mean you cannot claim listening to U2 is something unique when they force you to download their music on iTunes."

"Maybe you have to have heard old U2 high in a field full of crows in the nineties for it to count," she said, smiling, remembering listening to "Mysterious Ways" with Curtis. "You're not surprised I know him? Clearly, I'm not the kind of girl he hangs out with. Especially given the kind of clothes I'm wearing today."

The boy was confused. "This is a fifties diner. We do a retro event here called *The Breakfast Club* so everyone dresses vintage on Sundays."

"Oh," said Ruby. "Oh."

The boy smirked. For a second Ruby saw a young Curtis in him. She imagined bumping into the boy twenty years ago at Dan Heffner's house party, dropping acid along with the other boys his age that night.

"You've seen Curtis, but you've never introduced yourself? You also seem to know a lot about music."

He shrugged. "And say what? 'Whaddup, Mr. Simmons, sorry to interrupt you while you're pumping your gas, but can you sign my t-shirt?' The thing he loves best about coming through this town is that no one bugs him or acts like he is different. Folk 'round here are pretty fucking chill. Not that I care, but apparently Shania Twain lived in a cabin for weeks here, undisturbed."

"Hey, do you know his song, 'Ruby Red Skies'? It's an old one."

"Obviously."

"I'm Ruby."

He sank into the booth facing her. Ruby tucked her waves behind her ears, feeling self-conscious under his gaze.

"I legit just read an article saying he wrote that song about a sunset that looked like it was splitting the Earth in half."

"We sat on the hood of his car during that sunset and smoked weed, you know, back in the day when weed buds were raised in sketchy basements in East Van bobbing to Biggie and Tupac beats. Not like now, where the weed is artisanal, raised on Bach, and sold like Starbucks specials from some trendy hotspot."

The server was looking at her with fresh eyes, like he was really seeing her. She cleared her throat. "And we watched the sky turn into red ribbons. Just like he sang it, 'bleeding wounded clouds...'"

"'Ruby Red Skies,'" the boy finished. He pounded his fist on the table. "Man, that is fucking cool. I'm Dev, by the way."

"Cool. Dev. Nice to meet you. Do you have any idea where Curtis could be right now?"

"He takes yoga down the street. You can find the studio easily because it has a giant rainbow painted on the wall around the corner. He's probably there now. I think he's stupid enough to still try to pick up local girls there."

"I thought he might be in Williams Lake by now ..."

"I guess I should put your order in. *The Breakfast Club* crowd's coming in soon. I'm not sure about one thing, though," he said, giving her a half shrug.

"What's that?"

"Why you thought you don't look like the girl he'd go for. You're exactly how I'd imagine Ruby to look. Doesn't he have a tattoo of your name on his arm? I saw it in *Rolling Stone*. He has full sleeves done in dark blue ink but one red tattoo? I imagined Ruby would look like a pin-up girl, in my head, you know, on account of the glamour girl inked on his other arm? Yo, now I just sound like I'm obsessed," he shook his head at himself. "Hey, can I take a picture with you? Gotta have proof for my bandmates."

A pin-up, she thought, nodding and smiling for his camera before he walked away. *Glamour girl.* She pulled out her phone and decided to take her first-ever selfie to put up as a profile pic on Facebook. The one she had up now was of her and Belle laughing in the sunshine, blurry, the sangria set in front of them in clear focus. She focused the camera on herself. On the phone screen she saw cherries littering her dress. An arched, flirtatious eyebrow. A coy smile playing on red lips. For the first time since she was eighteen, Ruby felt indisputably beautiful.

Chapter 44

2017

"Are you here for *The Breakfast Club*?"

"I ..." Ruby put down the orange juice Dev had brought her.

"I'll need to squeeze into your booth. I came alone today, and if you're a single we should share, so we can give more people a chance to get a seat."

Ruby looked up to see a girl in black-rimmed Buddy Holly glasses and a polka-dotted red dress sitting across from her. Ruby looked around the restaurant. She'd been so focused on coming up with what she was going to say to Curtis Simmons that she hadn't noticed people had sauntered into the diner. A guy in a newspaper-boy hat and suspenders was standing across from her, talking animatedly to a girl in a tweed pencil dress. Ruby felt like she had slipped accidentally into a movie and forgotten her lines.

"Sure," she forced out. "By all means."

Big band music punctuated the air. Saxophones, trumpets, trombones, a snappy beat. More people were drifting in. A man in a twenties straw hat. A girl in a pinstriped dress and heeled oxfords. A guy with wing-tipped shoes. Ruby suddenly recognized the song playing. It was exactly the sort of music she listened to when Trevor was at work. The indisputable but perpetually overplayed swing classic: Glenn Miller's "In the Mood."

240

People were laughing, partnering up and starting to dance the Lindy. She saw a couple do a swing out, and the girl had the loveliest swivels. Two people started doing a tandem Charleston. She smiled, watching from her booth. "Is You Is or Is You Ain't My Baby" came on next. Ruby jolted — at once, she recognized Anita O'Day's maple syrupy and sharp voice. She took a sip of her factory orange juice, shaking her head at where she was now, and tried to imagine her opening line to Curtis. *It's been a long time ... Do you remember me?*

A guy in a boxy forties blazer came up to her. "Care to dance?"

"Oh," she said, thrown. "I don't know how."

"It's easy," he said over the jazzy tunes, pulling her to her feet. "We can do East Coast Swing. It'll be easier than dancing Lindy. Six steps versus eight. You'll get it once you get used to the music ..."

"I actually know the music well."

"What are you waiting for then? Yeah, there you go. Try not to bounce too much and just get a sense of the rhythm."

Ruby recollected all the times she had played this song at home. She had done the dishes to this song, cleaned the house to it. And when Trevor came home, as soon as she heard his car pull in, she had rushed to turn it off. Trevor would have said it didn't suit Ruby listening to jazz. That she was pretending to be someone she wasn't. Trevor had decided that Ruby had forfeited her sense of being able to tell if music was good because she had once liked Hole. After converting Kronsky and Heffner to alternative rock, Ruby was never allowed to change genres again.

She pushed Trevor out of her mind. Because she was familiar with this music, having listened to it in secret a thousand times over, she got the hang of the moves quite quickly and soon she felt like she and her partner were flying along. The song ended, and a different guy in a cap took her hand next just as Benny Goodman's "Sing, Sing, Sing" came on. Yet another swing signature song that would have almost everybody immediately tapping their feet, and Ruby felt like she had wings.

"I'll show you a few more moves. See, let's sort of step and click our heels forward, that's right, and move forward. Now let's move like a washing machine." For once, Ruby being a beginner at something was not annoying or a sign of stupidity. She was being supported.

"Like this? Whoa! That girl just went over that guy's back!"

"Yep. Okay, now look, when I kick my leg out you kick under! Yeah, you got it."

Ruby saw her eggs land on the table just as the guy showed her how to lean into him for a closing dip. With a nod of thanks to her partner, she rushed back to her seat to watch the advanced dancers, grinning as Dev gave her a thumbs-up from the breakfast bar. Ruby dabbed at the sweat at her brow with a paper napkin. What a rush! It was as though she had just gone through a time machine. It occurred to her that this reformulated version of the past suited her better than the present. She could not keep up with a world where women like Belle drank their vanilla chai protein shakes and wore five-inch platform stilettos. Smoothing down her cherry-covered dress, Ruby felt pleased with herself. Belle was so busy trying to emulate new things, she didn't appreciate the old. Belle could not have danced as Ruby had. They were different, and right now, Ruby was glad she wasn't in Belle's world, wearing ridiculously patterned leggings listening to remixed rap songs with autotune.

When Nina Simone's "Trouble in Mind" came on, the couples on the dance floor slowed down. Ruby sighed, taking in the energy of the down-tempo, bluesy song. She thought of all the days she'd spent listening to Nina, feeling the lyrics and the piano sink into her as she longed for the feeling of being in love. Belonging to someone. Someone belonging to her. Sharing an interest with someone. Had Trevor ever been a match for her? Was it even fair for her to expect he would be when she had thrown him into a life that shouldn't have been his to begin with?

The Breakfast Club, thought Ruby, wondering if she should drive all the way out here another time. John would like this place, Ruby suddenly thought, not that she would ever see him again after Belle had dumped him. Sunday, she remembered, was Belle's day to take a couple of back-to-back classes at the gym. Apply a face mask. Rest. Repeat. Sunday was Belle-day, but then what day of the week wasn't?

Her former best friend had always sought out perfection. In high school, Belle's carefully picked out ensembles were so orchestrated, they were unfashionable. She wore dresses that were too adult; too short; too try-hard. One time she wore a cheerleading outfit to school, another time, a French maid dress. In their twenties, however, Belle grew both into her looks and personality. Flirting shamelessly, overfriendliness, and much-too-short skirts had succeeded in getting Belle a variety of useful things: free samples of her expensive vitamins and creams, an entire paint job for her condo, and once, access to rental cars for a year. Belle had loved seeing Ruby's expression when she pulled up in a new vehicle every week.

But at her core, Ruby knew, Belle Du Ponte had always felt like an imposter. No matter how perfect she looked on the outside, inside Belle felt her genes weren't up to snuff, that if she were to have a child, evidence of her alcoholic, gambling father would come out or her bipolar mother would suddenly appear. Belle had repeatedly told Ruby that the best way to eliminate her fear was not to have children at all, live life according to her latest whim.

As time went on, Belle watched their high school classmates have multiple children with awe: how did they have an entire brood of children without at least one with a mishap, or one with Down syndrome, autism, or a club foot? Not one conjoined twin among them, no missing limbs, no intellectual disabilities? That family on television, the Duggars, with the nineteen kids especially stumped Belle.

She had often asked Ruby how had they produced such genetically perfect children? And Ruby, feeling Belle was being insensitive and ableist, had told her no one was perfect, that the Duggars had their own problems. She'd told Belle that kids with special needs weren't rejects, they had their own gifts, but her words had evaporated like melting snow.

Ruby knew that Belle's refusal to have children was because Belle didn't have the patience to raise anything less than perfect. Yet now, somehow, Belle had gotten over her fears and got pregnant. For Trevor, Belle was an obvious upgrade from Ruby; after all, Belle was exactly what Eleanora, Trevor's mother, would have wanted for him the first time around, had she had any say in the matter. It was Ruby who had stupidly revealed this insecurity to Belle. Ruby was the one who had expressed remorse she was not white and blonde, who had wished aloud to Belle for uncontested beauty by social standards, claiming that Eleanora would have shown her full love and acceptance had she been petite, if not at least fair skinned. Trevor, Ruby had always thought, had accidentally married what should have been a passing trend, and she was sure his mother agreed.

Belle had confirmation then, from Ruby herself, that Belle was better suited to be Trevor's wife. It was only a matter of time now before her former friend found herself at home in Trevor's designer kitchen (not wearing Ruby's god-awful robe, of course). Now that Belle was pregnant, she would soon use motherhood as an excuse to wear those stupid velour tracksuits from the 2000s decorated with gem designs. Ruby was sure that Trevor would put a giant rock on her finger, not a skinny ring with a questionable speck of a diamond. Although the Andrews' house was already trendy, Belle would have to put her stamp on it, which Ruby knew would be installing heavy, burgundy curtains and chandeliers in every room. Belle loved heavy, gothic, interior design. But Belle would only be uprooting Trevor's installations of modern, sleek lighting fixtures and airy, sheer drapes,

Ruby chuckled to herself. Ruby had nothing to do with anything pertaining to the house design, but Belle would still feel satisfied that Ruby's presence had been ejected from the house.

What Belle would not succeed in would be getting Ruby's food on the table without Ruby's help. Wasn't she the person who Belle panic-dialled when a new date was coming over for dinner? Belle was capable of making one decent gourmet French soup — her only real takeaway from her crash cooking course (that and generalizing that French men weren't as wild in bed as they came off in films), and so Ruby now pictured Belle getting ready to pour this perfectly concocted soup into small ceramic bowls in the Andrews house, all smiles with her latest teeth whitening job. Her new heavy, blood-red curtains framing the glass wall of the solarium. That real diamond glinting on her hand, matching the crystal teardrops hanging off the chandelier. Three-wick pinot noir candles from Bed Bath & Beyond casting Belle's skin in a pearly sheen, complementing the diaphanous underbelly of the fancy dishes Ruby only used on Christmas. Scooped like glazed oyster shells, the bowls would be waiting to be filled with salad to accompany her soup. Trevor might never see carbs again.

Ruby blinked hard, trying to erase the images from her head. The swing dancers and classic songs blurred into the background. Ruby could only see Belle in that glass house. Belle was always the better choice to live out the life Ruby once had. Even Ruby could see that.

Chapter 45

2017

Despite what Ruby had pictured, Belle was not yet situated in Ruby and Trevor's home. She was still in her own tiny condo in New Westminster.

"I'm a fucking asshole," Belle said. She was tucked into her purple bed, which was overdressed with velour sheets and countless aubergine pillows, all inspired by her love for Prince.

"No, you're not," Trevor said automatically, hoping this would quash the matter. It might be just clipping it at the surface. The root often went far deeper, as he knew from twenty years of marriage. It seemed the ability to reassure a woman constantly was turning out to be something he unfortunately needed in every relationship. Last night, it had been calming Ruby about Leah's well-being. He was growing tired of juggling all the women in his life. Discreetly sighing, he pulled Belle closer to him, tracing her thigh with his finger, closing his eyes to the strange photographs of Victorian women hanging at odd angles on the wall facing the bed.

Belle's room, along with the rest of her condo, had been charming when they first started their affair in the middle of October last year. Then, Trevor had thought Belle was simply a person who really liked Halloween, after all, the hallways in Belle's apartment looked like they were straight out of a New Orleans mansion from an old Anne Rice book. And while he was right — Belle was downright passionate about the holiday — he was wrong about the duration of her love; in Belle's condo, spookiness was an all-year affair. Sure, the sparkly pumpkins made from craft twining got packed away, but the dusty candelabras and antique trunks stayed on. He couldn't turn a corner without seeing a stack of thick volumes on zodiac signs, crumbling gothic candlesticks, or glassy beaded curtains that hung from doorways. Belle had taken her love for books like *Practical Magic* and managed somehow to turn it into a lifestyle.

"No, I'm the very worst," she moaned, and Trevor knew not only was Belle not in the mood for sex, he was also stuck in some conversation that would inevitably lead to the coming baby. "I can't stop worrying about the baby being born with some kind of defect."

Belle, waiting to slip into the life she had coveted for so long, was now plagued by her old worries about genetics and mishaps. Perhaps the doom predicted in a certain Poe poem was haunting Belle to the point she couldn't enjoy the life she had stolen for herself.

"This again?" Trevor pushed her leg off him and sat upright, about to leave. But in this condo, he had no den he could escape to, none of Ruby's leftover food in the fridge to dig a spoon into.

"I feel like we're going to be punished for what we did to Ruby." Belle started chewing her nails.

"Who is doing the punishing? The karmic universe? A god who is ignoring starvation around the world but is, for some reason fixated, at this very moment in time, on making sure Belle Du Ponte is punished sufficiently for her selfish behaviour?"

"I thought you subscribed to Buddhism. Aren't you all about karma? Ruby said it was you who bought that Buddha for the garden."

"I believe in meditation, but I don't think there is some dude writing down every bad thing you've done and then doling out punishments."

"You're starting to sound like Ruby." Belle twitched her mouth like her cat, Salem. "No good can come out of fucking over your best friend."

"So, your payback is having a child with issues?" Trevor pushed back the covers and threw down a pillow. Oddly, it was Indian print. Eggplant with squares of gold and sequin patchwork. It was nothing like the nondescript bedding his South Asian wife preferred. He had hated Ruby's pink curtained bedroom, but he valued her taste in bedding and the fact she had respected his minimalist decorating style. Would Ruby leave him her bed and duvet cover if she agreed to leave them the house? Was it fucking horrible that he was calculating this right now?

He looked over at Belle. Her honey hair had fallen over her forehead, and she looked vulnerable without having drawn on her eyebrows. Like a hairless cat or unwigged mannequin.

"Look Duck," he sighed, tracing one brow, fair and down feathered, "Even if something is wrong with the baby, we'll still love it. You just can't plan every detail out in life. All babies deserve to be loved. It's not that hard to love one. Trust me, I've done it before."

"But Leah is perfect," Belle said, as she pushed his hand away. "Our baby might not be."

"I thought you wanted all this."

She had. She was the one who had suggested the pull-out method and then had exhibited faux surprise that Trevor had gotten lost in the moment. Sure, she had gone back and forth with the whole Trevor thing, trying to end things with him on more than one dramatic occasion. But she had wanted a chance at the baby, the house, the man, and now that Leah was all grown-up, having Trevor to herself was possible. There was only pesky Ruby to consider, but Ruby had done nothing but complain passive aggressively about Trevor for years. She was doing her friend a favour in setting her free. Ruby and Trevor weren't in love; they were two characters playing out roles that had become prison sentences. If Belle hadn't come along, there would have been a Delia or a Susan or a Michelle. Maybe there already had been — Belle never thought it important to ask. Trevor seemed to be very easy to please; a few incidents of spontaneous sex and he had already told her he was in love with her. Trevor had been a very unsatisfied man when Belle had gotten her hands on him, that much was certain.

It was hard to feel real guilt — Ruby had become so goddamn boring, complaining about her fat ass and then eating bon-bons all day. Nothing exciting had happened to Ruby in years; not since Dan Heffner's stupid house party in grade 12. Seducing Trevor had been so easy; all Belle had to do was *look* his way one night and he had come undone. It was the easiest conquest she had ever engaged in, but unravelling Trevor from his domestic life, particularly getting him to part with his property, had been far harder. Trevor had not wanted to leave his dwelling. He had spent years designing every little detail about the place, from setting up a telescope in the solarium to arranging a meditation space in the backyard. A baby, thus, had been the only way to show Trevor that Belle was more important than Ruby with her goddamn casseroles made with Indian butter masala sauce.

"Did you know in Iceland nearly zero babies are born with Down syndrome?" Belle said instead, inspecting her ragged nails.

"Nearly zero, huh."

"They abort a hundred percent of babies that have the extra Down syndrome chromosome. There is a social consensus on the subject. By agreeing to this universal standard, no one has to feel bad about committing the act."

Now Belle had gotten Trevor's attention. He was looking at her so intently she cringed.

"You're not thinking of aborting this baby if something turns up on the tests, are you, Duck?"

"What? No!"

"You're sounding like the champion for eugenics. You do know Nazi Germany was founded on similar principles? Do you know something I don't about the tests? Have the results come?"

"No," Belle said. "That's really unfair, comparing my wanting a healthy child to Hitler's propaganda. It's perfectly legal to have an abortion if one wants to even if the child is healthy. You can't make me feel guilty for contemplating my rights."

She got up, aware that Trevor would see her perfect ass as she stood up to open the crushed purple velvet curtains a smidgen to let light into the bedroom. Half the reason she had picked Trevor as her mate was because he looked so much like her; the baby was sure to be angelic. Two blondes making a blonde child. Besides, Trevor had proved he not only shot swimmers, but pretty good ones — take Leah with her fair skin and Ruby's hair. Leah had even nicer hair than her mother, with a purplish-blue sheen threaded into the black.

"Are you telling me the truth?"

Belle turned around and touched the small belly forming above her pelvic bone. The Victorian painting hanging next to the framed window was a stark contrast to her nakedness. "The truth is ... I really want a White Spot burger right now. Can you arrange this?"

"You drive me crazy, Belle," Trevor said.

From the way he said it, she knew he thought it was better to be bugged by Belle ten lifetimes over than to have domestic stability with Ruby.

Chapter 46

2017

"I've Got You Under my Skin" by Dinah Washington was pouring the through the diner speakers. Ruby looked around, taking in the swing dancers spread along the checkered floor. The song started out mellow and then a jazzy part kicked in. She rifled through her bag to check her texts.

Nothing from Leah. One from Trevor. As if she had summoned him by thinking of him.

I need to talk to you. When are you coming back?

Fuck him, she wasn't going to discuss the house.

Don't know, she typed quickly, smudging the phone with grease. She wiped it quickly. *I have no immediate responsibilities. I'm taking time off.*

It's important, Rubes. Srsly.

Can't talk about giving you the house right now. Mostly checking texts in case Leah was reaching out.

Where are you?? Trevor's message read.

A diner. Ruby texted. She clenched her teeth. *I'm,* she hesitated and then punched in, *swing dancing.*

Swing what?

Never mind. She kept typing. *Is this about Leah?*

Yes and no.

Ruby picked up her fork and then set it down. *What the fuck,*

251

Trevor?? Is something wrong?

I went to grab a White Spot burger only to realize they only make brunch now. I decided to open up the test results I picked up recently while I waited for them to switch the menu over. You're dancing?

Tests? Ruby replied, wondering why, now that Trevor was her estranged husband, he was bent on explaining every minute detail in his daily agenda to her. Dev was offering her more juice. She shook her head at him. She put down her phone for a second on the table and then picked it up again, suddenly angry. *Look, I can't keep comforting you about Belle's anxieties about the baby. Belle's your problem now.*

A long pause. She dipped the bread in yolk. Let her shoulders relax. Rolled her neck to the jazz. Then peeked at her phone.

The tests were for me. Belle's already talking about a second kid. She's worried about my sperm quality. Says we are getting old. She keeps on talking about all the things that can be wrong with this baby. I'm starting to worry she's going off the deep end.

Injustices aside, Ruby found it amusing that Belle was getting to Trevor. Belle had always been loopy. Trevor just never had to deal with her directly. *We* are *getting old, Trevor,* she typed instead. *If she's so worried, why have a second fucking kid? She can't even handle being pregnant with one.*

Ruby, the doctor tested me. Turns out I DO have low sperm mobility. Worse than that. Do you remember that time I injured myself on a rope in gym? My balls felt like they were on fire? You must remember me talking about it. It happened about a year before we hung out.

No, she answered, annoyed that Trevor thought she would memorize his every tragedy when he didn't keep track of what book she was currently reading let alone who her favourite authors were. What did he really know about her?

No one told me back then that the injury would make me goddamn sterile! They stitched me back up and I got sent home. Just another dumb kid with a sports injury. I dropped gym class for a spare block after that and turned into a fulltime stoner. Now it turns out I have something called azoospermia. There's a huge chance it is too late to reverse the damage. Belle's baby can't be mine! John's more fertile than me with a fucking condom on.

Ruby wiped her hands with a napkin. This was certainly not something she could have expected, and she had to stop herself from impulsively typing, "serves you right." Her fingers were tingling. She recalibrated. *What do you mean?*

Trevor had texted again. *You weren't lying about Leah. BELLE'S BABY ISN'T MINE EITHER.*

Please stop FUCKING shouting. Ruby typed. *Does Belle know?*

No one knows I know that I'm not anyone's real dad, past or future. Like I said, I need to fucking talk. How important is this bloody trip of yours, Rubes? What the hell are you looking for, anyway??

Chapter 47

1610

"Where is he?"

"In the scullery of the Amber Fort, Rubina *jaan*."

"Is anyone with him?"

"Not that I know of. The Maharaja of Amber Court's royal kitchen staff want to cook for our camp, but Daniyal has insisted on boiling the skins from almonds for dessert himself. They are none too pleased to have him hover about and have given him a smaller, separate kitchen to work in."

Rubina nodded briskly at Heera. "How does he seem to you?"

"He seems healthy since we have arrived here to stay at the castle."

"I mean his manners?"

"Withdrawn. Quiet."

Rubina sucked air in. "I only wanted to make him happy." To this, Heera did not reply, so Rubina went on. "I thought it best Daniyal find out about Sabina's love for opium and her madness through me. How could he not have known about either? Surely if he is so serious about Sabina, he should know the truth! He was so eager to get away from me in the stock tent. I had to tell him something that would keep his interest, or he would have fled!"

"I feel worried because it is I who told you about Sabina's madness."

"Yes, but before I left the Agra Fort, I too saw Sabina in her opium haze. You met Daniyal when you delivered my message to him." She shook Heera's shoulders. "What, pray tell, did you think of him?"

At this, Heera blushed. "He was so very kind to me. Said I was a good child. Told me about losing his young sister and that I reminded him of her in some ways."

"You agree he is a good man?" Heera nodded. Rubina threw her hands up. "You see, I had to tell him the truth."

Heera chewed her lip. "Did your confessions dissuade him in his love for Sabina?"

"From your report of him, it seems my news has shaken him."

"Perhaps this is enough."

"Yes, but Daniyal still does not hold me in warm regard."

"Rubina *jaan*, you have become a dancing legend in the kingdom. The king knows your very name and has spoken it on his tongue! The king does not even know Sabina. Why are you wasting your time trying to persuade Daniyal to take notice of you?"

White pigeons flew in through the *zenana*, swooping under the marble bench Rubina and Heera were seated at. Heera extended her hand, so they might peck grains from her. Rubina shuffled her five-coloured gown, and they scattered once more. Heera frowned.

Rubina had no single answer for Heera. What had started as a plan to move from the harem quarters had turned into something more. Daniyal was a prize she wanted to snatch from Sabina. Daniyal was the man who had poisoned her mother. Daniyal was the talented chef that her friend Raj had thought she was capable of bewitching. Daniyal made her throat ache with longing and her stomach tickle with pleasure and pain. She dreamt of living alongside the river with him. She could not put her feelings into words, so instead she stared at the camels that were being hitched together in one long line near the east gate. They were headed down the hill to bring up fresh water and fruits.

"What is your plan now?" Heera spoke, dusting grain from her hands. The dry morsels fell onto the blue gown she had been wearing since they left Agra. Heera could not wash it properly as it was her only gown, and the colour had deepened with dirt and oil. A sweet air that smelled of honey blossoms travelled through the women's quarters. Rubina tilted her head back and swept her hair up, waiting for the breeze to dry the sweat from her neck.

"I must uncover more information on Sabina."

"What information?"

"That, Heera dear, remains to be seen." Rubina scanned the vast hill the fort was built on, skipping over the flowered shrubbery like a stone jumping on water. Her eyes settled once more on the Suraj Pol, where the sun rose from the eastern gate, painting the marble and red sandstone palace in shades of gold and rose. She tore her gaze away from the guards on elephants, hovering near the camels at the gate, to land on Heera. "And you, Heera dearest, must continue to monitor Daniyal *jaan* for me. I, in turn, will have to be truthful to Daniyal about my true feelings and declare my love for him."

"Your love?" Heera's large eyes widened incredulously.

"This confession," said Rubina, ignoring the girl's reaction, "will follow my grand performance at the Sheesh Mahal. May the most deserving woman win the heart of the court's royal chef."

Chapter 48

1610

Night fell on the Amber Fort. Tucked into bed chamber units in the *zenana* with Heera and a flock of younger girls, Rubina was feeling restless. She still had not gotten used to being trapped within the harem confines and thought often of her walks along the Yamuna back when she lived in Khushi's dance hall. How could that have been her life mere weeks ago? The Amber Fort in Jaipur was yet another new place to her. She had just started becoming accustomed to her room in the Agra Fort, where, at the very least, she had Raj's company and the ability to courageously explore the corridors. She tossed and turned once more before turning to Heera.

"Heera," she whispered, shaking the girl's shoulder.

The girl turned her back on Rubina, her dark blue dress rustling. Days had passed, and Heera still did not have access to gowns like Rubina; instead, she had hung the blue travelling dress near the steam of the hot baths and waited in her petticoat. Yet Heera still smelled pleasant, of pink roses. A juvenile scent lingered in her hair; a candied fragrance Rubina remembered well from the toddlers at the dance hall.

"Heera!" she hissed again, but the girl was fast asleep.

Rubina peered down the walled-in section of the ladies' quarter. A bird's eye view would show that the *zenana* was made up of several sectioned rooms, much like one of the king's large mouse mazes. These were filled with ladies who were housed together, but no doors separated the walls, only arched doorways. Thus, like a rodent, a lady could travel from bedroom to bedroom, round and round, searching for various companions to play cards or take garden walks with. Naturally, the women selected their closest friends to board with, and the youngest tended to gravitate towards others their own age. The maharaja of Amber's women had gladly accepted King Jahangir's women into their houses, excited to make trades of perfumed sticks and jarred kohl for inscribed bracelets from Agra. The wives and prized concubines of the maharaja had their own apartments. Maharaja Man Singh had these women situated at the far end of the ladies' quarters, in an area fenced off by landscaped rose bushes, including Bibi Mubarak, Mughal princess and niece of King Akbar, her father the foster brother of the great Akbar. Bibi Mubarak was undoubtedly one of Man Singh's most carefree and entitled wives.

Rubina rose slowly from her cot, wondering if Raj had been right about treasures being locked away here in the Amber Fort. If the maharaja had indeed been hiding loot from the king, where would he hide it? Hunting around would be a curious venture, but not one without consequence. Imagine the look upon Raj's face when she presented him a golden ball or bangle! Rubina smiled. She was the head dancer. She could claim she wanted to find a space to rehearse for tomorrow's performance if she got caught outside harem walls.

She exited the bed chambers. Outside, the two eunuchs, one with a mint-coloured turban and the other pink, guarded the arched entryway, but they had settled in for a game of chess. A lambskin chess board was laid out between them, with squares finely painted in turmeric and vermilion. Focused on the task of dumping ivory figures from the oiled cloth bag, they were less concerned with docile females escaping from behind them than they were a male intruder barging in from the front. Stories of daring villagers scaling the hill and jumping the wall to catch a glimpse of the gorgeous, possibly uncloaked concubines nearly always had a gruesome outcome. The peeping man was usually stabbed to death before the king could even sentence him to worse. On seeing them, Rubina froze. Then she floated past the guards, imagining herself as Khushi's vengeful ghost, pressing her body up against the outside wall of the ladies' quarters.

Outside, the pools were still. The harem garden was decorated in a fashion similar to the one at Agra Fort, but the Amber Fort, being built at the top of a high hill, was naturally more secluded from the city than was the fort at Agra. The shrubbery leading up to the grand palace was made up of flat bushes and desert-like sand, yellow and powdery. Once one was near the palace, one could see roses in full bloom thanks to the complex irrigation system and the hardworking gardeners who carefully planted roots — transported from as far as the Kingdom of England — in and around the palace. Both the maharaja and King Jahangir cared for aesthetics, but it was Maharaja Man Singh who was constantly building and adding to his structures. The maharaja liked the idea of creating multiple fanciful courtyards. The first main courtyard, which Rubina had now crossed into, was cultivated to attract a great number of butterflies and small birds, not that Rubina could see any by the moon's light. She could only smell lilacs and lavender as she rushed by the bluebells and bushes to re-enter the castle from the far west entrance, to explore further.

She had not really expected to make it this far. Past the rose bushes and main baths lay Maharaja Man Singh's wives' apartments. Amongst the grandest was Bibi Mubarak's. She was sure to have the best jewels in all the kingdom. Rubina entered her apartments through the outer baths, luxuriously outfitted with palm trees that acted as umbrellas shielding the bathing cauldron from debris. Nonetheless, renegade pink petals skimmed the top of the biggest bath.

The outdoor baths led to a marble-floored indoor bathhouse. Rubina saw the dressing room where she presumed Bibi Mubarak oiled and beautified herself. There was an intricately woven screen made of bamboo siding where a mirror and stool sat. Rubina crept to the dresser. It seemed she had no need to go any further to find treasures. A gold comb, small vial of pure rose extract, and turquoise scarf, lined with gems. Rubina hurriedly tucked them into her blouse. Raj would be pleased.

"Who goes there?"

Rubina did not dare move. The comb slipped and clanked onto the floor.

A fair-skinned woman dressed in wide golden pants and a matching blouse was speaking to her from the verandah. She was large, her curves defined, her waist pinched with a vermilion shaded belt. Her hair was as silver as the moon. Bibi Mubarak. She was holding a golden cup and paused to take a sip. "How brave you only just were, spying upon my quarters. Yet now, it seems you have no voice. Habib Hussein," she drawled in an odd deep voice that was no stranger to smoking strange substances, "capture this creature at once."

Chapter 49

2017

Ruby was caught up in emotion over Trevor's texts. She had left The Breakfast Club and wandered on foot until late afternoon, irritated, until the yoga class at the studio Dev had told her about was scheduled to start. When her cell rang, her body hardened with anger.

"What's all this nonsense, Trevor?" she said, cupping her hand over her mouth into her cell phone. Ruby stood on the left side of the yoga studio. Her back was pressed up against its brick wall, painted in rainbows. Trevor had riled her up so much, she could not concentrate on her plan to intercept Curtis as he entered the studio.

"I should be asking you. You lied to me for nineteen years about Leah. Don't you feel bad about that? Or do you just feel bad you got caught?"

"I didn't get 'caught,' Trevor. I was the one who told you the truth, remember? And oddly enough, no, I don't feel bad about telling you. Do you feel bad about lying to me about Belle?"

He sighed into the phone, so close that the phone strangled the sound. "It's weird, but I don't. I've known her as long as I've known you, and I guess it didn't feel like cheating. In the beginning, I didn't know if it was a passing thing, and I thought maybe I didn't have the conviction to disturb our lives in any long-term way. It's cliché, but I guess I knew I was playing with fire, and yet my feelings kept growing. I was tired of what we had become, just coasting along. I wanted passion. And when passion overtook me, I knew that I finally had the strength to end a dead marriage."

"Well, congratulations."

"You lied to me about the creation of an entire being. Hardly a time for you to feel fucked over."

"Look," she said in a louder voice, eager to make a distinction between her lie and his, "I *wanted* to marry you and have a life with you. I thought you wanted to be with me, too. I lied for us! Without my secret, looks like you wouldn't even have gotten to be a dad! Given that gym accident you never bothered to mention!"

"Wow. I did mention it, you just weren't paying attention. I was wondering how long it would take you to bring that up as a justification. I thought maybe you'd have some class and wait a bit, or never mention it at all. I didn't even know I had low sperm until today. But here you are, all justifying your bullshit," Trevor cleared his throat. "You basically *trapped* me ..."

"Trapped you?! I married you during your Eminem phase! You wore bandanas and quoted Tupac Shakur as life mantras to your friends. I don't think I had to *trap* you."

"You didn't have to lie to me." It was hard to hear him when a car rushed by, and she pressed her ear deeper into the phone. "I would have married you all the same, Ruby. That's the thing. I was crazy about you back then."

Back then. Ruby slid down the wall onto the pavement. There was chalk art on the sidewalk, and she stared at the squiggly pastel lines, dragging her fingers through a crooked yellow star. "You were crazy about me being some brown-skinned girl that completed your whole rap persona. Not the real me. I thought if I told you the truth you wouldn't have loved Leah the same ..."

"That's not true."

"Oh, please! To be honest, I didn't really know Leah wasn't yours until she was born. That's when I noticed the timing didn't add up.

She was born early with fully matured lungs. It was scary to tell you the truth with your mom there. We were already married."

"Exactly. I would have stood by you ..."

"I didn't set out to lie to you," she said hotly. "I was in a bad spot."

"Leah has the same hair as Curtis Simmons." His voice had gone soft. "But that pregnancy test that you took years ago was negative. Do you remember that night? You came in drunk to the Green Savers?"

"Of course I remember that night, Trevor." They had never, in all the years they had been married, talked about the drunk pregnancy test. "Just because things ended between us doesn't mean I lost all my memories. It was the nineties. Tests probably weren't as sensitive then, and I took it pretty early. And I have black hair, too, you know. Everyone thinks Leah has raven hair because I'm Indian." She stood up, dusted the chalk from her dress, and turned back to the yoga studio entrance.

"We both know Curtis had black hair that was almost blue. I never realized that until today. That is how stupid I am."

"It's still that crazy colour," she blurted out. "I'm actually looking at him as we speak. But maybe he dyes it now, who knows?" As quickly as he had appeared, Curtis had thrown open the door and disappeared into the studio.

"So that's where you are? You're with that fucking douchebag?"

"'Douchebag?'" she glanced through the building's large window. The walls inside were Japanese tea green with intervals of bamboo siding. It was such a peaceful place that it rivalled the forest. Behind the reception, people were crouching down, rolling mats onto the smooth wooden floors. She tried to imagine a time where her life was as simple as it was for the people in the studio. "It's not like he skipped out on me knowing I was pregnant," she said, trying not to think of what Dev and Brandi had said to her. "I'm not technically with Curtis. I can see him is all."

"Do you think he'll be pissed at you for keeping his daughter from him all these years? Or maybe he'll thank you for letting him have his youth and career while I did all the heavy lifting of raising his child? Never mind. Forget that fucker. Have you thought about what this will to do to Leah?"

"Obviously I considered these things," she bit back. She was relieved he hadn't mentioned the prospect of Curtis not believing her at all. "Regardless, Leah needs to know the truth, Trevor."

"Ah, the Purveyor of Truth."

"It takes one to know one," she said drily. A guy with a red beard nodded to Ruby as he opened the studio door, yoga mat strapped on his back like a bayonet. She nodded back, pretending she was having a casual conversation. Hipsters now took note of her, she thought, wishing Trevor could see she wasn't invisible anymore.

"Now that I know Belle's baby can't possibly be mine given my low sperm count, we could technically go back to our old lives, Rubes."

"Are you fucking serious, Trevor?"

"Why couldn't we? You could just resume your life with me again."

"And Belle?"

"Belle knows now the baby is John's. I told her. You, me, and Leah could be back at the house together, like before."

"What do we do, tell Leah it was a big bad dream that you had an affair? She's not seven, Trevor. You can't trick her and take back cheating. I love how selective you are about all this. Curtis can't know about Leah. But John can know about Belle's baby?"

"Leah's all mine, Rubes. You know that." his voice was gruff. "No one can take that away. Definitely not that washed-up rocker."

Ruby could hear Trevor's shaky breath coming through the phone. "Are you crying?"

"Belle had a test done," Trevor declared. "The baby has tested positive for Down syndrome. She's hysterical. She might not keep it."

"What?!"

"She is so upset about me telling her John was the dad that she locked me out of her condo," he choked out. "And out of anger she admitted she had the Down syndrome test done. She didn't even take the burger I went out to get her," he said, his uneasy laughter falling into the phone like rocks in a lake.

"She was always so worried she would have issues having a neuro-typical kid …"

"This has been quite the day," Trevor said, talking over Ruby, "And now I have a ticket out of this relationship. But the weird thing is, as crazy as she is, I don't even know that I want out. I miss our life, but I feel like I already miss Belle, too."

"Not your friend, Trevor. Estranged wife, remember?"

"We had tons of problems before Belle, didn't we?" Ruby didn't answer. "I wasn't nice to you. I took you for granted. I resented you because you gained weight, and you ask so many questions, and you don't get half of what I say. Take the wildfires." He was breathing deeply like air might run out. "I try and explain stuff about classical music and the environment, and you never get what I'm talking about."

"I take a while to get things," Ruby admitted, sticking her finger into the ashy air. The back of her throat tingled from inhaling smoke. Her chest felt heavy. "But you don't listen to me when I make good points. You miss out on the best part of me. You don't know anything about me, what I like or what I think or even how I actually fucking talk."

"You were the girl who knew all about bands and you were so cool when we met," he said, his voice wavering. "And having a baby changed you. I hated you for that. I didn't appreciate any of the grown-up you. Your cooking. Your cleaning. The fact you gave up your whole life to be a mom and wife."

"Yes, I was the under-appreciated maid."

"I missed that rocker chick I once looked up to," Trevor said gravely.

"But you also didn't let me be anything else. That was the person you decided I had to be for the rest of my life."

"I'm just saying I didn't fucking treat you well."

"No, you didn't," Ruby pressed the cellphone against her ear until it hurt. "You teamed up on me with my daughter and left me out, claiming I was too stupid to understand things." She paused and took a breath, deciding what she would say next. "If you are asking for me back, I'm saying no. Sneaking in your undying love for Belle and your lack of appreciating me is not much of a sales pitch. Not to mention you outright calling me fat."

"I didn't call you fat. What I meant was, I was a prick for judging you." He sighed heavily. "No second chance at us?"

"No," she said, testing out the solidity of the word against the phone. "I like getting to know me without you. I hate the house. It's always been your house. I hate feeling like a dumb clod when you and Leah talk. I hate the Buddha in the garden. I hate classical music. It grates on my last nerve. Vivaldi is more goddamn torturous to me than Metallica; I'm always in a bloody diamond commercial when I hear it. Honestly, I have felt like a house cat for years. I don't want to be a calico in your glass house anymore." Ruby started pacing in small circles.

"You feel like a house cat?"

"I want to learn how to swing dance. And wear vintage dresses without you saying with your eyes that my legs are too fat. I want to travel, too. To see all the places my mom talked about in her stories. You and Belle can have the house. *I don't fucking care.* I have enough money left from my mom's life insurance that I can live comfortably for a while anyway. I don't need you to take care of me or take out my garbage or check my oil. I can figure it out on my own. And for the record, I was lonelier in that house with you than I am on this road trip, meeting strangers. Have your dream house with its two staircases and the goddamn Carrara marble."

"Calacatta marble."

"Whatever, Trevor."

"The kid's John's, Rubes." He was sniffling. "Belle said she never wanted to see me again. As if I hurt her on purpose."

"For godsakes, Belle's just being dramatic. She'll come around."

"And what about you?"

She swallowed and stuck out her lower lip. "I don't want to be second best."

"This is a disaster," he said, not contesting any of Ruby's points.

"I think our loss of love for one another is more mutual than I thought. No offence, but I just realized I haven't loved you for years."

"Wow, Rubes. Harsh."

"I see Curtis again!" Ruby pressed herself up against the glass. "He's wearing a beat-up denim frayed coat over his workout gear. He has grey in his stubble! You can't see the grey in photos. How the hell did we all get so old?"

"Rubes, not your friend. Estranged husband, remember?

"I have to grab Curtis before the class starts!"

Chapter 50

2017

She needed to get off the phone. She was fiddling to open her purse, making room to jam the rectangular item in.

"Hang on there, Rubes," she heard, even though the phone was nearly in the bag now. Hadn't he heard her say she had to go?

"There is a bit more to tell you. Leah had it in her head to come find you. She knows where you are, right? Squamish?"

"I'm not in Squamish!" she squealed into the phone. "I told her I was coming to Williams Lake to find Curtis. I made it as far as Garibaldi and already found him. It's pretty smoky here already. Thank goodness I didn't drive all the way."

There was a pause. "How'd she react when you told her?"

"React?" Ruby said, feeling impatient. "She was mad about it. Told me I should focus on packing a fire-retardant suit instead of helping her choose clothes to take to Rick's. That was the last I talked to her." It was so refreshing to talk to Trevor without facades or walls up. They had been good friends, once, a long time ago, and now Ruby was starting to enjoy the adult feeling of being almost amicable with Trevor. She stole another glimpse into the studio.

"But she didn't have your exact plan?"

"No, I didn't even know my exact plan!"

"Well, that's just fucking great. Leah told me she wanted to find you. And get this. I encouraged her to drive. I thought after

268

everything you'd been through, you'd love the surprise of seeing her."

"What are you saying?" Ruby felt her body go slack.

"I'm saying she left hours ago. But now her phone's going straight to voice mail."

"But how could she know exactly where I was going? I was vague. All I said was I was going to Williams Lake. I'm in Garibaldi now."

"And I thought you were only in Squamish because you never bothered to tell me anything. You think I'd be ok with her driving to the fires? No one tells me anything in this house!"

What house, Ruby wanted to say, the three of them were not a household. Instead, she shouted, "You're telling me all of this now?! Why the hell didn't you open with this?"

"Like I fucking said, I thought you were in goddamn Squamish! Didn't you think it might be smart to tell me the truth in case of, I don't know, an emergency?!"

"I didn't think about it," she admitted, ignoring that he'd easily gone back to cutting her down again.

"Rubes, did you leave any hints about your trip in the house? Think hard. We both know how smart Leah is."

Ruby walked around the corner and tapped her hand on the mural wall, mulling this over. "Um, she likes working on the computer in your stupid man den. To write her papers for school."

"Well, the room does have great lighting, Ruby."

"Go check the browser history on the computer in the den."

"Okay." Ruby heard Trevor thudding as he moved around the house. "I'm pulling up the search history. Leah did do some research. *Rocker, Williams Lake.* When I click on that it leads straight to antique rocking chairs for sale. Next, let's see ... *rock star, Williams Lake.* Okay. First hit on that: *Curtis Simmons Plays Tribute Concert in Parent's Hometown.* Blah blah. I'm skimming it. It says his parents moved there after he graduated high school. Did he technically even grad with us? I remember that punk taking off to Portland before the year ended ..."

"Hurry up, will you?"

"Next article," he said, using an even voice to show he wasn't rattled. "Woah!"

"What?"

"Literally gives his parent's address on the net. The article says: *Curtis Simmons Makes a Donation to Save Mundy Park*. It starts, "'When Ted and Sachiko Simmons bought the only rancher on Queen's Avenue, Williams Lake, they did not imagine Curtis would grow up to save the city park.'"

"Oh my god."

"At least you know where she is driving to ..." he trailed off.

"Williams Lake, after all." Her throat closed.

"Wait! There's a pad with scribbling on my desk. It says *Curtis stopped at Garibaldi Lake*."

"Yes, that was me," admitted Ruby. "I knew from Facebook that it was the first place he went. I was doodling ideas. I think I also wrote down Rubble Creek parking lot because that's where you start the hike to get there."

"Hike?" Trevor said, in the hostile voice he often used with Ruby to show her how stupid she was being.

Ruby faltered. "I was just writing down ideas, I didn't actually plan to do the hike solo. I'm not that crazy."

"Well, Leah didn't know that. You circled Rubble Creek parking lot twice! She could be in the middle of the mountains by now looking for you. How could you be so stupid?"

"I had no idea she would come looking for me. She hasn't shown interest in anything I do for years. Telling her about Curtis was part of making me more interesting to her, you know?"

He exhaled. "I'm not mad at you, Rubes. I just want to find her."

"Yeah, me too."

"What's more important right at this moment, finding Leah or confessing to your stupid rock star guy?" She heard him pound down on something hard on his end of the line. "I'm Leah's *dad*, Ruby. *Me!* You and I might not get back together, but that part of the story doesn't have to change, you know? Why disrupt Leah's life with this info?"

"And what about Belle's baby? You want to still be the dad there, too? Part of your whole saviour complex?"

"John should know the truth. He can choose to be a part of the baby's life or not. I don't want to start a new baby off on another lie. Lies are not a good way to start anything. But talking to you, I realize you're right."

"What about?"

"I still want to be with Belle."

Ruby ran her tongue over her teeth and narrowed her eyes. Then she released the tension from her face. Although she knew she didn't want Trevor anymore, the rejection — him choosing her best friend over her — still hurt. Had she wanted him to fight more for her? No, she hadn't wanted him to stray in the first place. Even if she had only just realized how long she herself hadn't loved him, she still deserved a little more respect than this, didn't she? "You do realize you and Belle started your entire relationship on a lie, right? Judge me all you want, but just because you confessed John's the father does not make you better than me."

"Ruby," Trevor said, his voice finally cracking. "This isn't about who's better. What are you going to do about Leah? My stomach is in knots over here ... You can't take away who I have been for nineteen years."

Ruby turned the corner again and squinted into the studio. She saw Curtis, stretching his arms over his head like he didn't have a care in the world. She started digging through her purse for her car keys.

"Obviously I'm going to look for Leah. What do you think I'd do, Trevor?"

"Where are you going to start?"

"I'll start with Rubble Creek parking lot. It makes the most sense and it's closest to where I am."

"Good plan. And if she's not there?"

"We might have to see if we can get a search party going in case she went hiking. Also, I may have to go straight to Williams Lake on my own. Cover all our bases."

"This is crazy, Rubes. I'm going to lose my mind."

"Stay calm, Trevor. We'll get through this," she said levelly, before hanging up.

Heart pounding, she peered into the back of the yoga studio. Curtis was standing, looking lazy and cocky at the same time, chatting up a young Asian girl. Ruby watched as Curtis's eyes ran over the girl's breasts and thighs.

Ruby tapped her foot on the pavement, thinking.

She didn't want Curtis to be Leah's dad. In the hospital, all those many years ago, she had been right to listen to the doctor who had willed her with his silver eyes and furrowed brows to stay quiet. What she had thought were mistakes — getting pregnant as a teen with Leah, and then having Trevor raise Leah with her — were not regrets. She remembered what she had said to Harvey at the bar in Squamish, and she realized clearly that she would not change things even if she could. She paused for a second, feeling the gratitude of being freed from her own doubts on how her life had unfolded.

Then she closed her eyes and went cold, remembering the crisis she was in.

Chapter 51

1610

With Bibi Mubarak's one-word command, Rubina's eyes were uncovered, and she saw a room bathed in moonlight, filled with flickering candle flames. Blue curtains hung in the windows. Much too long for the windows, material draped on the floor in crinkled piles on either side. Sweet-smelling smoke rippled through the room in waves, coming from hookahs on the floor. There was no art here, only the black sky punctuated with jewelled stars shining through, visible through peekaboo shafts and octagonal windows cut into the ceiling and walls.

There were dancers and music. This was not the type of dance Rubina was trained in. This was Arabic music and dancing. Khushi had told her about the Al-Andalus style of dancing where women were merging styles from the Middle East with dance in the tribal fashion of vibrations that were hypnotic. It had been Khushi's dream to learn the art form. A man was singing from his throat with passion. Rubina recognized a few words. *Bismillah. Duniya. Habiba.* A deep percussion cut through the vocals. The women were moving only their exposed torsos, which were rippling in time to the drums. Their blouses were laced with full strings of pearls, coins, and dangling jewels. They had skirts with deep slits that exposed their legs. Rubina watched, transfixed, as their bodies undulated, and they shimmied their chests.

Men stepped forward. This was something Rubina had never seen — couples dancing together. The men began to twirl the girls softly, their hands on the top of their heads, like they were stirring pots. They dipped them low, and the women spread their arms back. These girls were not veiled.

Daniyal was one of the men. He was twirling a girl in time to the music.

"You were spying in my private corridors," Bibi Mubarak turned to Rubina, draping a plume of purple smoke over Rubina's face.

"This music," Rubina found herself saying, not bothering to wave the smoke away, "is enchanting. I have never seen men and women dance together."

"Habib Hussein, release her."

Rubina was so mesmerized she had forgotten that someone had been gripping her upper arm until the pressure ceased.

"The music is from al-Qandahār. The kitchen staff is from there. They do play lovely instruments, do they not? Of course, the two sexes do not dance anywhere else together, but these are my secret festivities, and I shall do as I please. I love the violins and the candle dances myself. If you stay longer, you may see one of those yourself. You do realize you will be locked in the prison for life." The last comment was made as a matter of fact. Bibi Mubarak did not have to use theatrics to get her point across; her words alone were weighty with power. Bibi Mubarak flicked back her silver hair in time to the music. "Taste your last night of freedom, slave girl."

"I am a dancing girl," Rubina said defiantly. Raj had taught her early on that the royals were impressed when a subject showed no fear. Rubina held up her chin and kept her eyes looking straight ahead. She hoped her lovely almond and gold gown would demonstrate that she was not any ordinary court member. Not sure if Bibi Mubarak had seen her stealing her personal effects, Rubina decided not to use the lie that she was looking for a dance rehearsal space.

Perhaps the night would yet turn in her favour. She realized what luck it had been for her to stumble upon such a den. With observation alone, she could train in the arts of dance expressed here from mystical tribes and lands. Imagine if Khushi could witness this.

"Every prisoner should be allowed one night of lovely things before imprisonment. It is what we believe here," spoke Bibi Mubarak as if Rubina had uttered nothing. "And the loveliest things in all the kingdom can be found here in Bibi Mubarak's chambers. I find it amusing that you intruders will risk your lives for one night of pleasure. You are the first from Jahangir's tribe to come to my lair, but many others have been imprisoned before you for sneaking into these quarters. Your king may rule the empire, but his rule does not affect my maharaja's immediate kingdom. Here, dancing girl, it is my husband Man Singh who is the ruler. Which means I am in charge."

"Fire!"

"Bismillah!"

The girls, Persians Rubina assumed, had moved away from their partners. They were placing hats made of lit candles carefully onto their heads. Rubina watched as they stood up and arched their backs, swaying to the music. The candles never wavered; rather, they burned more brightly, and Rubina saw flickering jewels dance right before her eyes.

Despite Raj's warnings about not showing fear, it was starting to take hold of her, much like the night when Prince Khurram had leapt down from an elephant to meet Khushi at the dance hall. Bibi Mubarak remained uncharmed by Rubina.

"Charming, right?" Daniyal was beside her, twisting the word Rubina was thinking of in her mind.

She swallowed the alarming feeling spreading over her chest. "You do not sound like your usual cranky self. I did not imagine you would be the type to enjoy secret gatherings."

Daniyal shrugged, moving her gently to the corner away from Bibi Mubarak. "I used to enjoy them when they were ours alone to enjoy. This is part of our al-Qandahār tradition. Bibi Mubarak caught us enjoying our festivities in the room where we store the ale. She demanded we join her other court members in these private corridors. And that the men mix with the women. Something unheard of in the court."

"Maharaja Man Singh's wife is not at all what I had imagined," said Rubina, watching as Bibi Mubarak put down her hookah and began clapping heartily alongside the girls.

Daniyal took a slow sip of rice wine from a copper goblet. He set it behind himself. Rubina saw from the way his eyes were unfocused that the wine had had its effect on this man whom Raj had told her did not ordinarily drink. His eyebrows were not furrowed. His mouth was relaxed.

"Bibi Mubarak enjoys the Persian parties and has us do dances to commemorate the Safavid dynasty," Daniyal said. "A part of me understands her genuine enthusiasm for the performances, but I do not enjoy being made to perform like a trained monkey." He looked behind her, as if searching out her shadow. "Where is the baby girl that you continually boss around?"

"Heera?"

"Why are you always sending her out to spy on me?"

"I have not deployed her to spy on you. Rather, I have her watch you to make sure you are in good health and spirit."

"I do not need your help, Rubina *jaan*. You will get that young one killed."

"I am the one in danger here!" Rubina seethed. "Not her! Bibi Mubarak has caught me on her premises. She has had me arrested. She says this is my last night of freedom! Does she have the ability to imprison me in the Amber Fort? For I am King Jahangir's dancing girl of Agra, not Jaipur!"

"Then why, by the great Akbar, are you stalking Bibi Mubarak's chambers in the middle of the night?"

Rubina reddened. "I promised Raj a jewel."

Daniyal shook his head. "Unbelievable. You and your stupid boy-made-of-girl. Good luck with Bibi Mubarak! You are always one to put your foot where it does not belong: my kitchen, the harem hallways made for the king, the stockroom at the camp where you had those ridiculous twins sneak you in. I am not surprised to see you standing right before the most dangerous and powerful woman of the Amber Court. What a fool you are!" He turned to walk away.

"Wait!" she pulled at his gold *angarkha* coat. Believe me, Daniyal," she took a deep breath and plunged ahead, "I wanted the best for you ... for us. I know tonight I got a bit distracted looking for something to surprise Raj with. But Sabina is not the one for you!"

"Why are you so intent on tarnishing Sabina's name? Have you any idea what Moti Ma will do to you if she finds out what nonsense you and your silly friend say about her daughter? Raj is not to be trusted. And Moti Ma is not someone you should dare cross."

"Daniyal, just hear me out! I have seen Sabina intoxicated on opium with my own eyes. I told you this in the stockroom at camp, but I feel you have cotton rags stuck in your ears. She is mad! She hears voices! Of ghosts! She cannot make you a good wife."

Daniyal came close to her. She inhaled, taking in his scent of fried cakes and sweet wine. Rubina was sure he was going to shake her violently or slap her. His fingers, which had come to rest on her shoulder, were perfumed with spiced ginger. He squeezed her shoulder so hard she felt her muscles twinge. He pulled her close, within an inch of his face. "You want something out of this."

"It is true," she said, trying to give her voice courage. She had wanted to wait until after she performed at the Sheesh Mahal, but the time to act was now. "I want you."

"What makes you think you will make a good wife?"

Rubina flushed. "I will put your needs before mine."

"But you are not doing that even now. You are putting your selfish desires before my happiness." He was swaying with her now, in time with the drums, still gripping her firmly, her body pressed against his. The night breeze came in through the sky panels and wafted gently into the room.

"I care for you," she said, her words carried away by the breeze. "I want the best for you. I am the best for you."

He was spinning her gently now, a hundred times over, like a child's top. Her bare feet were stinging but she kept up, looking at him to spot her turns instead of the audience as she usually did, keeping one arm hugged to her chest. When he stopped her, she was not dizzy. He landed his hand on her mid-back and gently lowered her. She opened her palms and grazed the floor with her hands the way the Persian dancers were doing. He pulled her up smoothly, his hands now on the back of her neck.

"Daniyal," his name got stuck in her throat. She was hoping to clarify her position further.

His lips were on hers. They were kissing.

"Daniyal," she whispered when their lips parted, "I love you."

"Shush." His voice was slurred. "The moment I saw you, I ..." he trailed off as if someone had stolen his thought.

She touched his cheek, focusing on the brown and green of his iris. They looked like the rusted and ripe colour contrasts used in the landscaped paintings the king commissioned the artists to do of springtime in the harem gardens, with the dusty paths winding between the greenery. Would he take her under the banyan trees as he did Sabina at Agra Fort, or would they discover a new place? Would they dance like this again? Surely Sabina could not move this lithely. Rubina would learn Persian prose if it was what Daniyal would like her to recite in the gardens. Surely, Sabina could not learn to wave her torso like the waves of the ocean as the Persians in

Bibi Mubarak's court could; surely Rubina would become dearer to Daniyal than his Sabina.

"I had feelings for you," he continued, "but you are corrupt." His sober voice was taking foothold. "You sneak. You lie. You go to places you do not belong. You do anything to better your own standing and think of no one other than yourself. How can you love a man who has murdered your mother? A man who has professed his love to another? A woman like you does not make an obedient wife. You have such a good life in the harem compared to that of a street dancer. You are the type of woman who will never find satisfaction with what you have."

"And a woman hooked on opium makes a good wife?" she lashed out. "I had no choice but to tell you! The harem will imprison me like it did my mother. I can leave with you, or I can move my way up, but I do not desire power or status. I desire you!"

Daniyal broke free from her. He was striding towards Bibi Mubarak where he performed the *taslim*, an honoured bow saved for his majesty, but which he extended gracefully to her. "My lady, I was the one who requested that the court's dancing girl attend our festivities tonight."

"You should have arranged her a proper escort then."

"Please spare her. She was confused about waiting for the escort."

"Daniyal *jaan*, her intrusion goes against court rules ..."

"However, I am certain she will not disturb our parties again," Daniyal said. "Lock her up for three lifetimes if she disobeys."

"How quick you are to condemn the future of the one you saved."

"This party is best kept private," Daniyal said. "I only look to serve you, Mughal princess and wife to Maharaja Man Singh."

"Soon she will leave with your camp. This punishment is not enough," Bibi Mubarak said, the tip of the hookah pipe touching her lip. Bibi Mubarak loved control and punishment. It was what she was known for. Her silver hair shimmered by way of candlelight.

"Her obsession for you is obvious. She must never have you or speak to you again. If she does, Daniyal *jaan*, her life is over."

Daniyal nodded. His voice was thick but controlled. "She will never. If she does, she will suffer for not three, but four lifetimes. Rubina's lifetime, and the lifetimes of her ghosts, as well. She will have no peace even in her afterlife should she disobey and try and see me. The doors to heaven will forever be closed to her." To Rubina he bent his body forward and touched his hand to his forehead. "*Adaab,* sister. Please stay away from me if you do not want to be imprisoned."

Bibi Mubarak smiled. "You have a deal. And do make sure she stays away from you in the Agra Fort. Or the dancer will be taken to the Elephant Garden and be trampled. I will be certain that everyone in Agra Fort knows of my decision. Every slave girl, every eunuch, every concubine. I will have eyes everywhere."

Rubina felt pain take hold of her stomach and she doubled over. Her mouth still tasted of Daniyal's sweet wine. Habib Hussein's arms were locked around her waist, already dragging her back to the harem to sleep next to Heera. The gold *dupatta* that matched her gown tore under the henchman's strong foot. She wanted to shout, *Ruko! Wait!*

But, hope dashed, her voice had fled with the very courage she had become known for.

Chapter 52

2017

Ruby had hoped she would find her daughter standing in the Rubble Creek parking lot.

Instead, she spotted Belle.

Her former best friend stood at the base of the wooden steps that led into a maze of Douglas fir trees, growing as close together as a pack of matches in a box. The glacier lake, Ruby knew, was a stunning mint-green body of water. It was hugged by icy mountains that were strung together like a line of crisp purple and white paper dolls. The lake was a long hike away, however, and it couldn't be seen from where the two were standing.

Belle was wearing a long floral dress that tugged at her bump, with gladiator sandals that told Ruby pregnancy had sneakily taken heels from her once-upon-a-time friend. Had Ruby just never noticed the tiny bump, or had the release of the affair allowed Belle's stomach to pop freely — her news, no longer a secret, rising to the surface? She had only just seen Belle, and over the course of a few hours, so many things had changed.

On a different day, in a different time, the two could be getting ready for a picnic. Ruby would have brought along hard salty cheese, gourmet crackers, ripe strawberries, and tart red wine, because Belle could never be counted on to plan ahead. In return, Belle would entertain Ruby with her stories of dating in the city.

But today there was an energy permeating from the two that suggested they would not venture past the stairs. The lake breeze blew gently through Belle's sandy locks. Grey, smog-heavy clouds hung behind her, giving the impression Belle was standing on a boat out on a stormy sea. Belle was a painting ready to be crafted, even in the misery she was projecting through her frown, or maybe more so because of it.

"Hi," said Belle trying to awkwardly hug her. Ruby resisted.

"Why are you here, Belle?"

"Leah wanted to find you. She said you circled the name of this place a couple times in your notes. I came instead. She's, well, she's at my condo. We switched spots. Hey, saying that reminds me of *The Parent Trap*. Remember how we used to watch that movie in eighth grade even though we were both too old for it?" She gave Ruby a smile as weak as half-steeped chamomile. "Took me an hour and forty-five minutes to drive here."

Ruby was embarrassed she'd also thought of the movie when it came to her and Belle's recent circumstances. Instead, she said, "What the hell do you mean, 'switched spots'?"

"I'll explain." Belle lowered herself carefully onto a rock. "She was a mess. You weren't around. By the time she contacted me, I'd already told Trevor I didn't want to talk to him anymore. It's been a hell of a day ..."

"What do you mean she's a mess?!"

"I made that sound much worse than it is." Belle tucked hay-coloured curls behind her ears. "Rick and she had a falling out. Anyway, I didn't think she should drive here to tell you that. We weren't even sure we'd catch you before Williams Lake. I drove straight here, no rests." The sun seeping in through the trees had dappled a leopard print design on Belle's face. "Leah's quite a detective. Finding the clues that you ..."

Ruby interrupted, "You want a prize or something?"

"What?" said Belle distractedly, raising her hand to her belly. "No, 'course not."

"I know you had the baby tested, Belle. I know that you don't care about danger right now because you probably want something bad to happen to you. Then you wouldn't have to make a decision on whether to keep the baby, right? You realize I know you better than anyone else, right? This drive is not an act of altruism on your part. It's you, testing your fate, like you're the main character in one of your witchcraft movie specials. You are so narcissistic you think the universe leaves you hints on what to do next."

"Trevor told you about the baby having Down syndrome?" She looked caught out. "I guess you also know that my baby's not Trevor's? I take him from you, and I can't even get the thing I wanted most: a part of him. That's why I'm not talking to Trevor right now," she mumbled.

"Do you know how worried we were about Leah? You couldn't have told either one of us that she was staying with you? We're Leah's parents, you know. I was this close," she pinched her index finger and thumb together, "to getting a search party together to look for her."

Belle didn't meet her gaze. Instead, she focused on metallic clouds overhead, which looked deceivingly full of rain but were just puffs of floating debris from the wildfires wafting by. "I didn't think about it."

"You don't think about much."

"Wait a sec, Trevor told you everything?"

"We've been married for twenty years; guess he found he could still talk to me."

"You two clearly still have a bond." Belle's voice was plain as oatmeal.

"He's with you, Belle."

"Yeah, he keeps saying that, but I keep hanging up on him." Belle's eyes glistened with tears. "How can it be that John's the father?"

Ruby sighed and sat herself down on the same flat, large rock, the flecks of granite woven into the stone sparkling. "Trevor couldn't give you a part of himself because he didn't have a part to give."

"But he gave you Leah."

Ruby stared at Belle, trying to gauge how much Belle knew. Belle's hyacinth-blue eyes looked blank. Ruby cleared her throat. "Yes, but that happened before Trevor's sperm count declined."

"So then why did you lie? About Leah not being his?"

"I was angry. People do crazy shit when they're mad."

"Also," said Belle, sticking up her gladiator sandalled foot so the metal clasp shone in the sun, "why are you looking for Curtis Simmons? I remembered he left to go to Portland in high school and you guys broke up. You guys have some unfinished business?"

"Well, aren't you and Leah suddenly Sherlock Holmes and Watson? Maybe you can start some future business together."

"God, you're just as snarky as you used to be in high school. I miss that Ruby! She always used to put me in my place." Belle raised a brow. "You're dressed differently too, like all retro and stuff. What's with the cherry halter dress and red lipstick? It's very Vivian Leigh. Did you lose weight?"

Ruby smoothed down her skirt, watching it bounce back up from the crinoline. "I'm the same Ruby. My bodily dimensions are none of your concern."

"Rubes, are you actually trying to get Curtis back? I mean he's never going to go for you. I'm not even saying this to be mean. I get this has all been a big hit for you, maybe made you a bit nostalgic for the old days. But maybe, if I'm being self-reflective, there's malice in what I say. That's what my therapist would say." She leaned forward and gave Ruby a confessional look. "You get a piece of Trevor and I don't. I obviously resent you. It doesn't matter. I'm aborting the baby."

"That's crazy!" Ruby said before she could stop herself.

"Goddamn it, I always knew this would happen to me; that there was no way I could have a regular baby, fair and square. I fell in love, and I fucked everyone over. Typical Belle! Ruby, I just can't do this."

"What do you mean you 'just can't do this'? You took my whole fucking life from me and now you 'just can't do this'? After spending your whole life proving you were too cool to settle down, you choose *my husband* to fall in love with? 'Typical Belle.' You say that like some white-girl tagline in a fucking sitcom. This is my life, Belle! Not a Netflix original series!"

"I know!" Belle shouted back, her words chillingly loud and free in the outdoors. Ruby could see an eagle soar against grey cashmere clouds in the distance, a black shadow-puppet racing over objects below. "I fucking know, all right? But I just can't watch my kid grow up and fail at being a kid, okay? It's not in me. For the record, I picked Trevor because of Leah, all right? He's a pretty wicked dad, and my own dad was a drunk. I guess I watched him all these years just loving the way he was with Leah. I never watched John or assessed him; he wasn't even on my radar."

A car had pulled into the lot, sending gravel jumping. Despite the wildfires, a pack of hikers filed out. "You did well, edging into the perfect family and cutting me out. But, if it matters," Ruby said, "Trevor and I were dead as a couple a long time ago. With or without you it was a relationship that could only be resuscitated once we became old enough that friendship could supersede sex." Ruby smiled sardonically. "Who knows, we might not have had to wait too long for that day to come."

Belle shook her head refusing to acknowledge Ruby. "I don't want him. I can't even look at him."

"Oh, that's rich, Belle. Fuck up my life and play the victim. Reject Trevor after he's thrown his life away for you. Make me, of all people, console you. And congrats on playing the hero too, keeping my daughter at your house after you played god intervening on my road trip."

"She came to me, Rubes. I didn't know what else to do." Belle wiped at her eyes with the back of her hand. "All Leah could do was talk about how much you had her best interests at heart. She was shaken up about Rick."

"Rick?" Ruby was questioning the trees.

"I think they might have slept together, and she realized what a prick he was. I just tried to be there for her. She was talking about how grateful she was they used a condom." Belle shifted her gaze to adjusting her sandal.

"She's *my* daughter, Belle. I wanted to be there for her."

"Then you fucking should have."

"The one time I decide to be like you and just take off," Ruby muttered.

"At least she isn't going to be a teen mom like you."

Ruby reeled back. "Definitely not the worst choice I made in life."

"No?"

"Quite clearly that was being your friend."

"I guess I walked right into that," Belle said, moving her eyes from her sandals to the tops of the ancient trees. "I was just saying, history isn't going to repeat itself."

"Fuck you," Ruby said squarely and stood up. And then, because she wanted to hurt Belle as much as she'd hurt her, she said, "Your poor baby!"

"For what it's worth, I came here to say sorry, and let you feel good about me getting what I deserve." Belle threw her hands up. "Because clearly this was karmic payback."

"That isn't what I meant," said Ruby. "I meant poor baby because you aren't giving it a chance to exist. And if you do, you will just look at it as a burden instead of a blessing."

"No matter what I fucking did to you Ruby Andrews, you do

NOT get to be the Pro-Life Police. You do not get to sit there and act all high and mighty, like you would deal with all this news better than me. Because you have already made a perfect fucking kid and you have no idea, and I mean NO IDEA what it is I am going through. Okay? All right? All you get to do is yell at me because I deserve that. So, go ahead."

"You think if I yell at you that will set the universe right? That me screaming at you frees you from your sins? You and your big ideas of karma and kismet. You're so deluded!"

Belle shrugged, the passion from her last words already dissolving like foam on freshly poured champagne.

"You need a lot more om-shanti-oms for that kind of redemption to happen. Surprisingly, I don't want my old life back. I don't want the house. Or Trevor. Or anything from you guys. Seriously, I don't."

"That doesn't help anything."

"It helps a lot. I'm not blocking your glorious union."

"You could fight for Trevor harder. Especially now that you know the baby isn't his."

"Ha!" Ruby laughed genuinely. "You think I'm that desperate? Don't throw Trevor away because you feel guilty."

"Now you want me to stay with Trevor?" Belle whispered. She dropped both of her sandalled feet into the gravel, causing powdered grey dirt to swirl in the air. "None of this makes any sense, Rubes."

Chapter 53

2017

Ruby had been looking up for a while at the smoky, greenish sky. "Remember that time we were drinking wine at my house and the television was on and Trevor came in and sat on the couch for a sec with us? A rich lady with a closet the size of a house was talking about her ridiculous furs, taking the host up and down the stairs, removing purses stored like museum artifacts out from behind glass cases?"

Belle nodded, looking confused.

"You said," Ruby said, making her voice high-pitched, "'that vintage Louis is the only stylish thing in her gaudy closet, and the Birkin is not even a real Tiffany blue like she says it is. Not only is the woman tacky, she's colourblind.' And Trevor said," Ruby adopted a hoarse voice, "'I would have done the shelves differently, and the lighting is all wrong.'" Ruby turned to Belle, ready to make her point. "We had all put aside the stupidity that we live in a society where a person has a closet the size of a house in the first place. But do you remember what I said?"

"No."

"I said, 'I'd be too lazy to walk over from my bed and change in another corridor of the house. What an inconvenience, to wake up every morning and trudge over and choose your clothes for the day from a closet the size of a department store.' I asked if you guys

288

thought she had another closet in her actual bedroom. You both didn't answer."

"What's the point of this story, Rubes?"

"The point is this: I've always been practical. Logical. I don't like change. I always follow the routine. I stayed in a relationship far past the expiry date because it's easier than announcing that something is terribly wrong with it. I lived in a house I hated because I was too unimaginative to think I had a choice to live anywhere else. I don't want Trevor. I don't want to go back to the way things are now, even if it's easier. Look," Ruby said, softer now, "I can't fix your baby for you, Belle." She swatted away a fly, purple, with a shiny, green back. "But we could all help you. Don't make a decision you'll regret."

"Like you'd help me after what I did to you. What are you going to do, babysit now? Have us over for Christmas? Make us lasagna at dinner parties? I look at it like this. Which would I regret more: keeping it or aborting it? At this moment in time, I feel like I would regret keeping it more."

It. Ruby clenched her mouth and sucked her lips inward. Songbirds were calling to each other from the trees above. The smell of pine resin and smoke burned down her throat. She exhaled, eyes watering from the wildfires. Ruby was mad at herself for caring about the baby. But how was any of this its fault? What business of hers was any of this? She was starting to sound like a right-wing nutter and Belle was right, she wasn't the Pro-Life Police. She released the tension in her lips. Forced herself to talk. "Look, I *know* Trevor. He'll never get over it if you do something rash. You won't be able to live with yourself."

"That isn't fair to say, Ruby." Her voice was feeble, shaking.

"At least tell John first, Belle." Ruby winced at how un-feminist she was beginning to sound by the minute.

"I miss you, you know." Belle's face was flushed. "It started with your food. I really miss your cooking. I didn't know, until Trevor smuggled some wraps from your deep freezer. He knows he's not supposed to eat your food. When he saw them disappear from the fridge, he thought I'd thrown them out, but really I'd eaten them."

When Ruby didn't say anything, Belle examined a twig, spray-painted golden by the sun, and kept going. "He said that one time you stopped cooking with garlic for a year. You were so tired of him not commenting one way or another when he ate your food. But one day, you yourself missed garlic so much, you sautéed half a bulb up in olive oil and a chunk of butter, all minced finely. You made a simple tikka curry. He almost died it was so good. That's what it's like with you Ruby. I don't miss you when I don't see you. I miss you when you are right in front of me. When I eat your samosa wrap or see your brown eyes. That's when I know how badly I've fucked things up." A tear slid down Belle's cheek.

"Where's John now?" Ruby said, refusing to be moved by this.

"He's in India."

"Email him and get him to call you."

"All I have is an address of an ashram." Belle wiped her face and pulled a small piece of paper from her purse, showing it to Ruby. "They don't even have wi-fi there. John doesn't have his phone turned on because he won't answer any texts — but maybe they aren't going through — what do I really know about international texting?" Belle gave her a half-hearted shoulder shrug. "Actually, I have a ticket just waiting for me at the travel agency. John put a non-refundable deposit down with the agent, but it's really good for anyone because ... I just ... well, never went to claim it. I chose to be with Trevor."

"What if I was the one to find him?" A rush of adrenalin washed over Ruby's body as she said the words.

"You? In India?"

"Stranger things have happened than a person of Indian descent going back to the motherland, you know." She snatched the paper

Belle was holding to inspect it closely.

Belle blinked at her.

"Look," Ruby reasoned, "I could use John's deposit."

"You want to go all the way to India?"

"What choice do you have, Belle?" Ruby bent at the waist to sweep brassy pine needles from the rock. "You all can reach this decision together. You don't seem like you are a hundred percent decided. I mean I'm not some right-wing conservative prude. I get it, your body, your decision. But there are an awful lot of people's lives that will be affected. At least make a decision with a clear head. It's fast travelling nowadays — I'd be there in a jiffy." As she thought of what she'd just volunteered to do, she realized the old Ruby would have never offered to do something so impulsive. So rash. So adventurous.

Belle met Ruby's eyes. "Does John even need to know?"

Ruby could only meet them for a second. "It's your call, Belle."

"I guess it wouldn't hurt. Trevor wants to raise it with me. But he's hellbent on John knowing. Maybe he knows a Down syndrome baby will need all the love it can get." She smiled sadly.

"Look Belle," Ruby said before she could take back the words, "I get we live in a world where we see people who have disabilities or who aren't neurotypical as a stigma and burden. Even medical labels shape the way we look at differences among humans as negative. Down *syndrome*. Autism spectrum *disorder*. Our society's preference for able-bodied people is totally causing your anxiety. You'll need to fight to get financial support and a whole bunch of other support. I don't know a lot about what you'll truly be up against. But," she took a deep breath and faced Belle head on, "I get the feeling even if you could swap them for something you consider now to be genetically superior, after you fall in love with them you will realize that that baby is the most perfect being in the entire world. You'll do anything for their health and well-being. But you'll never ever want to trade them for someone else."

"How do you know that?"

"Because Leah is perfect not because of her genes. She is perfect because she is Leah. At the same time," she cleared her throat and focused her gaze on the reflection of light bouncing off the parked cars and retraced her words, "at the same time, you're right to say I have no idea how you are feeling right now. We all want the best for our children. I get that you must be scared out of your mind right now. At least take the time to process everything logically — don't do that panicky running away thing you always do. Maybe talking to John will give you clarity, even if you decide not to stay pregnant." Once she had said this, she felt tension and anger release from her shoulders. Ruby realized, with a bit of surprise, that it wasn't just her own feelings at stake anymore.

"You'd really go? After everything I did to you?"

Ruby felt her body twitch at this comment. She folded up the paper with John's info. Ordinarily she'd never speak about her feelings to Belle without editing them first, but the events of the summer had taken a lot from her. So, she answered Belle candidly. "How do you know I'm just going for you?"

"What about your business with Curtis Simmons?"

Ruby didn't answer. All that could be heard was the slow rustle of pine needles that fell from trees. Thinking of flying to India, Ruby remembered the photographs in the shoebox she found when her mother died. The milky Taj Mahal. The sapphire sky peeking through the dusky red India Gate. Ruby's thoughts shifted quickly to the stories of Rubina. The places Rubina had been stood out stronger in Ruby's mind, like she had been there herself. The Amber Fort in Jaipur. The Agra Fort in Agra. She felt more connected to those places than she could vocalize. Those supposedly fictional stories meant more to her than real life.

"My business with Curtis Simmons isn't relevant anymore," she said, turning her back on Belle.

"Wait, Ruby? The info for the travel agency? It's on the same paper. I'll call them and make sure you can use John's deposit. You call and make the arrangements for when you want to fly out ... and, if you change your mind, I'll understand."

Ruby did not reply. Instead, she jumped in her car and reversed, looking through the rear window, making sure it was clear. It was a fast, confident motion, that of a skilled driver. Puffs of gravel dust rose behind the car. Just before she pulled out of the parking lot, she unrolled her window. "Belle?"

"Yeah?" The trees lining the path behind Belle were so thick they looked black.

"Take care of Leah."

She drove ahead, leaving Belle's reassuring reply to hang in the dry, rain-thirsty air.

Chapter 54

1610

The rains had been relentless. Water from the skies had poured down for sixteen days and nights. The dusty pathways, worn down by animals trekking through with carriages and goods, had turned into a small brown, gushing river. For the most part, on the return trip from the Amber Court back to the Agra Fort, King Jahangir's nobility and concubines were safe in their howdahs. These canopied structures had transformed into slick canvases where rain dripped down from either side, making circular fortresses of water. The footmen and slaves, however, were soaked thoroughly, as the rain battered down hard upon their half-naked bodies. The higher ranking the member of the Mughal dynasty, the more clothing the man was allotted. There was no need for the fanfare of *nakaray* and *dumanay*, the Mughal's favourite instruments, as the empire made its winding way down through the water drenched roads of hilled villages to return home to the Agra Fort, for the steady percussion of the heavy rain was music enough.

There was a small leak in Rubina's howdah, and by the time she reached the Agra Fort, she was soaking wet down to her undergarments. Heera had travelled in the same compartment as her on the last leg of the trip, as she had boldly rushed ahead to join Rubina in the headcount when the camels and elephants were being loaded with goods. This act of friendship had failed to impress Rubina, who had been looking forward to riding alone with her thoughts. She was still mulling over Daniyal trading their chance at a connection to save Rubina's life. But perhaps it had not been a sacrifice at all on his part. Perhaps his heart only belonged to Sabina. Rubina traced her lips, remembering Daniyal's hot touch. He had enjoyed kissing her — if nothing else, she was sure of that.

Now Rubina had to sit across from Heera and listen to her non-stop songs and chants, her rhymes and stories, and constantly refuse her efforts to engage Rubina in finger puppet games. She was still a child, Rubina thought, shivering in her wet clothes. Heera, a wet puddle of indigo ink gathering at her feet because the colour had run from her clothes, like a toddler, paid no mind to the rains.

"Sisterhood, yours and mine, is forever," Heera gushed, lacing her blue-tinged fingers through Rubina's. The animals had stopped tapping their heavy feet against the ground, which signified that the troupe had arrived at the entrance of the great castle. Yet something was amiss. Moti Ma had departed from her grandly decorated howdah hanging between two elephants and run, unhidden, ahead to the noble's howdahs. Such an act of breaking purdah was forbidden; however none of the foot soldiers were stopping her.

"Heera, I am your senior in rank," said Rubina, pulling her eyes away from the commotion reluctantly to meet her companion's. "As such, you must mind your manners. Though you refer to me as sister, a real sister must meet the same qualifications in the kingdom." Yanking her fingers from Heera's, she tried, once more, to decipher the situation ahead. Several attendants were running to Moti Ma. She had fallen to the ground in a heap. Was she ill? Hurt?

"I am sorry I rushed into your cabin uninvited," Heera said, her teeth chattering slightly, "I thought you would want some company ..."

"Yes, you thought. It goes without saying I have not had any rest since you joined me."

"It was bold of you to go after Daniyal Master in the Persian suite. It is hard not to be encouraged by your own courage to go after what you want," Heera pushed her sopping hair from her face.

"Persian suite? What do you know of that?"

"The Persian suite is the den where Bibi Mubarak has her dancers eat, drink, and dance in the region's customs. No one is in purdah there. It is a wild spot whereupon there is no division between men and women. And supposedly, the females dance with their hips, enticing men with a dance using bellies, which is more enchanting than opium. It is where you snuck in."

"I am well aware of what it is, but how do you know what happens there?"

"The other concubines all know you got caught, Rubina *baaji*. They also know that Daniyal Master rejected your advances, and that Bibi Mubarak has forbidden you from ever contacting him."

"They know?"

"Moti Ma was most displeased. It appears Sabina will be married to the royal chef immediately upon arrival."

"How do you know this?!"

"Daniyal Master asked Moti Ma for Sabina's hand. He sent a foot soldier off with the message to her from the Amber Fort. Moti Ma consented, provided he let Sabina stay with the harem for parts of the year."

The rain was coming down so hard that Rubina felt she was trapped in a glass bauble, like the ones that bobbed on the surface of the waterwork display fountains in the harem's garden. She strained to look through the heavy rain to make sense of what Moti Ma was doing. Nothing could be heard because of the loud rains. After a long while, a wooden plank was carried out from the castle entrance. On top, an object covered in a white cloth. Moti Ma was throwing herself at the men carrying it. No one was stopping her. The entire line of attendants in the camp was held up because of this commotion. Rubina felt her blood rush to her cheeks.

"Why did you not tell me this before, instead of filling me with your nonstop jabber about village idiot rhymes?"

"I did not want to upset you. I shouldn't have said anything at all. I only meant to show you how inspired I am by your bravery." Heera's head was down. Her shoulders and small frame were shaking. Her chest was still flat, so she looked like a young boy caught in the rain.

"I am not upset. I am surprised is all," Rubina recovered, pulling herself up. She did the same to Heera. "Look young sister — which is what you are to me, what you will always be. I am sorry to have written off your loyalties to me so easily. I just ... well ... I worry that if you defy the empire's laws so easily you will fall in trouble's way ... I do not want you copying me. I grew up in the streets of Agra, not some backward little village."

"How could I not want to be just like you?! You were saved when you snuck into Bibi Mubarak's den! You could have been beheaded! Or thrown into a dungeon! But Daniyal Master vouched for you. He must harbour some feelings for you."

Rubina shrank back into the bench, pulling her wet tresses from her face just as Heera was doing, considering this. "Do you think?"

As Heera was about to reply, a beautiful face suddenly obstructed Rubina's view of the wrinkled elephant bottoms and their fat feet sinking into the muddy pathways. She started at the sculpted eyebrows, and for the first time in days, smiled sincerely.

"Raj!"

"You are a wet mess!" he popped around and kissed her cheek. "Why are you in this compartment with a slave girl?"

"She is one of the prince's chosen women."

"She is but a soggy child! Never you mind," he said, squeezing his body into the howdah. His pink shirt and gold vest were splattered in wet drops. Heera was openly staring at the rubies tucked into his turban. "Did you hear?"

"Hear what? It has been raining for so many days my ears are filled with water," Rubina tipped her head to one side.

"Sabina *jaan*," he paused to smile, "is officially dead. She died of an opium overdose. That girl loved to drink her opium. Who knows what was mixed in. She had no taste tester as the king does, and contaminated product has been known to make its way into the palace." He shook his head to himself. "That is her *janaaza* you see being carried out. Prayers are being recited now and she is about to be laid down to face the *qibla*. Moti Ma has come undone. She is wailing, and you know the king will put a stop to this soon. For now, he is permitting her to carry on." New rings flashed on his fingers as he waved his fingers in time with his words.

"Dead?" Rubina's fingers shook.

"Now *chakli*, do tell me. Did you manage to bring me a bauble?"

"Raj!" Rubina chastised.

"Rubina *jaan* stole many things from Bibi Mubarak's dressing chamber to gift you," Heera rushed forward to say. "She will steal Daniyal's love, too. I am sure of it!"

"My, my, you have yourself quite the little fan. You robbed jewels from one of the King of Amber Fort's wives? I would expect no less from my little bird."

"Raj, pay this girl no mind. Do not distract yourself with trinkets right now! Sabina is no longer in this world! Her ghost could be listening!"

"You realize, do you not," Raj said, combing through the carriage in search of what Rubina had brought back, "that you, Rubina *jaan*, will have your royal chef now. Uncontested. Without issue. Your little shadow is right. Why, pray tell, is it so disastrously wet in here?"

Rubina slid against the slippery bench of the howdah as Raj jostled her in his search for his gifts. She peered through the flash of rain. Moti Ma had been pried away and the camp members were moving once more, unobstructed, towards the castle. She heard the whips scream through the air before they hit the wearied backs of donkeys. A plainly dressed eunuch suddenly appeared at Rubina's howdah with a golden parasol for Raj. Raj pulled his body from the howdah, frowning at his damp silk trousers and his failure in finding his trophies.

"Sadiq, you could not come sooner?" Raj chastised the younger eunuch.

"I will see you soon, Raj. *Adaab,*" Rubina said, more ceremoniously than usual to impress Heera.

Raj saluted her formally, happy to go along with her regal performance. "Indeed, you will. Grace to Allah that our dear Sabina *jaan* will have a safe journey to the other side. Go on Sadiq. Bow to Rubina *jaan.* She is one of the jewels of this fine kingdom."

Rubina smiled as the boy kneeled before her. It was not the *taslim* one would bestow upon the empress — such a tribute such could get the boy killed — but Rubina was happy with the gesture. "Raj," Rubina added, "do not let yourself forget that Sabina's worldly goods are of no use to her now, and Sabina will be buried in modesty as is the custom, just like every other person."

"Yes," Raj's smile spread. Rubina had meant to say this in jest, for Raj to see that his love of materialism was of no use in death. That, now, Sabina was no more special than Rubina herself. But from Raj's expression he had clearly taken this to mean that he had an opportunity to clear out some of Sabina's valuables before they were collected by others. "*Adaab,* sweet bird."

After settling in at the Agra Fort, Rubina's first priority was to send word to Daniyal. Rubina had tried, of course, to contact him through Raj, but Raj had returned each time shaking his head. Daniyal had his men escort Raj out of the kitchen. Bibi Mubarak's words had come to curse Rubina in a way she had never anticipated.

Daniyal was without Sabina now, in circumstances she could never have foretold, and yet, Bibi Mubarak had made it so Rubina was suffering more than she would have at the feet of an elephant. Raj returned, each time sullenly, not even managing to fill his pockets with sweet dates or hide cups of pudding away. He was forced to send Sadiq to steal things for him instead, and he did not enjoy this shift of power.

"One day," Raj promised Rubina, "I will be the first eunuch in command in this kingdom. And you, my dear, will be their favourite entertainer. Mark my words with the sharpest of arrows shot from King Jahangir's bow, Rubina. We must desert our plan to leave the harem. Now, we must rise to the very top of the dynasty."

Chapter 55

1610

Fifteen days of mourning followed Sabina's death. Throughout, the rains continued, pounding down on the gates, and overflowing the river that connected the gardens and ran through the innards of the palace. The servants had to remove buckets of water from the winding channels to keep it from spoiling the Persian rugs.

During the ceremonial prayers, Heera had not left Rubina's side. She had asked and received permission to move next to Rubina's bed chamber. Because of the observed mourning period, Rubina had not been requested to perform any dances, and she found herself taking comfort in Heera's childish banter. Rubina allowed Heera to braid her hair and fill her head with village stories, which entertained Rubina far more than she let on.

Though Sabina had not been a high-ranking member of the empire, Moti Ma had been the king's favoured concubine once upon a time. Her daughter's untimely death had heightened the kingdom's fear once more of the dangers of ingesting, either purposefully or accidentally, contaminated opium and alcohol. Though the royals partook mostly in wines, they preferred their subjects not do so, and as such, parties had stopped completely after Sabina's death. Rubina could only wait for the royalty to summon her for private parties once the fear of Sabina's vengeful ghost died.

At night, Raj came to spend time in Rubina and Heera's quarters. They would attempt to delight Rubina with poems and plays Heera had invented, which they would act out together, trying to distract her from Bibi Mubarak's curse. Like Rubina, Raj had first found Heera's antics childish, but soon after, he saw Heera's behaviour matched his easily. He was tickled by her village songs and accent, and Rubina found that the two mingled with each other enough to leave her to her own thoughts, which consisted only of Daniyal.

When Moti Ma had sent word that she wanted to visit Rubina's quarters on the sixteenth day after the camp had arrived home, Rubina had not thought much of it. She had been selecting some old dance gowns to gift Heera, who was most grateful as she still only had the one, faded inky dress in her wardrobe. When Sardar, one of Rubina's favourite eunuchs, arrived with the message that Moti Ma had come down from her apartments, Heera had been trying on the dress that Rubina had worn the night the guards had evicted her from Bibi Mubarak's den. Heera was studiously examining the rip where Rubina's golden *chunni* had been trampled.

"This should be quite easy to repair," her accent punctuated her words, a whistling lisp that Rubina had quite nearly begun to look forward to hearing.

"Moti Ma has arrived," announced Sardar theatrically, bowing forth from his hip. When he rose, he paid Rubina the compliment of a wink. "Dear, you have not visited me in the halls for some time. I have had so many fresh oranges for you, and you have not tasted even one," he spoke quickly, before the other eunuchs came up and filled Rubina's small chamber. "These oranges, they are said to be the sweetest yet because the king planted orange jewels in the soil next to the orange tree with his own fingers."

"That sounds divine," Rubina said, giving Sardar a private smile. "Why are so many people filling my quarters? Heera," she added, with a dismissive wave, "you may leave."

"Your quarters? My, you speak as if you are nobility. Such a lofty tone coming from someone so very unimportant." Moti Ma had appeared in front of her, arms crossed. Grief from her daughter's loss had caused the fat deposits to disappear from Moti Ma's cheeks, and now fleshy jowls hung in their place. "No need to send Heera away; it is she I am here for."

There was a time not long ago when Rubina relished being in Moti Ma's good graces. It was Moti Ma who had taken Rubina under her wing and helped her establish her role as a dancing girl. Rubina was thinking of this now, and Moti Ma, as if she was able to read Rubina's thoughts, spoke.

"Sabina was born a week after you were, Rubina, here at the castle. Your mother Khushi and I had great joy raising you girls together until you were young toddlers. Your shade was like tea leaves next to my cream-coloured daughter, because your mother is a Rajput. Together, you filled one another's spaces — where Sabina was light, you were dark, where she was heavy-footed, you were delicate. Then, as you know, Khushi had the great fortune of escaping her gilded bird cage. You and Sabina were both descendants of the great king's seed, but one of you remained trapped in these walls whilst the other was given freedom. Half-sisters with different fates. Both useless to the prince, as he cannot fornicate with you as he does with his other concubines, but nonetheless able to live in his father's harem, forever taunting the prince, for you were the two women he could never have."

Rubina did not know how to react to this information, so she remained still. Moti Ma sat on the bed and the eunuchs scattered like the sparrows in the king's garden, rushing to the open hovel that Rubina had never bothered to cover with a curtain like so many of the other girls did. Rubina had always thought her time in the harem to be temporary. She had believed Raj when he told her that she would find a way out, even though when she lived at Khushi's dance hall, she had wanted a way in. How stupid she had once been, enticed by the mesmerizing jewels lining the inside of a prison.

"I protected you by helping you earn the dancing girl's role, so you would have a titled role to play in court. Do you not remember it was I who helped you secure a dance rehearsal space after your mother died? So that when the prince tired of you, you would not fall ranks in the harem and become no better than a slave girl? And, for Sabina, I prayed she would marry the royal chef and have a well pampered life. It was her turn, after so long, to be free! Like you already had the chance to be! And then you," she pointed a yellow-tinged finger at Rubina, "tried to take Sabina's Daniyal ... After all I did for the memory of my friend Khushi."

"I did not know Khushi *jaan* and you had raised Sabina and me together ..."

"*Chup!*" Moti Ma's voice was thunderous in the dimly lit room. "Do not speak. You wanted Daniyal so badly you were willing to risk your life for a kiss. It is no wonder. You were raised in a brothel after all."

Rubina's eyes flashed. "Is that really so different from a harem?"

"The gall of you, to speak to me in such a disrespectful manner. It is one thing for us concubines to be disposable to the king, who is our godlike figure, who we serve as our master, and an entirely different matter for you to just give yourself openly to the common man. But I suppose I would expect no less from a girl who rented herself out in the dance hall."

"You must know I did no such thing." Rubina's cheeks burned.

"I have selected Daniyal a wife." Moti Ma's voice cut over her words.

"A wife?" Rubina said. She took a step back, hitting the red sandstone wall of her chamber.

"Heera." Moti Ma tested the name on her tongue as if it were a sugared date.

"Yes, Mistress?" Heera's borrowed gown fell in yellow waves as she stood up.

"You will be Daniyal's new wife."

Rubina watched Heera's face. She did not see shock. Instead, first she saw excitement. She would play this expression in her head for years to come.

"Me?!" Heera squawked.

"Yes, you."

"Daniyal cannot accept Heera as his new wife," Rubina said, her mouth moving before her head could stop the words. "She is but a child."

"Daniyal has already agreed," Moti Ma smiled. Her blackened teeth looked like bits of charred wood. "Heera? Pack your things."

"I have but one dress, Moti Ma," Heera said. "All of these fineries belong to my elder sister, Rubina *jaan*. Even the one I am wearing now. Not one is my own."

"But I gifted them to you," Rubina said dumbly. "They are all yours."

"You have no need for secondhand rags, my dear. Come with me, and we will have Sardar send this torn gown back to the owner."

"I am sorry," mouthed Heera to Rubina as Moti Ma led her away. "*Mu'aaf keedjiayy.*"

Forgive me, she said. Rubina turned away to face the candlelight so she would not have to respond that she never, ever would.

Chapter 56

1610

Raj lit one lone candle in Rubina's hovel. He had smuggled in a delicious array of nuts and dried pineapple and spread these on a silver platter he had lifted from the kitchen. Now that Heera had been claimed as Daniyal's soon-to-be wife, the ban forbidding Raj from stealing treats from the kitchen had been lifted. He placed a clay water jug that contained hidden fruit wine between them, on a white muslin cloth covering the flower motif threaded through the rug.

"Please do not say I should not have turned Moti Ma against me," Rubina moaned. She wrapped her hands over her stomach and leaned back against the red sandstone wall opposite her cot. "I made so many mistakes at Amber Fort. If only I had waited to profess my love to Daniyal until after we returned to Agra Fort ... Sabina would have been out of the picture and Moti Ma would not have known of my betrayal. I would have never brought on Bibi Mubarak's punishment forbidding me from meeting with Daniyal."

"Perhaps it was dreaming of your kiss that caused Sabina to overdose. Perhaps without the kiss Daniyal would still be marrying Sabina." Raj took a healthy swig of the jug and passed it to Rubina. "We can spend all night on the perhapses. But should we not spy at all on the wedding tonight? It is one thing you declined to dance, but ..."

Rubina faced Raj and pulled his shoulders towards her. "She is but a child, Raj. A mere girl. I could not bear to watch the festivities."

Raj looked out through the opening to the hovel, ever mindful of spying ears. "He blames himself," Raj declared, once he had established that the channels were clear. "For Sabina's death. He thinks even if she did not know of the kiss, his act caused her death. I think Daniyal is attracted to you far more than he was to Sabina. Daniyal knew in his heart of hearts that Sabina was weak in mind. But I am sure that Daniyal would have still chosen you even if he was haunted by Sabina's ghost for a lifetime had it not been for Bibi Mubarak's conditions. He cannot risk your life, little bird. His hands are tied."

"But why Heera?"

"Why anyone?" Raj shrugged, extending his legs. The pattern of golden birds on his pants was now smoothed out, and Rubina studied them: some of the birds were nuzzling, a few were beak to beak, others poised away from one another, scavenging for seeds. Such beautiful, carefree artwork in a world where Rubina had no control over her immediate environment. "Heera is like Sabina; her mind is yet undeveloped. Daniyal does not want to worry about falling for a woman who has her own mind. Like you. You are fire. He does not want fire. He wants to think with his mind now, not with his heart. But more likely, Moti Ma has made it so he has no choice."

"I do not want to live anymore," she seethed, tracing her finger over the lip of the jug, wishing it were the same poison that had killed her mother. "I cannot bear to live in this harem any longer."

"Rubina," Raj's voice was gentle, smooth as the clarified ghee that Daniyal made in his kitchen. "Fates change in an instant in this kingdom. You cannot throw everything away before knowing what tomorrow will bring."

"I ... cannot ... stand ... to ... see ... them ... together."

"I snuck a peak at her, and she looks horrendous. Even tailored to fit, the gown she is wearing is an oversized sack on her. The wedding crown of small pearls on her head is too large and keeps slipping into her eyes. And the henna and turmeric painted on her body look like a child designed it. In any case, you will not see her after today. She will be living in the apartments by the Yamuna River."

"I do not understand how the prince allowed Daniyal to take Heera. She was his concubine."

"Many things you will never understand. But the prince himself is smitten with Arjumand Banu. Until he is permitted to wed this gorgeous creature, he is refusing to be wed to another, let alone play with his concubines. Heera is, as you said, but a child. Perhaps he does not want Arjumand to find out about her. In any case, he was very willing to part with Heera when Moti Ma suggested Heera wed Daniyal. Prince Khurram sees the pain Moti Ma is in after the loss of Sabina, and it is obvious Moti Ma wants Heera to replace her own daughter."

Rubina's hands tightened around her own neck. "I will have to see Daniyal if I stay here, Raj," she moaned. "I love him, Raj. If only I had played my cards right. If only I had not pursued him so relentlessly, then, he might have been mine now ..."

"The what ifs will kill you, my dear." Raj raked his fingers through the wedding appetizer to search for jewellery. Gold rings were apparently laced throughout the mixture of nuts and sweets for the amusement of the emperor's subjects. "You could not have known that Sabina would die. Some say she was with child. Do you believe it?"

"I do not know what to believe anymore, Raj," she said, sinking into his lap and letting hot tears fall onto the golden birds embroidered upon his trousers. She lifted herself up and spoke truthfully. "I know only that I have lost the will to live."

"Then, my dear," said Raj, fishing out a gold ring hidden in the wedding sweet and savoury blend. He dusted off roasted almonds and candied fennels and admired the piece. "We simply must renew your motivation."

Chapter 57

1611 to 1626

While Prince Khurram, son of the current king, Jahangir, was still trying to make Arjumand Banu his wife, in 1611, his father went ahead and took for himself a new wife, Mehrunissa. Mehrunissa, as it so happened, was also Arjumand Banu's aunt. Although she was older than the usual marrying age of women in the kingdom and even married previously with a child, Mehrunissa commanded a beauty and grace unrivalled in the kingdom. King Jahangir gifted his bride the name Nur Jahan, which translates directly to "Light of the World." When the wedding shook the castle with endless festivities so ornate that the king wore a new vest of jewels every day of the week, Rubina was yet unaware the role Nur Jahan would come to play in her life. Rubina only did as she was obliged to do: perform in the wedding festivities when need be and occasionally, in the private quarters for the king and his new bride. She avoided the royal kitchens as if there was a plague outbreak in the corridor leading to them.

In 1612, Prince Khurram finally took Arjumand Banu as his wife. For a month, once more the castle was lit with celebrations that took up much of Rubina's time. It was hard for Rubina to remember the prince as the spoiled boy who had broken into Khushi's brothel years ago, seducing so many concubines, given how thoroughly enchanted with Arjumand Banu he now was. Jewels mined from the depths of deep quarries were exchanged between the bride and groom, who set up their marital home in Agra.

Hearing of their new home, Rubina missed the thrill of living in the centre of the city. She remembered Agra as a city filled with members hailing from many tribes: Afghan, Uzbek, Turkish, Persian. Even the odd European would rest at one of the capital's eight hundred *hammams*. Rubina did not know if Khushi's home for young girls — or as it was known to many others, the *nashaghar*, the drug house — still existed, but dancing as often as she did, she thought of that home less often than she did of the one she dwelled in now.

More and more, Nur Jahan was appearing at the *jharokha-e-darshan*, or Balcony of Appearance alongside the king, taking over his duties over the kingdom. Rubina imagined her clear view of the wealthy apartments alongside the Yamuna River would be that of cooling fountains and fragranced gardens, in one of which Heera was sure to be residing with Daniyal. When Arjumand Banu, who now Prince Khurram lovingly called Mumtaz, birthed her first child, Rubina was the one asked to dance for a women-only party in the harem. Ironically, it was the emulating of the dance she had witnessed the Persians perform in Bibi Mubarak's open-air night den that made Rubina truly famous in the kingdom. The fluid figure eights she made with her hips, the circular motions she created when she contorted her torso, her body isolations, all mesmerized the kingdom. Nur Jahan was dazzled when Rubina shook only her chest in shimmies or made her body shiver with vibrations, her exposed belly rolling like valleys and hills. Incense smoke always filled the halls she danced in, smelling of aloeweed, ambergris, and sandalwood. Rubina enjoyed catching glimpses of the fat white baby nestled in a bassinette made entirely of gold, rocked by the nursemaid.

When news broke out in the harem that King Jahangir's estranged son (and brother to Prince Khurram), Khusrau, was rising up once more against him, Nur Jahan and the king ruled that Prince Khurram and his now pregnant wife would have to leave Agra and stage an uprising against Khusrau. Rubina watched as Mumtaz left without hesitation to be next to her husband. If Rubina had been Daniyal's, she would have done the same. Rubina tried hard to push thoughts of him out of her mind and focused instead on new dance movements. The more pain she felt over Daniyal, the more intricate her footwork and steps became, and requests began coming in fast via messenger boys for her to perform in the main court. Whenever Rubina heard that Heera would be visiting Moti Ma in the harem, Rubina would drink with Raj late into the night in her private quarters, which by now had been moved to a larger space that was nearly the size of an apartment, separate from the conjoined harem. The two stayed there until they had news from Sardar that Heera had safely departed for her Yamuna apartments.

Now that Prince Khurram and his wife had been sent on a mission, Rubina found herself spending increasing time with Nur Jahan. The empress summoned Rubina often. In the intimacy of Nur Jahan's perfumed rooms, she heard of the triumph of Prince Khurram's campaign against his rebellious brother, of the children that Mumtaz seemed continuously blessed with, of even the loss of one of Mumtaz's beloved children to smallpox. Almost as soon as Mumtaz and Prince Khurram finally came back to live in Agra and were bestowed with jewels and regaled with feasts that raged day and night (at which Rubina performed extensively), Prince Khurram's stepmother, Nur Jahan, sent him off once again upon a new campaign. On this journey, Nur Jahan confessed directly to Rubina, Prince Khurram had undoubtedly murdered his own brother to secure his position for the throne, when he was only sent away to stop the mutiny.

Much of what the royals did eluded Rubina. As lavish as they were in their decadence, such as retiring amongst the gorgeous pink rose and bluebell cluttered hills of Kashmir, they were sturdy too, giving birth and riding out with day-old infants bundled upon elephants. Thus, when Nur Jahan told Rubina offhandedly that Prince Khurram and his wife were plotting to take the throne from his father, her husband King Jahangir, Rubina was not surprised. As she danced for King Jahangir, who lay sloppily against his divan, having just smoked opium, Rubina watched as Nur Jahan intricately plotted battle moves against the king's once beloved son, using a glass table and chess pieces in her quarters. Nur Jahan officially exiled Prince Khurram and Mumtaz from the kingdom in 1625. She demanded that two of the prince's sons, Aurangzeb and Dara Shikoh, be sent to live at the castle as the price of peace. It was a bold move, for Mumtaz had, by now, already lost three of her ten children.

By this time, through word of Raj, Rubina discovered that Heera had grown up to be a gentlewoman. Because of her malnutrition as a child, however, her body did not develop curves. She no longer wore her hair down. Rather, Heera coiled it high on top of her head and then pinned diamonds into it, so her bun looked like a jewelled snake. Heera's wealth and status had risen with her marriage, but she had not forgotten Rubina. Raj had said that Heera longed to see Rubina. On her next trip to visit Moti Ma at the harem, Heera had sent word that she was interested in meeting with Rubina. Rubina had also heard that the girl was still childless. It was undetermined if this was her own folly or the result of a marriage that lacked intimacies. Therefore, when Nur Jahan asked Rubina if she would like to join the Mughal camp to visit Kabul, she hurriedly agreed, just to avoid meeting Heera. Heera, Rubina was quick to remind Raj, was worse than dead to her, for the dead at least had her respect.

"Do you enjoy your time with me?" Nur Jahan asked Rubina. Nur Jahan never forced Rubina to spend time with her and the choice to do so was always Rubina's. The royal carriage, on its way to Kabul, jostled gently.

This was a far different trip from the one that had taken place sixteen years before, when Rubina had ridden at the back with unimportant, forgotten concubines. Now, as a favoured dancer and the closest of confidantes, Rubina was riding in the very carriage of the empress, the famed tiger huntress. Seeing that Rubina was not interested in increasing her rank by bedding men and that jewelled gifts did little to impress her, Nur Jahan had taken the woman and her odd eunuch into her closest circle.

"Yes, your majesty." Rubina stared at the fast-winding Jhelum River, the watershed coming down from the Kashmir mountains. The camp was passing through here on route to its northwest trip to Kabul.

"I see that you give all the gifts the king and I bestow on you to Raj. The boy has made a crown of flowered jewels to wear upon his head like a garden princess."

"Raj appreciates jewels more than I do, Empress. Besides, he does look rather beautiful in the crown."

"I cannot disagree with you." Nur Jahan sucked tobacco lightly from the pipe the Portuguese merchants had brought her. Raj was now Nur Jahan's pet more than he was her servant. She exhaled green smoke into the carriage. "If not jewels, what makes you giddy, then?"

Rubina shifted her eyes from the moving landscape outside to the empress. Nur Jahan was adjusting the pearly translucent scarf that hung from her crown. Rubina took in the queen's small lips and large eyes. The court paintings of her, influenced by Muslim, Jain, Buddhist, Sikh, and Hindu customs, did not exaggerate the hugeness of the empress's heart shaped face which was unnervingly identical to the old pictures of Hindu goddesses. When, as a girl, Rubina had seen the colourful paintings at festivals throughout Agra, she had thought the goddesses' faces could never exist in real life and that the artistic renderings were disproportionately comical. But everything about Nur Jahan that should have been unreal and disproportionate worked in her favour: her large eyes that popped out, her wide cheeks, her small chin, and her bowed lips. Nur Jahan was the one who brought into fashion the *nurmahali* dress, a sensation amongst new brides who were all rushing to be married in the garment She was a more skilled huntress than her husband. The advisers spoke to her about battles and property and matters of kingdom rather than consult the king. Men risked death by throwing themselves over the walled compounds of the Agra Fort just to catch a glimpse of her. Yet Rubina remained comfortably stoic in her presence. The queen treated her as a true friend.

Rubina pondered Nur Jahan's question. "Perhaps, Empress, for me it is the art of dance that is alluring."

The empress enjoyed the poetic way in which Rubina had spoken and Rubina was rewarded with a sly smile. "For me, it is power. Showing the men that a woman can rule a kingdom and make it like no other."

Rubina swayed back and forth with each step the elephant took along the muddy banks. The rains were beginning. It had not rained this hard since the downpour in Agra the day she discovered Sabina had died. Today, however, she was nestled in a cocoon of dry tiger furs, no doubt hunted by the empress herself. Rubina traced her hand along her arm, just to feel the perfect temperature of her skin, to ensure not a droplet of water touched her.

"Is it a man you pine for?" Nur Jahan continued, taking another puff. "The way you dance speaks of heartbreak, Rubina *jaan*. A man is such a useless creature to love. One will always find disappointment there. One must marry for power, never love." Nur Jahan's fair fingers were each encrusted with emerald jewels, to match the green lining that rimmed her pristine white lace multilayered gown.

A rainbowed sheathe of smoke filled the carriage. "I can make him yours, if it is a man you want. Pay no mind if he is married or widowed. Or even a man that likes other men. I can make him yours."

Rubina leaned back and her black curls splayed out against the fur-lined carriage. "I do not wish to force him as you do not force me to spend time with you. Furthermore, another member of royalty has placed a curse upon my destiny."

Nur Jahan was amused, and it was clear she wanted more information. The elephant stopped rocking, and Nur Jahan took the time to reposition her scarf upon her face, the scarf casting an opaque shadow on her face. "The camp has been set for us in advance. I want to know the whole truth. Do not forget I am the queen. I can undo any curse that has been put upon you."

Rubina considered this. Perhaps this was the time to try and undo the years that had been stolen from her. Who was Bibi Mubarak next to Nur Jahan? Never before had she been so close to the queen as she was in this moment, for today she was the queen's most trusted female friend. If Nur Jahan wanted to fix this, who was Rubina to stand in her way? Rubina swallowed. "Your majesty, I would be eternally grateful to you. But you must assure me that even if you do undo the curse, the will of my beloved to be with me has to be his alone."

Nur Jahan's reply was truncated by a battle horn. When Rubina looked out of the carriage, she saw the unimaginable. What appeared to be thousands of Rajput soldiers were standing along the hill, looking like fallen gods from the sky.

"Mahabat Khan," whispered Nur Jahan. Once a favoured general who had helped quell many rebellions against the empire, the empress had grown weary and doubtful of Mahabat's loyalty. There was a time that Mahabat Khan was trusted above all else. But Mahabat Khan was allying with the enemy now. And the enemy, undoubtedly, was the current king's most beloved son, Prince

Khurram. Prince Khurram, whom Rubina had remembered as a young man with a squeaky voice, had consolidated his power and was trying to take his father's crown. He was no longer the young boy seeking out women to bed in brothels like he had the first time Rubina had seen him. He was now dedicated to his wife, Arjumand Banu, and together they were determined to rule the empire, even if it meant destroying his own father.

Nur Jahan signalled for her personal eunuch. Raj hopped smartly from a nearby howdah and came at once to the empress's side, strutting over like one of the king's fine Arabian horses.

"Raj, send word that Mahabat retreat away from us. He is not to approach us. He may send down a messenger if he would like. But he must depart. I am not fooled by his bluff. One minute he grovels to me, the next he sides with Prince Khurram," she closed her eyes in annoyance. "I have more respect for the snakes in the jungle. At least they have made clear who their enemy is."

"Yes, your majesty." Raj, ever adorned in beautiful robes, relished his new role within the kingdom. He swished his cape around and walked along the muddy paths, his golden slippers wholly unsuitable for the rains.

Nur Jahan addressed Rubina, "Mahabat Khan has spent so much time combatting the opposition, I am convinced Prince Khurram has made the deal sweet enough for him to consider switching sides."

"Then are you not afraid, your majesty," Rubina ventured, "that Mahabat is planning something?" Only a few howdahs behind her, she presumed, Daniyal would be housed with his royal cooking staff. This was the closest she had been to him in years. The palms of her hands prickled at this thought.

"No," she said firmly. "I know Mahabat Khan. He is spineless. He will send down his complacent son-in-law as a sign of goodwill. He underestimates me. I will have that young chap arrested and flogged, and his wedding gifts stripped from him." She leaned forward and traced Rubina's jaw delicately, almost an erotic gesture of an intimate lover. "Mahabat will see I do not play games. He is trying to get close to us because he fears he has made the wrong choice in allying with Prince Khurram, who is weak and ill-trained to rule a kingdom. As always, he is trying to play both sides at once. Mahabat Khan wants to be an important man. If he helps Prince Khurram defeat us, he feels he will rise to be a remembered figure in history. If we work with him and allow him to rise in our empire, he will come to our side. He is like a child running from one side of the hill to another, trying to determine which side is sunnier. What a pathetic fool. I would never trust him again. I plan to erase him entirely. Only then can Mahabat stop torturing himself. But in due time, when he is least expecting it." She curled her lips in a small smile. "I do hope you were a better chess player than Mahabat is when it came to trying to capture your own love, dearest Rubina. If you were not, I do not sympathize with you."

"I have much yet to learn about life, my queen," admitted Rubina, as Raj returned to show that Nur Jahan's message had been effectively sent. The empress smiled warmly at him, her perfume reminding Rubina of pistachio almond pudding.

"We have arrived at camp, Raj," the empress drawled. "Forget about Mahabat Khan. Bring us fine wine and let us prepare for an evening of festivities. Mahabat Khan will have to go back to his tribe with his tail between his legs. If Prince Khurram and his Mumtaz hear that Mahabat Khan is trying to work with us by sending his own son-in-law as collateral, which I am absolutely certain will be his next move, I dare say they will not accept the poor fellow or his show of Rajput warriors back in their company."

"Mahabat Khan, as usual, tries to play two instruments at the same time," Raj interjected.

"Exactly! This is just what I was saying to Rubina *jaan*. Did you see how the Rajputs were lined up in a long row? If there were many, we would see a small row, for the Rajputs would be standing behind one another in a grove as thick as forest trees, ready to fight. He pretends, as he always does. Raj, go ahead and tell the others to go over the bridge so that they may set up camp for the day ahead. Does Mahabat Khan think he will dissuade me from sending our great army to the camp across the bridge?" She let out a tinny laugh. "Ha!"

Raj, looking as proud as one of the sapphire breasted peacocks that strutted along the outskirts of the harem, its enchanting feathers spanned out to showcase emerald, indigo, and turquoise eyelets, ran to complete his mission. Rubina settled back into the soft carriage, feeling secure. As always, her majesty was one step ahead. She had no need to fear. She lingered for a moment in the dry nest of the howdah, her fingers running through the hairs of the tiger furs, before finally following the empress to the nobility tents.

Chapter 58

1626

After Rubina had oiled her hair with rose extract and gone over what she would say to Nur Jahan about Daniyal the next time she spoke to her, she heard the unmistakable sound of fire licks. She straightened her arched back which had been bent, rehearsing a new pose. The crackling and deafeningly loud sound snapped fear into her. At other shows, Rubina had trained younger dancers to accompany her, but today, she was alone on this expedition. Rubina rushed out of the tent to follow the sound, only to find the bridge was on fire.

"Empress!" she yelled. On the other end of the bridge, she could make out the Rajput warriors standing, unmoving, like life-size statues.

Nur Jahan had grossly underestimated Mahabat Khan. There were thousands of glassy-eyed men staring back at her. The empress and the members of her camp were trapped. The bridge that they were to cross to meet the camp that had been set up for them was destroyed.

Rubina looked around. Nearly all the empress's warriors and slave men had made it to the other side of the bridge to set up camp, as Nur Jahan had ordered. The remaining camp, made up of the favoured nobles, royalty, and those who waited upon the first two groups, were now at the Rajput warriors' mercy. The blaze of the fire was so strong, plumes of black smoke were already cloaking the sky, darker than night. Though the rains were heavy, the bridge had been sheltered by a grove of trees and as a result the protected wood had burned as quickly as a funeral pyre ignited by the fury of oil. A man's voice cut through the smoke, chanting loudly in a sing-song voice, reminding Rubina of one of Heera's childish nursery rhymes: "King Jahangir, King Jahangir show yourself now! You big silly cow!"

"Rubina!" Raj was suddenly at her side, his blue turban slipping to one side of his head. His face, even after many years, had remained smooth, only a few wrinkles showing themselves under his eyes. "We are going to die!"

"Raj, get a hold of yourself! Where is the queen?"

"I do not know. The voice you hear is of Mahabat Khan! He is personally taking the king prisoner. Hide, Rubina. Save yourself!"

"I cannot! What of my love?"

"Who?"

"You know who I mean!"

Raj's face contorted. "Daniyal? You still think of him after all these years?" The charred smell of smoke was rapidly filling the air with the unmistakable scent of singed animal hair. "Rubina, the Rajput warriors have all been fed opium, as have their horses so they will battle us without fear! Forget Daniyal *bhayya*; he can look after himself."

Raj had taken her arm and the two began running towards the wooded area. Startled, they watched Mahabat Khan triumphantly push the captured King Jahangir into a dressed royal carriage, like a stolen bride. The carriage, finely decorated in pom poms and gold threading, looked like it was ready to lead a wedding procession. The two watched on as Jahangir's attendees, standing next to the carriage, were executed soundlessly. They fell to the floor like bags of rice. Two Rajputs, brass armlets shining upon muscular arms, took their place.

"I cannot watch this," Rubina whispered, as the Rajputs stepped smartly over the men. To her left, she spotted the glorious empress standing still, her white gown starkly obvious against the dark backdrop, a snow leopard amongst brown tree trunks. Although she was conspicuous, Mahabat's men had overlooked her in their eagerness to capture the king.

"Rubina, Raj, you must come with me," she commanded.

Trembling, the two rushed ahead. "Mahabat it seems," Nur Jahan said coldly, pulling the two closer to the trees in the wooded area, "has finally chosen a clear side. He has declared war on us as has our great king's son Khurram, his wife, and Arjumand. Mahabat Khan has outsmarted me. All this time I saw him as a weak man with no backbone and no ability to pick one side. I must reach Mahabat Khan! Perhaps I can still plead with him! He wants to rule alongside my niece and the king's son. Does he not realize what a foolish decision that is? The people support the rule of King Jahangir! They will not back the foolish action of a son overthrowing his father! Such utter disrespect for a father! For our king!"

"But your majesty," Raj said, cutting through Nur Jahan's emotion, "the bridge has been burned down!"

Away from the shelter of the tent, the rains were directly hitting the three. Raj's slippers were now caked completely in mud. Rose oil dripped from Rubina's braids and stained her petal pink gown. Their delicate clothes were soaked through, but they were not ashamed in their exposed state. The Jhelum River was raging with the extra flow of water. The centre of the bridge, covered by a canopy of trees, had completely fallen through, the fire proving stronger than the surrounding downpour. The fire, now hitting patches of water-soaked wood, seemed to have stopped burning across and burned high instead, towards the sky; the outer edges of the bridge held intact.

Nur Jahan did not pay mind to the whining Raj, nor to the rules of purdah, which forbade her to engage directly with the few members of the imperial army who had been left to guard her camp. She approached them now, boldly. The bodyguards begged her to wait for a male adviser to take the place of King Jahangir so that the men could await their next command.

"Ha!" she snorted. "Who do you think issues your commands in the first place? It is I who advises the advisers. You will follow my directions. I command you!" She hoisted her wet gown up and lifted herself bareback upon an elephant, preparing to cross the river. "If you care at all to save the kingdom, then you will follow me through the river to retrieve our great king! We do not need a bridge to cross. We will cross the river!" she barked at the imperial army.

Nur Jahan lowered a hand down towards Rubina. Raj assisted Rubina so that she could jump up behind the empress. And then Raj begged to stay back and wait.

"Make yourself useful, then," Nur Jahan said to the cowering Raj. "Fetch my newly born granddaughter from her nursemaid and bring her to me. The baby is safest with me. And bring me my bows and arrows."

Raj did as he was told. Nur Jahan hastily organized a battle, telling the army which way to disband once they were in the tributary. The empress wrapped the sheathe of arrows over her chest, and rested the bows that Raj handed her on the upper neck fold of the elephant. Raj ran into one of the nearby tents, emerging with a small bundle. Rubina had only ever seen Raj treasuring jewels, but here he was, carrying a being with more delicacy than she had known him capable of. The empress then took the wailing infant from Raj's shaking arms, holding it close to her while commanding Rubina to hold onto her waist tightly. Raj looked on, his face filled with shock.

"Take care of yourself, Raj," Rubina manage to choke out.

"'Til we meet again, little bird. I will look for Daniyal; do not worry yourself."

The empress and Rubina entered the river, which was tipping

excess water over on either side of the bank. The greenish muddy river appeared impossibly deep but covered the elephant only up to his neck.

Arrows from the enemy soldiers shot past, sinking here and there into the water, plopping and sometimes deftly slicing through solid forms. Rubina clutched onto Nur Jahan and watched as the arrows spitting out of every direction took down camels, imperial and Rajput soldiers, horses, and elephants alike. She looked on as men tumbled over, arrows piercing their necks or abdomens, falling to their instant death, or falling unconscious and drowning. Nur Jahan was not the least rattled. The river was quickly polluted with the metal breasted plates of soldiers and with swirling, rust-coloured blood. Nur Jahan clutched her granddaughter, ever eager to get to her husband, the king. When the baby was nearly sliced with an arrow which hit the elephant instead, she pulled out the offending item with her bare hand and emptied three rounds of arrows into a Rajput, who fell face forward into the river. Rubina found his scream to be far more troublesome than the sight of blood, which was shooting straight out from the side of his neck.

Nur Jahan was steady when she fired rounds, but the elephant stepped on something unstable in the river. It let out a trumpeting, thunderous protest. Rubina found she could not hold on, and she fell, tumbling into the river, her back hitting the water like a slap on the cheek.

For a second, all she could feel was the sensation of clayish water filling her nostrils. She opened her eyes to the bobbing parts of dead men: hands that would never hold another glass floated by; feet that would never march again sailed past. Miraculously, her body hit the bank of the river. She clutched the river's edge, lifting her head and gasping for air. Through blurred eyes, she saw the queen and baby being pulled off their elephant by four Rajput soldiers. The empress had been captured.

Though Rubina was vulnerable and in the open, the enemies were so busy capturing the imperial army they were uninterested in her damp body shivering against the muddy bank. How could she survive on her own in these parts? She felt weak and her fingers were tired. She looked at her body. How had another man's blood soaked through her clothing, in a pattern that spread out like a web? She examined herself closer. Something had got stuck on her dress. An arrow. Perhaps she had bumped into a dead body in the river. Her mind felt frozen, and she was trying to wake it up, make it solve a puzzle she was too tired to engage in. The rain softened the sandy earth that she was clutching, and once more she fell into the raging river.

"Rubina!"

The sound of her name was muffled as her ears filled with water. Silt filtered through her nasal cavity and her eyes opened once more in the grey water. She could make out loose dirt dancing in the river. She sank, slowly. Sand, shaken from the bottom, was rising. The particles were beautiful, each grain moving to its own melody. Like tiny dancers. Like her. Abruptly, she was pulled to the surface, gasping, the air cool on her damp cheeks.

"Rubina, are you okay?"

Daniyal.

"You came for me." She saw he had tears in his eyes. When she touched his face with her fingers, she left blood in their place. "We can be together yet. Our banishment can end, my beloved. Nur Jahan will end it. That is, if you want me to be yours."

"Do you not know you have been shot? An arrow has hit your chest. I saw you fall from Nur Jahan's elephant into the river."

"I did not feel it." She did not bother to tell him that the pain there had been constant for her.

"It is here." He touched her chest, and suddenly she felt searing pain.

"This is what I waited for my whole life," she moaned softly, as he struggled to keep her body from sinking back in the water. The land under his knees where he was crouching was growing softer. Bloated animal corpses floated by. The menacing smile of a camel. A donkey burdened with goods, tipped to one side, its belly round and covered with tiny hairs.

"I have always loved you," she said, the words coming through simply.

"Please, you are draining your energy talking."

"Did you love me? Or did you sacrifice me because you had no choice?"

His face was so close to hers she could make out where the brown and green parts of his eyes interlaced with one another. She traced his brow, unchanged but for a silver hair laced through his left brow.

"I loved you," he spoke finally, raindrops skittering down his nose and falling from his chin into the river. "But I am a loyal man. Yes, I felt for you more strongly. Your kiss was unlike any I have ever experienced, but I knew that Sabina would never have survived losing me. She was not strong like you, you who were made for the streets of Agra. When Bibi Mubarak suggested you sacrifice ever seeing me again for your life, it seemed a wise decision. It gave me no room to question who I was supposed to be with. Your life was just not worth sacrificing."

"That is where you were wrong. I needed you just as much."

"Perhaps I was wrong, because it pained me even more when I saw you never took a lover. For all your beauty," he clutched her oily black hair, spilling like ink in the water. "You stayed alone."

"I have been living like a ghost, Daniyal. Thinking of only you."

"I, in turn, have only thought of you. My relationship with Heera is only for show. She was but a child when I took her."

"But she is a child no more."

"Heera will always be a young girl in my eyes. We sleep in separate rooms. She needed a father more than a husband. In many ways, I gave her that."

Rubina's eyes were feeling heavy, "Tell me you love me again, Daniyal."

"I always did." His eyes were wet with unshed tears. "From the moment you and your stupid friend rushed into my royal kitchen," his voice was thick in her ears, "creating such a disturbance. No matter how hard I tried to push you away, you remained imprinted in my mind. My favourite pasttime was watching you dance. Even Heera knew this about me."

"I want time with you, Daniyal. To make you mine now."

"I will make you something in death then," he said softly, as her body began to go limp, life flowing away from her and into the current. "A monument in the Agra Fort so no one will forget you … so that everyone will remember you were my only true love. We could not be together in life. But we will be together in eternity."

He wasn't sure she had heard. Her eyes were closed now, her body completely placid. He released her body into the waters. She rose to the surface, like a fallen log. The river, only recently green and gritty, was now made up of a thousand different shades of red, changed by the blood of fallen men and dead animals.

Chapter 59

2017

Red letters. Beautifully scripted. Seva Ashram, they announced, under which was written: Eternal Promise of Forgiveness and Salvation. Located in a jungle and purposefully covered in jigsaw-shaped leaves in the brilliant hues of pickle, mint, chartreuse, amazon, and parakeet, it was tucked away like an Elven village in a fantasy novel. Ruby had never known there to be so many shades of one colour, and her eyes greedily lapped in the sight. The ashram's website, accessed via her phone, offered a meditative retreat focused on healing through well-being. This, it said, was achieved by practising traditional Indian lifestyle methods and infusing them with Western luxuries. A mouthful. Ruby didn't know what this meant, but she thought Belle might relate. It was almost a shame Belle had not come here with John, given her love of Starbucks soy vanilla lattes and brandname yoga apparel.

When Ruby had chosen how to pay for the ashram on the website (easy to spot icons featuring Visa, Mastercard, PayPal, and American Express), a good looking man with a light brown beard and long hair stared at her from her phone screen with an understanding look. He was dressed in loose Indian robes and his smile, stopping just short of his eyes, transformed into a piercing gaze. She found herself nodding back at him. The yogi's ethnicity was indiscernible, but he oozed the charisma of a politician or cult leader, a priest or a hippie, a man capable of leading many people in the volatile upheavals of any era, political or spiritual.

Other pages on the website featured lovely tables dressed in purple orchids, views of a jade ocean, dishes of salted delicacies, and neon orange juices. This, Ruby gathered, must be the Western luxury part. She scanned through the testimonials. One caught her eye. "Seva Ashram's impromptu social events connect lone travellers on a common quest for a harmonious life. The ashram allows you to reinvent yourself the moment you walk through the doors." The words were both convoluted and magical. She was sold.

The ashram had a man fetch her from the airport. Ruby felt content in her very green belted dress, the colour of a cut ripe avocado, which matched the jungle. She sank back into the van, fiddling with the small buttons running up the front of her vintage dress. It had been a long journey, and she had achieved that blissful level of fatigue only reached by journeying many miles. She had booked the first flight to India she could find after leaving Belle in the parking lot. She had travelled with the boxy 1950s trunk she had originally left home with, afraid that if she were to go home to pack properly, she'd change her mind — her car was now parked economically at a parkade close to the airport.

The van driver gently touched her arm. She gathered her trunk and stepped out at the ashram, taking in the multilayered leafy trees and smooth, mushroom-coloured stones leading to what appeared to be a simple bamboo hut in the jungle. She could smell the salty sea and the mossy promise of soon-to-come rain. Hear the faint chimes of church bells from a Portuguese-Goan cathedral.

When Ruby passed through the bamboo-framed doorway, she spotted a lady sitting at a modern reception desk with a paper-thin laptop. A modest water display sat in the centre of the lobby, along with many pots of purple orchids. Surreal web pages come to life.

"Welcome," said the woman, standing up and reaching over the desk to give Ruby a hug. "I'm Shanti." She had Nordic features and hair so blonde it looked like butter.

"Ruby An ..."

"To us, now you will be known as Asha." The woman dipped her finger into a bowl of rose water and turmeric and ran her finger through a self-made part in Ruby's hair. She pasted a small red *bindi* between Ruby's eyebrows. "What have you come here looking for, Asha?"

"John," said Ruby plainly.

"It is important to set one's intention before entering the ashram. If it is John you seek, it is John you will find."

"It really is John. I heard he's staying here. Perhaps you can direct me to his room?"

"If this man you speak of came into this ashram known as John, today he is someone new. Here, your past is forgotten. Today, you get to be a new person. Embrace this lucky day! Asha, your name means hope and desire. I'll take you to your room myself."

Ruby, finding herself too tired to argue with this logic and feeling that it was good to shed Trevor's surname, allowed Shanti to take her arm. They walked straight from the lobby into the outdoors. Behind the basic reception hut lay a complex village designed to be camouflaged by the jungle. The rooms were individual apartments each with private access to an artificial lake. Fat orange and silvery white koi skimmed the blackish green surface, following Shanti and Ruby's tour around the pebbled outskirts, chasing them like puppies. In the distance, there was a wooden gazebo large enough to be a restaurant, sitting over a cliff.

"We have our events there," she said pointing in the direction of the gazebo. "And dining is available there in the day. But many prefer to take meals in their own room."

The gold sun had created yellow pearls that sparkled upon the distant ocean's surface, visible just beyond the cliff. "We have a social coming up you might want to attend. If you are up to meeting others, that is. There," she pointed to a bank of grass overlooking the ocean, "is where we will be practising yoga at sunrise and sunset." She peered at her watch. "If the rains hold up. Leaves you a couple hours to get ready for sunset yoga. But I imagine you need rest? If you require spa services, ring me up front. Or likewise, a Goan delicacy. Asha, do you speak Konkani?"

Ruby shook her head no.

"I've learned a few phrases myself," Shanti offered. "*Mau zo gao* Norway.*"

"I'm from Canada," said Ruby, immediately able to translate. She hadn't meant to sound flat, but she couldn't conjure up any more enthusiasm. Shanti rewarded her with a smile all the same.

In unison, the two stepped over a small cobblestone bridge and reached Ruby's room, the door facing the pond, which acted like a courtyard linking all the rooms. Shanti placed the key in Ruby's palm. It felt like a cool coin in her hand. The koi gathered near the edge of the water as if waiting for Ruby to say hello.

"I hope you find what you are looking for, Asha," Shanti said.

Chapter 60

2017

"The receptionist's name is not Shanti, it's Ulla," Dani said in her snarky Irish accent. "She's fecking the guru and has boughten a little too deeply into what this place is selling."

The other students were rolling up their yoga mats and putting them into wicker baskets, the orange light from the newly risen sun outlining their profiles in crimson. The sky was the colour of rose quartz, threatening to turn blue any second. "She's useless. Who are you looking for again?"

Ruby found Dani's melodic, on the verge of annoyance, Irish accent strangely soothing. She walked with Dani over the trimmed grass, allowing the ground to massage her feet before she slipped her swing-era shoes back on. "This guy John? He has brown hair and dimples. Very fresh-faced." Ruby patted her cheeks. "I tracked him down and apparently he's staying here."

"For now," Dani quipped back, "I'm going to ignore how much you sound like a stalker and tell you nobody here looks like that. The one guy that does is named Mike and he's from Australia. Shanti calls him something else, but the rest of us ignore Shanti's naming rituals. Anyway, I'd like to get to know Mike better, if you know what I mean."

"I didn't think it would be such an impossible task to find someone here."

"So, you going to the social, like?" Ruby liked how Dani ended her sentences with "like." Dani went on, unphased by Ruby's thoughts about the quaintness of an Irish manner of speaking. "The yogi here believes in enjoying luxuries in moderation, so he's letting out the drinks tonight. This place isn't like the other ashrams, you know?"

"This is my first experience."

"This place isn't bad, it's more spa-ish than a full immersion where you would go fully native and do away with modernity. I'm trying to get over my marriage ending after one year."

"Gosh, mine just ended after twenty. This place must be filled with desperate housewives."

"Try rich girls trying to find themselves. I think we might be the only two heartbroken girls in the lot. The theme at tonight's social is the Roaring Twenties which they call the Gatsby party. Wasn't necessarily the best time for India, with the British occupying it, and the English girls all accessorizing their flapper girl outfits with Indian charms. But, hey, do you have something I could borrow then, for the social tonight?"

"Is this because I am Indian? You've already sort of called my people 'natives.' Do you figure I'll have some anklets that jingle in my suitcase?"

Dani smiled patiently. "I'm asking you because you are literally the only person I have spoken to since I arrived here. You're the only person that is wearing like a vintage dress instead of hundred-dollar leggings. Who fecking does yoga dressed like their going for high tea? And what do I call the native people of the native country, then?"

They had entered the gazebo via the sandy trail. It was beautiful to be in a space unencumbered by walls, with a roof to protect you from the elements. A young man served them a bowl of pineapple and mango slices. A light breeze drifted in. Tables were rimmed with black and gold ribbons and with candles placed in rhinestone flower holders. Preparations for the evening, Ruby supposed. She speared a piece of mango and marvelled at its golden ripeness.

"This place is onto something with the early morning workouts. I feel refreshed," Ruby admitted.

"Is anyone watching us?"

"I don't think so." Besides herself and Dani, there were only two other girls who had also taken the sunrise yoga class, eating yogourt and granola at another table. When she looked back at Dani, she saw the ribbon lining the table was gone, as was the crystal decorative piece cradling the candle.

"I'll drop off our headpieces to your room tonight. Hey, don't look at me like that. Everyone steals something to make their costume more 1920s. It's tradition. Say, yours is the room across the bridge, like?"

"Yeah," Ruby said.

On a normal day a couple of weeks ago, it would be evening time in Vancouver. Trevor would take the dinner she made him and eat in his den. The sky, visible from the windows that had no blinds, would be the shade of apricots. Leah might be studying at the dining room table, bordered by two sets of French doors, looking down at the sunken living room as she pored through textbooks. Ruby would be cleaning the grass from Leah's soccer cleats and preparing to watch reality television alone on the couch in the family room, tucked far away from everyone else in the right wing. Leah might pop in and talk to her about Rick. Not to Ruby, rather at Ruby. Ruby would press pause on her PVR and grab some candy tucked in a jar. She had hidden treats around the house from herself and found them in odd places, like forgotten eggs in an Easter hunt. While she was eating them — Twizzlers or Reese or Snickers — she wouldn't feel so alone anymore.

How, then, had she ended up staying in an oceanview room guarded by chunky, speckled fish? How was she under a sky that turned a thousand different colours, performing a new light show every few hours? Sitting across a young, snappy Irish girl who was casually stealing table décor, with whom she had gotten along better in under half a minute than she had with people she'd known for years? Ruby popped another bite. This fresh pineapple tasted so much better than the artificial pineapple candies she kept in the jars.

"I hope you have something that looks remotely 1920s. I have one black cocktail dress, but I have to make it work," Dani was saying.

"Weirdly enough, I do," mused Ruby, remembering all the crazy dresses she had packed when she had left for Williams Lake. "Look, you think there is anywhere else I could find John? You think he'll do the next yoga session?"

"Did you really come all the way to this ashram to hunt down a guy? It seems sort of desperate, like."

"Dani," she sighed. "I have something important to tell him that is time sensitive." It was not beyond Ruby that all she'd done this summer thus far was chase down fathers to tell them they had babies. Apparently, all of them liked yoga sanctuaries. "I'm desperate, but not in the way you think me to be. But with everyone renamed, my hunt seems impossible."

Dani sighed. "The last place I went to stipulated complete silence, so I suppose they can call me what they like so long as I can speak. Aren't you even a bit curious what my Sanskrit name is?"

"Come on, Dani. I need your help."

Dani sealed her lips together in thought. "Well, there is a day hike going on today. Trekking through the jungle. If he's here, he might have left to go on that excursion. But I'm telling ya, no one I met looks like your John mate. No fresh-faced cuties, I'm sure of it."

"Can I still join?"

"The hike? They left at 5 am. Are you fecking kidding me? You'd have gone, like?" Dani intoned, sucking mango juice off a fork. "It's bloody monsoon season. The rains are coming."

"What else am I supposed to do?"

"Get pissed drunk with me."

"Hard pass."

"Suit yourself. I have candies, too. But you seem like a health nut."

"I do?" Ruby held an arm out, shaking it to see how much it jiggled.

"If you buy a bloody detox package, don't come find me later. Our friendship will be over. And it's Khushi, by the way."

"What is?"

"My Sanskrit name. It means happiness."

Ruby left Dani and walked to the far end of the ashram grounds, hitting the edge of the field where a lusty grove of coconut trees led into the jungle. The air here was thick and pungent, but easy to breathe in. Sauntering along the outskirts, she could smell sautéed garlic coming from the ashram kitchen (Dani had promised this was one of the only ashrams that did not restrict garlic or chili). Ruby understood why John had come to Seva; it really had managed to distill the best parts of the east and west to create a unique environment.

Being so far from home, she had thought she would spend her time consumed with thinking of all the people she had loved and left behind in Vancouver. But her mind only had room for immediate sights that were right in front of her. Birds as brightly coloured as Christmas bulbs. Leaves large enough to canopy a small hut. Butterflies the size of her palm. Fallen coconuts instead of the orphaned acorns littering the forest beds of Vancouver.

When hunger struck, she snuck into the gazebo on her own, dining on a mushroom chili fry and Portuguese rice custard. She had never felt so hungry. Or so good about feeding herself sustaining food to her heart's content. As she licked the last of the lemon rinds and vanilla sugar from her spoon, she watched the workers setting up for the Gatsby party coming up in the evening. They stood on stools, weaving coloured lights through the rafters and hanging paper moons. Busy crafting a night of magic.

Maybe she would go tonight after all.

Chapter 61

2017

By the time she made it back to her room, sunset was fast approaching. Red veiny clouds lit up the sky. A light rain had added shine to the rocks on the cobblestone bridge. She was far away from Vancouver's wildfires. The koi were kissing the pond's surface, lips puckering, greeting Ruby when she returned home as if they had been waiting for her. She should have been tired without a nap but she felt alive. Invigorated. A plastic bag hung on her doorknob. Ruby reached in. Inside was a velvety black headpiece. An art deco leafed motif made of rhinestones was attached to its side.

Ruby sighed, fingering the smooth texture of the ribbon as she entered her room, wondering how table settings could be turned into something so beautiful. Setting it down to sparkle under the tableside light, she upended the entire contents of her suitcase onto her bed. The sunset passing through her room made it glow, like a Klimt painting. Everything she had packed to go to Williams Lake was now spread out before her, except for her passport, which Shanti/ Ulla had locked away for safekeeping. Her hand brushed over the satin camisole flapper dress. Drop waisted, gem work decorated the top and fringe was layered on the bottom. Trevor had claimed it looked like a nightie. Almost everything Ruby had packed consisted of things Trevor hated (too bright! too old-timey! too much like a negligee!). She supposed the last years she was with him she had been rebelling against his idea of what she should be, hoarding away things she'd found in costume stores or thrift shops, and somehow, she'd ended up packing all these offensive finds with her to take on her trip. Pinching the thin fabric between her fingers, she draped it over the bedframe.

Stepping into the shower, Ruby washed herself with the mango infused toiletries the ashram attendants had left for her. When she finished showering the sweet, musky smell of the jungle from her skin, she wrapped herself in a towel and stopped to look out of her window at the koi pond, now disturbed by angry rain drops. The winds and rains had come, as Dani had predicted, in heavy sheathes, painting over everything with the spite and wrath of a hundred gods.

Slipping into the 1920s dress, she shimmied a little so the lower fringe could fan out. She put on the beaded pearl choker she had packed to go with it and applied a rich brown lipstick called Antique Talkies. Carefully, using the bathroom mirror, she drew wings onto her eyelids using her eye liner. She placed the headband Dani had made across her forehead and knotting it at the back, slid the stones to the side. She made a face at herself. Something was wrong. Her hair looked heavy. She took the pair of eyebrow scissors she kept in her makeup bag and began cutting. Wavy locks fell into the bathroom sink. She stopped when her hair ended above her shoulders, leaving a blunt cut with wavy, mismatched lengths. A dishevelled bob. Grabbing a towel from the bathroom, she hurriedly wiped the jungle earth off her red buckled shoes. She slipped her key, cash she had obtained at the airport exchange desk, and a tube of lipstick into her vintage white clutch purse and braced herself to face the rains.

The first thing she saw were the tissue-thin moons hanging in the gazebo where she had taken her meal not too long ago. The coloured lights of the strings shone through them: green, blue, pink. With the backdrop of the black sky acting as walls in the open-air space, everything inside looked brighter, more festive. Dani, dressed in a simple cocktail dress with a black and gold headpiece, the sister companion to Ruby's own accessory, toasted Ruby. Once Ruby was under the domed ceiling, the rain wasn't as loud — it hit the rounded wooden roof of the structure, slid over, and calmed a bit. It seemed the people who had craved a vacation with minimal interactions had been teased out of hiding with a promise of alcohol. This lent the gathering the feeling of a real speakeasy: a group of people drinking in an ordinary place that had been transformed into something unusual.

Dani made some quick introductions. Mike. Melissa. Eduardo. Kristina with a K. Nikhil, whom everyone called Nik. Shanti/Ulla was in the corner with the man Ruby assumed must be the guru, as he was the only one dressed in robes. Most of the other men were dressed in linen and assorted colours of khaki pants but had somehow managed to buy straw hats from the local boys or designed ties and suspenders using various stolen materials from the premises. One girl confessed to cutting her summer maxi dress at the knees. Another had painted the masseuse gloves she'd lifted from the spa with nail paint. Feathers from colourful birds found on the lawn were tucked into hats or used as ornamental headpieces. Drinks, served in gorgeous, ridiculously shaped glasses, added to the whimsical ambience.

Dani tapped Ruby. "Your mystery man isn't here. I told you."

"Mike does look a bit like John," Ruby admitted, sipping something very red from a long, tube-shaped glass that looked like it belonged in a science lab. The rains mixed in seamlessly with the sound of jazz, like an instrument you didn't know was missing until you heard it. "No dimples, though. Could be John otherwise."

"Except that he isn't," Dani stated. "I told you, no other bloke has brown hair and an angelic face."

"Plain face."

"Okay, plain face, like," Dani conceded in her Irish lilt. "Try to have fun, Ruby. It isn't like every day we find ourselves in the middle of a Goan jungle that has somehow managed to transport us back in time to the twenties. Find out how people stole things and made them into twenties items. It's quite a conversation starter."

Ruby gave her a "fine, I will" smile and again sipped her fancy elixir. Jazz standards came and went. The guests toasted life, death, nothing, and everything. More drinks were served — tangerine, dubonnet, canary yellow. Thoughts were beginning to get clearer rather than fuzzier. She stared at the moonlight quivering on the ocean, showing that the body of water was indeed a moving thing, alive and shivering next to the dark jungle.

Ruby wandered toward a man with a brown beard leaning out against the wooden ledge. She set her clutch and drink there, stretching her arms out to catch rain drops. She tried to think of a question to ask him, as Dani had suggested, in an attempt to be social. His elbow touched her. Rattled, she looked up. Up close, his beard was intertwined with rust and copper.

Ruby fingered one of her just-cut locks, feeling where the strands sharpened softly at the tip. She waited for the Americano brown eyes to look at her. When they didn't, she took a deep breath. "Hey there," she said softly, nudging him. "What Sanskrit name did you get when you came in?"

"Jai," he said, still looking out. "It's the first initial of my name, too, so I didn't feel like a total poser using it."

"Quite the beard you have there. Makes you pretty hard to find."

"Eh, I forget about it. But people keep telling me I have one." He stroked his face, turning to her suddenly, registering her last sentence.

"Belle isn't here," Ruby said quickly, when John took her in. "In case you're wondering."

"I'm not. Jesus, Ruby, what are you doing here?"

Background laughter sprinkled the silence between them. Ruby had always thought the sea to be noisy in the day: what with sea bird cries and waves slamming against the shore, but the ocean at night seemed even livelier. The rains were falling harder, and the sea was overflowing against the sand, covering the areas she had walked across earlier. The ocean sound carried, even over the jazz notes.

"Uh, you told me to check this place out?"

He scratched his head, baffled.

"I may or may not have stolen the deposit you put down for Belle's ticket. On account of her being with my husband now."

He crumbled against the railing as if someone had punched him. "Oh! I had doubts that night, but I didn't think she would do that to you. She broke up with me over text message."

"I'm so sorry," it was Ruby's turn to say, "but I have come to realize that with or without Belle's interference, Trevor and I wouldn't have lasted together in any healthy way."

He turned to face the jovial crowd. "Actually, Belle and I were never really a match either. I kinda knew that after I danced in the solarium with you the night of the dinner party. I didn't want to stop dancing to pretend music with my girlfriend's married best friend. How crazy is that? But I'd already invested in tickets to India thinking I could make Belle into who I wanted her to be."

Ruby found herself laughing at the absurdity of what he had said. Her hands went to touch the cropped wavy edges of her hair.

"Your hair looks great," said John. "And the outfit; it's completely you. Is this the flapper dress you said you bought but never wore anywhere?"

"Yes," she said, surprised he remembered. "The truth is I have a remarkable talent for buying impractical costumes from Halloween close-out sales. Before I went on my crazy adventure, I decided to pack every ridiculous thrift store find I had and wear it. Hence," she looked down and pointed, "the red three-buckle shoes that look like I came off a set of Wizard of Oz."

"Actually, it all goes together quite well," he said, waving his hand over her. "Gosh, standing here with you, in this small square of the world, surrounded by jungle, beaches, and the ocean, life feels hopeful, somehow, right?"

"Hopeful?"

"Hopeful that there is still a part of Earth yet uncorrupted by super malls and giant parking lots."

Ruby directed her hand toward Dani and the others, who were doing a mock Charleston dance. She exhaled, relieved to have found him. "It feels incredible that we've been taken right back to the past. To a time where we'd done less to fuck up the world ... environmentally at the least."

"Meh, we idealize the past. Those kids in the Roaring Twenties had no idea what was coming to them in terms of catastrophes."

"Back then it felt like the good was good, the bad was bad. It was easier to know what stood for what."

He tutted. "It's easy to think of the past as binary: the good guys went on to fight Hitler. The bad guys were the Nazis, but it really wasn't that simple."

"I'm beginning to see nothing is."

She had meant specifically the mess of her life, but encouraged, he kept going. "There were people caught in all kinds of crossfires back then, especially after the Second World War. There wasn't a perfectly good and bad, so to speak."

"Aren't you the guy who argued that Schrödinger's cat was dead at my dinner party? That there was no 'in between'?"

"That's a different issue," he said earnestly. "No one talks about the displaced ethnic German peasants whose homes were taken over by Polish occupiers. No one discusses the gulags where many Germans were made to pay for their mistakes, some who committed them, others who were innocent; or the camps in Siberia where real and imagined traitors starved or died; or how about the children who were separated from their parents on all sides ... Nope, we always boil it down to the good guys versus the bad guys."

It was just like John to inject heavy politics into a casual conversation, especially when she had hoped for his full attention on the matter at hand. Wasn't this exactly what Trevor had hated about John from the first moment they met? But as usual, his words woke Ruby up. She found herself being dragged into John's chaotic thinking, and spit out, "You can't possibly be letting Nazi Germany off the hook for allowing Hitler come to power. That's like forgiving America for Trump!"

"Europe was a complicated place back then. I'm saying, rather, that we forget the footnotes, like even the women in the French resistance, fighting to hide Jewish children or helping the allied air pilots escape. But Trump, Jesus, I don't get that at all. Maybe we should have remained nomadic tribes wandering the plains instead of forming countries by battling and pillaging."

Somewhere, in the corner of her mind, she remembered Trevor echoing a similar sentiment when it came to the wildfires in BC — about how the permanency of human settlements had caused so much destruction in its wake. How weird it was that she was hearing these words echoed back to her and reformulated after all she had been through. How different those words sounded to her today, from where she was standing. When Trevor said them, she hadn't understood them. But she wasn't the same person anymore. They sounded completely different coming from a person who enjoyed talking to her rather than at her. "Sad how we have just gone on to more war and destruction," she said, adjusting her flapper headpiece, which was falling into one eye.

He nodded, unfazed by the bewildering emotions she was trying to hide. "Combat has gone from hand to hand to bombing cities from planes. Look, I think we'd have done the same to each other in the past if we'd had those weapons. I guess the 1920s aren't about going back to a simpler time for me, just one with less means to do more horrible things."

"It just *feels* like the past was a simpler time. This music we are hearing now," a jazz trumpet interrupted her sentence just then, "it's so romantic and it makes me forget all our problems. But I guess the *Titanic*, as beautiful as it was, was just a precursor for the awful cruise ships thrashing through our oceans now. I heard of one recently called *Norwegian Bliss* that is the size of three football fields and can carry 6,000 people." She laughed bitterly. "Why do we need such a ridiculous thing? I guess in the past we were already designing our over-indulgent futures. The *Titanic* we remember as poetic. *Norwegian Bliss*? A nightmare."

"The past becomes us. We imagine items in sci-fi shows and then we create them. And we also become the past. We redo movies set in the past with our own idyllic image of days gone by, and whatever trends we have today get mixed in. As if we know the 1930s better than they knew them." His hand brushed her nose. "Hey, there are raindrops on your face. How'd that happen?"

"Gosh, watching the monsoon rains fall upon the ocean is really something else." Her hand went up to touch her nose where he had just done the same, and she felt embarrassed, thinking it was sweat from the humidity rather than the rain. "I dreamt of the sea last night. Usually, I dream of people or events. But last night, I only saw the open waves; I felt sure it was specifically a place that no boat had yet trespassed. I wasn't in human or animal form; I was just a presence looking down on the rippling water. There was no marker of time. It could have been easily today or a thousand years ago."

John was giving her the same full, intense attention as he had at the dinner party. She couldn't believe how easy it was to fall into meaningful conversation with him.

Encouraged, she went on. "This ocean," she said, "it went seemingly endlessly in all directions with an unimaginable depth. And I didn't have a fear of any kind at all. I don't think my vision came from memories. I think it was more an answer to where life vanishes when we die. I have been thinking of death a lot lately. My mom died when my daughter, Leah, was a newborn, and I guess I never dealt with it."

"That's tough."

"Anyway, dreaming about the ocean, I feel like in death we become the waves. And each wave," she continued, registering that John was really listening to her rather than looking at her like Trevor always did, like she was crazy and delusional, "is alive and represents a person. It's hard to articulate, but I imagined my mom's soul becoming absorbed into the water. I've always wondered how we just simply aren't anymore when we die. And I'm not religious, so I never hoped for a heaven or reincarnation. Waves I can buy into. Does that make sense?"

"Yeah." He combed his beard with his fingers, looking out at the ocean. "When we capture the sea in a photo or painting, it is impossible to illustrate the true movement of it. Sometimes, we might even picture it in our minds as something glassy and still. Unless I have just been on a speedboat or surfing, I forget the way the sea shifts. But if you look, really look at the sea, you'll see it's a million squiggly lines of rippling waves that are always moving. Even on the quietist night. If your theory is true, we are sure making a mess of places for our souls to go; polluting the oceans with our cargo ships that supply our endless demands for consumer merchandise, filling the sea with one-use plastic bags, and overfishing every living thing out of there."

"Yeah," Ruby agreed. They both looked out at the rain. "Before we talked tonight, I was thinking the same thing, about how alive the ocean looked. Maybe tsunamis are the souls of the ocean uprising?"

John smirked. "A sea-bellion."

She laughed. And then a comfortable pause. "It's so easy to talk to you."

"As if we are back at your house."

"My house is not mine anymore, John. Gosh, I really should

address how it is I ended up here."

"Ending up in an ashram in Goa dressed like a flapper girl."

"Exactly." She turned to look at the rain to sort her thoughts out. "When I found out about Trevor, I first felt betrayed, but what are my problems compared to the end of the world? You wouldn't know it standing here now, looking at the rain hitting the ocean, but BC is up in flames ... I drove through parts the fire had touched. Made me sort of change my perspective about things a little. We're literally destroying the world we live in."

"BC is on fire?" he said, and before she could confirm he shook his head at her,

"It isn't you destroying the world we live in. It's the corporations and our allegiance to an economic system based on plunder." He gave her a disillusioned smile, and she remembered him at her dinner party, arguing with Trevor over merlot. "How I think of it is this." He separated his hands and made circular motions with them. "There are planes on the top half of the Earth, just flying no matter how many seats are bought, going to destinations. They maintain a rigorous schedule. Then there are cruise ships and large fishing ships on the other side, the bottom of the world, on the sea, doing the same thing, going all the time. In the middle, on land, there are factories puffing out smoke to make Happy Meal toys and other nonsense we don't need."

Ruby raised her finger in the air. "Like the pizza wedge floatie. Where you lie in a pool on an inflatable slice of pizza with all your friends and they join up and you make a pizza pie? Those kinds of silly inventions, there are stores and warehouses in China full of them. Ridiculous items being made that no one needs but you have to have. New 'needs' being manufactured all the time."

"Sure, like the pizza wedge floatie if you like," John agreed, and Ruby couldn't help thinking Trevor would have been irate had she made the same point with him, particularly because she had brought plastic pizza into the conversation. "It's a consumer's world even when we run out of natural air and have to consume bottled air," John continued.

"People are already buying air in China. I saw it in the news."

"And now BC is on fire you say," John said.

"It is. And I just feel like I finally understand the true crisis of it all, and now I can't look away anymore. But despite the fact that the world is burning down, I feel like you of all people deserve to know something."

Chapter 62

2017

For a second, she thought they were in the solarium the night of the dinner party. Maybe because she saw the banner of the black sky behind him as he talked. Or because of the similar way he looked at her and made her feel. But then she realized she was thinking of the dinner party because "Fly Me to the Moon" was playing.

"Hey," he said in a low voice, "care to dance?"

Sinatra's voice was filling every inch of the open-air space, mixing with the monsoon rains and crashing waves. John led Ruby in a basic swing dance, and she followed easily.

"I had this song in my head for days after the dinner party," Ruby admitted.

"It's a good one. I think we both wanted to get off planet Earth that night."

"True."

"There's another good one I like by him: 'I've Got the World on a String.' It's a positive, happy-go-lucky one. About having the whole world in front of you. Kind of the opposite of this song where we want to be flown off the world and into space."

"I prefer this one."

He spun her three times effortlessly. "Hey, I feel like you've had some practice since last time."

"A few songs only, a bit of a crash course — I was thrown right into swing dancing."

The earthy smell of rain mixed with John's sweat, along with the undercurrent of a mango fragrance. She started, suddenly remembering the scent from the night they first met. Did he hoard the lotions from his previous visits to the ashram and use them in daily life? She chuckled. The song ended and John dipped Ruby.

"Hey," he said, "do you want to look at ruins with me? I have plans to fly out tomorrow morning and go to the Agra Fort. You said you always wanted to go."

"You remember me saying that?"

He laughed, leading her off the dance floor and back to the ledge where her purse and drink were sitting. "Ruby, I remember a lot about that night. And all of it concerns you."

"My mom," she fiddled with her headpiece, "used to tell me stories about this dancing girl named Rubina who lived in the Agra Fort during the Mughal Empire's reign. Gosh, I loved those stories."

"So that's why you picked up swing dancing so fast? It's in your blood?"

She blushed. "Doubtful any of what I remember about the dancing girl is true."

"I've heard of her."

"What do you mean?"

"The dancing girl. Her story's in the traveller's guide."

She felt her stomach flip for the second time. "Rubina?"

"Honestly, I don't remember her name. There was a blurb on a dancing girl and how she grew up in a brothel house and against all odds came to be the court's favourite performer. She got trapped by the ruling king's enemies during a war. Hmm," he meandered off, "there might have been a love story that went along with it, but I can't remember more. I'm sure I can look it up in the guidebook again."

They both stared out at the rain, falling so fast it came down in blurry white lines.

"I was named after her," she said finally.

"Ruby ... from Rubina. Makes sense."

"He went back for her, you know," Ruby said softly.

"Who did?"

"Daniyal. The royal chef. The love of Rubina's life. He went back for her and tried to rescue her from the river, but she'd been shot in the chest."

"You seem to know the stories better than the history books," John said.

"That surprises me more than you know."

"Well, apparently, this dancer of yours is one of the only non-royals to have a burial plot statue around the grounds of the Agra Fort. Only lovers used to build such monuments in remembrance for one another, so you must be right about Rubina's great love. Take the Taj Mahal Shah Jahan made for Mumtaz. I guess that's how love was proclaimed in those days. In death, not in life."

"Ah, Prince Khurram and his undying love for Arjumand Banu ..."

"I didn't even know they had other names."

"Those were their real names," she said.

"I'd love for you to share your stories with me. We could check to see if one of the local guides has more info on the dancer. Maybe we could get a walk-through of the dancing girl's quarters in the Agra Fort. I heard that back then the concubines lived with eunuchs."

"Wow, Rubina's actual living quarters!"

"I don't imagine the quarters are more than sectioned-off places divided by stone. You'll have to use your imagination to go back in time. With your mind's eye you'll have to paint in jewelled pillars and silk cushions into the ruins. But it'll still be breathtaking, I'm sure."

"Crazy," said Ruby. A calmness washed over her. She realized

John looked confused. "Sorry, yes, I'll come with you," she rushed on. "There's frankly nowhere else I'd rather go."

She reached over the ledge until the rain hit her fingers. John touched her shoulders and turned her. His lips brushed hers lightly. Simply grazed.

Then, she felt herself pull up to him in a way she had never thought she was capable of doing. She was taking control, and it felt exhilarating. Their lips just meeting turned into a deep kiss. Rum. Salt. A touch of mango from the ashram's soaps and lotions. He stopped to look at her. She touched a finger to his face, and it sank easily into his hidden dimple. It fell in just as she imagined it would, back at her dinner party at the beginning of July.

"I have to tell you something," she forced herself to say. "It's about Belle."

"I don't want to talk about Belle right now."

"I have to tell you, John." She squeezed her eyes shut as if jumping off from the gazebo and into the ocean. "Belle's pregnant with your baby. And it might have Down syndrome."

"Oh," he said, stepping back. There was a pause while he digested the information.

"Are you okay?"

"I work with kids with autism, Ruby. Some have Down syndrome. So, I know better than anyone how resilient and gifted such kids are. In a weird way, I always thought I'd be the best parent for a special needs child."

"I seem to have dumped a lot on you," she said. And when she saw for once he had nothing to add, she went on. "Belle always thought she'd have a child with special needs too," she said quietly. "It was an obsession that came true, but I'm not sure it's something positive for her."

"How is Belle?"

"Not great, to be honest. She isn't sure she wants to keep the baby.

That's why I came, to offer you a chance to talk to her before she decides what she'll do."

John's shoulders tensed. She saw conflict in his face. "Look, I'll call her, and tell her what I told you," he said, his voice determined not to give in to emotion, "but ultimately this is her choice."

Ruby nodded. "I know that I have no say in this, and that I shouldn't make her feel bad for her choice. I might already have made mistakes in that department," she said falteringly. "I don't know how to navigate any of this. I went from being angry at Trevor and Belle's betrayal to shifting my cause to something else entirely." Pausing, she remembered how conflicted she had felt in the parking lot when she had argued with Belle. "I want to take the baby from Trevor and Belle and raise it myself. I feel like I'm only now beginning to see how much love I'm capable of giving and of who I can be. I feel like my life is just starting, and I can't wait to see where it goes. Like I was asleep for many years and only just woke up. How insane is that after everything they did to me?"

John looked at her a long time. He squeezed her shoulders and said, "It's her choice, Ruby. We can support her and love the hell out of the baby if she keeps it. But it's her choice to make. No matter how upset you are, you can't control her decision. We need to be there for her. Whatever she decides."

"But you'll talk to her?"

"Of course."

She thought of deciding to keep Leah. About initially lying to Trevor about Leah. About now agreeing to guard Trevor's secret that Leah was not his biological daughter. Then she remembered Harvey's words in the Squamish bar — people having a way of disappointing you. About how she had a habit of putting her energy into things that she had no control over. And how she wanted to change that, start putting her energy towards progressive things. Slowly, Ruby nodded.

"Let's travel to Agra," he said.

She couldn't speak just yet, so she nodded again. The rain fell like a curtain around her. It was so easy to lose people, she thought. She'd lost her father to Julia. Curtis to fame. Trevor to Belle. Belle to Trevor. Leah to life. Her mother to death.

But when she felt John's hand take hers, she felt like she'd finally found herself.

Epilogue

In British Columbia, wildfires in the summer have become our new normal. In the summer of 2017, we were ordered by the radio to stay indoors or suffer permanent lung damage. The sky turned the colour of chlorophyll, and smoke burned our throats. Capitalism and climate change were not topics that were discussed in great depth; rather, the news focused on the rage of the fires, the velocity, the rescue missions, and the evacuations. This alarmed me.

That summer I decided to write a novel with the forest fires in the background, formulating how one Indo-Canadian woman might process her world burning down, quite literally around her, while dealing with her own personal crisis. Writing about Ruby made me wonder how her life would have been different had she been born more than four hundred years prior. The European medieval era is often a source of great inspiration for writers, but the presentation of the Eastern counterpart is less popular. Sure, many tourists make a pilgrimage to the Taj Mahal, but how many know the history of Shah Jahan and his Mumtaz, of how Shah Jahan pursued his father's crown, or of the decadence of the Indian courts? We do not readily know of the king's wife, Nur Jahan, or her warrior abilities. I became fascinated with the time period of the Mughal Empire in the seventeenth century and wanted readers to enjoy learning a part of India's history. I thus chose to portray a modern Indo-Canadian character that gets pulled into the story of a dancer who moves out of a brothel to live in the royal court amongst a tiger huntress queen who is thirsty for power. I wanted to contrast what the pressing environmental threats would be for one person living in 1610 versus one in 2017.

By plunging into her past, Ruby realizes what life was like for Rubina living through the reign of a monarchy in perilous times. I wanted Ruby to feel shaken up when confronted with the challenge of looking at her culture through a new lens, noting that over the years she has prioritized comfort over adventure and stopped valuing her own identity in the context of her marriage to a white husband. Ruby's goals change over time, and her desire to control Belle's decision highlights the recent global threats to women's right to abortion, but also sheds light on the value, or lack thereof, that people with special needs have in our world. Ruby comes to the transformative realization that she isn't allowed to control Belle's decision. Over time she notes that the one thing we can control as a society – our impact on our natural environment – is not something we take as seriously as we should. I am hopeful that the recurrent threats posed by the wildfires will finally become an urgent call for action.

To elaborate the importance of this, while Ruby's story is fictional, I stayed true to the details surrounding the spread of the fires during the summer of 2017 in BC. I have, however, made up places in the town of Garibaldi which Ruby visits en route to Garibaldi Lake. You will not find a yoga studio or Dev's diner there. While you will still find some buildings, the town has been abandoned due to concerns about a natural lava dam called The Barrier, which could potentially overflow with waters during heavy rainfalls and flood nearby townsites. Garibaldi (also known as Garibaldi Townsite) was thus evacuated in 1980. A town ruined by rains and environmental hazards was appealing to me to use in a book exploring such themes.

Though the characters I write about in the seventeenth century, such as King Jahangir, his wife Nur Jahan, Prince Khurram (Shah Jahan), and his wife Arjumand Banu (Mumtaz) existed in history, Rubina, like Ruby, is fictional. Other fictional characters include Daniyal the royal chef, Raj the eunuch, Sabina the opium addict, the twin eunuchs Sukh and Dukh, Moti Ma, Hira, and Khushi. The only real historical characters in the novel are the royal figures, such as Bibi Mubarak, Man Singh, and Mahabat Khan. I have remained true to historical dates and events. Therefore, the battle that occurs where Mahabat Singh betrays Nur Jahan and King Jahangir did, in fact, happen, as did Nur Jahan's capture by the opposing army. Of course, the surrounding incidences and conversations happening in and during these times are fictional as are the liberties I have taken with character depiction.

Travelling through India and exploring castle ruins, seeing the Agra Fort, visiting museums featuring weapons, art, and history, and talking to the many experts on the Mughul Empire all helped me create this novel. I am especially grateful to the knowledgeable guides of India. Imagining the lives lived within the skeletal ruins allowed me to come up with Rubina's story.

Acknowledgments

I have many people to thank who helped *Ruby Red Skies* be where it is today.

To my dearest friends, Jennifer (Quynh Le Dang) and Leonardo Ngo (In Loving Memory), Maureen Kihika, Anthony Ndirangu, Christine Lai, Jessica Curtis, Dawn Chan, Ajan Khera, Roger Chen, Alex Shaka, Kylee Carreño, Michelle Aguasin-Ustaris, Dr. Lisa Smith, Gleb Krotkiy, Claudia Hernandez, Tasleem Rajwani, Karen Wu, Jen Schaefer, Manav and Emily Bhardwaj, Sari Nobell, Ayla Mellios, Lukasz Wozniak, Giuliana Alayo Casas, Shawn Ayres, Víctor Manuel Monterroso-Miranda, Kat Tuason, Stacey Kumar, Surindra Sugrim, Curran Faris, Allison Flannagan, Maddi Wilson, Jason Starr, David Vosper, Nadine Kelln, Dr. Huamei Han, Dr. Habiba Zaman, Sandra McIntyre, Robin Maggs, Darrel Yurychuk, Linda Kassendy, David McKee, Leanne Sherwood, Paul Toth, Jodie Haraga, Dino A. Poloni, Ryan and Karen West, Deborah MacKenzie, Kevin Rey, Elisha Ramstad, Bec D, Annika Vriend, Dr. Sean Ashley, Tami Storey-Cooper, Calvin Bill, Sothea Puth, Benoit Boyer, Nia Brown, Carla Naar, Samone Kennedy, Nathaniel Roy, Raquel Lahrizi, Inder Singh, Alisa Lvin, Heather Greenlay, and finally, Emily Carpenter, for believing in all the possibilities that would come of this book.

To the Khoja community, which continues to support me in every way they can.

I am thankful for Simon Johnston, a fellow writer and someone I can count on.

To all my friends at Royal City Swing and Rhythm City Productions and the international Lindy hop scene for making me feel welcome and inspire me with ideas for Ruby.

To Halie Scaletta and Carine Carroll at Samba Fusion and all my Samba Fusion ladies: for passion, acceptance, and unity.

Librarians make the world better for both writers and readers, but I am particularly thankful for the ones at Guildford Library, White Rock Library, and Ocean Park Library.

Rishma and Sonali Johal and the Johal family, for our shared Indian dance history and your boundless support.

To Jind Singh, for believing in my writing and giving me the opportunity to share.

The entire Douglas College Department of Anthropology and Sociology and extended family! For always being excited for what comes next and for epic parties.

Dawn Schabler, who will call me as soon she finishes reading my novels.

Noriko Hagiwara, for standing behind my creative decisions.

Ashvinder Lamba, for dropping in from all over the world, whenever.

To Ashiya Khan-Sequira, for books clubs and always keeping in touch.

Candice Montgomery, for long conversations that pick up where they stopped.

Michelle Koebke, for artistic photography that is one of a kind.

Jolene Boyd, the person who I wrote letters to for many years and who always shows up.

Daniela Alexandra Abasi, for pushing me to get my work out there!

Elizabeth Dylke, because soup and "How Bizarre" never gets old.

Rosemary Winks, for being there through the chaos and the calm, and still believing.

Elizaveta Nesgovorova, for long talks (and seaside walks) about literature and writing.

Demi DeBoer, for friendship.

For Vielda Morris, for showing up in every single way.

To Kathryn O'Neill, Jana Wall, Sean Witzke, and Philippa Joy, for home.

To Fazeela Jiwa, my development editor, who has always believed in my projects and never been afraid to tell me exactly what she thinks.

To Amber Heard, my copyeditor, for helping me find the right words.

To Brenda Conroy, my proofreader, for your final touch, patience, and careful eye.

To Tania Craan, for the best cover I could have imagined for this book.

To Jessica Herdman, for text design and for our wonderful back-and-forths on ideas.

To Beverley Rach and the entire crew at Roseway Publishing, for taking a chance on me.

To my family: Aleksandra and Kazimierz Burkowicz, Shirin and Amir Suleman, Mumtaz, Zishan, Shaif, Shabir, and Khalisa Hemraj. Fatim and Ali Hemraj. In loving memory of Rizwan Hemraj and Mohammed Hemraj. All for endless support.

My brother Nishat Sherif, thank you for helping me in every way you can.

To Farah Asaria, my cousin sister, who, even with a twelve-hour time difference, will always be down to read a book synopsis and hear about a new book idea. I appreciate you!

To my parents, Naseem and Zahoor Sherif, who trekked with me through various regions in India, which helped me shape my ideas for this novel.

To my husband Jakub Burkowicz, who is always the first reader of my first completed manuscript and who offers me honest critique, whether I want to hear it or not.

To my children, Anjay, Alek, and Augustyn Burkowicz, who inspire me endlessly.

And, to my readers, many of whom have reached out to me over the years to share their thoughts on my work. I am grateful to have you all still turning the pages.

Lastly, a huge thank you to Parvez Mahmood, retired Group Captain of the Pakistan Air Force. An expert in Mughal Empire history, he has written several articles featured in *The Friday Times* in Pakistan. Mr. Mahmood was kind enough to read the entirety of Rubina's section and help me get things factually correct. From topics such as the Mughul travel procession to the languages used in the time period, Mr. Mahmood was able to continuously able to answer questions and provide information. I was lucky to consult with him and will be forever grateful for his patience, knowledge, and thoroughness.

Research

Books

Kathryn Lasky, *The Royal Diaries: Jahanara, Princess of Princesses* (New York: Scholastic Inc., 2002).

Niccolao Mannuci, *Storia Do Mogor, Vol. 2: Or Mogul India, 1653 1708* (London: Forgotten Books, 2017).

Ruth Ozeki, *For the Time Being* (New York: Viking, 2013).

Diana and Michael Preston, *Taj Mahal: Passion and Genius at the Heart of the Moghul Empire* (New York: Walker, 2007).

Subhadra Sen Gupta, *Varanasi: A Pilgrimage to Light* (New Delhi: Rupsi & Co., 2004).

Indu Sundaresan, *The Taj Mahal Trilogy Series: The Twentieth Wife, The Feast of Roses, and The Shadow Princesses* (New York: Atria Books, 2013).

M.G. Vasanji, *The In-Between World of Vikram Lall* (Toronto: Doubleday Canada, 2003).

Victoria & Albert Museum, *The Indian Heritage: Court Life & Arts under Mughal Rule* (London: The Herbert Press, 1982).

Podcast

Ideas from CBC Radio: "World on Fire: What wildfires tell us about living in the forest and a challenging climate."

Websites

Amer Fort, Jaipur

www.transindiatravels.com/rajasthan/jaipur/amber-fort-jaipur/

Amber Fort

http://www.culturalindia.net/indian-forts/amber-fort.html

BC Wild Fires 2017

https://globalnews.ca/news/3585284/b-c-wildfires-map-2017-current-
location-of-wildfires-around-the-province/

Bharatanatyam: Indian Classical Dance

http://www.indianmirror.com/dance/bharatanatyam.html

Chequered Past

http://www.thehindu.com/features/friday-review/history-and-culture/
Chequered-past/article16888328.ece

Coin of Emperor Jahangir

https://www.ashmolean.org/coin-emperor-jahangir

Courtyards of Amber Fort

https://www.indianetzone.com/69/courtyards_amber_fort.htm

Description of Bharatanatyam

http://rangashree.org/bharatanatyam-description.html

Folk Songs and Dances of Iran

https://folkways.si.edu/folk-songs-and-dances-of-iran/
central-asia-islamica-world/music/album/smithsonian

From Babur to Bahadur Shah Zafar, this is what the Mughals loved eating

https://timesofindia.indiatimes.com/life-style/food-news/from-babur-to-
bahadur-shah-zafar-this-is-what-the-mughals-loved-eating/photos-
tory/75476498.cms

Hall of Mirrors, Sheesh Mahal

https://www.alamy.com/stock-photo-hall-of-mirrors-sheesh-mahal-in-
amber-palace-also-known-as-amber-fort-22953794.html

History of Amber Fort

https://jaipur.org/2016/08/05/history-of-amber-fort/

History and Chronicles: Akbar and Man Singh — The Fight

https://angel1900.wordpress.com/2015/12/28/
akbar-and-man-singh-the-fight/

How is Babur Related to Timur and Genghis Khan?

https://www.quora.com How-is-Babur-related-to-Timur-and-Genghis-Khan

How the Mughals Travelled - II

https://www.thefridaytimes.com/how-the-mughals-travelled-ii/

India. The Mughal Empire. Costume and Fashion History
https://world4.eu/indian-mughal-empire-costumes/
Interactive Maps: Wildfires
https://www.wltribune.com/news/
    interactive-map-paints-b-c-wildfire-picture/
Jaipur's Amber Fort: The Complete Guide
https://www.tripsavvy.com/jaipur-amber-fort-guide-4123752
Kandahar: Historical Geography to 1979
https://iranicaonline.org/articles/kandahar-historical-geography-to-1979
Kohinoor is not the biggest diamond in the world!
http://www.catchnews.com/national-news/kohinoor-is-not-the-biggest-
    diamond-in-the-world-1461237704.html#:~:text=Found%20
    near%20Guntur%2C%20Andhra%20Pradesh,105.602%20
    carats%20(21.12g).
Language Log
http://itre.cis.upenn.edu/~myl/languagelog/archives/005276.html
Learn More About Wildfires
https://www.nationalgeographic.com/environment/natural-disasters/
    wildfires/
Legendary Goddess Shila Devi, Amer Fort Rajasthan
https://navrangindia.blogspot.com/2016/06/legendary-goddess-shila-
    devi-amer-fort.html
Map of India: Raja Man Singh Biography
http://www.mapsofindia.com/who-is-who/history/raja-man-singh.html
Medieval Facts: Lighting, part three: Oil Lamps
http://jillwilliamson.com/2010/05/
    medieval-facts-lighting-part-three-oil-lamps/
Medieval Underwear: Bras, Pants, and Lingerie in the Middle Ages
https://www.historyextra.com/period/medieval/
    medieval-underwear-bras-pants-and-lingerie-in-the-middle-ages/
Mughals on the Move - I
https://www.thefridaytimes.com/mughals-on-the-move-i/

My Jaipur: Rulers of Jaipur
http://myjaipur.weebly.com/rulers-of-jaipur.html
NWS Lightening and Fire
http://www.lightningsafety.noaa.gov/fire.shtml
Portrait of Raja Man Singh of Amber
https://www.metmuseum.org/art/collection/search/453180
Royal Family of Jaipur
http://www.royalfamilyofindia.com/jeypore/
The Barrier Remains a Concern
https://www.piquenewsmagazine.com/whistler-news/
   the-barrier-remains-a-concern-2486371
The Tragic Consequence of Half Truths in Indian Subcontinent
https://gernailsaab.blogspot.com/2020/04/the-tragic-consequence-
   ofhalf-truths.html
Thirty Beautiful Mughal Paintings for Your Inspiration
http://webneel.com/mughal-paintings
Vancouver Symphony Orchestra Facts
http://www.vancouversymphony.ca/about/facts-and-figures/

YouTube
Mughal Emperor Family Tree
https://www.youtube.com/watch?v=zu5UcqvY1Cg
Narges Dehghani: Kamancheh, Iranian musical instrument
https://www.youtube.com/watch?v=vAYb_GU7Vcs
Tasnif Hanuz Hosein Nourshargh "Ghamar" persian traditional folk
   music Great Hall
Tchaikovsky Moscow: https://www.youtube.com/
   watch?v=k0BDZ0fuklk
Travelling within the World: Belly Dancing History
http://travelingwithintheworld.ning.com/group/bellydance/forum/top-
   ics/bellydance-history?commentId=2185477%3AComment%3A10
   4506&groupId=2185477%3AGroup%3A23298